Dedicated to our spouses and children,
the inspiration for our perspiration.

Waiting for an Echo

Echoes at Dawn

by

Jann Rowland & Lelia Eye

One Good Sonnet Publishing

This is a work of fiction, based on the works of Jane Austen. All of the characters and events portrayed in this novel are products of Jane Austen's original novel, the author's imagination, or are used fictitiously.

WAITING FOR AN ECHO: ECHOES AT DAWN

Copyright © 2014 Jann Rowland & Lelia Eye

Cover art by Dana Rowland

Published by One Good Sonnet Publishing

ISBN: 0992000025
ISBN-13: 978-0-9920000-2-8

ACKNOWLEDGEMENTS

We would like to give thanks and recognition to everyone who has helped bring us to this point:

Our families, for their love and support and for allowing us the precious time we needed to write.

Jann's sister Dana, for creating the cover art and assisting with proofreading.

Lelia's brother Pete, for providing general commentary.

And finally, we would like to thank everyone who has provided encouragement along the way.

We really appreciate your support.

"I would hurl words into this darkness and wait for an echo, and if an echo sounded, no matter how faintly, I would send other words to tell, to march, to fight, to create a sense of hunger for life that gnaws in us all."

— Richard Wright

Chapter I

*M*eryton. It was the same old town he remembered from five years before, and those intervening years had not changed it in the slightest. Of course, Meryton was typical of any other small market town which could be found in every corner of the kingdom, containing dusty streets which turned into a veritable quagmire after a rainfall, tiny shops with little or no quality or charm to them, and dreadfully ordinary locals whose lives were just as drab and boring as the town in which they lived.

Still, Meryton—and any other town like it—was nothing more than a means to an end for an enterprising young man such as himself. And at this point in his history, enterprising was exactly what he needed to be.

Though he had never been rich—no thanks to *someone* he could name—he had been holding his own until recently, with the freedom to do as he pleased. Then, after a streak of bad luck with cards and a few poor choices at the horseracing track, his hard-won resources had been all but depleted. With no other choice before him and a mountain of debts behind him, he had left his establishment and set out into the world to make his fortune . . . again.

But he did not let the repetition darken his mood. He could always find people to swindle, credit to run up, and a few widows or maidens with whom he was duty-bound to share his charms. And if the women who caught his eye had money, then so much the better.

In some respects, however, the chase and all that came with it was a bother. Feminine delights could be readily found at the many establishments he frequented, and as for the other things involved in the chase, he would just as soon spend his time at the gaming tables. No, the chase was a means to an end, not the end itself, and though he would have preferred not to be bothered by it again, his circumstances and appetites—not to mention his tendency to go through money as if it were water—necessitated his imminent performance.

Because the chase had been difficult and fruitless thus far, he was ready to break from his search to conduct a conquest which promised more than a little pleasure. That was the reason he had come to Meryton.

Over the past five years, he had often found his mind wandering back to this insignificant little speck which barely appeared on any map. And somewhat surprisingly, it was not the thought of past triumphs, conquests, or extraordinary luck in gaming that kept the town on his mind. It was the girl who had managed to escape him. Few had ever evaded him after he had set his sights on them, which was, he supposed, why his thoughts had returned to her so often despite the passage of time.

She had been a pretty little thing less than five years before, and the period he had spent "courting" her had been most enjoyable, for she was not like most other young women of her age. For one, she was not a bashful young lady who blushed prettily while agreeing with every word which proceeded out of his mouth—his wife, to his mingled amusement and disgust, had been *very much* that sort of woman. No, this girl he remembered had been intelligent and unafraid to show her intelligence by challenging his opinions and stating her own with decided confidence. *That* in and of itself set her apart from just about any other young lady of her station . . . and made the idea of her surrender all the more satisfying.

Now, after five more years of maturity, he could hardly imagine how she would appear, but he was wagering that her youthful prettiness had grown into an uncommon beauty, and he very much wished to sample the delights she had to offer. It truly was a shame that she had lacked the monetary inducements necessary to satisfy his needs.

He strode into town with the confident strut he had carefully cultivated over the years, and he frequented a few of the shops, just enough to observe and gather information. It was at a taphouse that he finally heard all he needed to know; he then quietly left town, mounted the horse he had left tied to a tree just on the outskirts, and took the road heading north.

The journey was barely a mile from Meryton and took him only a few minutes on horseback. When the manor came into his view, he smiled to himself before schooling his features into his customary charming demeanor. He dismounted in front of the door and knocked, handing his card—one of the few he still possessed—to the maid who answered.

In only a few moments, the maid had returned, and he was led into the well-remembered parlor to greet the inhabitants.

"Mr. Wickham!" exclaimed the matron of the house.

He smiled and greeted her with aplomb, noting that only one of her daughters seemed to be in evidence—the youngest one, unless he missed his guess. He could not even remember her name, not that she had mattered much to him back then; she had only been eleven at the time, and though he appreciated them young as much as the next rake, even he had his limits.

"How do you do, Madam?"

"I do very well, Mr. Wickham. I had not heard that you were again in the area."

"I have just recently returned, Mrs. Bennet, and am very glad to see you again. Is your family all well?"

"They are, indeed, Mr. Wickham."

Then her face suddenly clouded over, and she regarded him with a scowl. "And how is Mrs. Wickham?"

It had taken longer than he would have thought, but it appeared the memory of his time in Meryton—and the reason he had left—had finally penetrated the fog of Mrs. Bennet's mind. It was clear a certain amount of flattery, combined with an induction of pity, was in order to win the clueless woman over long enough to extract some information from her.

"Unfortunately, Mrs. Wickham is no longer among the living, Mrs. Bennet," replied he, allowing a glum expression to fall over his face.

Mrs. Bennet appeared to be taken aback. "I am very sorry to hear that, sir. Please accept the condolences of my entire family."

"I thank you, Mrs. Bennet. It was a tragic loss. Mrs. Wickham, who had recently found out she was with child, went out riding and was killed when her horse reared and threw her to the ground. And I was so looking forward to becoming a father . . . ."

Enthralled by the tale, Mrs. Bennet clucked her tongue and murmured her sympathy for his loss, in response to which Mr. Wickham thanked her, allowing silence to fall over the room.

At length, Mrs. Bennet roused herself to call for tea, and sitting once again in her chair, she looked at him with frank appraisal.

"In spite of your loss, sir, you appear remarkably well. I understand Mrs. Wickham was heiress to an estate in Surrey. How do you find life as a gentleman running an estate?"

"I enjoy it very well indeed," replied Wickham, though he had never spared a moment's time for the upkeep of the estate. "The estate is very prosperous, and while it does consume a certain amount of my time, I have an excellent steward to assist in its running." In truth, the estate his wife had inherited was nowhere near prosperous enough to warrant a steward, and he had sold it two years earlier to fund his activities.

A manic gleam of greed appeared in Mrs. Bennet's eyes, and she gazed at him in a calculating manner, exactly as he had intended.

"So, do you mean to come and ask after Lizzy?" asked the young girl at Mrs. Bennet's side, speaking up at last. "Perhaps you have changed your mind and wish to pursue her again?"

"Oh, hush, Lydia," was Mrs. Bennet's reply.

Lydia! That was the girl's name. She appeared to be about the age that Elizabeth had been when he was here before. Furthermore, she was blessed with womanly attributes similar to that of her elder sister. In fact, she resembled Elizabeth quite closely—much more so than any of her other sisters, unless he remembered incorrectly. She also seemed to lack even an iota of her elder sister's wit and intelligence.

"Do not concern yourself, Mrs. Bennet," said he, unconcerned over the girl's words. "I *had* thought to call concerning your family, after all."

"Ah, yes," responded Mrs. Bennet. "Unfortunately, at present, only my Lydia is at home."

That did not sound promising. If Elizabeth were already married . . . Of course, that did not truly signify. Among his conquests were numbered not a few widows and several married women. Should Elizabeth be willing—or perhaps even should she not be *quite* willing—her marital status would not bother him in the least.

"Yes, Mr. Wickham, only I am home," acknowledged Lydia with a considering eye. "Jane and Kitty are in London with our aunt and uncle, while Mary and Lizzy are in Kent. Mary has lately married, so Lizzy is visiting her. I am afraid I am the only one of my sisters available to greet you, sir."

Though the girl was all but batting her eyes at him, Wickham was far more interested in the information she had imparted about her eldest sister. Elizabeth—the one who had resisted his advances—was still unattached. An opportunity was there, and he would not pass it up.

"Ah, Kent—what a beautiful region."

"Are you familiar with the country?" queried Mrs. Bennet.

"Indeed, I am," replied Wickham. "Pardon me, but whom has your sister married?"

"She has married my husband's cousin, Mr. Collins. Mr. Collins is the rector at Hunsford parsonage, where the esteemed Lady Catherine de Bourgh serves as his patroness. As he is the heir to Longbourn due to the entail, Mary will be the mistress of this house after I am gone. I once detested the very thought of that entail, but I suppose it is in truth not so very terrible a thing."

Hunsford! Wickham smiled at the thought. So, Elizabeth was in Hunsford, not a mile or two from the great estate of Rosings, which he had visited as a boy in the company of his godfather's son, Fitzwilliam Darcy.

Wickham nearly scowled at the thought of the man. Darcy was certainly no longer a friend of his, and they had not come across each other in some time now. Still, Wickham made it a point to never forget anyone who had wronged him . . . and the payback he owed the master of Pemberley was long overdue. Given the man's many offenses against Wickham, that revenge merited special consideration indeed.

He brought his mind back to Elizabeth and reflected that it truly did not signify *where* she was when he pursued her. Kent would suffice in every way, for there were as many lonely heiresses there as anywhere else. Meanwhile, with any luck, Elizabeth Bennet would soon be his in every way possible. He might even keep her, though she could not increase his fortune; after all, she affected him like no other ever had.

Once he had received his desired intelligence, he conversed easily with the two ladies until the time for a polite visit had elapsed. Having put up with her for the past half-hour, he now considered Lydia Bennet flighty and stupid, not worth his time to pursue—not when there were greater treasures to obtain. Mrs. Bennet invited him to stay for dinner, but considering the fact that Elizabeth had been her father's favorite, he doubted the master of the estate would appreciate his attendance. He declined, saying he had business in town that evening and giving every assurance he would call again later in the week. Of course, he had no intention of ever keeping that promise.

Only moments later, he was back on his horse, pointed toward London and the challenge which waited beyond. There was enough time left, he thought, to make it to an inn he remembered on the outskirts of town which was known for its fine ale and even finer maids. There, he would stay a day or two and plan his next move. He smiled to himself. His stop at Longbourn had turned out to be very profitable indeed.

Chapter II

The journey from London to Kent left Elizabeth feeling very tired, but at last she arrived at Mary's new home on the third of March. Despite her fatigue, however, Elizabeth felt her spirits lighten when she saw her sister's happy face from the carriage window.

After stepping out onto the ground, Elizabeth embraced Mary warmly.

"Lizzy, I am so glad to see you!" exclaimed Mary in delight once they had moved apart. "Part of me feared you would not come."

"Nonsense," said Elizabeth. "I have been thinking about you quite often, and I am glad I shall have the opportunity to see how you are situated in your new home!"

Turning, Elizabeth saw her sister's husband glowering at her, though he placed the barest of smiles on his face when he noticed her glance. "My cous—" began he in greeting, only to pause and correct himself, "—my sister Elizabeth."

"It is a pleasure to see you again, Mr. Collins," said Elizabeth politely, though she could not help but refute the comment in her own mind. She would have much preferred to never see the parson again, but she supposed it was not to be helped. He was, after all, married to her sister.

"Lizzy, you simply *must* see our home!" said Mary. "Lady Catherine de Bourgh has assisted in much of the decorating, and I think you will be pleased by it."

"Her ladyship is most kind to us," noted Mr. Collins stiffly, his air somewhat haughty. He seemed intent upon playing the part of a petulant child, and it was all Elizabeth could do to suppress a laugh.

Elizabeth could more than handle a grumpy Mr. Collins — far better she experience *that* side of him than the one which lauded every detail of his patroness's home. And so, happy for her sister, if not for Mr. Collins himself, Elizabeth exclaimed over the furniture and the garden, giving continual assurances that she believed Mary was doing very well for herself as Mrs. Collins. While Elizabeth might still have had some doubts, she could ascertain that her sister *did* seem content with her new place in life, and for that, Elizabeth was grateful. The dark looks given to her by her sister's new husband were quite easily ignored.

Elizabeth's first few days in Hunsford passed in a rather unremarkable fashion. Though the Collinses lived only a lane away from the fabled property of Rosings Park and were beneficiaries of the condescension of its residents, they were not in any way well to do, which meant that they did not enjoy the same style of life as the de Bourghs.

That this was no hardship for the practical Mary was evident, and Elizabeth rejoiced to see her settled into her new life. The circumstance was also somewhat fortuitous for Elizabeth, as it afforded her the opportunity to examine Mary without the interruption of others.

Mary, it appeared, was very pleased with her new life. She had immersed herself in the role of a parson's wife and was diligent and careful in the performance of her duties to those in her husband's flock. Indeed, Elizabeth had never seen Mary so content before — it appeared to be the life for which she was intended, though it did not wholly surprise Elizabeth, who knew how pious Mary had always been.

More surprising was the evidence of a new maturity to Mary's outlook on life. Whereas previously she would have spouted banal platitudes from Fordyce's sermons with impunity, she now appeared to have gained a new appreciation for and understanding of the Lord's words. Rather than speaking the sometimes dreary and overdone homilies to which she had often subjected her family in the past, she was now more likely to quote directly from the Bible, if she quoted anything at all. In fact, many of her opinions were given from her heart rather than the written word, and although she remained as pious as ever, the self-righteousness that had once characterized most of her speech was gone. Elizabeth found she liked the new Mary very well indeed.

As for Mary's relationship with Mr. Collins, Elizabeth saw nothing to give her concern and everything to give her hope that all was well on that front. Despite Elizabeth's expectations, Mr. Collins actually appeared to be a good husband to Mary. He treated his wife with courtesy and deference, always listening to her opinions and sharing his own with perfect grace, if less than perfect intelligence.

As for the behavior of Mr. Collins in general, he was basically the same man in essentials—still lacking in wit and carrying himself with a pomposity which would not have been warranted had he been the prince regent himself. Yet though neither his mind nor his manners were improved, it was clear that he was already deferring to Mary in their marriage. With expert skill, she was able to guide him while still allowing him to be his own man, and in the process, she had some success in curtailing some of his more embarrassing tendencies. The arrangement undoubtedly made her life much more agreeable than it otherwise would have been.

Mr. Collins did not have much to say to Elizabeth herself. From the time of her arrival throughout the first week of her stay, he was coldly polite and distant to her, never exerting himself to say much beyond the usual civilities. Though unable to account for his behavior, Elizabeth was not in the habit of questioning something which brought her peace. While Mary tolerated his idiosyncrasies and more than occasional stupidity, Elizabeth knew she herself would have been tempted to strangle him within the first fortnight had their roles been reversed.

As it took only a few days to determine that Mary was happy, Elizabeth soon allowed herself to enjoy her stay. The parsonage was comfortable and well laid out, and the garden around the house was quite large and very beautiful, even in the early spring. Elizabeth spent many happy hours in the garden in particular, reading a book or walking and talking with Mary. And when the closeness of the house— or the presence of its master—became too much, the woods around Rosings Park were exquisite, and Elizabeth enjoyed taking the opportunity to lose herself amongst the forested paths.

She had been in Kent for almost a week when the first invitation arrived to dine at Rosings that Sunday after church. Or rather, when the *summons* to dine with the de Bourghs arrived, Elizabeth corrected herself after she perused the note Mary had shared with her. Clearly,

Lady Catherine was not a woman who requested; she demanded and expected to be obeyed, especially by the obsequious person of her cleric.

The walk to the manor house was accomplished with the accompaniment of Mr. Collins's long-winded monologue concerning the glories of Rosings Park. Nothing was beneath his notice; he regaled them with information concerning everything from the number of windows and the amount the owner had spent upon them, to the color of the roof tiles, to the comfortably arranged and eminently fine furniture, to the number of servants the estate employed. And though Elizabeth thought his discourse was in poor taste, she tried not to pay attention to his rambling raptures on the wealth of others. Instead, she tried to concentrate on the delightfully vibrant countryside in which the estate was situated.

When they were accepted through the main doors of the house, Elizabeth peered around at the interior with great interest. As she had expected, the materials used in the house's construction were the finest, built with the highest workmanship money could buy. Then, as they were led deeper into the house, the glimpses she caught of the various rooms told a slightly different story. The furniture was solid and surely expensive, but by and large, it appeared to be massive, with excessively ornate filigree carved upon its surfaces—undoubtedly fine, but overly pretentious to Elizabeth's simpler taste.

The servant who greeted them said that Lady Catherine was expecting them, indicating as well that her ladyship had other visitors, namely James and Elia Baker, both of whom Elizabeth had never met.

"Oh!" said Mary. Then, speaking in a low tone as the servant led them to the drawing-room, she said to her sister: "I apologize for the surprise, Lizzy. I had not realized Lady Catherine meant to invite the Bakers tonight."

"Do not concern yourself, Mary," said Elizabeth softly. "After all, neither you nor I can have any influence on such a great lady in the matter of whom she deigns to invite for a dinner party."

Mary gave her a wry smile in response and informed her quickly: "Mr. Baker is the master of Stauneton Hall, which lies on the other side of Hunsford from Rosings Park. It is a moderately large estate of some rumored six-thousand pounds per annum. Mr. Baker and his sister Elia are the only surviving members of their family. Their parents and a younger sibling died during an outbreak of cholera some ten years before, leaving Mr. Baker as the master of the estate at fourteen. His sister is two years his senior and is quite . . . interesting in her conversation."

Elizabeth peered at her sister, wondering at her description of the young lady, but they had come to the drawing-room and were being announced by the servant, so she did not dare pry further. Mary looked at her, as if she might venture a little further information, but then their attention was caught by the imperious voice of Lady Catherine demanding that they pay their respects.

"Mrs. Collins!" said the great lady. "Please do not skulk in the doorway! We have been acquainted long enough to make such hesitation unnecessary."

"My apologies, Lady Catherine," replied Mary with a hint of deference; any hint of intimidation, however, was decidedly *not* present, a fact which encouraged Elizabeth. "I was merely speaking with my sister."

Lady Catherine sniffed but motioned for them to come closer. "Ah, yes, I do recall that your sister was coming to visit you. Well, do not stand there gaping; come forward so that I may know her better."

Lady Catherine's manner was nothing less than should have been expected from the stories Mr. Collins had told of her, but it also did nothing to endear her to Elizabeth. That she was an arrogant and meddlesome old woman with a high opinion of herself and an exaggerated sense of her own importance was immediately evident.

However, Elizabeth was unwilling to offend her sister's patroness, and so she approached and curtseyed to the lady.

Mary calmly made the introductions, and Elizabeth returned the greetings of those present in a polite manner. Feeling Lady Catherine's eyes boring into her, Elizabeth returned her frank and appraising look with a placid one of her own. Though she might have been the daughter of an earl, the overbearing woman would *not* intimidate Elizabeth Bennet!

"Indeed. I have heard much of you, Miss Bennet. Your sister has distinguished herself as Mr. Collins's wife and mistress of his home. I do hope that you are as competent as your sister has proven herself to be."

Though she betrayed no reaction, Elizabeth wondered if Lady Catherine's words were censorious, or if she were merely behaving as was typical of one who held herself to be superior to everyone. Deciding it did not signify, Elizabeth responded thus:

"Thank you, Lady Catherine. I always knew Mary would acquit herself well in her new role. I am happy to hear that you feel likewise."

This response seemed to satisfy Lady Catherine for the moment, as she redirected her attention to Mr. Collins, who gladly made his obeisance to her. Elizabeth turned and made the further acquaintance of Lady Catherine's daughter as the Baker siblings spoke with Mary.

In Anne de Bourgh, Elizabeth found a sickly young lady who was nevertheless willing to enter into a pleasant conversation. It was moments into their discussion when Miss de Bourgh made a comment which confused Elizabeth exceedingly.

"I am glad you have joined us, Miss Bennet. I believe another addition to our party will be a welcome one; after all, the only other young woman of my age in the area is Miss Baker, and with your sister always engaged in the concerns of the neighborhood, as is her duty, we only have each other for company. I look forward to getting to know you."

"Given the company, I had thought you would have heard all about me already, Miss de Bourgh."

Miss de Bourgh snorted indelicately into her hand and cast a disparaging glare in the direction of the parson. "Perhaps if I were my mother, I would have—he tells her *everything*, after all—but I do not have much to do with your cousin."

A twinkling smile was part of Elizabeth's reply. "Yes, he can be rather tedious."

"Downright sycophantic," was the other woman's less than kind whispered response. "I am afraid that Mr. Collins and I do not see eye to eye, and I find his behavior around my mother disgraceful. Of course, she enjoys his attention, but I prefer a parson to be of a more independent nature; I believe such a parson to be better suited to caring for those under his influence. Mr. Collins does not sneeze without my mother's permission, making him nothing of the sort."

Elizabeth stifled a giggle at this apt description of her cousin. "I see that you and I are of one mind on this subject."

The ladies shared a smile, and they began to speak of other matters. Within a few moments, the Bakers had joined the conversation, and Elizabeth became better acquainted with them as well. Elizabeth immediately identified the young man, James Baker, as someone with a high opinion of his own charms. He was a pleasant conversationalist, however, and was clearly intelligent, and as he did not allow his flirting to cross any boundaries of propriety, Elizabeth was content.

Elia Baker was another sort of person altogether, though she did possess some similarities with her brother. She was kind and pleasant and appeared almost eager to meet and converse with the new members of the party. She was very beautiful, with flaxen hair, green eyes, and an effervescent personality, and Elizabeth thought it was truly a wonder why she was not yet married.

However, although Elizabeth immediately liked the young woman, she quickly understood what Mary had meant with her cryptic statements about the woman's conversation. Miss Baker was quite flighty, and she sometimes made comments which appeared to show a rather shocking lack of understanding and which even, on occasion, bordered upon utter stupidity. For instance, when Elizabeth and Miss de Bourgh had begun to converse about music, Miss Baker burst in with a comment to the effect that she really did enjoy music, as it was "so very musical." Elizabeth looked upon her in wonder at the comment, but Miss de Bourgh merely continued blithely on.

It was not long before the company was called into the dining room for dinner. As Elizabeth would have expected, the cuisine was fine, the conversation was dominated by Lady Catherine, and the flattery was commanded by Mr. Collins. But Elizabeth was content nevertheless; Mary seemed happy with her life just as it was, and Elizabeth was more than willing to continue to support her.

Chapter III

The next day, Elizabeth was invited to Rosings for tea with Anne de Bourgh. Mary was busy attending to an ill parishioner, but she had encouraged Elizabeth to go without her. Elizabeth, who knew Elia Baker was to be present, had agreed to do so, as she was curious to see whether the young woman would continue to make occasional inane comments or whether the previous day had been unusual.

The weather was glorious and clear, and Elizabeth very much enjoyed the short walk, in part because it was unmarred by the presence of Mr. Collins, who seemed to appear at the most inopportune times in a gloomy cloud of dark looks and grumbled greetings.

At Rosings, she sat down to tea with Miss de Bourgh and Miss Baker. Both women seemed genuinely glad to see her, and the latter said: "I do hope you had no difficulties in your journey here today, Miss Bennet."

Elizabeth frowned. "I did not, thank you. My sister's home is not far from here."

"But there are so many tragedies which can befall a young woman walking," persisted Miss Baker. "A bootlace can break, a dress can rip, an ankle can twist—why, I am always so pleased when these misfortunes do not come to pass!"

Elizabeth glanced briefly at Miss de Bourgh and then back at the other woman. With a slight smile, she said: "I am a strong walker, I can assure you, and it is very seldom that I have experienced any such misfortune as those you have listed."

"I am glad to hear that," said Miss Baker warmly. "I dare say Miss de Bourgh has the proper idea, as she does not venture outside unless she is to ride in her phaeton."

Elizabeth saw the tight look on Anne de Bourgh's face, and she felt sympathy well up within her for the sickly young woman. Lady Catherine's daughter did not have much choice in her mode of travel, for she was not well enough of body to go traipsing about the countryside as Elizabeth did. Miss Baker's remark was insensitive, yet Elizabeth did not know whether the woman recognized that.

"Well," said Elizabeth, unsure how to alleviate the sudden tension, "I am certain the grounds of Rosings look just as appealing from the inside of a phaeton as they do when walking. But there are certainly a multitude of indoor pursuits to keep one entertained. Do you paint, Miss de Bourgh?"

After giving a somewhat wary look to Miss Baker, Miss de Bourgh answered: "I do paint a little, though I have not dedicated the time to it which might be desirable."

"Your paintings are lovely," said Miss Baker, "but I must say that I rather dislike the activity. Paint is very wet, and it does drip so."

Elizabeth refrained from commenting on this; instead, she turned the conversation to other matters.

They all spent a pleasant afternoon together, but there were those strange recurring moments of tension interspersed with the same displays of Miss Baker's lack of understanding which had occurred the day before. Though Anne de Bourgh and Elia Baker seemed amiable enough in company, they also appeared to be rather wary with one another. Elizabeth was not certain of the reason for such guarded behavior, but she tried to keep the conversation light, and both ladies appeared to be enjoying themselves.

The mood of the afternoon soon changed, however, when Lady Catherine joined their party.

"Anne," said she, "you must be careful not to overexert yourself with conversation. Miss Bennet, I am certain you find my daughter to be an excellent conversationalist and appreciate the honor of speaking with her—she is very generous with her time, condescending to speak with those below her station—but I am afraid her poor health does not allow her to stay out of her chambers for long."

"I am fine, Mother," said Miss de Bourgh with what Elizabeth believed was a note of consternation in her voice.

"Nonsense, Anne. You need to rest. At least sit quietly for a while until you regain a little of your color."

Elizabeth looked at the young woman. While Miss de Bourgh *was* pale, she was no paler than she had been when Elizabeth arrived. They had been seated for most of their time together, so there was no particular reason for the young woman to be feeling peakish. Elizabeth was about to open her mouth to say as much when her ladyship spoke again:

"Certainly, I do plan to see my dear Anne very well situated soon. Indeed, it will be a happy day when the estates of Rosings and Pemberley are united."

Elizabeth felt something strange rise up in her chest, but she quickly smothered it. Lady Catherine, oblivious to her reaction, continued to talk: "You know, Miss Baker, I do have such high hopes for my daughter's future with Mr. Darcy. He does dote on her so. Why, I have seen her frequently immersed in the book he was so kind to give her the last time he visited. They say Shakespeare is the food of love, and my dear Anne is a proficient in Shakespeare."

Elizabeth looked to the two other women. There was almost a grimness to Elia Baker's face, though the expression disappeared before Elizabeth could determine its meaning. Miss de Bourgh, however, was steadily avoiding meeting anyone's eyes, and Elizabeth did not miss the slight redness to her cheeks.

"He has not proposed yet," murmured Miss de Bourgh at last.

Lady Catherine waved a dismissive hand, though she seemed slightly irked. "It is only a matter of time. Darcy knows it was the dearest wish of his late mother. She and I planned the union while he and Anne were in their cradles. He knows it is his duty to maintain the family's exalted status, and he understands the debasement he would bring to himself and his noble line by marrying one of lesser station."

Elizabeth might have imagined it, but it seemed as if Lady Catherine's gaze flicked briefly toward Elia Baker before returning to her daughter.

"I heard one of the gardeners was having trouble with those pretty little flowers," said Miss Baker suddenly. "What are they called again? I am afraid I can never remember."

At this chance to illustrate her knowledge, Lady Catherine began to discuss the details of the flowers in question, extolling their virtues and the well-meaning efforts of the gardener in question.

When it was finally time for Elizabeth to depart for Mary's home, she could not help but feel relieved. Spending time in the presence of Lady Catherine was draining, especially since her ladyship appeared to be less than pleased with Elia Baker. Elizabeth herself was by no means left untouched by the Lady's displeasure; Lady Catherine took care to criticize her upbringing, her posture, and even her skills on the pianoforte (though that last amused Elizabeth, as Lady Catherine had not yet heard her play).

Through it all, Elizabeth held herself proud and steady, though she would have liked very much to stand up to the meddlesome woman. It was only when she was at the parsonage that Elizabeth allowed herself to relax and consider what she had heard. Foremost on her mind was what Lady Catherine had claimed about Miss de Bourgh's being Mr. Darcy's intended. Was it true? Did he mean to marry his cousin? Elizabeth was aware that duty was of supreme importance to him. Would he perform what he believed to be his duty? Or did he even feel it to be his duty? He had certainly never spoken of an understood engagement to Miss de Bourgh, though that was perhaps not surprising given his general reticence. She tried to push these thoughts from her mind, yet she could not help but feel as if, somehow, it were crucial that she learn for certain the truth of the situation.

Chapter IV

*J*ames Baker stared outside the window of his study at Stauneton Hall, deep in thought. A small smile was tugging at his mouth — one might almost have called it a smirk — and his fingers lightly held a piece of paper covered in the neat writing of a male hand.

The arrival of a letter from Fitzwilliam Darcy did not come as a surprise to James Baker. In fact, though they did not correspond often, he had been expecting the man to write him. Baker had sent him a letter not long before due to his sister's insistent — dare he say *nagging*? — urging. Elia had wanted to know when Darcy would be returning to Rosings, and Baker had not been uninterested in attaining knowledge of such information himself. After all, Baker had to listen to his sister bemoan Darcy's absence when the man was gone.

It had certainly been very difficult living with Elia these past few months. She had been looking forward to a season in London, and then a lingering illness had left her incapacitated for some time. When at last her convalescence at home was complete, the prospect of Darcy's Easter visit to Kent had loomed on the horizon, and Elia had made the decision to stay at home in hopes that Darcy might decide to come early. At least having some assurance of the man's return would decrease the frequency of her complaints, though it would by no means completely quell them. And Baker was not wholly opposed to spending time in company with Darcy—or even Darcy's cousin, Colonel Fitzwilliam—due to the dearth of tolerable male companionship in the area. Given the interest Darcy had frequently shown in Baker's sister, it was to be expected that the Bakers and the Darcys would be on friendly terms.

No, it was not surprising that Darcy had written him. The majority of the contents of the letter were unremarkable as well. Darcy visited Rosings every year at Easter, though his visits had of course become more frequent once he had begun to take an interest in Elia, and in this particular letter, Darcy noted his intent to return to Kent. Baker chuckled to himself at the thought that Darcy was already a slave to the whims of two women, though perhaps it was telling that the man had not arrived as soon as both her ladyship and Elia would have wished.

Baker felt a small measure of relief upon reading the information concerning Darcy's anticipated arrival date, as imparting the information to his sister meant he would have some respite from her continual harping. But he found himself most interested in something that would have appeared insignificant to someone who did not know Darcy well.

The letter mentioned that Darcy knew Rosings would likely be having other visitors and that he hoped they were well. There even almost seemed to be a question in that, as if Darcy wanted a response ensuring him that these "visitors" *were* indeed well.

Baker was quite aware that Rosings had only had *one* new visitor of late, and that was Miss Elizabeth Bennet. Mr. Collins appeared to hold some grudge against the woman—and Baker had his suspicions as to why that might be—yet he had revealed, with some prodding from Baker, that Miss Bennet was a gentleman's daughter, though she was one without much dowry of which to speak. In fact, though he had initially been reticent to impart any information, Mr. Collins had quickly been induced to reveal that his wife and Miss Bennet were daughters of his cousin, whose estate he stood to inherit upon the man's death. For Darcy to take such an interest in her—for him to not only know her itinerary, but to also inquire about her well-being—well, it was interesting, to say the least.

Baker dropped the letter onto his desk, where it lay among countless other scattered documents. In fact, "amusing" might be a better word than "interesting." If Darcy did indeed hold some interest in Miss Bennet—and Baker could not exactly blame him, as the woman was quite handsome and quick with her tongue—then Elia's plans for her future as the mistress of Pemberley might dissipate swiftly indeed.

The letter had almost made it seem as if Darcy were more concerned with Elizabeth than Elia. And considering Darcy had appeared to be on the verge of proposing to Elia when he was last in Kent, that meant matters were going to become very heated soon.

Baker smiled to himself—no, it was definitely a smirk this time—and swept out of his study. His sister was down the hall and saw him, and she came quickly toward him, like an eagle swooping down upon a mouse.

"Have you heard anything from Mr. Darcy?" asked she breathlessly. She obviously knew that the post had arrived.

"He said he will be here before too long," said Baker with a shrug. "He will probably arrive on either the 16th or the 17th."

"You are certain he is coming, James?" persisted she.

"Yes," answered he, wiping a hand over his brow. "He will be here." *If not to see you, then to see Miss Elizabeth Bennet,* thought he to himself. The corners of his mouth rose even higher in amusement.

"Oh! I must have a new dress made!" exclaimed Elia, clasping her hands together in excitement.

"Yes, yes," said he, waving a hand dismissively as he walked away. "Have a dozen dresses made. Just be a little more careful with your budget this time. I would rather you not draw up debts with every tailor in the county."

"James!" called out she after him. "I wished to talk to you more about my dresses!"

But he ignored her and continued on.

Sometimes, he wondered if she was as foolish as she acted. Still, whether she was or was not a fool could be of little concern to him. He was simply glad that he was not duty-bound to stay behind and listen to her describe in detail the anticipated design of the dress she intended to have made. If that had been the case, he would have been certain to seek an early grave. There was little he hated more than listening to unending descriptions of feminine fripperies.

Chapter V

*A*nne de Bourgh was no fool.

She had been sickly all her life, and although several of the most prominent physicians in the country had been hired to examine her, none had been able to offer a definitive answer as to why she was so frequently ill, and so her malady remained unknown. It was chalked up to a weak constitution and a tendency toward catching the colds and agues that swept through the neighborhood from time to time, robbing her of any vitality she might feel and subjecting her to a lonely existence. Her mother, eager as she was to control everything and everyone, had used that malady ever since Anne was a child to restrict her pursuits and curtail any kind of exercise she may have wished to undertake, even though at times Anne had felt that a little exercise would do her good.

As a result of her forced inactivity, Anne had developed the ability to closely observe events about her. From the moment Elizabeth Bennet had entered her mother's sitting room, Anne had known that she was a confident person of decided opinions and intelligence, and an evening spent in conversation had not disabused that notion. Though it was true that Miss Bennet was well below Anne in terms of societal consequence, such things did not mean as much to Anne as they did to her mother, and she was grateful that she had met someone who could break the monotony of her life.

By contrast, Elia Baker—whom Anne had known for some time—was a much flightier creature, prone to somewhat idiotic actions and comments. Yet Anne could often see something else in Elia as well—a gleam in her eye, a forced quality to her inane comments, or a studied nonchalance when a discussion turned serious. All of this told Anne that although Elia was decidedly silly and rather uninformed, she was also quite conniving. The way Elia had behaved around Darcy certainly seemed to suggest that she had designs upon him.

This was something Anne could not countenance. Darcy was *her* betrothed and *her* cousin. Anne expected—depended upon!—Darcy doing his duty and making her an offer, saving her from the casual tyranny of her mother.

Thus, when Anne and Miss Bennet were shown into the sitting room at Stauneton Hall, Anne's trained eye was immediately able to discern that Elia held a letter of some sort. Given Elia's reaction when they had entered the room—hurriedly concealing and then slipping the letter into a crevice in the couch—it was not something she wished her guests to see. It seemed unlikely that it was something relating to Miss Bennet since Elia had only known her for a week, which made it natural to conclude that the letter was specifically not intended for *Anne's* eyes. The irony of the situation was not lost on Anne, for if Elia had simply closed the letter and put it aside, Anne would not have thought anything of it; however, the woman had foolishly drawn attention to it.

Burning with curiosity, Anne greeted her friend with as unaffected a manner as she was able, and the three sat down and began to converse.

Anne had to acknowledge that Elia was a consummate hostess, adept at putting her guests at ease and attentive to their comfort. Within moments, a tea service had been delivered, and the three ladies sat with their refreshments, enjoying idle chitchat.

At least, Anne *tried* to enjoy their discussion. Worried as she was over the contents of the letter that she could even now see poking out from the corner of the cushion—tantalizing her with its mere presence—Anne could find no true enjoyment in the proceedings. She had long been suspicious of Elia's intentions toward Darcy, and she felt that if she could get her hands upon the letter, then she would finally be able to confirm her conjectures and warn the woman off.

Just when she thought she would go mad with the desire to know the letter's contents, her salvation came in the form of a summons for the mistress of the house to attend to some matter with the servants.

"Oh, I do hate having to deal with the servants," said Elia with a frown. "They are so lowborn and uncouth. If they were of higher breeding, my life would be so much easier and more comfortable."

And with that piece of inanity, Elia departed, leaving her two guests alone in the room together. Anne and Miss Bennet exchanged a significant glance—neither commenting that if the servants *had* been higher born, they would *not* be servants—and then settled in, speaking on insignificant matters while waiting for the return of their hostess.

At length, their conversation seemed to falter, and to Anne's delight, Miss Bennet rose and indicated her intention of inspecting the pianoforte on the other side of the room. She then wandered over to the instrument, leaving Anne with the perfect opportunity to do what she had been desperate to do since arriving.

Carefully, listening to ensure the mistress was not approaching the room, Anne spared a glance at Miss Bennet, who was running her fingers over the keys of the instrument. Thankful for the lack of attention, Anne eased to the side of the couch, slipped the letter from its position, and opened it up.

She recognized the handwriting immediately; though she and her cousin were not regular correspondents, she had seen a number of his letters, though most of them were directed toward her mother. Not having the time for a leisurely read, she skimmed down the letter's length and noted some of the passages.

London engagements . . . visitors to Rosings . . . Easter . . . pray that you and your sister are well . . . Miss Baker!

Anne stopped reading and glared at the offending letter, seeing the name of the woman she suspected of duplicity emblazoned upon the page as though it were monogrammed and embossed in gold. It was true! Elia did have her sights set upon Darcy, and the sentiment—if the letter specifically asking after her was any indication—appeared to be returned.

A rage descended upon Anne, and she thought back to the times she had been in company together with Elia and Darcy. Darcy had only paid *Anne* the attention due a close relation, but she could remember several instances of him smiling at Elia and even chuckling at something the woman had said. Anne's disposition was much more serious than that. Could she blame him if he wanted someone who could bring a smile to his face?

But though she knew she was being selfish, Anne was desperate to change her cousin's mind. She was under no illusions as to her own desirability. Years of poor health had robbed her of any vitality or beauty she would have otherwise possessed, and Elia was, after all, a very handsome woman. Anne was not the type of person who got caught up in ideas of sentimentality. She thought she and her cousin would do well together due to their close familial ties and general ease with one another . . . but now she wondered if such a marriage of convenience would be enough to offset the prospect of physical attraction or—dare she even say it—love. She had always counted on her cousin's sense of honor and duty to induce him into marrying her, thereby saving her from the control of her mother. But with Elia now doing her best to distract him, Anne was not certain he could still be counted on to adhere to that duty.

Startled by the sound of footsteps in the hallway, Anne folded the letter and put it in the crevice of the couch where it was before. But while the physical evidence of her snooping was hidden—Miss Bennet remained at the pianoforte and appeared to have noticed nothing— inwardly, Anne was still furious over her cousin's defection. She was not certain she could keep her countenance composed in light of the other woman's now exposed deceit.

When Elia appeared back in the room, she approached the couch, and Miss Bennet left the pianoforte, sitting across from them in the chair she had occupied previously. Yet although they attempted to resume their previous discourse, the atmosphere in the room had changed.

Finally, after hearing another stupid comment from Elia concerning the desirability of friends, Anne could stand it no longer.

"Elia, I understand *your brother* corresponds with my cousin Darcy a great deal."

There was no outward response from the other woman, but her eyes flicked to where the letter was hidden, and then, apparently satisfied it had not been disturbed, she turned her attention back to Anne.

"Oh, he corresponds with so many people I hardly know how he can keep track of it all," said she with a titter. "I do declare that if I were to receive so many letters, I would soon find my head spinning with all those words on the pages, and letters are so very wordy, after all. I am truly grateful it falls to his lot and not mine."

But Anne was not to be deterred, and the woman's stupidity was truly beginning to grate upon her nerves.

"But I have it on good authority that my cousin *has* exchanged letters with your brother," said Anne. "It should be a great comfort to you that the master of such a magnificent estate, versed in all business matters, should *condescend* to write to your brother."

Only a hint of displeasure could be seen in the tightening of Elia's eyes at Anne's patronizing tone. "I am sure my brother would indeed be comforted by such a thing, Anne. However, I keep out of the running of Stauneton Hall, and my brother stays away from the running of the house, so I really could not say whether, or to what extent, they exchange letters."

Anne sniffed in disdain. "I expect my cousin to join us very soon."

"Yes, I believe that he often visits at Easter, though recently I have noticed that he has visited more often."

"That he has," said Anne through gritted teeth, "and I must say that I derive much pleasure from his visits." She turned to Miss Bennet. "You saw my cousin in London recently, I understand. Surely he must have mentioned something of his plans to visit?"

"Indeed, he did," was the response, though Miss Bennet appeared to understand the thrust of Anne's words. "He informed me he will follow my arrival and stay for several weeks."

"Yes, it is so," confirmed Anne. "My mother and I enjoy his visits ever so much."

Anne leaned forward, speaking almost conspiratorially. "In fact, it is my understanding that my cousin's recent increase in visits has occurred because he has a specific purpose in mind. Surely you have heard about how our marriage has been arranged since the time we were infants? When Darcy's mother was alive, it was her favorite wish that the houses of Darcy and de Bourgh be united in matrimony."

A pair of nods — Elia's being somewhat curt — met her declaration.

Anne smiled. "All indications are that he believes it is time to formalize our relationship. I expect a proposal from him in the course of this visit."

"In that case, I must congratulate you, Miss de Bourgh," said Miss Bennet.

Elia, however, appeared to be somewhat put out. She hid it in an instant and plastered a most insincere smile upon her face. "Oh, I should be very happy for you, Anne, but you must not put your confidence in Mr. Darcy. Men are so inconstant, you know, and I fear your hopes should be dashed if he does not make the expected proposal. Your mother has spoken of this *'arrangement'* at great length, it is true, but my understanding is neither of you are bound by it, and in my opinion, he has never shown any inclination to oblige. In fact, Mr. Darcy may have someone else in mind — he may even mean to make an offer to Miss Bennet here."

Miss Bennet's shocked gasp was immediately heard, and she hastened to assure the other two ladies that Mr. Darcy had made *no* such intimations to her, but Anne, though cognizant of the fact that the young woman was very comely, felt she had nothing to fear from *that* quarter, as she believed the woman to be beneath Darcy's notice. Darcy *was* very proud, after all, and surely he would not sully his line by marrying a young lady of no consequence.

"I assure you, *Miss Baker*, that my cousin is very aware of his duty and will take this familial obligation very seriously. And Miss Bennet, though everything that is good and pleasant, would not dream of attempting to stake a claim on such an illustrious person as my cousin. Indeed, I could wish that *all* young ladies of my acquaintance were so aware of their station in life."

Miss Baker's frown bore testament of her displeasure in the face of Anne's insinuations. "I am sure I do not understand your meaning, Miss de Bourgh."

"And I am sure there can be no mistake, Miss Baker. I am well aware of your ambitions and your intention to steal my intended, and I cannot emphasize strongly enough what a mistake such an endeavor would be. Not only would my *mother* take a dim view of such an attempt, but Mr. Darcy has far too much sense to pursue some fortune-hunter with nothing more than flaxen hair to tempt him!"

With that, Anne stood and quit the room. In the back of her mind, she realized that her behavior had not been what she would have expected of herself, but she had been unable to help it. Elia Baker was a brazen adventuress, and Anne would not put up with it!

Yet Anne recognized her inherent vulnerability, and she was fearful for what the future held. She *had* to escape from her mother's influence. Perhaps it was time for her to take hold of her own fate.

Chapter VI

lizabeth watched in shock as Anne de Bourgh quit the room. Then she slowly turned her head to peer at the woman across from her.

Miss Baker was staring at the doorway with a flinty glare upon her face, an expression which Elizabeth would never expected the young woman to bear. Then again, Elizabeth would never have expected Miss de Bourgh to act in such a manner either.

Elizabeth was not insensible to the tension which had pervaded the room since their arrival, nor was she ignorant of its cause. When Elizabeth had first passed through the doorway, she had seen the letter Miss Baker held, and she had also witnessed how Miss de Bourgh had later pried into Miss Baker's affairs. Embarrassed by the blatant impropriety of what Miss de Bourgh was doing and not wishing to draw attention to herself, Elizabeth had feigned ignorance of what had occurred and kept her silence.

Aware of her own time spent conversing with Mr. Darcy and knowing how it would be viewed by the other women, Elizabeth felt that she needed to leave and take stock of the situation in solitary contemplation. Perhaps it would be best if she were not in company with Elia Baker and Anne de Bourgh much in the future.

Standing, Elizabeth stated her intention to depart. Miss Baker turned and gazed upon her with an unreadable expression for several moments before she smiled and rose to her feet.

"I am sorry you were witness to that."

"It is quite all right," said Elizabeth.

"It is not all right, I beg to differ," contradicted Miss Baker with a frown. "I would hope that—regardless of what may pass between gentlewomen—we would all endeavor to keep our discourses polite."

She sighed and continued: "I worry that our friend Anne is feeling the effects of her enforced confinement with her mother. I am sure you have not missed the fact that the lady dominates Anne and allows her very little freedom."

At Elizabeth's noncommittal response, Miss Baker smiled. "I sometimes fear that Anne leads a cheerless existence, and I believe she may put too much stock in this cradle betrothal of which she likes to speak. But perhaps it is best to continue no more on the subject. I would not have this unpleasantness make you feel unwelcome. Please, do say you will call again tomorrow."

Elizabeth hesitated. "Oh, I should not wish to inconvenience you—"

"It is no inconvenience," disagreed Miss Baker with a wave of her hand. "Oh, perhaps the servants may feel differently, but they *are* here to serve *us* are they not?"

Elizabeth could only agree with such a statement.

"Then *do* say you will come again. I believe I should like to know you better. And please, feel free to bring your sister along with you."

Left with nothing but to acquiesce, Elizabeth agreed, and after a few more moments of farewells, she departed, reflecting that Kent was much more interesting—and less restful—than she would have imagined.

Thus, it was with no small amount of trepidation that Elizabeth returned to Stauneton Hall the very next day. After the outburst from Anne de Bourgh, Elizabeth was not certain what to expect, and since Mary was feeling unwell, Elizabeth was forced to face the estate's mistress alone.

However, her anxiety turned out to be unnecessary, as Elia Baker acted as if nothing out of the ordinary had happened at all. She greeted Elizabeth with utmost kindness, ushering her to a seat and plying her with questions. It did not take long for it to become apparent that Miss Baker had no more desire to talk about what had happened than Elizabeth did. And so, Elizabeth allowed herself to enjoy her time with the woman, reflecting that what Miss Baker lacked in understanding was made up in kindness.

Soon, the two women had veered into a somewhat strange

conversation involving their likes and dislikes.

"I dislike jam tarts," proclaimed Miss Baker. "They are much too fatty for my tastes."

Elizabeth smiled. "But they do make such a magnificent treat at a picnic."

"Picnics!" cried Miss Baker. "Oh, heavens! I have never understood the appeal of a picnic. To sit out upon the ground . . . why, there are ants and other disgusting little creatures to be found there! And do not forget about the squirrels — and the hedgehogs — and all the other small creatures which may sneak in and steal your food, tickle your legs by crawling all over you, and generally create mess and unpleasantness. I should much prefer to eat inside."

Elizabeth stifled a laugh. "The blanket is to be placed underneath you to ensure that no insects disturb your meal. And I dare say that small creatures would give a party of humans a wide berth rather than attempt to steal food. I might also add that it can be amusing to feed the odd squirrel which may peer at you from the edge of a clearing."

"Feeding squirrels?" cried out Miss Baker with a shudder. "Good heavens! Why ever would you do that? And all it takes is one little ant to utterly ruin a person's appetite! But that is enough discussion of picnics. Come, Miss Bennet, do you have any suitors applying for your hand?"

Elizabeth could not help but flush. "I am unattached."

"What sort of suitor do you prefer?" Seeing the increasing redness of Elizabeth's face, Miss Baker tittered. "Miss Bennet, it is just the two of us. Do you prefer a man of fortune?"

Elizabeth's thoughts flashed inexplicably to Mr. Darcy, but she quickly pushed them aside. "No, I much prefer a pauper."

Miss Baker did not seem to understand Elizabeth's playful tone. "Oh, surely not!" cried she. "How would you live if you married such a man?"

At times, Elizabeth truly thought that Miss Baker was as insensible as she appeared. "I am sorry, Miss Baker, I was merely attempting to tease with my answer. In truth, I believe a mutual regard more important than financial considerations."

"You are one who is caught up more in ideals of romance, then!" exclaimed the other woman. "In that case, perhaps you prefer a man of sunny disposition, one who pleases and is pleased by all. Or might you prefer a man who is rightfully proud of his place? Someone of tall stature, perhaps, whose dark brooding creates an air of mystery?"

Elizabeth suddenly choked on air. Elia Baker began patting her, trying to assist her, and she finally managed to control her breathing. Was the other woman intentionally trying to describe Mr. Darcy? Did she have an idea of how much time Elizabeth had spent with him?

At last, certain she could speak without embarrassing herself, Elizabeth said: "I have no preference. As I said before, I think a mutual regard is by far the most important consideration, and I have met many good men of different social dispositions. My opinions of them were never determined by fair complexion or dark hair, I assure you."

Miss Baker stared at her for a few seconds, her face unreadable, and then she smiled. "I hope whoever I marry shall be a dark and enigmatic sort of man, for then I shall be required to divine his mysteries. A woman might as well dream!"

"Indeed."

"However, a woman must also be careful when indulging any fantasies." Miss Baker's tone had suddenly become serious, and Elizabeth shifted uncomfortably in her seat, not certain why a feeling of unease had suddenly come over her. "Dear Anne, poor thing, has allowed herself to believe in her mother's dream that she will marry her cousin, and she has taken that dream upon herself, deluding herself into thinking it is a reality." Miss Baker shook her head sadly. "No, Mr. Darcy will never marry her."

"I have spent some time with Mr. Darcy, and I do not believe the subject has ever come up. I cannot say I know what Mr. Darcy will and will not do," said Elizabeth carefully.

"His waistcoats are fine, are they not?"

"Wh-what?" stammered Elizabeth, confused by this non-sequitur.

"I have told my brother many times that Mr. Darcy's tailor must be skilled indeed."

"I must say I have never especially noticed his waistcoats," said Elizabeth.

"And his buttons are so very shiny. I have always admired a good shiny button."

And then the conversation turned to other fashions, and the hint of darkness in Elia Baker's conversation—and Elizabeth's sense that something was slightly *off* about the other young woman—dissipated.

Before long, Mr. Baker entered the room and greeted them.

"James!" cried Miss Baker. "You simply *must* discuss the keeping of our grounds with Miss Bennet. She has a particular fondness for the outdoors, and I am certain she would be delighted to hear whatever you have to say on the subject."

Mr. Baker raised an eyebrow in obvious skepticism, but he allowed his sister to usher him over to sit beside Elizabeth.

The shrewd gleam in Miss Baker's eyes was unmistakable, and Elizabeth could not help but be made uncomfortable by the notion of the woman serving as matchmaker . . . especially since the match Miss Baker was making involved her brother! Elizabeth had not spent enough time in Mr. Baker's company to be able to understand him to any great degree—she had only been in the neighborhood for a few days, after all—but she would not be rude to him, no matter how ill at ease she was.

"Mr. Baker," said Elizabeth with a small smile, "are you fond of the outdoors as well?"

"I do enjoy riding my horse," said he after a second's pause, "but I am afraid I should not know a rosebush from a thistle."

Elizabeth gave a small laugh. "Surely it is not as bad as all that."

"Perhaps not," said Mr. Baker as he offered her a grin. "But it is not much better."

"I would not say I am well versed in botany, but I do know the names of several common plants found near my father's estate."

"Is she not charming, James?" said Miss Baker suddenly. "And so agreeable. I dare say I have not heard her speak a single unkind word."

Elizabeth's cheeks became warm. "I am no saint, I can assure you." *Jane* was, certainly, but Elizabeth was not even close to sainthood. If only Miss Baker knew what Elizabeth's character sketch of her was!

"And modest, too!" said Mr. Baker with a laugh.

"Careful, Mr. Baker," said Elizabeth. "I might think you were teasing me."

He grinned at her. "And would that be so terrible?"

"That would depend entirely on what sort of woman I would wish you to see me as. Perhaps I would like to be coy . . . or perhaps I would like to pretend I have delicate sensibilities. A woman need not face restrictions when deciding what personality she wishes to present."

Mr. Baker cocked his head, amusement shining in his eyes. "And a woman cannot simply be herself?"

Elizabeth looked at him in mock astonishment. "Of course not! It is a woman's prerogative to act as something other than what she is in order to keep a man guessing. You must not believe all women enjoy flattering male vanity?"

He let out a bark of laughter. "You intrigue me, Miss Bennet."

"There—you see? Already, I have done something unpredictable."

They continued to speak together, and Mr. Baker seemed to be somewhat amused with their conversation. However, Elizabeth suspected it had less to do with what they were discussing and more to do with his sister's matchmaking attempts. Elia Baker was continually pointing out the good qualities of both her brother and Elizabeth, noting everything from a mutual love of tea (which was quite ridiculous to mention, as there were few people in England who *disliked* the beverage) to the way the color of their eyes went together so perfectly (which was also ridiculous, for reasons which need not be mentioned).

Elizabeth tried to enjoy herself. Mr. Baker was a pleasant enough companion, as was his somewhat unique but apparently well-meaning sister. However, despite his mild interest in her—for she did not believe it was anything *but* mild—she did not feel entirely comfortable with him. Perhaps he was too boyish for her . . . or perhaps he simply failed to challenge her. In conversations about literature, he fell short, not being especially interested in reading, and his opinions on events of the day, while intelligent, were not especially insightful. And above all, though he appeared to be interested in what she had to say, many of his replies carried that slightly condescending air which Elizabeth had often associated with a self-confident man conversing with a woman. Still, she did try to enjoy his company. As she had told Miss Baker, she was an unattached woman. She might as well try to determine whether it was possible for her to have any feelings for this young man; after all, he was handsome enough and a pleasing conversation partner. He was certainly closer to her station than a lofty man such as Mr. Darcy.

And so she teased him and laughed with him, though a small part of her, to her frustration, kept comparing him with Mr. Darcy. She tried not to think about the fact that he rated less than Mr. Darcy in every single category except one: Mr. Baker's amiability. No stretch of the term "amiable" could ever make it fit Mr. Darcy. And surely that was a failing on Mr. Darcy's part, was it not?

But that one "victory" for James Baker felt hollow to Elizabeth.

Chapter VII

The rest of the week passed, and when it had, Elizabeth was left to reflect that the time had gone by very quickly indeed. It hardly seemed like she had been in Kent for an entire week—so much had happened that she felt as if it had instead been a month!

The disagreements of the previous few days appeared to have severed the acquaintance between the two young ladies of the area, both of whom Elizabeth had met with individually since the day of their falling out. Neither of the two women mentioned the other if it was avoidable; indeed, they both acted almost as if they had no awareness of each other's existence. Elizabeth, eager to stay clear of their disagreement, was quite happy to sit with each lady without the presence of the other, though she took great care not to give any appearance of choosing sides.

Miss Baker continued with her attempts to forward an acquaintance between Elizabeth and Mr. Baker, and though Elizabeth found the man engaging and polite, his behavior reminded her of *another* young man she had once known. It was nothing she could put her finger upon, and she certainly did not feel *unsafe* in Mr. Baker's company, but she did get the decided impression that his ways were a little rakish. He was a charmer, without a doubt, engaging in his manners and cheerful in his demeanor, and that in and of itself made Elizabeth wary.

Apart from taking on the role of matchmaker, Miss Baker continued to act as if nothing out of the ordinary had happened. However, Miss de Bourgh's behavior had undoubtedly changed. Though she had not been especially talkative or friendly before, now she was reserved almost to the point of taciturnity, causing Elizabeth to wonder why Miss de Bourgh even bothered to invite her to visit. With Mary, Miss de Bourgh was somewhat less aloof, maintaining the polite, though distant, manner which she had always shown her. Now that Miss Baker had been revealed as a rival, it seemed that Miss de Bourgh viewed *all* single young ladies as potential threats to her stated intention of marrying her cousin. And perhaps Elizabeth seemed to be more of a threat than most. After all, Elizabeth had recently spent time in the company of Mr. Darcy while in London.

However, Elizabeth found that she was unaffected by the heiress's change in demeanor. Anne de Bourgh could act and think as she pleased, after all, and there was nothing Elizabeth could do—or wished to do—about the matter. She was in Kent to support Mary, not to make herself agreeable to the local ladies.

Elizabeth found a great sense of joy and satisfaction in visiting Mary, and they began to forge a closer relationship. Though unable to agree with Mary's choice of husband, Elizabeth could not help but observe that married life seemed to agree with her younger sister, who appeared to have blossomed almost overnight.

Of Mr. Collins, Elizabeth saw little. He was much as he had been in Hertfordshire, though his groveling behavior toward Lady Catherine was such that one might have almost believed her a deity rather than the meddlesome, imperious woman she truly was.

A week after her arrival in Kent, Elizabeth was returning with Mary from the village, where they had been visiting with the local parishioners, and they were just about to enter the gate to the parsonage when a horse came trotting toward them. Both sisters edged to the side of the road to avoid the dust kicked up by the horse's hooves, only to be surprised by the sound of a voice hailing them.

"By my word, Miss Bennet! And Miss Mary, if I am not mistaken. Good day to you both!"

Turning, Elizabeth peered up at the horseman in alarm and found herself gazing into the face of the last person she would have expected to see in Kent.

The gentleman, who was sporting a wide smile, dismounted and bowed with a flourish. "I cannot tell you how good it is to see you— and to find you in the best of health as well!"

The two women exchanged a glance before curtseying back to the young man. Mary's countenance evinced displeasure at seeing the man which was the equal of Elizabeth's own. At least Elizabeth could count on her sister's assistance in ensuring they parted with the scoundrel as soon as possible.

"Thank you, Mr. Wickham," responded Elizabeth, though she spoke with a singular lack of enthusiasm. "Yes, we are indeed well, as you can see."

While Elizabeth would have been happy to never again cross paths with this particular gentleman—and indeed, she detested the very sight of him—she would not create a public display by being rude.

"I had thought you to be in Surrey, sir. What brings you to Kent?"

Ignoring her lack of welcome and frosty tone, Mr. Wickham flashed his usual grin. In the past, the smallest smile from him had fairly melted her heart; now, of course, those same smiles had no effect on her other than to infuriate her. "I was, but I recently passed through Meryton, and I decided to stop to visit with your family, who informed me of your presence in Kent. Since I also had business here to attend to, I was hoping I might come across you. This is truly a fortunate happenstance!"

"Fortunate, indeed," murmured Elizabeth, thinking that it was, in fact, just about the worst circumstance she could possibly imagine. Of course, she was not at all fooled into thinking that he had come across her by "happenstance."

Mary, however, was not inclined to be polite to Mr. Wickham, and she asked him with obvious skepticism: "You mean my father allowed you to enter the house?"

He waved her off in a nonchalant manner. "Your father was not available at the time, Miss Mary. I visited with your mother and your youngest sister, though I must own I was surprised and disappointed not to see *you*, Miss Bennet."

"I am sorry, Mr. Wickham," replied Mary, "but though you *say* that you have visited my family, you still refer to me by my maiden name. Perhaps you have not heard, but I now respond to the name 'Mrs. Collins.' I have been married these last three months."

Mr. Wickham bowed low. "Indeed, I believe I do remember your mother telling me of the joyous event, and I apologize for not addressing you as you deserve. I congratulate you and offer my felicitations on your marriage, Mrs. Collins."

Elizabeth colored at his statement about wishing to see *her* and was silent, wondering how she could dispose of this uncomfortable situation. He obviously had no desire to leave her and be on his way.

Mary, however, had no trouble asking him to be gone. "Perhaps you should attend to your business, *sir*, and leave us to ours. I believe everything between you and my sister which needs to be said has already been said."

"Nonsense! I would enjoy the chance to catch up with old friends. My business is not *that* urgent, you understand, and I much desire the opportunity to become acquainted with you again, as I did with your mother and sister. Surely you would not wish to send an old friend away without becoming reacquainted."

"I think that perhaps it is best that we do not," said Mary, completely unyielding. "You did not leave our family under the best of circumstances, after all, Mr. Wickham, particularly with regard to Elizabeth. Besides, I understand you are *married* now. Perhaps you would be well advised to depart immediately, lest your *wife* misconstrue the meaning of your attention."

"Alas," replied Mr. Wickham with a heavy sigh of melancholy, "Mrs. Wickham has been deceased these past three years—a tragic accident with a horse, you understand."

"I am very sorry to hear it," said Elizabeth, exerting herself to speak.

Mary, however, said nothing, merely contenting herself with glaring at the young man. Mr. Wickham, for his part, seemed determined to pretend her attitude did not exist. He focused his attention upon Elizabeth, who was made uncomfortable by his scrutiny.

As they were thus engaged, an open coach which had been approaching them stopped, and the voice of Lady Catherine blared across the intervening space.

"Mrs. Collins! You should not be standing by the side of the road in all this wind. I dare say your hair shall be a mess—and your dress will become quite the sight—if you continue so with this attitude."

Elizabeth shared a glance with her sister. Though Mary was obliged to pay deference to the lady due to her husband's position, she was not oblivious to the fact that Lady Catherine was a pompous busybody whose declarations sometimes contained not a hint of sense. After all, both Elizabeth and Mary were wearing bonnets to protect their hair, and their dresses would not be any worse for the wear in so little wind as existed that day (not to mention Lady Catherine and her daughter were traveling in an open carriage themselves). Elizabeth turned away to hide a scowl as her sister answered that they were about to enter the house. It was because of this that Elizabeth was in a position to see Mr. Wickham focus his attention to the two new arrivals and smirk at them.

"Mr. Wickham!" cried Lady Catherine. "I have not seen you in many years — since before your father passed away, I believe."

Mr. Wickham's bow was smooth and only hinted at deference, something which the lady did not appear to notice. "Indeed, milady. How do you do?"

"I do very well, Mr. Wickham. But then again, I always do well — maladies are for the lower classes, after all. What are you doing in this part of the country?"

"I had some business in Kent and happened across these lovely ladies, with whom I have a prior acquaintance."

Her ladyship's appraising glances between Elizabeth and Mr. Wickham were hardly subtle, and Elizabeth had to stifle a groan. Lady Catherine *could not* be thinking of matching her with Mr. Wickham!

Yet she quickly found a curious part of her mind rearing its head. How had Lady Catherine come to know Mr. Wickham? Had she been acquainted with his family? Unfortunately, Mr. Wickham had never truly been forthcoming with the details of his own life, so Elizabeth found she knew relatively little of him.

"Well, if you have a prior connection with the two ladies, then perhaps you should come to Rosings and dine with us. I normally would not extend such an invitation, but as you know them *so well* . . ."

Elizabeth longed to correct the lady and induce her to rescind the invitation, but she doubted Lady Catherine would listen to her even if she did, so she merely pursed her lips and held her tongue.

Mr. Wickham's reaction to the prospect was all enjoyment. "Lady Catherine, I believe such a scheme would be most delightful. I gratefully accept."

"Well, I am happy I could be of service," replied the lady, directing a knowing look at Elizabeth. "The Collinses and Miss Bennet have been invited three days hence, and you shall be welcome at the same time. Please understand that I do not put up with tardiness!"

"I do remember your appreciation for punctuality. I shall endeavor to arrive at the proper hour, milady."

He flashed a grin and turned to speak a few words to Miss de Bourgh as well. Their discussion was carried on with some interest on the lady's part, and Elizabeth had the impression that although Lady Catherine was familiar with the gentleman, Miss de Bourgh had not the slightest idea who he was.

Lady Catherine began to speak to Elizabeth and Mary, and the conversation continued in a desultory manner for a few minutes before they separated. Lady Catherine and her daughter went toward

Rosings, while Mr. Wickham, after bidding the ladies of the parsonage an elaborate farewell, mounted and rode away in the opposite direction.

Though it appeared Mary would have liked to discuss the situation in more detail, she was called away to deal with some matter of the servants the moment they entered the parsonage, leaving Elizabeth by herself to reflect.

Mr. Wickham was back. Though she would have expected to feel anger and revulsion at the thought, in truth she felt overcome by weariness and disinterestedness. The man would do what he would, but Elizabeth would not be fooled again. Still, it would be difficult to enjoy herself with him present, as it would dredge up all of the old memories that were better left forgotten.

Between Mr. Wickham's return and Mr. Baker's attentions, Elizabeth was very much afraid she might find herself caught in between two rakes, one of whom had hurt her in the past.

But one thing was clear: she would not allow a man to hurt her in such a fashion again.

Chapter VIII

The day of the dinner at Rosings approached swiftly, much to Elizabeth's dismay. She found herself indulging in vain hopes — namely, that time would stop, Mr. Wickham would meet an untimely delay in the form of a mild accident with a horse, or she would be afflicted with a terrible cold that would preclude any possibility of her attendance at the dinner. Unfortunately, these hopes did not come to pass — and the ground also failed to open up and swallow her whole — so Elizabeth was doomed to an evening spent in the company of the man she had once believed she might one day marry. Being forced to look upon him and recall her naïveté in the realm of love was painful for her, but she had little choice in the matter. She did not wish him to know how much his presence affected her; she refused to give him that satisfaction.

Thus, Elizabeth went with Mary and Mr. Collins to Rosings, determined to hold her head up high. She caught more than one knowing look from Mary, but neither sister mentioned the sensitive subject weighing down the air around them, and Elizabeth felt very grateful for Mary's forbearance. Mr. Collins certainly would not be sympathetic, and Elizabeth did not wish to hand him something he could lord over her — not that she believed him intelligent enough to truly realize what such knowledge could mean in regard to his effect on her level of misery. She did, however, believe him petty, and she thought it possible he could stumble onto the realization of what had happened in his attempts to snub her.

Rosings was much as it usually was—it was filled with the same ostentatious and slightly uncomfortable furniture, the pretentious and overly showy decor, and the domineering and overbearing presence of Lady Catherine. Anne de Bourgh was still cold as she had been since the incident at Stauneton, Mr. Collins was his normal eagerly obsequious self, and Mary remained calm and thoughtful and blind to the social faux pas which Mr. Collins committed every time he opened his mouth. To all this, Mr. Wickham and his insincere flattery and charming manners were added, making the company even more tedious than it had been previously.

It was Elizabeth's misfortune that she was required to sit beside Mr. Wickham at dinner, but she had known such would be the case when she arrived.

With a knowing smile, Mr. Wickham said to her: "I feel very fortunate to be part of this meal. I had rather hoped to spend more time in conversation with you, Miss Bennet."

"I am certain you did," murmured Elizabeth with a glare which clearly told him that the pleasure would *not* be mutual. Mr. Wickham either did not recognize the insult or completely ignored it, though her suspicions leaned toward the latter as being more likely.

Elizabeth's eyes lifted and met the sympathetic gaze of her sister across the table. Elizabeth gave a brief nod of reassurance, for she was well able to withstand the man's attentions, regardless of what had happened between them before. It was a matter of feeling ill at ease. That was all. Before she knew it, the night would be over, and she would be secluded in Mary's home, with Mr. Wickham out of her life forever. The little voice that warned her he might be lingering in Kent for a time was one she quelled.

The soup was served, and both Mr. Collins and Mr. Wickham declared it to be very good. When it was time for the main course, the chorus of flattery from both men grew louder.

"My! What a glorious table we have before us!" exclaimed Mr. Collins. "Your ladyship always has such an eye for complementary flavors. Though I am only a humble cleric, with an unrefined palate that has not been properly cultured in the nuances of spices, I dare say not even the royal table could hope to compare with the bounty you place before us."

"I must second the opinion of Mr. Collins," said Mr. Wickham smoothly. "Your selection is much to be praised. I dare say you must keep only the finest cooks."

"That is certainly the case," confirmed Lady Catherine, obviously quite pleased at the prospect of a new admirer.

"Finding a proper cook can be a difficult task," said Mr. Wickham, "but you appear to have managed quite well, your ladyship."

"I should say so. I refuse to settle for anything less than the best. If you are going to do something, then you might as well do it in the proper fashion, and my table shall never be anything but proper."

"I could not agree more, Madam."

Although both men were free with their praise and flattery, the difference between the two was striking. Mr. Collins was in his element, constantly acclaiming everything which came to mind, and his words sometimes flitted from one subject to the next without any discernible sequence; his words flowed instantly from whatever was passing through his mind at the moment, so desperate was he to continually show his patroness how thankful he was for her favor. Mr. Wickham's flattery, however, was relevant to what was occurring at the time, and his attempts at increasing Lady Catherine's vanity—as though it were not already bloated enough!—were therefore smooth and bespoke of intelligence and purpose, though Elizabeth had no way of determining what that purpose was.

As the meal progressed, Mr. Wickham and Lady Catherine proceeded to engage each other in an exclusive conversation in which the former built up the vanity of the latter, continuing to exercise his charisma to its utmost. Mr. Collins, when he attempted to insert his own compliments into their dialogue, found himself cast aside by an abrupt statement from her ladyship. He then began to glower in barely disguised anger at the object of his patroness's attention.

Elizabeth was initially amused by the situation, especially since it meant Mr. Wickham was not addressing her, but she soon began to worry about Mr. Collins. After all, if the man were to have an outburst that displeased Lady Catherine, then it might harm Mary's situation, and Elizabeth did not want that. So, drawing upon what must have been the patience of a saint, Elizabeth began to speak to Mr. Collins, thereby forcing him to focus some of his displeasure on her. It was not a pleasant way to spend the meal, but at least it was preferable to being the object of Mr. Wickham's flattery.

After dinner, they retired to the drawing-room. The men chose not to separate from the women, and Mr. Wickham immediately turned on the female-pleasing charm Elizabeth knew quite well.

"Mr. Collins and I are very fortunate," noted Mr. Wickham with a smile. "We are surrounded by lovely and talented women. It is a wonder we can speak at all."

The expression on Mr. Collins's face darkened, and Mary jumped in: "Lizzy, you must play the pianoforte for us." She looked at Lady Catherine. "My sister plays quite well, Lady Catherine, and I am certain you would enjoy it."

"Very well. Go to it, child," said Lady Catherine, gesturing toward the instrument.

Repressing a sigh, Elizabeth moved and sat down at the pianoforte. There was only one piece of music available, which appeared to be testament to the fact that the instrument was seldom used, but she was simply glad the song was one with which she was familiar. As her fingers began to press against the keys, she noted out of the corner of her eyes that Mr. Collins was talking to Lady Catherine, likely trying to flatter himself back into her good graces. Mr. Wickham, on the other hand, had moved toward Anne de Bourgh, presumably to converse.

Mary assisted Elizabeth by turning the pages, and she murmured: "Are you well, Lizzy?"

Elizabeth gave an almost impish smile. "I am fine, Mary, thank you. Somehow, however, I do not believe anyone wished to listen to me play."

"I wished to," said Mary firmly.

"Would you like to play?"

Mary shook her head. "I would rather listen to you a little longer."

After Elizabeth continued for a few minutes more, she finally stopped and looked at her sister. "Are you ready to face the rest of the room?"

"I suppose I am," said Mary with a smile.

The two ladies turned and left the pianoforte. Mr. Collins was still flattering the seated Lady Catherine, though that was nothing out of the ordinary. Miss de Bourgh and Mr. Wickham, however, were standing against a wall out of sight of Lady Catherine and Mr. Collins, deep in conversation. Mr. Wickham was leaning a little closer to Miss de Bourgh than was strictly proper, but when he saw Elizabeth, he smiled brightly and called out to her: "Miss Bennet, Mrs. Collins, please join us! The music with which you favored us was truly excellent. Of course, I remember your talents quite well, Miss Bennet, and the intervening years have only improved your performance."

Inhaling deeply, Elizabeth walked with her sister over to Miss de Bourgh and Mr. Wickham. The night had not been ideal, but at least it had not been too terrible. She was, however, strangely missing the taciturnity of Mr. Darcy; even when he was at his most dour, she felt she would far rather face him than listen to the sycophantic conversations of Mr. Collins and Mr. Wickham.

Once, Mr. Wickham had meant the world to her. Now, however, she marveled that she was the same girl who had relished every dance and every word from him. What she had not understood before was that silences could sometimes be infinitely more interesting than even the most artful discussion.

Her carefully placed smile faltered as she realized Mr. Darcy had not yet arrived at Rosings. Was he coming soon? And when he came, would she see him? Or would Lady Catherine be so enthralled at the chance to support an alliance between Miss de Bourgh and Mr. Darcy that suddenly the Collinses—and Elizabeth—would not be quite so welcome at Rosings? If that were the case, it would not come as much of a surprise.

She tried to think of this as a blessing, but she could not convince herself that she did not want to see Mr. Darcy at least one more time.

Chapter IX

$\mathcal{T}$he carriage ride to Kent seemed interminable, and though Darcy knew it to be short—a mere four hours—somehow he felt as if it were a journey of prodigious proportions.

Part of the reason, of course, was due to the fact that he was traveling to Kent alone for the first time in his memory. In the past, Colonel Fitzwilliam had always accompanied him on his annual visit, but this year, unfortunately, his cousin had been summoned back to his regiment on urgent business. Darcy was not certain of the reason for the summons—and hoped the man would not be sent to the continent—but he had been given every assurance that Fitzwilliam would join him again this summer or perhaps even sooner, which fortunately seemed to suggest that he would *not* be in the middle of the fighting.

The fact that Fitzwilliam would not be joining him at Rosings this year had darkened Darcy's mood, for he counted on having a friend and confidante to fortify him during these annual visits. Their aunt, after all, *did* have a tendency to make them uncomfortable, and Darcy was aware that Fitzwilliam generally joined him with the primary purpose of providing Darcy with support. Furthermore, it was *this time* in particular when Darcy could have used the assistance, making the timing irksome at best.

Darcy expected this particular visit to be especially unpleasant, and Lady Catherine's usual displeasure at his unwillingness to commit to marrying his cousin would pale in comparison to what she would feel when he told her once and for all that he had no intention of wedding her daughter.

Darcy had thought long and carefully on the subject—indeed, little else had been on his mind for the past several months—but the more he considered the notion, the more convinced he became that marrying Anne was not what he desired and was, in fact, just about the worst thing he could do for his future happiness. He loved and respected Anne as a cousin, but they were too similar in temperament and character to make their marriage a happy one. Of course, Lady Catherine would no doubt trot out that old argument about how she and her sister had planned a union between their heirs from the time they were both in their cradles. However, Darcy knew it had been otherwise—his father had told him that Lady Anne *had* indeed discussed the *possibility* with her sister, but she had never agreed to a formal engagement. For this, Darcy was grateful, for *if* his mother *had* agreed to such a scheme, he knew he would have been honor-bound to abide by the agreement; his sense of duty would allow for nothing else.

As for his more particular choice, Elia Baker was a fine woman of a very good pedigree, she had an impressive dowry, and marriage to her would bind Darcy not only to the Bakers, but also to their distant cousin, who was an esteemed duke. Therefore, she had all the necessary requirements to be considered a good match by any definition. In addition, the woman was cheerful and engaging, and she made for pleasant company—not to mention she was his complete opposite. She also amused him, though his amusement was primarily due to her sometimes unintelligent comments. Still, he enjoyed her company, and he was aware that he could do much worse in his quest for a wife. It did not hurt that she was quite beautiful as well.

As for the other young lady he would see in Kent—well, Darcy had resolved not to think *too much* of Miss Elizabeth Bennet, difficult though that was proving. His resolve seemed to disappear in her presence, and he found himself wishing to speak with her and to hear her opinions. She intrigued him and challenged him intellectually more than anyone else ever had. He had been so disconcerted by his lack of control where she was concerned that he had even delayed telling her that he would be joining her in Kent, as he was not certain he would actually be attending his aunt this year due to Miss Bennet's beguiling presence. He was unable to control his desire to converse with

Elizabeth Bennet when she was nearby, and he could not subject her to the displeasure that would rain down on her should Lady Catherine suspect even a hint of partiality.

Of course, he was not partial to Elizabeth Bennet in anything other than an intellectual fashion—no more than she was partial to him. Her eyes did not sparkle more than usual in his presence, and the welcoming smiles with which she favored him were the same as those she gave to everyone else. No, they felt no mutual attraction; they simply enjoyed one another's company and intelligent discourse. Besides, she was certainly *not* an appropriate prospective partner in marriage; after all, she had no dowry to speak of, her relations included a sycophantic parson and a fortune-hunting mother, and she had no connections to bring to a marriage. If he were to consider marrying her, *all* the advantage would be on her side and none on his. In light of that fact, he would not expose her to the disappointment of hopes which could not be filled.

In the end, he had decided to honor his yearly commitment and go to Kent. Anne looked forward to his visits every year, and Lady Catherine's anger would be almost unbearable if he did not attend her. Furthermore, he knew that Lady Catherine was an indifferent manager of the estate at best, and if he did not go to Rosings to look the situation over, he would have an even more difficult time sorting it out when he did finally return.

If Rosings still existed then, he thought, somewhat cynically.

Besides, he *did* enjoy seeing Anne, even though it necessitated time spent with his aunt. He would simply have to take great care with Anne's feelings in all of this. Although he had spent a lot of time in her company, the subject of their supposed marriage had never come up between them, and he was not certain what her reaction to his rejection of her would be. It was this lack of knowledge which had been the most difficult part of the process of coming to a decision about his future.

However, the facts remained: she was not a good match for him, and Miss Baker more closely fit his needs in a wife. In addition to all of those concerns, he was not even certain that Anne could carry a child safely to term. His need for an heir was the consideration which had perhaps trumped all others, especially with *two* estates destined to be inherited by his children, should he marry Anne. No, he was certain this decision was for the best.

It was because of these thoughts that the trip to Rosings passed in such a dreary and seemingly long manner, and when the carriage finally pulled into the drive of his destination, Darcy had worked himself into a foul mood. He wanted nothing more than to seek his room and brood in silence, but he knew that Lady Catherine would not allow him such a luxury. Resigned to spending the evening in company when he would have preferred nothing more than his room and a good book, Darcy supervised the unpacking of his trunks, and once he had bathed himself from the dust of the road, he descended the stairs to brave the welcome of Lady Catherine.

The first thing he found upon entering the drawing-room was perhaps the last thing for which he would have hoped: Elizabeth Bennet was there, speaking with his aunt and cousin. Still in an unsettled state, Darcy nonetheless exerted himself to politeness and greeted the ladies. Unfortunately, his aunt was much as she had ever been.

"I see you have finally arrived, Darcy," stated she after the necessary pleasantries had been exchanged. "I had thought you would be here earlier in the day, but you young people always insist on sleeping late and then arriving at your destination at a most inconvenient hour."

"I am afraid you are mistaken, Lady Catherine," said Darcy, affecting a patience he did not feel. "I made very good time indeed and left once I had finished a small piece of business which presented itself at the last moment. I *did* arrive soon after the luncheon hour, after all."

Lady Catherine merely sniffed and did not deign to answer directly. "Well, you are here now — that is what is important. Of course, you did not bring your cousin with you. I suppose he is off carousing with the officers of that regiment of his."

"Actually, I saw Fitzwilliam before I left London, and I am certain that whatever his business was, it was of the most serious nature. I believe he indicated he had written a note to you apologizing for his inability to travel with me, but whatever he is doing, I am certain it is not 'carousing with the officers.'"

"I suppose not," was her reply, after which she was silent.

Knowing her dislike for being contradicted, Darcy suspected she would likely be silent for some time unless some other topic overcame her petulance. He was grateful for small blessings, and every stolen moment in which she would be silent was to be cherished, for such occasions were few and far in between.

"Cousin, I believe you have met Miss Bennet before, have you not?" spoke Anne.

"Oh, yes," interjected Lady Catherine, pushing past her previous displeasure, "I had forgotten of the young lady's presence." She turned to stare at Elizabeth as though she were a criminal who had stolen into the room under their very noses.

"We do share an acquaintance," said Darcy. "How do you do, Miss Bennet? I hope you find Kent to your liking."

"Indeed, I do," replied Miss Bennet softly. "Lady Catherine and Miss de Bourgh have been very accommodating and kind. I hardly know I have left home due to the gracious welcome they have shown me."

A glance at Lady Catherine showed her preening under the praise, while the sparkle in Miss Bennet's eye showed that she understood exactly what she was doing . . . and that she was amused his aunt was lapping up the praise like an enthusiastic puppy.

Anne, on the other hand, was watching him intently, though her gaze moved to Miss Bennet every so often. Darcy wondered what she was thinking. Could she have some inkling of his . . . camaraderie with the young woman? And if so, did she feel threatened by it?

Determined that he would show no especial favor to the young woman—particularly in Lady Catherine's presence—Darcy returned his attention to the conversation to hear his aunt addressing Miss Bennet.

"We were happy to receive you, Miss Bennet. You are not precisely of our sphere, it is true, but you are pleasant enough company and appear to know your place. Your sister has been a true benefit to the parish, as she undertakes her duties to her husband's flock with a seriousness I find most pleasing. You should be very proud of her."

Darcy was embarrassed by his aunt's speech. *Perhaps* Miss Bennet was not of the first circles, but to state such directly to a gentleman's daughter was very rude indeed. Miss Bennet, however, appeared to accept her words with grace, ignoring the less than diplomatic ones in favor of the praise for her sister.

"I am, Lady Catherine," said Miss Bennet. "I have always thought Mary would be an excellent wife to some fortunate man. She is very pious and attentive to the words of our Lord, which makes her perfect for her role. I am very happy for her."

"As you should be. I hope that you will be as diligent in your duties as a wife when you are married. Your young beau seems to be good for you. I believe you will make an excellent pair, and as I am familiar with the ways and means of pairing those persons who are complementary with one another, I am never wrong about such things."

That received Darcy's full attention. Miss Bennet had been in Kent for a matter of two weeks, and she already had an admirer? Try as Darcy might, he could imagine no one in the area who would take such a quick and decided interest in her. The only unmarried man of her station in the nearby area was James Baker, and not only did he not mention anything of the sort in response to Darcy's letter, but he was also not one who appeared to be ready to settle down with a wife. In truth, though Darcy *did* end up spending a certain amount of time with Baker whenever he visited, it was primarily due to the lack of other suitable male companions. Darcy considered him to be somewhat of a rake, and though Baker's targets were not usually daughters of gentlemen, if he had taken an interest in Miss Bennet . . . The very thought caused a disquiet to manifest itself as a pit in the bottom of Darcy's stomach. He shook his head to clear it and focused on the conversation again.

"I believe you are reading too much into Mr. Wickham's actions, Lady Catherine," was Miss Bennet's rebuttal. "I am certain he is only passing through and has not shown any particular interest in me. In fact, I would much prefer that he did not."

Almost choking on his tea, Darcy coughed quite violently, causing his aunt's attention to turn to him.

"You really must learn to sip your tea as is polite, Darcy," stated she. "You shall certainly cause yourself to drown in your own beverage if you consume it too quickly."

Ignoring the inanities of her words, Darcy focused his attention upon Miss Bennet and asked:

"*Mr. Wickham* is here?"

She appeared taken aback by his vehemence, but she boldly faced him. "Yes, Mr. Darcy. He arrived a week ago and was in this very room a few days later dining with your aunt and my sister and her husband."

"Whatever for?" demanded Darcy, unable to hide his surprise.

"Why do you question who I invite to my table?" challenged Lady Catherine. "Certainly, Mr. Wickham is not of our sphere—he is not even of Miss Bennet's sphere!—but he *is* an acquaintance, and one can only be polite. Besides, he was paying Miss Bennet particular attention."

His aunt's smirk was quite unpleasant, but Darcy had no time for her absurdities. He peered at Miss Bennet, trying to ascertain what sort of situation existed between her and Mr. Wickham. He *would not* allow her to be drawn in by that scoundrel.

Miss Bennet, however, appeared to sense his displeasure. "I assure you, Mr. Darcy, that I have no interest in furthering an acquaintance with Mr. Wickham, nor do I think he is interested in one with me."

Lady Catherine appeared as if she were about to protest, so Darcy spoke up, neatly diverting the conversation to one about Rosings and the situation of the estate. Lady Catherine appeared pleased at being able to update his knowledge — and thereby show him what a benefit it would be to him if he should marry Anne, no doubt — and the previous conversation was forgotten.

Although Darcy gave the appearance of interest in her information, inside he was seething and could concentrate upon little but the fact that Wickham was in the area and paying attention to Miss Bennet. *That* was a situation which he could not countenance in the slightest.

He had not seen the scoundrel since the meeting almost five years before in which Wickham had requested the value of the living Darcy's father had provided him in lieu of the rectorate at Kympton. The only communications between them after that time had been Wickham's request for more money — which had been firmly rejected, of course — and then a final abusive letter; after that, Darcy had not heard another word. He had hoped he would never see his childhood companion again, knowing what a wastrel the man had become.

Wickham was a rake of the worst sort, which meant that all the young ladies in the area were in danger, including Elia Baker and Anne in addition to Miss Bennet.

Uneasily, he cast his gaze upon both his cousin and Miss Bennet. The latter was affecting an air of unconcern while trying to appear interested in the conversation of Rosings, which had nothing whatsoever to do with her. The former, though, was watching the proceedings with great interest, and Darcy witnessed her often staring at Miss Bennet and then alternating between her and himself with a small frown upon her face, as though trying to puzzle something out.

It was at that moment that Darcy decided that his original plan of proposing to Miss Baker would not do. With Wickham prowling around the area, any deviation from their normal routines and activities could give the man an opportunity to commit whatever perfidy he was here to perpetrate. No, it would be much better for Darcy to keep his own counsel and watch Wickham carefully when he was around *any* of the young ladies.

As the conversation progressed, Darcy found himself observing Miss Bennet as she interacted with his relations, and he knew one thing — he *would* keep her safe.

Chapter X

A few days passed before Darcy spoke with Elizabeth Bennet again. His aunt was pleased to see him and seemed reluctant to share him with outsiders, and he had begun to wonder if she intended to completely ignore everyone she considered beneath her notice in favor of trying to bring *him* under her domain in their stead. But with a little subtle prompting from Darcy to remind her of their neighbors—which included two daughters of a gentleman—a dinner invite was at last sent to Hunsford and duly accepted. As for the Bakers, although Darcy suggested that their attendance be requested as well, the idea was met with cool disapproval, particularly from Anne. Though nonplussed at the de Bourghs' changed attitude toward their neighbors, Darcy shrugged and did not pursue the suggestion.

Darcy welcomed the company for the change it promised. Anne had been behaving strangely—in ways beyond simply her altered feelings toward the Bakers—and his aunt seemed more officious than usual, all of which had made him long for Colonel Fitzwilliam's presence even more. At least the colonel was skilled at bringing humor into any situation. Darcy had begun to wonder if *anyone* living at Rosings ever truly smiled.

His aunt's parson, the parson's wife, and Miss Bennet arrived for dinner, and when they were all at last seated at the table, Darcy found the conversation to be somewhat of a relief. Lady Catherine had already asked him a number of prying questions, and she now seemed content to turn her focus on their guests in order to ascertain whether they were facing any quandaries which necessitated her advice. Mr. Collins appeared more than willing to grace Lady Catherine with the minute details of his life, and Mrs. Collins occasionally chimed in with statements or questions that were designed to either curtail her husband's sometimes fumbling eagerness or please her husband's ever-lofty patroness.

As Darcy watched Miss Bennet, he noticed her quietly eating her food. She would speak when spoken to, but she offered no conversation of her own; certainly, dinner talk was more than covered by Lady Catherine and Mr. Collins alone without anyone else needing to add to it. He found himself wondering what Miss Bennet was thinking. Were her thoughts concerned with Wickham? Darcy still had not seen the man, but that did not mean he was not skulking about, engaged in his usual distasteful pursuits and attempting to extend his influence over any women nearby.

At one point, Miss Bennet looked up and saw Darcy gazing at her, and she smiled. He gave her a nod, and she returned her attention back to her plate.

Not long after that, Anne engaged him in conversation, but it was brief, and she soon returned to her silence.

Once they had finished dinner, they retired to the drawing-room. Miss Bennet sat on a sofa in a position which was separate from where his aunt sat holding court, he noticed with some amusement. After hesitating briefly, Darcy took a seat near her.

Gazing at her, he asked: "Are you still a great walker, Miss Bennet?"

"Indeed, I am, Mr. Darcy. I find there is nothing that clears one's head as well as a walk."

"And you remain an avid reader, yes?" For some reason, he was certain that what he recalled of her could not be true, as if she were something he had conjured up in a dream.

"Yes, I am," acknowledged she with a smile. She lowered her voice, as if divulging a secret. "But I am afraid Mr. Collins does not have much of a library to speak of. Religious texts are fine enough to read, but I had much rather spend a little time with the Bard."

"And what are your favorites, Miss Bennet? His sonnets?" Their conversation was moving just as easily as it had in London.

"'Shall I compare thee to a summer's day?'" quoted she with a smile. "Shakespeare's sonnets are enjoyable, certainly. But one must not forget his plays. 'If we shadows have offended . . .'"

"'Think but this, and all is mended,'" finished Mr. Darcy. The corner of his mouth drew upward. "Do you like Robin Goodfellow, Miss Bennet?"

The expression on her face was almost a smirk. "I might."

"I should not be surprised. He is, after all, a mischievous character."

"Why, are you telling me that I delight in mischief, Mr. Darcy?"

"I am afraid that is something of which you are already well aware," said he lightly. "If a love potion were put in your hands, I should fear what you would do with it."

She laughed. "Perhaps you are right. After all, I might decide I should like to see what *you* are like when in love, Mr. Darcy. Somehow, I could not see you composing love sonnets for your lady."

"You are quite right. I should not even know where to begin."

"You would need to begin with her eyes, I think. How about—'Your eyes, they shine so brightly, like the stars—'"

He shook his head. "I think even I could write a line better than that."

Miss Bennet looked at him with a challenge sparkling in her eyes. "Are you certain, Mr. Darcy? You do not strike me as a romantic."

"'A brilliant glen is hidden in your eyes—'"

"Nephew!" called out the shrill voice of his aunt. "Of what are you and Miss Bennet speaking? You look as if you are trading secrets."

"We are discussing poetry," said Darcy calmly, though inside he was cursing his aunt for interrupting the easy conversation between him and Miss Bennet.

Lady Catherine was staring at him and Miss Bennet with what seemed to be a suspicious look. "I was not even aware you liked poetry." She fixed her gaze on his conversation partner, and her lip curled into a slight sneer. "Miss Bennet, you should provide us with some music. I was not able to truly listen to you when you played the last time you dined at Rosings."

"Yes, your ladyship," said Miss Bennet as she stood and moved toward the instrument. Darcy was of the impression that she would have sighed if she had been able to do so without drawing his aunt's attention.

He watched as she examined the pianoforte. She searched, but apparently the search did not yield any music, and after a moment, she became a little flustered. Darcy was about to speak up when he saw her direct a glance at his aunt—who was once again conversing with the parson while surreptitiously watching Miss Bennet—before sitting down at the instrument. She closed her eyes and placed her fingers on the keys and then began playing "While Shepherds Watched Their Flocks by Night" from memory.

Though the hymn itself was neither somber nor lively, there was something remarkable about the passion she managed to put into it. The caresses of her fingers seemed to breathe life into the pianoforte, and Darcy could hear the progression of words in his head just as clearly as if she had been singing them.

His aunt, however, had barely listened at all to Miss Bennet's playing before she saw fit to proclaim: "Miss Bennet, it is still many months before such a display would be appropriate. Why do you play a Christmas hymn?"

"Perhaps it is because there is no music at the pianoforte and she is playing from memory," interjected Darcy.

Lady Catherine sniffed in disdain. "She should have several pieces memorized so she may play them when there is nothing else suitable at hand. A Christmas carol is not appropriate for a spring evening." She listened critically for several moments before speaking again: "I do believe that your fingering is as deficient as your taste, Miss Bennet. You could undoubtedly use more practice time. I dare say you would do better if you would spend your days in front of the instrument rather than traipsing throughout the countryside."

Darcy's countenance darkened as he watched something flicker across the young woman's face. She continued to play, but something of the vigor was lost.

Turning to look at his aunt, Darcy said: "I believe she handles the instrument admirably, and her choice of music is light and pleasing."

Lady Catherine shook her head. "You do not know music so well as I do. There is something lacking—"

"I am surprised at your words, Aunt, as I do not recall you possessing a proficiency at *any* instrument. There is nothing at all lacking in Miss Bennet's performance."

"No, Nephew, you see—"

And then, Darcy, unable to listen to any more of his aunt's criticism, began to sing loudly:

> "The heavenly babe you there shall find
> To human view displayed,
> All meanly wrapped in swathing bands
> And in a manger laid . . .
> And in a manger laid."

His aunt's face was all astonishment. Her chin dipped down as she tried to speak, but no words issued forth from her mouth—perhaps because of the force of Darcy's voice. Her annoyance then grew to an almost palpable point, yet she was obviously not willing to displease her nephew. She simply raised her head and glowered at Miss Bennet, as though the young woman were the cause of her imagined troubles.

For her part, Miss Bennet appeared just as astonished as Darcy's aunt, though she masked it much better than Lady Catherine did. While her playing never faltered, Darcy thought he could detect a flicker of gratitude in the depths of her eyes. A warmth which had nothing to do with the fine spring evening spread through Darcy; he was pleased he had been able to assist against the officious—and even vicious—pronouncements of his aunt.

As Darcy continued to sing, he glanced over at Mr. Collins and was surprised to see the parson was glaring at the Miss Bennet.

Mr. Collins then actually moved toward Miss Bennet and said to her in a low voice (which Darcy could just barely hear by stepping forward): "Have you bewitched Mr. Darcy? Why is he singing as *you* play?"

Darcy moved even closer to the pair, and Mr. Collins flushed upon noticing him. "M-Mr. Darcy," stuttered the parson.

"What were you saying, Mr. Collins?"

"Nothing of consequence, Mr. Darcy," said the man in a small voice before retreating to a safer region of the room.

It was all Darcy could do to keep from scowling. The parson disgusted him.

And to be frank, his petty aunt often disgusted him, too.

Chapter XI

*M*ary Collins, née Bennet, was content with her life. After growing up as the middle of five daughters and frequently hearing comparisons between their beauty and her lack thereof, she had surprised everyone by marrying before any of her sisters. Thus, it was not Jane's handsome countenance or Elizabeth's playful personality which had first attracted a husband, but Mary's practicality and pious nature.

Oh, she was aware that naysayers—had they known the true story—would have pointed out the fact that Jane had been Mr. Collins's first choice, but Mary discounted that consideration out of hand. Mr. Collins *had* been enamored with Jane's fair appearance, but there were few men who were not. Beauty had little to do with compatibility, however, and Mary was convinced that Jane would not have made Mr. Collins a good wife. There was nothing at fault in Jane's manners or her character, but Mr. Collins required a wife who was capable of subtly guiding him, and Jane was far too self-effacing and thought too well of others to do anything of the sort.

Mary had been pleasantly surprised when she had arrived at Hunsford. The parsonage was not large, but it was comfortable and clean, and the gardens were delightful. As for the parishioners, who had gone without a pastor's wife for many years—the previous parson having been a widower for more than a decade—they were welcoming and grateful for anything she did on their behalf. It had not taken long for her to decide that her life would be a pleasant enough one.

Of course, Mary had to acknowledge that her husband was not particularly gifted intellectually. Yet he was, in general, a good husband. He was solicitous of her comfort, and he was industrious, spending time writing his sermons, working in his garden, and tending to the people of the parish. Furthermore, he was quick to ask her opinion about the matters over which he presided and had realized that she could help him a great deal in all aspects of his life.

The near-constant presence of Lady Catherine served as the one area in which there was potential for misunderstanding and discord in the Collins's marriage. Mr. Collins was so deferential and downright obsequious when it came to his patroness that Mary knew within moments of seeing them together that she would be unable to wean her husband from Lady Catherine's influence as she had initially planned. Therefore, if she could not induce him to rely more upon her counsel than the lady's, then she would have no choice but to ensure she was agreeable to the lady.

Drawing on every ounce of patience she had, Mary went out of her way to ensure that Lady Catherine never had anything about which to complain, and she followed her ladyship's instructions to the letter, even if she felt Lady Catherine was in error. Keeping harmony, after all, was more important a consideration than always having her own way. Still, she was pleased to discover that she could guide Mr. Collins away from the lady's advice at times, encouraging him to take a slightly different tack than that which the lady had intended. The perils of this approach were great, so she only used it when handling a matter of import in which she felt the lady's directions would be harmful.

Yes, Mary was happy in her new life, and the arrival of her sister made her happiness complete, even if Elizabeth—whose behavior Mary truly could not fault—did not seem to garner Lady Catherine's approval. Since Elizabeth was not to stay long in Hunsford and had held her outspoken nature in check, there would be little lasting effect on Mary's relationship with her husband's patroness.

The final piece of the puzzle which would guarantee Mary's happiness had been confirmed that afternoon. She had been feeling somewhat poorly for the past few weeks. Suspecting a very welcome condition, she had visited the apothecary, who had pronounced her to be expecting. Happier than she had ever been, Mary returned home that afternoon, anxious to tell her husband the joyous news. The conversation, however, did not proceed in the manner she had expected.

"Mary, come into my bookroom, please," directed her anxious husband as soon as she entered the house. "A matter of a most serious nature has occurred."

Concerned, Mary followed Mr. Collins to his room and sat across the desk from him as he paced the small space behind the piece of furniture. His face was pale, and he was sweating; in fact, he had been a little unwell the past few days, but this day, he was looking much worse than he had been.

"What is it, Mr. Collins? Are you ill?"

"I am well, my dear," replied Mr. Collins as he waved off her concern. "I received a letter from my cousin Delilah Hampton this morning which has worried me greatly. In it, I learned that her mother, Sophia, has taken ill, and they do not know if she shall recover."

"Sophia is your late mother's sister, is she not?"

"She is. After reading the letter, I immediately hastened to Rosings to ask Lady Catherine's opinion and hear her wisdom, for she is knowledgeable about so many things that I knew she would be able to guide me as to the proper course of action. Her ladyship's advice mirrored my own thoughts on the subject: I must go to London and visit my aunt."

It was so like Mr. Collins to value the lady's opinion over that of his own wife, but by now Mary was accustomed to the fact that anything of import would be decided upon by his patroness and relayed to Mary afterward. She did not always like it, but she was forced to accept it nonetheless.

"Of course you must go," said she. "Am I to understand that Lady Catherine has given you permission to absent yourself from the parsonage?"

"Indeed, she has." His voice took on a pompous tone, and he straightened as he spoke of his mistress. It often seemed to Mary that the only time he was straight in posture and completely confident in tone was when he was quoting his patroness verbatim. "Lady Catherine was gracious in condescending to advise me on the subject, but so she always is. 'Mr. Collins,' said she, 'of course you must journey to London to visit with your lady aunt. Family is so very important, after all, and your cousin will be fortunate to have your assistance and will undoubtedly take comfort in your presence. I suppose no one takes as much true enjoyment in the company of those of close familial ties as I do. I take great delight in my nephews' visits every year, as you well know, and I have advised them many times that they should come more often. Be that as it may, nothing must come in the way of family obligations, and I therefore command you to leave as soon as may be.'

"It is wonderful that I am so very in tune with my good patroness that my thoughts on the matter agree with hers so closely, though I am but a modest cleric and not as well versed in the ever-fluctuating ways of the world as she. I am determined to depart for my cousin's house forthwith. Therefore, I shall be leaving early tomorrow and will likely not return for at least a week's time."

Mary was crestfallen. She had looked forward to informing her husband of the imminent arrival of an addition to their little family, only to learn that he was to leave the next day. Making an immediate decision, she resolved to keep the news to herself until he returned, as he would need to focus his energy upon his aunt and not concern himself with her.

"Of course you must go, Mr. Collins," said she with a smile. "I shall prepare for your departure in the morning. You must make certain to keep me advised as to any changes in your aunt's condition."

"I shall," replied Mr. Collins, his face lightening in a fond smile. His countenance was not handsome, but when he showed his affection for her, it altered his face in a way which made it much more agreeable. "I thank you, my wife, for being so understanding and for supporting me during such times of need."

"You need not thank me, sir. It is the least that any wife could do for her husband."

Mr. Collins accepted her words with a smile, but when he turned and glanced out the window, his smile ran away from his countenance, and a firm mask of disapproval descended in its place. Bewildered at this sudden change in his mood, Mary moved to see what had caught his attention and was not surprised to find her sister approaching the parsonage from the direction of Rosings. What had undoubtedly caused Mr. Collins's displeasure was the presence of the gentleman with whom she was walking.

The pair reached the gate, and Mary witnessed Mr. Darcy stop and open it for Elizabeth. Then he took her hand and bowed over it before retreating in the direction of his aunt's estate while her sister entered the house. Knowing Mr. Collins had not been pleased over what he considered Elizabeth's improper advances toward Mr. Darcy, Mary attempted to smooth over the worst of his ill-humor by directing the conversation toward other matters, but Mr. Collins was quiet after the incident, never regaining the happy mood which had possessed him previously. At length, Mary was able to convince her husband to take a short nap before dinner, which helped in dissipating his displeasure.

The subject of Elizabeth was one in which Mary had been quite unable to sway Mr. Collins. Mr. Darcy's startling display during their last invitation to dinner at Rosings had cemented in Mr. Collins's mind that Elizabeth was somehow attempting to draw Mr. Darcy in. The fact that Elizabeth had been quiet all evening, rarely initiating any conversation, had not entered his mind. And while Elizabeth had been careful to display no marked preference toward Mr. Darcy—thus satisfying Lady Catherine that she had no designs on the lady's nephew—Mr. Collins still subscribed to his theory of Elizabeth's duplicity and had taken every opportunity to remind her of her lowly station and her unsuitability for the nephew of his patroness. Elizabeth had thus far borne his censure with dignity and restraint, but Mary, who was well acquainted with her sister's moods, could see it was beginning to wear on her. Perhaps the prolonged absence of Mr. Collins was coming at a fortuitous juncture after all.

Dinner that evening was subdued, with Mary directing the conversation in as neutral a manner as possible. The subject of Elizabeth and Mr. Darcy was not brought up at all, though Mr. Collins did make a point to expound upon the proper behavior of *unmarried* young ladies on more than one occasion. Elizabeth, obviously understanding his reference to herself, wisely kept her own counsel, though her mouth did tighten in displeasure more than once during Mr. Collins's monologues.

The next morning, Mary saw her husband off with some relief. The days away from Kent would undoubtedly restore his equilibrium, and by the time he returned, Elizabeth would only stay a few more weeks before leaving.

After Mr. Collins's departure, Mary was in the midst of speaking with her sister when they were interrupted by the bell announcing a visitor to the parsonage.

It was the beginning of a very interesting morning, for while Mary was not a studier of character as her elder sister was, it was almost impossible for her to miss the various emotional undercurrents caused by their visitors. And as none of the visitors had come to see *her*, Mary could largely sit back and watch the scenes as they played out.

The first caller was James Baker, and though Mary had lived in the neighborhood for almost four months, she still was not certain she had the measure of him. At first glance, Mr. Baker almost appeared to be a rake, and rumors of his exploits with the young ladies of the area — and in town — were plentiful. If even half of them were true, then Mr. Baker was to be watched with Elizabeth.

Quickly, however, Mary had begun to determine that though Mr. Baker seemed ready enough to call on Elizabeth, his heart truly was not in it. He smiled and flirted and made himself agreeable, and he obviously found her attractive and pleasant, but for whatever reason, his interest in Elizabeth appeared to be lukewarm. At least, that was what Mary thought. It *was* difficult to tell, after all, as Mary had never witnessed him speaking with any other eligible young ladies, save for Miss de Bourgh. Still, Mary did not believe she was wrong in judging the level of his interest. Moreover, she was convinced that Miss Baker was at least somewhat to blame for Mr. Baker's attention to Elizabeth, though Miss Baker's true agenda in encouraging her brother was somewhat of a mystery to Mary.

Elizabeth's feelings were easier to understand. Though she spoke with Mr. Baker animatedly and with enjoyment, she did not show any true measure of regard — certainly not what Mary had witnessed those years ago when Elizabeth had been courted by Mr. Wickham.

Speaking of the scoundrel, it was not until *he* arrived that the dynamic in the room changed. They had seen Mr. Wickham only a few fleeting times since his arrival in Kent (and not at all since Mr. Darcy's arrival). Elizabeth, though she had heard nothing specific, had described to Mary what Mr. Darcy's behavior had been whenever Mr. Wickham's name was mentioned, which seemed to indicate that there was some form of disagreement between the two. Though Mary did not trust Mr. Wickham, and he continued to show Elizabeth the same smooth and playful attention that he had in the past, it was of some comfort to Mary to see that Elizabeth was not affected by him in the slightest.

When Mr. Wickham was announced, he greeted them with the most outrageous flattery before being introduced to Mr. Baker. The gentlemen were both somewhat quiet for several moments as they appeared to inspect one another thoroughly. It was after Mr. Wickham apparently dismissed the master of Stauneton Hall and focused on Elizabeth when Mr. Baker's hackles were raised. Rather than leaving due to the arrival of another visitor, as was polite, Mr. Baker instead began competing for Elizabeth's attention, giving Mr. Wickham dark looks that were returned in kind and generally causing her to regard them both with exasperation.

The most interesting scenes, however, took place once Mr. Darcy had arrived. With the way the morning had been proceeding, it seemed almost inevitable that the man should show up, Mary reflected. It was simply that sort of day.

After Mr. Darcy was shown into the parlor, his face immediately reddened in anger, and he stared at Mr. Wickham.

"What are you doing here, Wickham?" demanded he before any introductions could be made.

"The same as you, I should imagine," was the insolent response. "I have known these excellent ladies for some time now, and I am simply visiting to renew my acquaintance."

Eager to avoid a confrontation, Mary spoke up and drew both men's attention to her. "We have not seen you much in recent days, Mr. Wickham."

"I was finishing my business in the area," replied the man. "But once it was completed, nothing could keep me away from the agreeable company I find here, and the prospect of basking in your sister's presence was too much of a chance to pass up." The last was said with a bow and a devastating smile at Elizabeth, who colored and looked away.

"If that was all, you should not have come, sir," said Elizabeth with some rancor.

"Just what is your game here, Wickham?" asked Darcy angrily. His countenance had become even darker with Mr. Wickham's declaration of regard for Elizabeth, and now he appeared ready to strangle the man. "Is there not some *rock* under which you should be hiding?"

"Just because *you* cannot be civil in company does not mean that I should avoid my friends, Darcy. There is no reason to be rude."

"With you, Wickham, there is *always* reason for rudeness. Now I suggest you find that rock I mentioned and return to it immediately. I do not appreciate your imposing yourself upon ladies of quality, and I will have you at the end of my blade if I must!"

A spasm of fear crossed Mr. Wickham's countenance, only to be quickly replaced with a look of studied nonchalance. "It appears I am not welcome here by *some* of the company, Mrs. Collins, so I am afraid I must take my leave."

"*Those* are the first true words you have spoken since you arrived, Mr. Wickham," responded Mary, coming to a sudden resolution. He obviously made Elizabeth uncomfortable, and she would not have her sister bothered by the man who had already hurt her once. "Given your history with my family, I must ask you to leave and not return."

Though he appeared momentarily angry, his displeasure was soon masked. "I am sorry you feel that way, Mrs. Collins. I have only ever been polite to you."

"And you have never had anything but your own selfish interests at heart, sir," said Mary in response. "I can have my husband endorse my demand upon his return, should you wish to have the matter confirmed by the head of this house."

"I assure you, Mrs. Collins, that no such measures are required."

With that, Mr. Wickham rose and quit the room. Elizabeth heaved a sigh of relief, and the company relaxed and descended into desultory conversation. Mr. Baker returned to his previous form, seemingly recognizing that Elizabeth did not require him to protect her from Mr. Darcy, and that second gentleman, for his part, retreated into the mask he had sometimes worn in Hertfordshire, though he did rouse himself whenever Mr. Baker spoke to Elizabeth. He appeared wary of the young man, though not to the extent he had been of Mr. Wickham, and he seemed relieved when Mr. Baker made his excuses and departed. He was focused on Elizabeth, and though he did not speak often, he paid her more attention—his gaze fixed almost always upon her—than he had ever done with Anne de Bourgh.

Lady Catherine had waxed poetic upon the expected union between Mr. Darcy and her daughter, but since Mary had come to the area, she had also heard of some expectations of a match between the gentleman and Miss Baker. Obviously, the lady had not learned anything of them—one did not bring up such rumors in Lady Catherine's presence, after all—but that did not mean they did not exist.

But what of Mr. Darcy's continued scrutiny of Elizabeth? Did he have some knowledge of Mr. Wickham and wish to protect her, or was there actually a kernel of truth to be found in Mr. Collins's continued diatribe about Elizabeth catching the great man's eye? Elizabeth—despite what Mr. Collins said—was obviously not to blame for Mr. Darcy's notice of her, for she made no attempt to garner any more of his attention than he already seemed willing to give. But after a morning spent observing them, Mary believed it was equally obvious that there was something more to Mr. Darcy's scrutiny than mere protectiveness.

By the time the gentleman had departed, Mary felt as if she was bathed in uncertainty. She did know, however, that there was much more going on under the surface—and that the situation bore watching.

Chapter XII

Not long after facing that insufferable blackguard at Hunsford — and still wishing keenly that he *had* been able to have the man at the end of his blade — Darcy went to dinner at Stauneton Hall.

Lady Catherine and Anne had both rejected the invitation, and the former had even encouraged him to do the same. He had refused — he *was* considering marrying Miss Baker, after all, and he would not allow his aunt to dictate his life — and when he saw Miss Baker, he offered an excuse for both his aunt and his cousin, not wishing to offend her.

In truth, however, he was puzzled. Miss Baker's once-amiable relationship with Anne appeared to have dissolved completely. He was uncertain what had happened to produce such a drastic change, and when he had tried to pull Anne aside to ask her about it, she had deflected his questions. It was obvious she did not wish to talk about it. But Darcy knew it had to be something serious indeed, as severing a friendship was not something to be taken lightly among their social circles. Though the two women did not seem inclined to make the estrangement public, it was disturbing nonetheless.

Surprisingly, however, it appeared that Elizabeth Bennet was on friendly terms with both women, for he knew she had visited both ladies even after his arrival. Although Darcy was not quite certain how

Miss Baker viewed Miss Bennet, he knew that Anne was friendly with her, if somewhat distant, though that was what he would have expected from Lady Catherine's daughter. For a moment, Darcy almost considered asking Miss Bennet for an account of how the two young ladies had come to have their falling out, but knowing that such an application was not entirely proper—and that Elizabeth might not wish to speak of such things—he abstained.

Darcy and Miss Bennet were the Bakers' only guests that night. Whereas Darcy had to give an excuse for the absence of his aunt and cousin, Miss Bennet had to offer one for her sister and brother-in-law. Mr. Collins had apparently left to visit an ill relative, and Mrs. Collins was not feeling well herself. As a result of these absences, dinner felt like a most intimate affair.

After they were served their first course, Miss Baker appeared determined to monopolize Darcy's time and instantly set upon asking him questions about what had happened since they had last been in company together.

"After all," said she, "it has been practically an age since we last spoke. I dare say I could have made a thousand reticules in the interim!"

"I suspect you exaggerate, Miss Baker."

"Perhaps you are correct. The stitches are so small, and I would probably have pricked my finger into such a wretched state if I had tried to sew so many purses! You would not wish to look upon my hand in such a case, I am certain!"

"Then let us be glad you did not attempt such an endeavor." He stared at the woman with the hint of a smile tugging at his lips. She was very pleasing to look upon, and his interactions with her always filled him with dark amusement. Yet as he moved his gaze to Miss Bennet, he felt the vestiges of humor disappear. Yes, Miss Baker made him darkly amused. But Miss Bennet made him truly amused—and utterly enchanted. Even now, she was speaking animatedly with Baker. Not even that man seemed completely immune to her charms.

Though Darcy's acquaintance with Baker was nothing like Darcy's friendship with Bingley, he was well aware of what sort of man Baker was. Baker was often spontaneous, and he frequently pursued things he believed would have a bit of fun in them. It would not be utterly unexpected for Baker to make a sudden proposal to someone as playful as Miss Bennet. After all, a life with her would certainly never be boring. Though Baker did not seem enamored of the young woman, it was likely he would recognize there was pleasure to be had in the frequent presence of Miss Bennet.

Baker was not exactly a rake, yet he did immensely enjoy the company of women. Part of Darcy worried that he might take advantage of Miss Bennet, yet he pushed the notion away; he knew that Baker would never hurt a gentlewoman. Baker did keep at least one eye on his reputation, after all, and besides that, he was not immoral. Baker would never set out to ruin a young woman.

Still, the thought of Baker and Miss Bennet being together bothered Darcy. Baker was not quite intelligent enough to truly match Miss Bennet on intellectual grounds. If it came to setting their minds against each other, Miss Bennet would be the victor without question. If they did marry, however, all the advantages would be on Miss Bennet's side from a social viewpoint.

"Do they not make such a lovely pair?" cooed a soft voice.

He turned to look at Miss Baker, who had evidently noticed him staring at Miss Bennet and Baker. He was not certain how to respond. He suddenly wished to ask if they were engaged, but he pushed the question aside as ludicrous and remained quiet.

Fortunately, Miss Baker did not wait long before speaking again. "I have told my brother more than once that Miss Bennet would make a fine wife. She is a lovely young woman, is she not?"

He looked back at Miss Bennet, who was trying to hide a smile as Baker leaned toward her with a conspiratorial expression to tell her something. Then, Miss Bennet laughed, her bright eyes shining as she responded to whatever Baker had said, and Darcy felt his mood simultaneously lighten and darken—something that appeared to happen far too often when in the company of that young woman.

"Yes," murmured he, "I suppose she is."

Miss Baker soon called his attention back to her as she began to complain about the unfortunate soiling of her favorite handkerchief, and Darcy—though bothered by the direction in which his thoughts were traveling—could not help but think that conversation with Elia Baker was nothing like conversation with Elizabeth Bennet.

But what he needed in his life was the beautiful young Miss Baker. Combining her connections with his own would mean a bright future for any of his heirs.

As he tried to concentrate on what Miss Baker was saying, he found himself staring at Elizabeth once again. Miss Baker was the perfect match for him. So why was he continuing to think about Miss Bennet's bright eyes?

Chapter XIII

*I*t started as a typical day for the master of Longbourn. He arose early, as was his wont—all the ill health in the world could not cause his body to sleep late, it appeared—and retreated to his bookroom, feeling as if a cloud of gloom were hanging over his head.

At times, it seemed a difficult life for Mr. Bennet. Oh, he was of a privileged class, he knew, and even his small estate, which could not make his family wealthy, allowed them to at least live a more comfortable lifestyle than many could boast.

No, Mr. Bennet's particular form of complaint against the world had more to do with two things in his life: his health and the absence of four of his daughters.

He remembered when, as a young man, he had enjoyed a constitution similar to that of his acquaintances. Though he had never been particularly active, he had at least been able to do whatever he wanted with little or no fuss. His current state could not be attributed to any specific event or period in life. It merely seemed that as he became older, his body was not functioning as well as it had when he was young. He was aware that infirmity was an affliction with which all were forced to contend as they aged, but it did not follow that a man of less than fifty years should constantly feel as though he had run for miles every day when no others of his acquaintance and of a similar age appeared to be as constantly ill as he was.

But though he had tolerated this weakness of body for some time now, it was not truly that which affected his melancholy. Rather, it was the lack of his favorite daughters by his side.

They were becoming beautiful young ladies, and he knew the time was approaching when they would find worthy young men of their own. He would no longer be the most important man in their lives. Despite the blessed nature of such an event as matrimony, however, Mr. Bennet was discontent.

It was selfish, he well knew, but he wished to hold on to his daughters for a few more years, enjoying their society and watching them as they continued to mature and grow. But it was not to be. After all, Mary had already left the nest, Jane appeared to be well on her way to being engaged to that Bingley fellow, and Elizabeth . . . Suffice it to say that Mr. Bennet did not think Elizabeth, with her playful personality and her beauty (which *he* considered a match for Jane's), would fail to attract some young man with enough intelligence to understand that her worth meant far more than the meager dowry she would bring to a marriage. And Mr. Bennet was certain that even Kitty, with her flowing wit and her determination, would find someone who would discover in her a gem worth more than all the gold in his vaults in spite of her perceived disability.

It appeared that his worrying for Elizabeth was a thing of the past. While her letters had been cheerful, as was her wont, it was his letters from Jane which illuminated the true situation of his eldest daughter. Though Jane wrote that it had been necessary to drag Elizabeth into society that winter, she had gone with grace and dignity and ever-increasing interest. He had been worried about her lack of enthusiasm for attending assemblies, as she had been so inclined to seek out society in the past. But now, though the past was perhaps not forgotten, at least she was on the mend. The damage done to her by that scoundrel was finally no longer holding her back, and she appeared to be willing to once again live her life rather than wallow in bitterness.

Given his thoughts about his daughters, it was not surprising that when the post came and Mr. Bennet sat down to read Elizabeth's newly arrived letter, he found that the contents shocked him exceedingly. It appeared that not only had Wickham — the aforementioned scoundrel — called on Mrs. Bennet and Lydia without their informing Mr. Bennet of the man's visit, but that they had also accepted him into their home with nary a thought as to what had happened in the past. Mr. Bennet was not normally a man given over to fury, tending much more toward amusement and sarcasm, but reading the words from his eldest about how Wickham was importuning her yet again filled him with such anger as he had not felt in years.

Throwing the letter down on his desk, Mr. Bennet crossed the room in a few clipped strides and flung open the door to his study. "Mrs. Hill!" barked he.

The housekeeper hurried down the corridor from the direction of the kitchens, obviously bewildered at the master's sudden change in demeanor. She stopped in front of him and curtseyed perfunctorily, waiting for his instructions.

"Good morning, Hill," said he, attempting — belatedly — to put the woman at ease. "Please have Mrs. Bennet summoned to my study immediately."

"Immediately?" asked Mrs. Hill. "The mistress is still abed, master — "

"I care not if she is on her deathbed," rejoined Mr. Bennet. "Wake her and tell her that her presence is required in my study *now*."

Curtseying, Mrs. Hill scurried away to do as instructed.

"If Mrs. Bennet is not here within five minutes, she will lose her allowance for a sixmonth," called Mr. Bennet after the retreating housekeeper. "In fact, you may tell her I said that!"

Scowling, Mr. Bennet closed the door and returned to his desk, where he sat in fury, his eyes raking over the papers which contained the offending news about his daughter's betrayer. Fortunately, Mrs. Hill must have conveyed his words to his wife, for a few moments later, Mrs. Bennet hurried into the room, her nerves already fluttering and her wails easily discernable well before she entered the study.

"Oh, Mr. Bennet," keened she, "what has happened? Are you dying? Did something happen to our girls? Oh, what shall become of us?"

"Mrs. Bennet!" rebuked Mr. Bennet. "My health is still as it was, and our daughters are very well. If you mention one more word about my health in the next two weeks, I shall confine you to your chambers until you are able to demonstrate that you have managed to have even one sensible thought in your head!"

At mid-flutter, Mrs. Bennet halted, her mouth wide open in the act of wailing yet again. Apparently, she noticed something in her husband which was not often seen, for she stilled her protestations and sat in her chair and waited for him to speak. She still wrung her hands nervously, and her eyes darted from him to her hands in her lap, but it was far better than was normal for his wife.

"Now, I have a question I wish to ask you," stated Mr. Bennet. "Please tell me, or am I incorrect, did Mr. Wickham visit this house in the past fortnight?"

Surprised, Mrs. Bennet gazed up at her husband, as though wondering if this was the cause of all the fuss. "He did, Mr. Bennet, and we had a very agreeable visit with him."

"Please inform me, Mrs. Bennet—who exactly is 'we?'"

"Why, Lydia and I, of course," said Mrs. Bennet, as though she thought her husband a simpleton.

"So, you allowed that . . . that . . . *libertine* entrance into this house?" said Mr. Bennet, his voice rising in his anger. "Why would you do such a thing, Mrs. Bennet? He should have been run off by the stablehands with pitchforks for daring to show his face on our doorstep!"

"But he was such a pleasant young man," cried his distressed wife. "And he was so particularly attached to our Lizzy."

"Do you not recall how he left her," demanded Mr. Bennet, "when she had every right to expect an offer from him? Do you not recall how long it has taken Elizabeth to get over her disappointment? How she has shunned society and retreated into herself? Our Lizzy was a sparkling and witty young woman who was sought after at any ball, and now she can barely bring herself to even attend such an event, let alone dance. And you welcome the rogue who brought her to that state into our home?"

"Lizzy is well, Mr. Bennet," cried Mrs. Bennet, waving him off as if he were a small child. "Mr. Wickham is now a widower, you know. He told us of how he met his wife and the sudden manner in which he fell in love with her. You cannot fault a man for his feelings, can you?"

Not believing what he was hearing, Mr. Bennet gaped at his wife.

Either not seeing or not caring about his stupefied state, Mrs. Bennet continued:

"Now, however, he has returned, and his feelings for Lizzy appear to be as strong as they ever were. I dare say that if we encourage them in the slightest, we may hear wedding bells for our eldest before long."

"Mrs. Bennet, I have heard inanities from you aplenty, but I never dreamed you could be *this senseless*."

Mr. Bennet was actually shaking from barely suppressed rage, and Mrs. Bennet, though perhaps not completely understanding her husband's anger, at least appeared to have finally recognized that he was most seriously displeased.

"If you could think for even a moment that I would consent to such a marriage—assuming Lizzy herself should be irrational enough to give her own consent—then you are more foolish than I could have believed possible. The man hurt and exposed your daughter to ridicule after paying exclusive attention to her and, I dare say, engaging his own honor in the matter. Leaving her for another when he had led her on in such a manner was *not* the action of a gentleman, despite how he may protest his 'sudden love' for this other woman.

"And while you may not have thought of the matter in the slightest, I would remind you that although Mr. Wickham displayed his charming manners and agreeable nature to the neighborhood, he was most reticent in sharing anything about his past with *anyone*, even our Lizzy. He was most adept at *assuring* us that he was a gentleman, but he was most *deficient* in proving himself worthy of the title. Did you ever hear of him talk of his family, his estate, or anything of substance about his past?"

When Mrs. Bennet shook her head mutely, he continued:

"He did not. And I think it likely that he was not explicit because there was nothing to share. Mr. Wickham's actions, far from proving him a gentleman, are, when one closely examines them, more in line with his being a fortune hunter."

"How can you say that, Mr. Bennet?" exclaimed his wife. "He was most gentlemanlike in his manner and address—"

"And nothing like one in his actions! He could easily have considered Elizabeth the heiress to this estate when he first came, for we endeavor to avoid any discussion of the entailment with any newcomers. But it appears to me that he found out and then turned his attention to some other woman he could marry for her fortune. It seems probable he has exhausted that woman's money and is actively seeking more. Why he is pursuing Elizabeth now, I know not—he is aware that she does not have the resources to keep him financially secure, after all—but it cannot be good.

"I can also tell you that Elizabeth's farewell with Mr. Wickham when he left was not pleasant, and he proved his lack of propriety without any doubt."

Mrs. Bennet was stunned. "Why was I not informed of this?"

"Because Elizabeth knew you could not be trusted not to proclaim the event in every parlor in Meryton!"

Knowing he was causing his wife distress, Mr. Bennet nevertheless continued. Mrs. Bennet was not a vindictive person, and she generally meant well, but she needed to know that her actions were not having the effect she intended. Indeed, he had allowed her to carry on thus for far too long.

"Mrs. Bennet, I am sorry to dismay you, but you must begin to think about your actions and words before blindly prattling on without any thought of the consequences. Elizabeth was afraid—quite rightly—that she would be tainted by Mr. Wickham's actions, though the man was not able to do what he obviously intended. He importuned her most inappropriately and was sent on his way. Should the impropriety of his insinuations have become public knowledge, however, other members of our society could very well have ignored Elizabeth's response entirely, and the effects to Elizabeth's reputation—and that of all your daughters—could have been disastrous.

"Now, believe me when I say, Madam, that if I hear that even a single syllable of what we have discussed today about Elizabeth has been spoken of in town, you will be cut off from your allowance forthwith."

Mrs. Bennet's gasp of dismay, coupled with her horrified expression, led Mr. Bennet to believe that he had proposed a punishment which was above anything else he could possibly have devised. If that was the case, then so much the better.

"I am most displeased that you did not inform me of his call. In fact, had Elizabeth herself not chanced to mention it in one of her letters, I might never have known of it at all. What possessed you to tell him where he could find our daughter? Are you completely insensible to the distress his sudden arrival caused our Lizzy?"

Mrs. Bennet's countenance paled, and her husband thought she was about to swoon. He smiled grimly. Hopefully, she was beginning to understand the consequences of her actions at last. Confident he had her complete attention, he proceeded to inform her of his decision regarding Elizabeth's erstwhile suitor:

"In the future, Mrs. Bennet, if Wickham shows his face here again, you are to inform me *immediately!* Under no circumstances are you to engage him in conversation, invite him to tea, or even meet his eyes in passing, and that stricture goes for Lydia as well. I will deal with the brigand the next time he appears, and I shall do so in a manner which will leave no doubt as to the extent of the welcome he will receive in this house and in our lives. Am I quite clear?"

Though Mrs. Bennet was stunned almost speechless, she nodded her head dumbly and made her way from the room posthaste. Mr. Bennet suspected he would not be seeing much of her for the next few days, and that suited him very well indeed.

Unfortunately, Mr. Bennet did not feel any calmer after dealing with his recalcitrant wife. His worry over his eldest and the thought of how

Wickham might be importuning her again caused his thoughts to enter into such an upheaval that he spent the rest of the morning brooding on the stupidity of the specimen of femininity which he had had the poor judgment to marry. He even began to consider writing to Mr. Darcy—who he had learned from Elizabeth was visiting Lady Catherine in Kent—to inform him of Elizabeth's past with Wickham and beg him to be on guard for any evil tendencies in the man's behavior. Soon, however, an unexpected visitor interrupted him from his solitary thoughts. Mrs. Hill entered the room upon his acknowledging her knock and stood aside while Mr. Collins revealed himself.

Eyebrow raised, Mr. Bennet welcomed his son-in-law to his study, wondering what the man could be doing in Hertfordshire. Elizabeth's letter had said he was visiting some ill relation in London, not gallivanting about the countryside. What could be his purpose in coming here?

Mr. Collins was not an exceptionally bright individual. In fact, to make such a statement would be akin to claiming the ocean between England and her former colonies was a mud puddle. Mr. Bennet had never felt that fact more keenly than at the present moment, as he stared at the sweating figure of the man sitting across the desk from him. Collins looked quite ill, sneezing and coughing into his handkerchief while wheezing his protestations that he was very well indeed and had merely come down with a small indisposition. Considering Mr. Bennet's uncertain health and tendency to catch the agues which at times swept through the small community, the presence of a less than healthful—and less than intelligent—man in his bookroom was decidedly unwelcome.

Though Mr. Bennet would have preferred to postpone the pleasure of the parson's company—perhaps permanently!—it appeared he did not have a choice. And so he waited for the man to come to the point.

"Mr. Bennet," began the pompous man when the pleasantries—such as they were—had been exchanged. "I am here today to call upon you to discuss something of the most serious nature, a matter which is causing me the most grievous distress imaginable. It concerns appalling behavior of which, if I had not witnessed it myself, I would not have believed a sister of my most excellent wife to be capable. Though my Mary is of the best disposition and highest moral fiber, I regretfully, though it brings me pain to speak of her favorite sister thus, must conclude that your eldest daughter does not possess the same upright standards as her younger sister."

Through narrowed eyes, Mr. Bennet glared at the sweating and sneezing countenance of his son-in-law. The man wilted slightly under his pointed gaze, but he held his eyes up with a slightly petulant huff.

"Of what can you be referring, Mr. Collins?" queried Mr. Bennet, his unfriendly feelings toward the man clearly showing in his abrupt demand. "I have received letters from both Elizabeth and Mary since Elizabeth arrived in Kent, and they have assured me that they are quite content in one another's company. Surely you are not accusing my eldest of unkindness toward her sister."

"No, indeed not, Mr. Bennet. My cousin Elizabeth and my dear wife Mary indeed do very well together, and their sisterly fellowship is eminently proper and pleasant. I most humbly apologize if I have concerned you on that account. I do not speak of specific injuries perpetrated against my wife by your eldest—no, not at all. It is other circumstances which have caused me distress . . . and, by association, which have caused distress to my most excellent patroness."

"Then you have come on an errand to complain of Elizabeth at the request of your patroness. Really, Mr. Collins, can you not be your own man? Must you always hurry hither and thither spouting the banalities of that woman? You more closely resemble a dog submitting itself to its master than a man."

The paleness of Mr. Collins's features became a mottled red in anger. "I assure you I am not, Mr. Bennet. In fact, Lady Catherine knows nothing of my errand here today. *I* am a clergyman, cousin, and I am due the respect of my office. As for my patroness, she is due the respect given her by dint of the position she holds and the nobility with which she was born!"

"And here I thought that a man was due only the respect of which he was deserving," was Mr. Bennet's retort. "Please say what your purpose for coming here was, Mr. Collins, but leave out your fanciful thoughts of respect—and your imaginations about Elizabeth—and come to the point in a rational and *accurate* manner."

Though apparently on the verge of apoplexy, Mr. Collins wiped his brow with great agitation. He looked about ready to collapse with whatever ailment he had been stricken, and Mr. Bennet wished to have him gone.

"I do not know why I have come here; indeed, I do not," whined Mr. Collins. "She is your favorite, and you will see no evil in her, I am certain. I am sorry to say that the preference of a father toward certain of his children is a most harmful thing at times, though I may gladly note that my father's preference for me was always of a most upstanding and noble character.

"Regardless, I must inform you that my cousin Elizabeth has behaved in the most abominable manner possible since her arrival. She is impertinent and disrespectful toward *my* lady patroness when she ought to be silent and grateful for her ladyship's attentions and advice, which have not been inconsiderable and which have been most graciously bestowed. In addition, she has been most brazen in the use of her arts and allurements to entrap Mr. Darcy, her ladyship's nephew, and in so doing, she has grievously injured her ladyship. Your daughter knows of Mr. Darcy's engagement with Miss de Bourgh and has willfully ignored the arrangement already subsisting in order to ensnare a husband of the highest circles and the greatest fortune. The Bible tells us we must forgive, and so we shall, but she should be censured, despised, and cast from your family immediately to reap the rewards of her infamous behavior!"

"Mr. Collins!" thundered Mr. Bennet. "You will now be silent! I shall not stand by and allow you to defame my precious daughter any further. I have it on good authority that although Elizabeth has been in company with Mr. Darcy, he has not breached propriety, nor has she had any wish for him to do so. Whatever you believe is happening between them exists only in the imaginations of yourself and your patroness and has no reflection on reality. Now, be silent, or I shall have you removed from this house immediately!"

Mr. Collins's eyes protruded from his head most alarmingly, and though his mouth worked silently, no sound proceeded forth. He appeared about to respond when a frothing appeared from between his lips, his eyes rolled up into his head, and he collapsed, insensible, on the floor.

Though Mr. Bennet would have almost preferred to have kicked the man as he lay there, he sighed and pulled the bell cord, summoning assistance.

Mr. Collins was removed from the floor of the bookroom and installed in the room furthest from the occupied family apartments. A doctor was immediately sent for to see to him.

Mr. Bennet did not go to visit the man—it would not do for him to come down with whatever Mr. Collins had contracted—but the time he had spent listening to his son-in-law's rattling breaths was cause for some alarm. While he could not bring himself to spare Collins a moment's concern, he *did* care about Mary's comfort and happiness.

Once the doctor had examined his patient, the diagnosis was confirmed. Mr. Collins had contracted pneumonia.

Chapter XIV

$\mathcal{E}$lizabeth was concerned for her sister. Mary, who had always been of a healthy and robust constitution and who had seemed hale when Elizabeth first arrived in Kent, had taken to being sickly of late, and there did not appear to be anything that could be done for her relief.

Trying to be of assistance to her sister, Elizabeth took to doing much of Mary's work around the parsonage, hoping that her support would allow Mary to rest and regain her previous vigor. She conferred with the servants when necessary, helped with the preparation of the menus, and assisted in the parish whenever required. She already knew that Mary was well respected by the members of her husband's flock due to her devotion to her duty and her willingness to do anything required by those under her care, and in this, Elizabeth tried to emulate her younger sister.

But nothing worked, and Mary, though she did not worsen, persisted in her poor health. It was all so maddening! The illness could strike her at any moment of the day or night, often sending Mary into the water closet, where she lost whatever she had managed to eat, or into her bed, where she would collapse in exhaustion. And though Elizabeth was quite concerned, Mary refused to send for an apothecary, insisting that she knew exactly what was wrong with her and that her condition would improve with time.

The situation went on for more than a week after her husband's departure, and though the time spent out of Mr. Collins's company was quite welcome indeed for Elizabeth, Mary seemed to feel his absence keenly, and her condition was certainly not helped by it.

Finally, on the morning exactly a week and a day after Mr. Collins's departure, an express arrived from Longbourn. As Mary was still abed due to the early hour, Elizabeth paid the courier and asked that he tarry in the kitchen for a few moments in case there was a reply to be made. The messenger gratefully accepted the invitation, and Elizabeth, fearing what the letter might hold, repaired to the sitting room. Taking a deep breath, she opened the missive, which was dated the previous day.

My dearest daughters,

It is my sad duty to inform you that Mr. Collins is gravely ill. I had retired to my bookroom after luncheon when Mr. Collins surprised me with his visit and an application for a private discussion with me. I shall not concern you with an account of that meeting. Suffice it to say that during the course of our tête-à-tête, we both became rather animated, and Mr. Collins, who had seemed rather unwell from the outset, collapsed on my bookroom floor. He was immediately installed in one of the guestrooms, and a doctor was summoned. I wish I could tell you that there is no need to fear, but the doctor says that Mr. Collins has contracted pneumonia, and the prognosis is uncertain.

Mary, my daughter, I grieve and sympathize with you in this difficult time. Lean on your sister for support, as I believe her presence with you at this moment is truly a gift from God. You may be certain that Mr. Collins will be given the best of care while he is under my roof, and every possible action to restore his health will be taken.

I shall write again when I have further word. Take heart, and hope for the best.

Your Father,
H. Bennet

To say Elizabeth was shocked and grieved would have been a rather large understatement. She had not noticed anything amiss with Mr. Collins when he had left, but then again, she had always attempted to spend as little time in his company as she possibly could. And now the man had been struck down by a potentially fatal illness.

Above all, Elizabeth worried for her sister's well-being and state of mind. Mary had almost wilted since the departure of her husband, and her already poor level of fitness was in danger of being exacerbated by their father's report. For a moment, Elizabeth even considered withholding the news for fear of her sister's reaction, but she discarded the notion immediately. Not only was Mary entitled to know what had happened to her husband, but if the worst should happen, Mary would never forgive Elizabeth for not telling her about their father's letter when it had arrived.

With a sigh, Elizabeth stood and, checking the time, saw she had a few moments before Mary would be up and about. She penned a quick response to her father, asking about the health of Mr. Collins and the extent of the threat to him. After seeing that the letter was delivered to the messenger with instructions for the return journey, Elizabeth made her way to Mary's room, determined to support her sister in any way possible.

Mary was in her room, where the maid was styling her hair. Her color appeared better than it had for several days, and Elizabeth wished it were not necessary to give her grief. She very much feared Mary's reaction.

Dismissing the maid—who had completed her task in any case—Elizabeth tenderly embraced Mary and led her to a nearby chair. She did not know how to impart the news, yet she did not see the point in any further delay, so she decided she might as well be somewhat direct in her approach to the task.

"Mary, I am sorry to say it, but I have just received some difficult news from Longbourn."

"Is it about Papa?" said Mary with a gasp.

"No, Mary, he is well. Unfortunately, it is about Mr. Collins."

Confused, Mary simply stared at her sister.

"According to Papa, Mr. Collins arrived to speak to him yesterday afternoon. I do not know what his errand was, but some time after arriving, he collapsed in Papa's bookroom, and a doctor was called."

Mary's face whitened in horror. "Is he . . ."

"He is alive," soothed Elizabeth. "The doctor has diagnosed pneumonia but could not say anything more than that. Perhaps you should read the letter for yourself."

Mary fairly snatched the missive from her sister's hand. Elizabeth watched her as she read, seeing Mary's expression grow more horrified and noticing the way she pressed a hand to her mouth as the tears began falling from her eyes. After reading the letter, Mary stared unseeing at the piece of paper for several moments before it fell from her suddenly nerveless fingers. She flung herself into Elizabeth's arms, weeping her heartbreak, and Elizabeth, knowing there was nothing else she could do, held her sister and rocked her in her arms, crooning nonsensical sounds of love and support.

It was not long before Mary's distress brought on another one of her attacks, and though she heaved, little was expelled from her stomach due to the fact that she had not yet eaten anything that morning.

Elizabeth saw that her sister was changed into her nightgown and once again installed in her bed. She sat with Mary, holding her sister's hand and drying her tears with her handkerchief, lending what support she could to the stricken young woman.

At length, Mary turned her head toward Elizabeth, and her pale face formed into a sad smile. "I thank you, Elizabeth, for the prodigious amount of care you have shown me and the duties you have taken upon yourself."

"It is the least I can do, Mary," replied Elizabeth with a soft smile for her sister. "We are sisters and thus must care for each other and share our burdens."

"It is wonderful, Elizabeth. You truly are the best of sisters."

Blushing at the praise, Elizabeth patted Mary's hand. "I only do what I must, Mary. You have not been well, and I want you to rest and regain your strength. I will correspond with Papa and keep you informed of your husband's condition. We must all pray for the best."

The responding expression from her sister was thoughtful and a trifle calculating. Elizabeth, uncertain what her sister was thinking, stayed silent and waited for Mary to speak, wondering what it all meant.

"Elizabeth, I have a confession to make to you. I had intended to keep it secret until my husband returns, but I believe, due to his sickness, you should know."

Cocking her head to the side, Elizabeth gazed at her sister inquisitively.

"I see I have managed to tweak the infamous Lizzy curiosity," said Mary with a slight smile.

"Indeed, you have, Mary, and I should think you had best share your intelligence with me before the infamous Lizzy 'temper' makes its appearance."

Mary laughed. "Papa was correct—it truly is a God-given gift to have you here with me now. I am so grateful." She hesitated a moment, looking down at her hands, and then she spoke again:

"I know you have noticed my sickly state in recent days. Do you not have any inkling as to what ails me?"

"I do not," stated Elizabeth, her earlier grumpiness over her sister's insistence that she would not see an apothecary returning.

"It is common in my condition," continued Mary. "For you see, Elizabeth, the reason I have been so ill lately is because I am with child."

The expression on Elizabeth's face was suffused with a heartfelt joy. Mary was to be a mother, and Elizabeth the new baby's aunt!

"That is wonderful news, Mary!" cried Elizabeth, embracing her sister with enthusiasm. "I am so happy for you!"

"Thank you, Lizzy. I had hoped to tell Mr. Collins when he returns, but I am glad you are here and are the first to know."

"And you will tell Mr. Collins, God willing," said Elizabeth firmly. "I thank you for confiding in me, Mary, but this news, coupled with the manner in which you have been unwell, induces me to believe we should have the apothecary visit and examine you."

And so, Mary's protestations notwithstanding, Elizabeth called for the apothecary, declaring that she would not take any chances with the health of her sister or her sister's unborn child.

The apothecary was very happy that Elizabeth had insisted he come, as he pronounced the pregnancy to be a difficult one and said the strain of the news of her husband's illness was further taking its toll upon the young mother-to-be and, by extension, her child. He prescribed strict bed rest and some draughts for Mary and advised her she should only be up and about if she felt truly well. He also stated he would begin examining her at least twice a week in order to confirm her health and the continued well-being of her child.

Elizabeth, who was now running the house in Mary's stead, was adamant that the apothecary's instructions be followed to the letter, and she had little trouble persuading Mary that staying in bed was for the best, as the young woman was exhausted and listless due to her fear for her husband.

Of course, news of this sort could not be kept a secret, and though Elizabeth was not quite certain, she suspected that the servants spread the gossip throughout the town. It was later that afternoon when the parsonage was invaded by the nearby ladies paying their respects to the young wife. Of most interest, however, were the appearances of the female denizens of Rosings Park and Stauneton Hall.

Elia Baker arrived first, and though she was still a little silly and vain, she seemed genuinely concerned for Mary and expressed her sorrow for the trials the other woman was experiencing.

But when Miss de Bourgh and Lady Catherine arrived before Miss Baker left, it was obvious the temperature in the room had slipped below freezing in almost an instant. Miss Baker and Miss de Bourgh were uniformly cold to each other, and Lady Catherine, while seeming mostly oblivious to the two young ladies' attitudes, nevertheless treated all as though they were of no consequence in the world. She spouted off meaningless platitudes and inane advice on how Mary could cope, how Mr. Collins would recover, and how she herself, by virtue of her exalted status, could *never* fall ill in such a manner. Elizabeth could not stand two minutes of the woman's company before she was wishing Lady Catherine would leave them in peace.

It was not until almost the entire time of their visit had passed when Elizabeth noticed that Miss de Bourgh had added little to the conversation other than a few trite words of supposed comfort to Mary and some glares at Miss Baker. Such was perhaps unsurprising given Lady Catherine's propensity to dominate any room with her conversation, but the lack of any communication from the young woman—even with Elizabeth, whom she had spoken with in a friendly, if somewhat superior, manner in the past—*was* unusual.

She was not able to dwell upon the puzzle for long, however, as the ladies soon departed, leaving Elizabeth to care for her sister. The demands of the household then took hold, and Elizabeth found herself busy for most of the rest of the day. In her heart, she kept a prayer. Though she had never been close to Mr. Collins, she prayed for his health and safe return. She could not bear to see her sister suffer thus.

Chapter XV

*I*f Elizabeth had been dreading giving her sister the news of Mr. Collins's illness, it meant nothing in comparison to the sheer horror that overcame her upon reading the express she received on the sixth of April.

Elizabeth was leaving Mary's room when the message arrived. She had intended to request that the maid attend her sister. Mary was feeling well enough to go outside, and Elizabeth was eager to walk with her in the fresh air. Elizabeth believed that being bedridden was one of the worst things that could happen to a sick person, for it gave the situation a whiff of despair and the hint of being hopeless, even if the illness was not overly severe. Since Mary had not been outside much lately, Elizabeth thought it all the more important that she escape the confines of the house. Fresh air could only do her good. Unfortunately, their pleasant walk was not to be.

When the letter she had received was in hand, she went and sat down in the drawing-room, not certain what exactly the missive would hold. She suspected only that it had something to do with Mr. Collins. Unfortunately, she was right.

Dearest Lizzy, began the letter in her father's script. Seeing another letter from her father so soon was enough to fill Elizabeth with dread, yet she continued to read, her fingers tightly clutching the paper.

I write specifically to you and not to Mary because the news I have to impart is not fit for her to learn from a piece of paper. Yet I must have out with it: Mr. Collins has passed away. The apothecary believes the man's exertions had something to do with his passing. If Mr. Collins was so ill, I do not know why he insisted on traveling to speak with me, yet it seems he was faithful to his patroness unto his end.

His body will be borne to Kent so that Lady Catherine de Bourgh and the members of his parish shall have their own closure. I do not know that Mary will wish to look upon him one last time, but if she does, then she shall have her opportunity.

I am far more skilled at laughing at the foibles of others than offering sympathy, yet I ask that you give my condolences to your sister. I am feeling slightly unwell myself, but I do not believe I have a similar illness. The apothecary, however, has told me to rest and not exert myself, and after seeing the example of my cousin, I cannot disagree with his orders.

Elizabeth clutched the letter to her chest, trying not to think about the possibility of her father being struck with pneumonia. She brought the piece of correspondence back down, and after reading her father's last words—"Give Mary my best"—she closed her eyes. She was already worrying for Mary's health, and now she had to tell her that her husband had died! She feared her sister's reaction, but she had to give her the news without delay.

Inhaling deeply, Elizabeth folded up the letter and stood. After storing it in her reticule, she walked to Mary's room. Her sister was alone inside, sitting in a rocking chair and softly crooning a lullaby as her hand moved gently back and forth across her stomach. She looked happier than Elizabeth had seen her in days, and it nearly broke Elizabeth's heart to know that she would have to tell her sister that life as she had known it was over. A parsonage was nothing without a parson, and Hunsford could thus no longer be Mary's home.

"Mary," said Elizabeth at last with a gentle tone as she closed the door behind her.

"Lizzy," answered Mary warmly, her cheeks slightly pink, likely from the realization that her sister must have heard her. But then she saw the sober expression on Elizabeth's face, and she frowned. "Is there something wrong?"

"Oh, Mary, I am so sorry. I received news from—from Longbourn. It is about Mr. Collins."

Mary stared at her, reading the expression in her eyes. Then her mouth tightened. "He is gone, Lizzy?" asked she softly.

"I am afraid so, Mary."

The bereaved woman turned away. Elizabeth was just barely able to see as Mary began to chew on her lips, and then she witnessed the glitter of falling tears.

Elizabeth moved to embrace her sister, who began crying quietly into her bosom. "I am so sorry, Mary," said Elizabeth soothingly. She did not know what else to say; all she had to offer was platitudes. Mary was newly married and with child—it was a wonder she did not collapse into an inconsolable puddle.

"I know what you thought of him, Lizzy," came Mary's muffled voice. She pulled back her head and looked at her sister with tear-stained cheeks. "But he was a good man who was kind to me. I was happy with him. I shall . . . I shall miss him."

Elizabeth squeezed her sister up against her, gently rubbing her hair. "I am glad he was kind to you, Mary." And it was true. She was glad that he had been able to give Mary—the Bennet daughter who had so often been ignored—some measure of contentment. Elizabeth had truly held nothing against him except for his fawning nature and utter lack of anything resembling intelligence. Even when he had been petty toward her, she had often simply turned it to a private source of amusement. Though the world might perhaps be a little more intelligent with his passing—which was a terrible thought for her to consider when her grieving sister was in her arms—she wished he were still alive, for Mary's sake.

They sat in silence for a long time, and when the maid knocked, Elizabeth sent her away. She wanted her sister to have the chance to compose herself before she faced anyone.

When they finally left the room, Mary's eyes were dry, but there was an expression of deep sorrow on her face that struck Elizabeth to the bone.

The day passed on, and the look on Mary's face did not change. Two days later, when Mr. Collins's body was returned to Hunsford, her expression was still deeply sorrowful. He was buried almost immediately, but not before she took the opportunity to look at his face one last time.

It was considered unseemly for women to attend funerals, so Elizabeth stayed at home with her sister, who remained very quiet. Mary ate at Elizabeth's prompting—after all, Elizabeth told her, the baby would need nourishment—and they talked of nothing of consequence. Both women wore clothes of mourning, but Elizabeth was in truth mourning not the departed, but the happiness her sister had lost.

Later, Elizabeth heard that Mr. Darcy and Mr. Baker attended the funeral. Though she dared not share her thoughts with Mary, the news almost made her smile. Mr. Collins would have been very happy indeed to learn that the nephew of his esteemed patroness had been at his funeral.

The weather outside was sunny and warm.

Chapter XVI

The very day after the funeral of the late parson of Hunsford, Mr. Darcy descended the stairs of Rosings and entered the dining room, early as was his wont. The previous day had been trying. Even though he had not known his aunt's parson to any great degree, the ceremony had brought back memories of the funeral of his own father. He was, therefore, looking forward to a morning ride about the estate, hoping the exertion would rid his mind of the memories and, perhaps, the thoughts of young ladies which had been dancing in his head the past several months.

It was with great surprise that he found himself confronted by the person of Lady Catherine when he entered the breakfast room. As far as he could recall, his aunt *never* awoke this early. Rather, she generally preferred to sleep later and would often take a light repast in her personal chambers.

"Good morning, Darcy," stated she.

"Aunt," said Darcy with a bow. "I must say this is a surprise."

She waved him off impatiently. "I can hardly stay abed when there is so much to do this morning, Darcy. I have several young men coming to meet me this day, and I must be ready to receive them."

Eyebrow raised, Darcy regarded his aunt, who was calmly sipping her tea. *This* was not the woman to whom he was accustomed. "Young men? For what purpose will these gentlemen be calling on you today?"

"Why, for the purpose of filling Hunsford parsonage with a new rector," exclaimed Lady Catherine, her expression suggesting she thought him witless.

"That seems rather . . . precipitous. Mr. Collins has been in his grave less than a full day, after all."

"And the Lord waits for no man, Darcy. You should know this. I refuse to be anything less than fully attentive to all concerns within the sphere of my influence and mean to choose a parson as quickly as I can. I dispatched a note to the seminary as soon as word of Mr. Collins's death arrived, and I instructed them to send three likely candidates to visit me . . . according to my specifications, of course. I shall not endure a pastor who cannot run the parish in the manner to which I am accustomed. I have very exacting standards, you know."

It was all Darcy could do not to snort at her self-important pronouncement. He knew *exactly* the type of man which his aunt wanted to fill the vacant parsonage, and it was *not* the sort of man Darcy would ever choose to employ. Should he make himself available to greet the candidates — which he was less than inclined to do — Darcy was certain the men would be almost indistinguishable from the recently departed Mr. Collins.

"Your dedication to your duty is admirable, Aunt," said Darcy. Lady Catherine, of course, missed the slightly sardonic edge to his voice and inclined her head, no doubt thinking it was only her due.

"Very well then, Nephew. I shall be off at once."

Darcy blinked. "You are leaving now?"

"Of course. Because I must install a parson as soon as may be, there must be a parsonage available for him to occupy. And since Mr. Collins's wife and her sister are still in residence, they must be told that I require them to depart. I shall not leave that task to a servant — such a course of action would be most improper, indeed."

He knew the parsonage would be required for its next occupant, but to force a grieving widow out of her home the day after her husband had been interred was not only cruel, but unchristian as well. Lady Catherine was not the most tactful person — not any more than a stampeding bull — yet Darcy was wary of giving her offense. It would be best for all concerned if he accompanied her on her visit.

He stated his intentions to his aunt, who told him that he need not trouble himself. Darcy, however, was firm, and a few moments later, they were both ensconced in the carriage for the short ride to

Hunsford.

Once they arrived at the parsonage and stepped out onto the ground, Darcy noted the mourning wreath which adorned the door and felt a moment of silence for the departed might be appropriate. Lady Catherine, however, took no notice and knocked impatiently.

Once the maid had opened the door, Lady Catherine entered immediately, demanding to see the mistress. The maid led them to a sitting room and asked them to wait while Mrs. Collins was summoned. Lady Catherine did so with obvious ill-temper, causing Darcy to cringe at his aunt's overt display of poor manners.

At length, Miss Bennet entered the room. She was wearing a light gray dress in respect for her brother-in-law's passing, and her countenance was pale and fatigued, no doubt due to the events of the week and the fact that she was likely alternating between managing the household and watching over her grieving sister (during the night, too, unless Darcy missed his guess). Still, she appeared to no less advantage in her present state, and indeed, he felt more disposed toward her than ever before with this example of her caring and capable nature.

"How do you do, Miss Bennet?" asked Darcy.

"I am well, sir, I thank you," was her tired reply.

"And Mrs. Collins?"

"Well enough, given the circumstances." Miss Bennet's eyes shrouded over in pain. "She is with child, and I am afraid she is having a most difficult time with it. I fear for her if this should continue."

"I did not know she was with child," commented Darcy in surprise. Her husband had died while she was carrying his child? The strain must have been difficult indeed.

"That is most unfortunate, Miss Bennet," interrupted Lady Catherine in her customary superior tone. "Be certain to tell your sister that she must rest and not overexert herself. Only thus can she ensure that the child remains healthy and that she does not endanger herself."

Though she checked her reaction, Darcy could see the way Miss Bennet repressed the urge to say something sarcastic. As an avid walker, Miss Bennet was not likely one to advocate that which had been suggested by Lady Catherine. Neither was Darcy, for that matter.

"I shall be certain to impart your . . . instructions to my sister, Lady Catherine," was Miss Bennet's diplomatic response before she began to rise to her feet. "Now, if you will excuse me, I really must check on her. I thank you on behalf of Mrs. Collins for your kindness in calling upon us again in our time of need."

"Miss Bennet," said Lady Catherine in a more than usually insolent and condescending tone, "you have misapprehended my purpose for calling here this day. I do sympathize with Mrs. Collins for the death of her husband, but Hunsford now no longer has a parson. I mean to rectify that at once. You and your sister must vacate Hunsford immediately—by Friday at the latest."

Darcy winced at the way his aunt, lacking in anything even remotely resembling tact, presented her demand. Miss Bennet fixed Lady Catherine with a baleful glare.

"You would push a woman who has just lost her husband from her home less than a day after he was buried? Where is your compassion, Madam? I do not believe I have ever witnessed such a display of utter disregard for the feelings of others!"

Lady Catherine had never been addressed in such a manner, and her countenance showed it. She cried out in indignation:

"I have never been accustomed to such language, Miss Bennet! I am truly sorry for your sister's loss, but I must fill Hunsford, and that necessitates your sister's removal from this house!"

"Lady Catherine, I am afraid I must agree with Miss Bennet," interjected Darcy. "Surely an arrangement could be devised where they may stay a little longer while still allowing you to have your new rector."

"What can you be suggesting, Darcy?" demanded Lady Catherine. "The new parson cannot stay in Hunsford *with* the two ladies. You can never be too attentive to these sorts of things, after all. They could be considered compromised if they were to do something so foolish as that."

"We must be able to conceive of another solution. Perhaps the parson can stay with one of the families in the neighborhood, or perhaps you can allow him to use a room in Rosings until the ladies can depart."

Lady Catherine looked aghast at such a suggestion. "Stay at Rosings?" demanded she. "Surely you cannot mean that, Darcy. A rector staying at my estate? I should think not!" She shook her head at the very thought. "No, Mrs. Collins and her sister must simply return to their father's house. It is not as though they do not have another home to which they can go. I am certain their father will be pleased to take them in again."

While Miss Bennet appeared as if she wished to dispute Lady Catherine's assertions, she sighed and appeared to deflate slightly. "Perchance we could travel to London and stay with our aunt and uncle."

"There," cried Lady Catherine triumphantly. "You see, Darcy? Miss Bennet has suggested an excellent plan. In fact, to speed your journey and make it more comfortable for Mrs. Collins, I shall send you on your way in one of my carriages."

"You are very kind, Aunt," murmured Darcy, though he was hard-pressed to keep from grimacing.

Miss Bennet was clearly fretting over the developments. "I thank you, Lady Catherine, but even with a comfortable carriage, I worry for my sister. She has had a difficult pregnancy thus far and has been very ill, especially since word of her husband's death arrived. She may now be carrying the heir to Longbourn, and I fear for the child's health if we should be required to journey to London at this time."

After the event, Darcy was never certain what possessed him to respond in the way he did. While Lady Catherine blathered on about how the springs in her carriages were of the highest quality and how the ride would be so comfortable that they should hardly know they were moving at all, Darcy was only able to think about Miss Bennet's expression of concern for her sister and the entrancing brown eyes which gazed at the floor in worry. Aware that he would very much like to know her better—and acutely cognizant of the untruth of the insulting words he had spoken concerning her appearance all those months ago—Darcy formed a resolution in an instant and acted upon it before he had time to consider it carefully.

"In that case, perhaps you and your sister should stay at Rosings until she is able to withstand the journey."

Miss Bennet glanced up at him with surprise, and a grateful expression came over her face. Lady Catherine's feelings toward his solution, however, were the exact opposite.

"Stay at Rosings?" cried she. "However can you suggest such nonsense, Darcy? I shall not have the wife of my former parson staying with me at my estate house!"

"That wife is also the daughter of a gentleman, Lady Catherine. And as you have so astutely pointed out, she is no longer a pastor's wife."

Lady Catherine sputtered in indignation. "Regardless, they . . . It is not proper!" She shook her head and seemed at a loss for words.

"My dear nephew," stated she finally, gaining control of her emotions, "this is not seemly. You cannot possibly insist upon such an arrangement. She shall have no trouble making the journey back to London to her uncle's house."

"On the contrary, Lady Catherine, even a journey of short duration can cause a woman who is already experiencing difficulty to lose her unborn child. I must insist upon this. We cannot in good conscience subject her to a journey now of all times."

Lady Catherine's eyes narrowed, and she was silent for a moment. Though Darcy had rarely insisted upon anything in the past, she was aware of the assistance he provided and the influence he wielded. She appeared as if she were trying to swallow her walking stick, but she nodded jerkily before agreeing:

"Very well. They may stay at Rosings. But I will have my own physician examine Mrs. Collins, and as soon as he deems her fit, she shall return to her uncle's house in London."

"I believe that would be acceptable. Do you not agree, Miss Bennet?"

Elizabeth immediately acquiesced and thanked Lady Catherine for her condescension, but her face ran through the gamut of emotions, and Darcy had the impression that had she any other recourse available to her, she would not have accepted the invitation.

They spoke for several moments longer and determined that the sisters would decamp to Rosings on Friday. Then Darcy departed with his aunt, glad he would be afforded more time in Elizabeth's company.

When they had entered the carriage, Lady Catherine turned to Darcy and spoke:

"I am surprised at you, Darcy. I had not thought you to be the champion for ladies who are beneath you in consequence and in the eyes of the world. What made you take up their cause in such a manner?"

The real thrust of her question was, of course, to determine whether he had insisted upon their removal to Rosings for reasons that might threaten her matrimonial plans for Anne. Apparently, his aunt had not forgotten about the night at Rosings when he had come to Miss Bennet's rescue by singing a Christmas hymn.

"It is only proper, Aunt," responded he, careful to appear nonchalant. "Surely you would not wish for your parson's wife to miscarry when she could have remained safe at Rosings. It is the Christian thing to do."

Her expression softened slightly, and after peering at him for a moment more, she looked out the window. "Yes, I suppose you are correct. Very clever to have thought of it, I must say. When we arrive back at Rosings, I shall have rooms prepared for them in the servants' quarters, where they may be out of the way."

Scowling, Darcy glared at his aunt, wondering if she had always been this ungracious. "You cannot possibly be considering such ignominy for our guests."

"Why should I not?" queried she. "With their station in life, they cannot expect anything better. They should be grateful to have a roof over their heads at all! I am perfectly within my rights to remove them and order their belongings discarded by the side of the road if I so chose. Of course, I, who have always been celebrated for my generosity, would never perpetrate such shame upon anyone. But they cannot expect my best rooms. The servants' quarters shall do very well for them indeed."

"It is an insult, Lady Catherine," growled Darcy. "If you mean to put them up in such shameful lodgings, then you had almost better send them packing to London."

"Why, Darcy?" an exasperated Lady Catherine demanded. "What has you suddenly taking up their support and succor? What are they to you?"

"They are acquaintances of many months," stated Darcy. "Beyond that, they are gently born ladies, and they cannot be expected to stay in such accommodations. I am quite determined, Aunt. Please do not tempt my displeasure."

"Very well," said Lady Catherine with a long-suffering sigh. "They shall stay in the guest wing, but under no circumstances shall they be allowed to stay in the family wing."

"That would be appropriate," agreed Darcy. "They are *not* family after all."

Lady Catherine huffed and then fell silent, ignoring her nephew for the rest of the short journey. Darcy found that he could bear the silence very well indeed. He did not often impose his will upon his stubborn aunt, but the insult she was contemplating was not to be borne.

Besides, with Wickham likely still lurking around, Darcy would feel better if he had Miss Bennet close at hand. It would not be right to allow that rake to ruin such a woman as Miss Bennet. Someone needed to look out for the young lady's welfare.

Chapter XVII

After the Bennet sisters moved into Rosings, it took a few days for them to settle into a routine. They were installed in the guest wing in rooms next to each other, and then they were largely left alone by the women of the house, though Lady Catherine and her daughter did, somewhat grudgingly, attend to the obligations required of hostesses toward their guests. Darcy attempted to be as civil and attentive as possible, but as he did not wish to incite his aunt's resentment, he endeavored to keep his attentions sparing.

Though Miss Bennet often descended for dinner with the family, Mrs. Collins rarely did so. This latter development seemed to suit Lady Catherine and her daughter very well indeed. It was clear Lady Catherine considered the sisters to be interlopers, and Anne, while not overly unfriendly, was not exactly welcoming toward them. Though Darcy would have expected no less from his aunt, he could not understand his cousin's attitude. Still, he did not inquire as to the cause of it, preferring to hold his tongue and wait to see if the reason for her behavior revealed itself. If it did not, well, it truly did not signify.

Much to Lady Catherine's chagrin, her doctor had pronounced Mrs. Collins unfit to travel at this time, and he strictly forbade her from going to London. As a result, her ladyship was forced to keep to her pledge to allow the two young women to remain at Rosings until such time as Mrs. Collins was judged to be able to withstand the journey. Given the difficulty she was experiencing, Darcy expected that determination would not occur any time soon.

It did not take long for Darcy to notice that Miss Bennet spent a lot of time with her sister, constantly ensuring she was comfortable or soothing her when grief appeared to be pressing down too heavily. The effort involved in this was taxing on Miss Bennet's spirits, and Darcy resolved at last that he would try to distract her a little from the burdens that had been placed on her.

Remembering a conversation with Miss Bennet concerning her interest in horses, Darcy attempted to persuade her to allow him to teach her to ride, though it was difficult to convince her that she could spare a few moments away from her sister. She appeared to be of the opinion that no one could possibly serve in such a capacity as well as she, and she seemed determined not to allow Mrs. Collins out of her sight. However, Darcy was persistent, and after he had enlisted her sister's assistance—Mrs. Collins being concerned for Miss Bennet and her lack of exercise and noting that her sister had rarely gone so long without her outings in the past—he was finally able to induce her to accompany him.

On the day of their outing, Mr. Darcy escorted Elizabeth to the stables where two horses—a black one and a white one—were waiting. Both horses were saddled, and the black steed was shifting in place, snorting a little and scraping a hoof across the ground. The white horse, however, was examining them calmly and curiously.

"You do not have to do this, Mr. Darcy," protested Miss Bennet for what might very well have been the tenth time. "I am not precisely a novice."

"You must pardon me, Miss Bennet, but the old nags used as plow horses on your father's farm are very different from the kind of horses kept in the stables belonging to me and to my aunt. You must learn to ride a proper horse."

Her eyes flashed in annoyance, and he began to regret having spoken as he had. He was elevating himself and his aunt while debasing Miss Bennet's own connections. He opened his mouth, chagrined. "Miss Bennet—"

"Very well, Mr. Darcy," interrupted she, sounding none-too-happy. "I shall ride one of your aunt's horses. I do hope I shall not be riding the black one. He seems too unhappy a mount for a *beginner*. Tell me—what are their names?"

His brow furrowed slightly, Darcy decided to ignore her tone—he *had* provoked her, after all. He turned and guided her closer to the two mounts. "You shall ride the white one. Her name is 'Glittering Stream.' The other horse is called 'Silver Lining.'"

Miss Bennet turned to him with a small frown. "But he is not silver. Not to mention the fact that those are perhaps the most ridiculous names I have ever heard. Surely you did not come up with them, Mr. Darcy."

Darcy smiled and said softly: "Appearances can be deceiving, Miss Bennet." He reached out to stroke Glittering Stream's nose. "And yes, your conjecture is correct. These horses are not mine, nor would I ever name a horse in such a manner. They are from Lady Catherine's stables."

Elizabeth shook her head but remained quiet, prompting Darcy's responding grin. Nothing further was said, and a few minutes later, they were mounted and riding out in the field. Miss Bennet proved to be a quick study, and she handled Glittering Stream with grace. Laughing as she pushed her horse into a trot, she threw a warm look back at Darcy.

"You were correct, Mr. Darcy," cried out she. "This is nothing like riding my father's horses!"

Had Darcy been walking, he might have faltered at the sight of that smile. Fortunately, however, he was on a horse . . . and thus able to continue on with no visible signs of being affected by the fiery young woman riding ahead of him. Yet he *was* affected.

There was something in her smile and the gleam of her eyes that did *something* to Darcy. It was as if a happy expression on her face had the force to twist his insides, steal his breath, and stop his heart. Her form was pleasing to the eye—it had certainly grown on him—yet it was seeing her happy, even if only for a moment, that truly had an effect on him.

Trying to shake himself from his observation of her, Darcy kicked his own horse forward and pulled up alongside Miss Bennet.

"I am glad it pleases you," offered he, not certain what else to say.

But she did not seem to notice his awkwardness. Instead, she spread her arms out alongside her like wings and laughed as her horse carried her forward.

"Miss Bennet!" cried Darcy in alarm. "Please!" A strange fear was gripping his heart. Riding a horse at a trot on a side-saddle was dangerous enough when a horsewoman was skilled—to do something that might cause an offset of balance was even more so.

She brought her arms back down and threw a look at him which he could not read. "I am sorry, Mr. Darcy. I did not intend to upset you."

"Perhaps we should go at a walk," suggested he, unable to keep the tightness from his voice. She did not argue with him.

The day was sunny enough that the incident did not keep Miss Bennet quiet for long. Soon, she and Darcy were talking pleasantly, and he found himself hard-pressed to keep up with her wit.

They had been riding for less than half an hour when they saw someone in the distance. Upon taking a closer look, they learned that the figure was Elia Baker. They approached her on horseback—Darcy with some regret—and she smiled warmly at them.

"It was such a glorious day," said she after greetings were exchanged, "that I wished to walk outside. I can see neither of you were able to resist the day's call either."

"I thought you were not fond of walks," ventured Miss Bennet.

Miss Baker tilted her head. "Not even I can resist nature all of the time. If I should tumble, I dare say there will always be someone to assist me." She gave Darcy a bright smile.

Darcy looked briefly at Miss Bennet before returning his eyes to Miss Baker. "Would you like to ride with us?" They would have to return to the stable to obtain a horse, but Darcy felt obligated to make the suggestion.

"Oh, no," said she with a dismissive laugh. "I do not ride. Horses are dangerous beasts. They can crush your feet! And besides, I should not like to lose my bonnet in the wind." Her eyes met with Darcy's, and she gave him an almost secretive smile coupled with a very coquettish look. "Perhaps, Mr. Darcy, you should like to accompany *me* instead."

Darcy did not even pause to consider her idea, and it was not her rudeness in suggesting he exchange his current companion for her company which caused him to be so decisive. He was enjoying himself far too much with Miss Bennet to leave her. "I am afraid I cannot do that, Miss Baker. I am giving Miss Bennet riding lessons, and I cannot desist now. Perhaps we may walk another time."

"Perhaps," said Miss Baker in a detached way.

They exchanged goodbyes, and Darcy and Miss Bennet brought their horses back into a walk. Darcy glanced back at Miss Baker and noticed that although she had plastered a congenial smile upon her face, she seemed put out that he would not accompany her. Perhaps he should have felt guilty at having displeased her, but he knew it was a rift he could repair later, if indeed a rift had been created.

As Silver Lining carried him forward, Darcy could not help but compare Miss Baker and Miss Bennet in his mind. In intelligence and appearance, the two ladies could hardly be more dissimilar. Miss Bennet was, beyond a doubt, the superior in intellect. And as for appearance, they were both attractive, yet Miss Baker was a lighter beauty, whereas Miss Bennet was a darker beauty. A few months earlier, he would undoubtedly have considered Miss Baker the superior of the two in appearance, but now he was not so certain. Both ladies seemed pleasing in face and form.

Was it possible for him to be attracted to such differing women? Considering the idea troubled him.

It did not help his confusion to recall that he had been attracted to darker coloring in the past.

Chapter XVIII

$\mathcal{T}$he day was beautiful, a wonderful blend of bright, glorious sunlight; soft, gentle breezes; and the remarkable sight of blooming flowers and budding trees, all of which spoke to the nature of the season taking hold of the countryside. Here and there across the landscape, the greenery of early spring was returning, pushing past the recent winter season, and the spring planting of the farmers of the estate was beginning in earnest. The view from the second floor of the manor—which stood upon a small rise itself—was magnificent, allowing almost the whole of the estate to be seen. However, though the view was inspiring, Fitzwilliam Darcy saw none of it.

Despite his insistence to pay a certain young woman no more mind than any other acquaintance, he found himself powerless, his thoughts continually bent toward her without any conscious decision on his part for them to do so. The object of his reflections was, of course, Miss Elizabeth Bennet.

He stood at the window of his room, watching as Miss Bennet strolled through Lady Catherine's formal gardens. While she walked, her fingers delicately traced a newly sprouting flower, or her hand trailed through the water fountain, seemingly without a care in the world. Though he could not see her expression—her bonnet hid all attempts to do so—Darcy could visualize her smile and the true delight which would illuminate her face when she was engaged in an activity she loved, even one so simple as walking outside. She still spent much of her time caring for her sister, but as Mrs. Collins's health had improved somewhat, Miss Bennet could be found in her favorite pursuits more often than she had the first few days of their stay. It was then, when her cares were forgotten for a moment and she was at her ease, that her true beauty could be seen. It was the beauty with which he had been so entranced on the day of their outing on horseback.

Looking down at the papers in his hand, Darcy pushed thoughts of Elizabeth Bennet to the back of his mind to consider the words written upon them. Or at least to consider as much of the words as he could make out through the blots.

Chuckling to himself, Darcy lifted the letter once more. Penmanship was not precisely Bingley's strength, a thought which was charitable to say the least. More than one of Bingley's friends at Cambridge—Darcy among them—had been known to comment that deciphering Bingley's hieroglyphics should be a required course for anyone with whom he was acquainted. And though Darcy had corresponded with him for several years, he still felt it a trial to make out the man's words.

In the letter, Bingley rambled on for several paragraphs about how well his courtship of Jane Bennet was proceeding, how much of an angel she was, how much he was enjoying himself, and how he greatly anticipated the day in which he would finally propose and make her his. He then went on to ask after Darcy, inquiring as to how Darcy's plans were proceeding and how close he was to finally making the choice which he had been delaying for some time. He closed with an offer to provide assistance whenever required, citing the help and care Darcy had often given to him during the course of their friendship.

Now, Darcy knew his friend quite well indeed. Bingley had many fine qualities which made him the perfect companion for Darcy. He was perfectly at ease in most social situations, whereas Darcy often struggled; he was of a happy, carefree disposition, while Darcy was serious and sober; and he had need of someone to assist him with business matters and navigating through the shark-infested waters of high society, which Darcy was more than capable of doing. They were a very compatible pair, each one's strengths balancing and improving the other's weaknesses.

But whatever Bingley was, subtle he was not. He had known—for Darcy often confided in him—of Darcy's state of mind when he had left for Kent. He had been aware that Darcy, in spite of the fact that marrying Anne to fulfill his duty was a strong inducement, had been considering proposing to Miss Baker, as his feelings for the young heiress were much more in line with what he should feel for a woman he was considering making his wife. The idea of marrying Anne was the product of his aunt's wishes, not his own. And he was not even certain exactly of what Anne's feelings consisted, nor was he certain that his mother had actually desired this connection for him. There was nothing in her will to suggest such a thing, after all, and she had never mentioned it to him during the course of her life.

But now his sudden and burgeoning feelings for Miss Bennet—though, to be honest, those feelings were not *sudden* at all—had become a major fly in the ointment. And he was completely at a loss. He did not know what to do.

Bingley's letter had indeed come at a most opportune time. Darcy desperately needed his friend's advice and guidance if he was to have any hope of resolving this muddled situation.

Darcy could only think of the three women in question with some measure of exasperation. Marriage should have been a simple matter. He merely needed to find a woman who was compatible with him, who was capable of managing his home, who possessed a significant dowry, and who had the necessary connections and accomplishments to further his place in society. It was, unfortunately, more complicated than that.

Of the three, Anne was the easiest to judge in light of those considerations. She had virtually no accomplishments; her connections would not help him, as they were the same as his own; and they did not have complementary temperaments. The last consideration was certainly important, as he had always desired a lively woman who would induce him to be happier himself. Anne was far too much like him. The only inducement that Anne brought to the table was her dowry, which, of course, consisted of Rosings itself. If Darcy's only thought was to increase his wealth and consequence, then Anne would be the obvious choice; with her, he would become one of the richest men in the kingdom, considering all of his other holdings. It did not help that Lady Catherine, on this visit, had been especially insistent that he finally fulfill his duty and propose to Anne. Indeed, the lady's hints could only be called "hints" to the most obtuse.

Miss Baker, by contrast, was everything Anne was not. She was bright and sunny, congenial and playful. In that regard, she was almost his perfect match. Her below-average intelligence was troubling, perhaps, but that could be ameliorated by a patient husband who was willing to share his experience and knowledge of the world. Regarding the other considerations, he was certain she was acceptable, as her dowry, while certainly not the richest he had ever seen, was still significant, and her connections were impeccable. When one weighed Miss Baker's overall merits, she seemed like the easy choice.

And finally, he considered the unexpected possible match — Miss Elizabeth Bennet. Her suitability as a prospective wife was perhaps the most difficult to determine. She had no dowry to speak of and no connections, both of which were of major importance to a man of his station. However, he suspected she was actually the one with whom he was best suited in terms of emotional compatibility. She was intelligent and passionate, and if he married her, then they would always have the closest of relationships. She would never be a mere adornment on his arm in society. And he knew that she — with her compassion, fiery determination, and indomitable will — would be more of a partner to assist with running his holdings than merely a woman to manage his home.

A part of him could not help but think that as far as pure feelings were concerned, Miss Bennet was rapidly outdistancing the other two women for the foremost place in his heart. Was that not the most important consideration?

Thus his quandary, which he hoped advice from Bingley would help resolve. It would be good, indeed, to have his friend available to assist him. An invitation to attend them at Rosings would be just the thing. Lady Catherine would perhaps bemoan his attention to "those of the lower classes," but Darcy knew that she would accede should he press the issue — the manner in which the estate of Rosings would decline if he were to withhold his services would be enough to ensure her cooperation, as would the subsistence of her hopes to someday have him as a son-in-law.

The issue decided, he sat down at his desk — after one last look at the woman walking in the gardens below — and composed a letter to Bingley, inviting him to visit Rosings at any time convenient. He truly missed his friend, and he would appreciate his company.

Once the letter was written, he went to address the prospect of a visit with his aunt, and though she acted as he had predicted, still she agreed at last that perhaps Rosings could benefit from a diversification of company.

Chapter XIX

*H*ad Elizabeth only needed to worry about Mary during their stay at Rosings, then that alone would have been enough to trouble her. Unfortunately, Elizabeth's life in Kent consisted of more than tending to her sister. It was a necessity for her to be in company with the other occupants of Rosings, and the two permanent residents of the estate were not disposed to treat her with any sort of kindness.

Anne de Bourgh, for instance, rarely spoke with Elizabeth, and when she did, she tended to be condescending, if not downright rude. She clearly held a grudge of some sort against Elizabeth, as the friendlier relations they seemed to have shared in the past had evaporated. Now, her enmity was contributing to the strained atmosphere at Rosings.

Lady Catherine was no better . . . and was, in many ways, worse. She believed Mary and Elizabeth were intruders in her home, and she was steadily becoming more overbearing than she had been previously. Since Mary frequently stayed in her room—partially to avoid the tense environment and partially because of the difficulties her unborn child was causing her—Elizabeth usually had to face the brunt of Lady Catherine's hostility alone. Though Mr. Darcy often appeared to be ashamed of his aunt's ill breeding, he did not seem inclined to rein in his aunt's rudeness, and while spending time with him did actually help Elizabeth's state of mind somewhat, still it was not enough to counter the behavior of Lady Catherine and Miss de Bourgh, and Elizabeth found that the last of her nerves were being grated away.

One day, Elizabeth found herself in the drawing-room with Miss de Bourgh when Lady Catherine interrupted them. As the little conversation that had been taking place was stilted, Elizabeth did not particularly mind the interruption. However, somehow, as her ladyship was suggesting new accomplishments for Elizabeth to take up, Miss de Bourgh managed to extricate herself from the room without either Lady Catherine or Elizabeth noticing. When the former finally *did* realize the absence of her daughter, she began harping on Elizabeth: "Miss Bennet, where is Anne? You must have seen where she went! Tell me where she is at once! Have you hidden her away from me, Miss Bennet?"

"I am not your daughter's keeper, Lady Catherine," said Elizabeth softly, fighting to keep her annoyance from showing in either her countenance or voice. "I only know what you do—that she was here with us a little while ago."

"You must have seen where she went, Miss Bennet," persisted Lady Catherine. "Did you encourage her to go outside before I came into the room? She knows she should not do something so foolish as that. The weather is not good for her health. She needs to stay indoors and not exert herself. Miss Bennet, you should not have told her to go—"

"Lady Catherine," said Elizabeth through gritted teeth, "as I have stated before, I *am not* your daughter's keeper. She is an adult, and as such, she does not require me to mind her, if indeed I were inclined to do so. I do not know where your daughter is. I have been in the room here with you for the last hour."

But Lady Catherine persisted in blaming Elizabeth, who at last—fuming about the older woman's behavior—took her leave to escape outside. A few more minutes with Lady Catherine might have been enough to unleash Elizabeth's temper. Though it would have been satisfying to lash out at her ladyship, Elizabeth was dependent on the woman's begrudging hospitality until Mary was fit to travel. But that did not mean she had to feel kindly toward her. Charitable behavior, after all, was not truly worthy of thankfulness when it was forced, and Elizabeth believed that while Lady Catherine would have preferred to have the sisters gone from her house, her hand was stayed for some reason. She almost suspected Mr. Darcy's involvement in the mystery, though she knew he could have no reason to care for her and her sister's welfare, even if it had been at his insistence that Lady Catherine had allowed them to remain at Rosings at all.

She was wrapped up in such thoughts when she began to proceed toward the front doors of the house, and as she passed outside, she came across Anne de Bourgh.

"Miss Bennet," said Miss de Bourgh tightly, her face flushed.

Elizabeth, in as ill of a temper as she was, did not bother making any queries of the other woman. Instead, she merely told her: "Your mother is looking for you, Miss de Bourgh." And then, barely waiting to hear a response, Elizabeth continued forward.

She planned to walk to clear her head, feeling the brilliance of nature would be enough to bring her to more a pleasant state, but unfortunately, she was not destined to a solitary enjoyment of bright skies and verdant plants, for she had not gone far from the house at all when she came across Mr. Wickham.

She was startled to see him, to say the least. Not only had she not expected to come across another person on her walk, but she had also thought Mr. Wickham had already left Kent. Why was he still lingering in the region? What purpose did he have for doing so? Surely Mr. Darcy's enmity for him would have sent a lesser man scurrying from the county with his tail between his legs—though, to be truthful, she did not think there were *any* such curs in existence which were lower than Mr. Wickham.

These thoughts ran swiftly through her head. In her desperation to get away, she considered feigning that she had not seen Mr. Wickham, but they were too close to each other when she noticed him, and she would not leave abruptly, tempting though it was. Despite her ill temper, she would attempt to hold on to the vestiges of polite behavior.

And so the two walked toward each other, Mr. Wickham bearing a smile much like a pleased cat might wear upon spying a crippled mouse. Elizabeth's own expression was far darker.

"Miss Bennet," greeted he easily, "how do you do on this fine day?"

"I am well, Mr. Wickham, thank you."

His grin grew and became almost a leer. "Might I walk with you, Miss Bennet? I could not ask for a better companion."

Something about his expression made her feel discomfited, and she knew for certain that she did *not* want to walk with him. If he was trying to resume where he had left off long ago in Hertfordshire, then he was destined to be severely disappointed. Her history with the man notwithstanding, she liked to think that even if she had never met Mr. Wickham before, age and maturity had lent her a more discerning eye, and she would have been able to detect his rank insincerity and flattering ways without difficulty.

"Mr. Wickham, I must confess I had hoped to walk alone and clear my head."

"Come, Miss Bennet," said he, his voice filled with that charm which grated on her nerves, "could you not use a companion? Such sights as this are better appreciated with another at your side."

She let out a sigh. She was unsure what to do to dissuade him, and she feared he meant to be persistent. Fortunately, she was saved from having to extricate herself from the miserable situation by the sound of an approaching horse.

Turning, she saw Mr. Darcy trotting toward her on Silver Lining. It appeared that he was often out riding of late, so she was not utterly surprised to see him, but she *was* surprised at how grateful she felt for his presence. The dark look on his face, however, was anything but heartening.

The horse stopped in front of Elizabeth and Mr. Wickham—for a moment, she almost felt Mr. Darcy wished to run the other man down—and Mr. Darcy dismounted and took the reins in hand.

A period of intense staring then commenced between the two men. Whereas Mr. Darcy's gaze was filled with extreme displeasure, Mr. Wickham's appeared to be filled with something more akin to hatred.

Finally, Mr. Darcy said: "Wickham."

Mr. Wickham, his countenance darkening, returned: "Darcy."

Mr. Darcy turned to give Elizabeth a slight greeting—almost as a sort of afterthought—before bringing his dark stare back to focus on Mr. Wickham. "What are you doing here?" asked he stiffly.

Mr. Wickham narrowed his eyes. "I was merely engaging in a pleasant walk with Miss Bennet."

"I do not believe you have any business being on or near my aunt's property, Wickham, and I suggest you leave." Mr. Darcy's voice was cold as iron.

Mr. Wickham's gaze flicked away from Mr. Darcy's—almost in fear, Elizabeth thought—and he turned slightly. "Miss Bennet, I believe I should go. Unlike certain persons, I have no wish to cause a scene." Then, after glaring at Mr. Darcy, Mr. Wickham walked away with clenched fists and a stiff back.

When the other man was finally disappearing from sight, Mr. Darcy told Elizabeth darkly: "You should not be walking with him."

Elizabeth turned her head to face Mr. Darcy, offended. Lady Catherine was already making every attempt to control Elizabeth's movements and opinions, and now the woman's nephew was trying to do the same! It was too much to be borne! Perhaps she was required to grit her teeth and nod at everything her ladyship said, but she was under no such strictures with Mr. Darcy.

"I beg your pardon, Mr. Darcy," said she in a voice filled with barely restrained fury, "but I shall walk with anyone I please."

Mr. Darcy appeared surprised that she should not have simply accepted his statement. "Mr. Wickham is not the sort of man with whom you should associate, Miss B—"

"Mr. Darcy," interrupted she, "I shall not allow any man to dictate my life in such a matter as this. I am fully capable of choosing whom I wish to have as a walking partner, and I do not take kindly to such officiousness as you are now displaying! I will decide what society I shall keep and what society I shall shun." Inhaling deeply, she turned away from him. "Now, if you will please excuse me, I wish to resume the walk which I had started before you and Mr. Wickham interrupted me!"

Fuming, she stalked away from him, not even looking back to see how he had reacted to her outburst. She was too wrapped up in her anger to care. Had Lady Catherine not been fraying her patience, perhaps she would not have reacted in such a fashion, but as it was, she felt her anger growing to immense heights.

She had believed—despite herself—that perhaps Mr. Darcy was an agreeable companion; after all, they had spent many pleasant hours in each other's company conversing in London. Since his arrival in Kent—and her own move to Rosings—the amount of time she spent with him had increased accordingly. Frequently, they came across each other in the library, where Elizabeth went to escape from Lady Catherine. When Mr. Darcy entered to replace or take a book, he would often discuss poetry or prose with her. It had led her to soften toward him, yet now she was suddenly reminded of why she had initially disliked the man. His pride made him believe his way and his opinions best, but she refused to stand idly by and allow him to limit her autonomy. He was, indeed, a maddening subject to study; sometimes, he was pleasant and easy to speak with, and other times, he was controlling and difficult.

Her thoughts moved to Mr. Bingley and Jane, and she recalled how the former had told her that one of his friends had pushed him into abandoning her dear sister. There was no question in her mind that Mr. Darcy had been that person, and thinking of the almost ruinous extent of his meddling made her even more furious. First, he had sabotaged her sister's happiness, and now, he was trying to control Elizabeth's life!

She could hardly wait for Mary's child to be born. Then, they could finally return to Hertfordshire, and she could put this entire mess behind her. She could act as a loving aunt and cheerfully forget about all the men who had brought her such misery . . . and about Lady Catherine, who would always be frustrating to no end!

Chapter XX

The days following her confrontation with Mr. Darcy, Elizabeth kept her distance from the insufferable man. This seemed to suit Mr. Darcy well indeed, as he was nothing more than frostily polite to her in return. Neither ever went beyond what was acceptable and proper, but the distance between them was wider than it had been in the past several months. Of course, this development did not escape Lady Catherine's sharp eyes, and though she clearly did not know the reason for their sudden estrangement, she was not made unhappy because of it either. On the contrary, she became marginally politer to Elizabeth as a result and stopped watching her as closely as had been her wont since the sisters' move to Rosings.

As for Elizabeth's feelings regarding Mr. Darcy, on one level, she knew that he had been looking after her, trying to protect her reputation if nothing else, and she could not fault him for that. Indeed, he seemed so antagonistic toward Mr. Wickham — something Elizabeth, who considered herself a victim of the man, could understand — that she wondered if he knew something of Mr. Wickham beyond the information to which she was privy.

On another level, Mr. Darcy absolutely infuriated her. He was a competent and extremely capable man, certainly. But that competence led him to the belief that he invariably knew best. His warning against

Mr. Wickham might have been better received if it had been delivered in a more tactful manner. Perhaps it would not have been accepted with complete composure, but at least there would have been an absence of the antagonism his discourteous demands had provoked in her.

Elizabeth felt she was owed an apology, regardless of what Mr. Darcy's intentions had been, and she was determined that he would receive no further attention from her until it was obtained. He could not be allowed to suppose that his behavior would be dismissed without proper amends being made. And knowing how great his pride was, Elizabeth suspected the rift between them would be permanent.

Another change those days wrought was the return of Mr. Baker to Rosings, though Elia Baker continued to stay away. It was an unfortunate consequence of the composition of the society in the area, perhaps, but Mr. Baker was the only other young man within close proximity of Rosings. As such, it meant that he, almost by default, became Mr. Darcy's primary source of male companionship. And though Elizabeth did not consider the two men truly compatible in their dispositions or interests, they were often found together riding, playing billiards, or partaking in any of the other entertainments in which young men took pleasure. Elizabeth supposed that the reason Mr. Baker had not been in evidence as much before was because Mr. Darcy had been engaged quite often with *her*, busying himself with their riding lessons and other such matters. But now that she was essentially not on speaking terms with Mr. Darcy, he was free to once again revert to his normal pursuits.

Mr. Baker, when among company at Rosings, often paid attention to her, but his intentions were difficult to ascertain. It was clear to Elizabeth that he liked her. Their conversations were often lively and interesting, and he sought her out whenever he had a chance. His admiration, however, seemed a halfhearted thing at best. He could laugh and flirt, lavishing her with attention, but it all seemed superficial, and his emotions appeared to be but little engaged. The look in his eyes, though friendly, did not show the level of admiration she would have expected from a man who appeared to be purposefully seeking her out.

One thing was certain—Mr. Darcy's scowls when she was engaged in discussion with Mr. Baker were pointed and rather unfriendly. It appeared to cause a certain tension between the young men as well; they would often arrive at Rosings quite easy in one another's company, only for their good cheer to vanish once they came upon Elizabeth.

She was not certain what was occurring between them, but she wished they would cease their maddening behavior. If his attitude toward Mr. Wickham and Mr. Baker were any indication, Mr. Darcy was acting much like an elder brother, determined to critically examine any potential suitors and be displeased with them regardless of their standing or intentions. That was assuming there was no other reason for him to disapprove of Mr. Wickham, of course. What exactly Mr. Darcy had found wanting in Mr. Baker, Elizabeth could not be certain, but she was irritated with his behavior. Her one source of retribution — which undoubtedly exacerbated the tension between them — was her perverse delight in taking every opportunity to converse with Mr. Baker, laugh at his antics, and raise an eyebrow in Mr. Darcy's direction whenever she felt his unfriendly gaze upon her companion. Perhaps it was beneath her to act thus, but sometimes she could not help it — the man aggravated her so!

On a fine late spring afternoon, Mr. Darcy and Mr. Baker returned from a ride and found that the occupants of Rosings had retired to one of the larger sitting rooms. Mr. Baker immediately approached Elizabeth upon entering the room and proceeded to engage her in conversation, while Mr. Darcy fell into his usual brooding silence as he watched them. Of the other occupants of the room, Mary was sitting quietly, a book open in her lap, and Lady Catherine was positioned in her regal, throne-like chair, pontificating on anything and everything in the unqualified tone of authority which usually characterized her discourse. Only Anne de Bourgh was missing, having retired to her room some time earlier.

The company continued in this attitude until suddenly Lady Catherine stopped and glared about the room. The longer she stared, the more speculative her look became. Elizabeth watched this continue for several moments before she saw an offended expression slip over the lady's face and heard her speak:

"No, no, this will not do!"

Mr. Darcy was startled out of his thoughts. "Of what are you speaking, Aunt?"

"Why, it is this room," responded she, as if it were the most obvious thing in the world. "I cannot imagine how it escaped my notice before, but whoever is responsible for the layout of the furniture did *not* consult me, for I would never stand for such blatant misplacement."

"The furniture, Lady Catherine?" spoke Mr. Darcy, with some

confusion. "It appears much as it ever has."

"And *that* is indeed the problem," insisted his aunt. "This furniture is placed in a completely erroneous manner. Why, look at that sofa! The position in which it sits is completely reprehensible considering the way the light falls in the room. No, indeed, it will not do. It must be moved."

By now, the entire company was staring at Lady Catherine as though she were standing on the table, dancing and singing bawdy tunes in a seaside tavern. Only Mr. Darcy, who was undoubtedly more familiar with the lady than any of the other occupants, appeared unsurprised, which made Elizabeth wonder if her ladyship might be prone to this type of impulsive behavior.

"In fact, it must be moved," declared Lady Catherine. "I insist upon it."

Mr. Darcy gave an almost imperceptible sigh and rose from his chair. "I shall call the footmen—"

"No, indeed," interrupted Lady Catherine. "There is no cause for any further delay. You and Mr. Baker, I am certain, shall be more than capable of moving the furniture without any trouble at all."

Though Mr. Darcy's expression was unreadable, Elizabeth's quick glance at Mr. Baker revealed he was not put out by the lady's suggestion in any way and in fact appeared to find the situation almost humorous. He turned toward the other gentleman, his question expressed in nothing more than a raised eyebrow. Mr. Darcy's responding shrug prompted a smirk. Both gentlemen rose, Mary vacated her seat on the sofa, and the two men positioned themselves at either end of the large and overly ornate piece of furniture.

Of course, it was impossible for Lady Catherine to leave the movement of the furniture to the gentlemen. Even after she had explained to them in excruciatingly explicit detail exactly what she wished done, she found it necessary to instruct them even further—and in close proximity to where they were attempting to do as she commanded. As usual, no facet of the endeavor was beyond her notice, and she expounded upon everything from the proper grip to the exact pace which they must take to ensure the proper and easy movement of the sofa. Unfortunately, she was standing a little too close to the furniture when the gentlemen started to lift it, so intent was she on making her opinion known.

The first hint of trouble occurred when the sofa began to shift in the gentlemen's arms, as a slight popping sound could be heard. Soon after that, once the gentlemen began to drag the heavy piece toward its ultimate destination, the sound of further popping issued forth, and the bottom and sides of Lady Catherine's dress appeared to fall apart of their own volition. Looking down, Elizabeth could see the end of Lady Catherine's lace caught upon one of the sofa's castors, and as the gentlemen moved, the stitches gave way, dragging the lace from the woman's dress, strewing it haphazardly across the carpet, and exposing the uneven line of the fabric which the lace once hid. It was truly a sight to be seen.

The great lady looked down at the carpet in astonishment, her face caught in an expression of horrified offense at the fact that her furniture and dress could conspire to betray her in so infamous a manner. It was not until the sofa had reached its destination—and the greater part of the lady's lace had been forcibly removed from her dress—that the straining men realized there was something amiss. Having set the sofa down on the floor heavily, Darcy peered back at the line of lace lying across the carpet and then up at Lady Catherine, who was staring at it in mortification.

Now, it must be said that the lady was incensed with the treatment her gown had received. But though her sense of outrage had been provoked, it was clearly warring with the necessity of staying agreeable to her nephew, and after a few moments, her indignation died a most unceremonious death. She said not a word; rather, gathering whatever dignity she retained, she dispensed an imperious sniff at the gathered witnesses to her disgrace and then left the room, trailing a long line of rent and ruined lace in her wake.

Upon her departure, there was nothing further to be done. Mr. Baker excused himself and quit the house, while Elizabeth, noting that Mary was shaking with fatigue—though it could just as easily have been suppressed mirth!—conducted her sister to her room to rest. However, not feeling weary in the slightest, Elizabeth decided to visit the library in an attempt to distract herself from the amusing scene which had played out before her very eyes.

It was but a moment after entering the library when she discovered she was not alone; apparently, Mr. Darcy had had the same thought as she. Though she was still angry with the gentleman, the sight of him caused a small giggle to escape her lips, and she turned away, desperately trying to hold on to her composure.

"Miss Bennet?" queried Mr. Darcy. She could almost hear the confusion in his voice. "Are you unwell? Shall I get you something for your relief?"

Elizabeth laughed out loud, unable to retain her composure any longer, and Mr. Darcy, though he was perhaps loath to laugh at a family member, appeared to be fighting a smile of his own.

"I dare say your aunt learned her lesson about standing too close to moving furniture," said Elizabeth between laughs.

For the first time, Mr. Darcy responded with a chuckle of his own. "I do not doubt she has. In fact, I believe she may think twice before asking me to move her furniture again."

"It is a lesson worthy of learning, indeed, Mr. Darcy!" proclaimed Elizabeth, still laughing.

They continued sharing their amusement for several more moments until another thought struck Elizabeth.

"I believe your aunt must be most pleased, indeed," said she, a wide grin etched upon her face.

"Whatever do you mean, Miss Bennet?" replied Darcy, a slightly suspicious expression warring with his still amused mien.

"Why, your aunt does so love to be of use, and I believe she has been today. The best thing for us all after the last few days was to indulge in a good laugh, and she has been the means of providing it for us!"

"I hardly think that was her object," said Darcy with a further chuckle. "But I dare say you are correct in your estimation."

This was the Mr. Darcy she could converse with quite cheerfully, Elizabeth reflected. It was clear that he should indeed laugh more often, as it rendered his face uncommonly handsome when he did. A lady could verily swoon when presented with the sight of a brilliantly smiling Fitzwilliam Darcy.

Chapter XXI

The mirth produced by the dismantling of Lady Catherine's dress had an unanticipated effect on Elizabeth, softening her toward Mr. Darcy in a way she was barely prepared to acknowledge to herself. The next day, she found her head filled with thoughts of the man, and she began to wonder how precisely she should view him. And then something occurred which threw her mind into further confusion: she saw Mr. Darcy speaking with Elia Baker, who had come to Rosings for a morning visit.

He seemed pleased with Miss Baker's presence, talking to her in a low voice and nodding in acknowledgement of much of what she said, acting much more attentive than was his usual wont when in company. Elizabeth saw something in their expressions and conversation that made her feel sick at heart.

Before coming to Kent, Elizabeth had never heard any rumors of a blossoming relationship between Mr. Darcy and Elia Baker. Anne de Bourgh, however, had quite blatantly begun to view Miss Baker as a potential rival for Mr. Darcy. Judging by Miss Baker's suggestion that Mr. Darcy abandon Elizabeth while he was riding horses with her, Miss Baker seemed to believe that Mr. Darcy cared greatly for her. Yet Elizabeth had never truly thought them viable as a couple until now, for she had not believed Miss Baker suited Mr. Darcy. But even she could not deny that *something* appeared to exist between them.

Elizabeth had almost begun to care for Mr. Darcy. It was difficult to own such feelings, even to herself, but it was the only explanation for why his interactions with Miss Baker caused such distress. A part of her remembered that she was still angry at him due to his officious commands concerning Mr. Wickham and his suspected role in separating Mr. Bingley from Jane, yet that part of her kept recalling how they had laughed together . . . and how complementary their tastes and opinions were. She was coming to a realization that she and Mr. Darcy actually suited one another very well indeed.

Absentmindedly, she reached up and took a book from the shelf. She recognized it as a rare edition of John Milton's *Paradise Lost* from an outing she had once taken with the Gardiners, but though she opened it up and stared down at the pages, she still could not tear her thoughts from Miss Baker and Mr. Darcy.

Perhaps she was not skilled at reading the man, but Mr. Darcy's response to Miss Baker appeared somewhat ambiguous. Before today, she had believed he enjoyed Elia Baker's company, yet she had not been sure that he had any particular regard for the woman. Now, however, she was beginning to doubt that assessment. *Could* he intend to marry Miss Baker?

Elizabeth's right hand clenched a page of the book. She knew she could not measure up to Miss Baker, even if the woman appeared to be somewhat lacking in intellect. Miss Baker was beautiful and of good station, and her connections were impeccable; there was no reason for Mr. Darcy's interest to ever wane. In fact, Elizabeth could not help but think he was similar to her father in that respect. Mr. Bennet had also shown interest in a pretty yet flighty young woman. Could true happiness ever be found in such a relationship?

Elizabeth sighed. History suggested that happiness *could not* be found in a marriage built on such disparity, though she was forced to acknowledge that Mr. Darcy was not at all like her father. While her father had found a certain contentment, he did not seem to be happy. "Unhappy" was not precisely a term she would use to describe him either. He usually preferred the company of books to that of his wife, and even if Elizabeth's mother was daft, she must have come to that realization herself at some point. Would Mr. Darcy end up the same way with Miss Baker as Mr. Bennet had with his wife?

"Miss Bennet?"

Elizabeth jumped, her right hand flinging out to the side.

Unfortunately, her fingers were clutching one of the book's pages too tightly, and when she jerked it to the side, the piece of paper was ripped out.

Elizabeth stared down at the torn page in mortification, not even daring to look up and acknowledge Mr. Darcy's presence. Instead, she whispered to herself: "Oh, no. What have I done?"

"Miss Bennet," said Mr. Darcy, hesitation evident in his voice.

"Oh, Mr. Darcy," said she in a panic, finally lifting her head up to gaze at him. Her heart was beating rapidly. "I have done something terrible. This edition of *Paradise Lost* is very rare indeed."

"It was my fault, Miss Bennet. You must allow me to replace it."

"No," said Elizabeth adamantly, shaking her head. Mr. Darcy covering up her blunder was out of the question. "I do not need your assistance, Mr. Darcy. I shall somehow procure a copy and replace it."

He shook his own head in return and began: "Miss Bennet, I startled you—"

"Mr. Darcy, it was my own fault. The blame belongs to me alone." Though Elizabeth's voice had become calm, inside she felt very distraught indeed. Books were expensive items, and this one was even more so. Coming up with the funds would be difficult enough, but finding the book would be a challenge she was not certain she could manage. Her only hope was to write to the Gardiners for assistance. Her uncle might be able to help her, yet she feared the search for the book would take far too long, even if she could obtain the money to purchase it. Still, she was determined to decline Mr. Darcy's offer of assistance. It was mortifying enough that he had witnessed her clumsiness.

He observed the book for a long moment before venturing once again: "Miss Bennet—"

"Please excuse me, Mr. Darcy," said Elizabeth, wanting to be away from him and to escape her humiliation. Why did such a thing have to happen to her? Sometimes, she felt she had the worst of luck. At least he had not seen fit to scold her as one would a naughty child, though she felt that her behavior was not unlike one. Destroying a book, indeed!

She escaped immediately to her room. Her embarrassment was only heightened by the fact that she knew the book would not be easily replaced. Within moments, she was starting a letter to her uncle to request assistance in procuring a similar copy of *Paradise Lost*.

Despite her willingness to take responsibility for the destruction of the book, Elizabeth took great care to avoid Mr. Darcy as much as she possibly could the day following the incident in the library. The mortification she had felt upon ruining an obviously expensive book was acute, and the idea of facing him so soon after her utter humiliation was a difficult one indeed.

So it was that Elizabeth avoided Mr. Darcy the entire day. Even the next morning, she was still not in a mood to face him, and as a result, after breaking her fast with Mary in her room, she took the first opportunity to escape the house and go on a long walk. Mary appeared to be doing was well as could be expected, and Elizabeth was convinced that she could leave her sister for a short while without any ill effects. Beyond that, she was in desperate need for some time alone to think about what was happening in her life.

She stepped from a rear exit and began making her way through the formal gardens to one of the wilder paths which led up through several copses of trees, already feeling lighter than she had in days.

A flash through the trees caught her attention, and she stopped to look in the direction where she had seen the flicker of light, contemplating whether she needed to take an alternate route. After all, she did not wish to inadvertently come across Mr. Darcy when the whole purpose of her walk was to avoid him. Yet though she studied the scene for several moments, searching to see what had caught the sun's light, she finally gave up when nothing presented itself.

Putting Mr. Darcy out of her mind completely, Elizabeth began walking again, and soon she was in the woods, glorying in the stillness of the air, the chirping of birds, and the fragrances drifting along the light breeze which tickled her cheeks and ruffled her hair.

She walked in this attitude for some time before someone appeared around a bend in the path. Elizabeth stifled a groan as she saw the insincere smirk of her former paramour. She did not even bother plastering a smile on her face. Instead, she scowled at him, determined to make the encounter as brief as possible.

"Good day, Mr. Wickham," said she before attempting to move past him on her walk.

He was not about to allow her to escape so easily. He bowed with a gallant flair, reaching out to grasp her hand and place a kiss on its back. "How do you do, Miss Bennet?" exclaimed he. "I must say you are a vision of true loveliness on this beautiful day."

Elizabeth pulled her hand from his grasp and turned a stern glare upon him. "Mr. Wickham, I have not given you leave to take such liberties, and I would implore you to keep your flattery to yourself.

Now, if you will excuse me, I wish to continue on my walk."

"Miss Bennet," said Mr. Wickham as he reached out and stopped her attempt to move away, "I am very grieved indeed that you think me anything but sincere. I once held the greatest of affection for you, and I would do so again, should you give me any encouragement."

His expression took on a sad quality, and he dropped his hands to his sides. "I can only conjecture that Mr. Darcy has poisoned you against me, as is his wont. Truly, the man hates me beyond measure and takes great delight in blackening my name wherever he goes."

This claim, of course, piqued Elizabeth's interest. She had wondered for some time at the reason for their distaste for each other. However, knowing Mr. Wickham was nothing more than a silver-tongued devil blessed with agreeable manners, she was certain she would not obtain the full story from him. As a result, the only option was to excuse herself and leave him behind.

"This might be true, except for the fact that Mr. Darcy has not spoken a word to me of his past dealings with you. And I am sure, Mr. Wickham, that you require no assistance from him in blackening your name. Your own behavior all but ensures it."

A slight tightening of his mouth indicated his displeasure, though he never wavered. "But are you not curious as to how Mr. Darcy became so ill disposed toward me?"

When she hesitated a moment, Mr. Wickham continued, a mournful expression plastered upon his face.

"I believe I have never told you much of my past. The unfortunate reason is that it was far too painful for me and that I had desired to forget, as much as possible, the disappointment I suffered at the hands of your Mr. Darcy."

Elizabeth very nearly spoke up to cut him off, yet she felt he would not be satisfied until he recounted the whole of the story to her, and so she held her tongue.

"I was not born a gentleman," continued Mr. Wickham, "though I have been fortunate enough to ascend to that rank. My father was the steward of old Mr. Darcy—Fitzwilliam's father—and I had the very good fortune to have Mr. Darcy as my patron. Fitzwilliam and I grew up together, playing together and spending the bulk of our time in each other's company. In fact, I believe that at one time we were as close as brothers.

"Unfortunately, such happy circumstances were not to last. As we grew older, our relationship grew more and more distant. And when we went to Cambridge together, we were almost strangers.

"You may wonder at my ability to attend such a prestigious institution. It was due to the good will of the elder Mr. Darcy alone that I was so favored. He sponsored me in my education, showing his great love and affection for me, and he desired very much that I should make the church my calling for the future. And I dearly would have loved to do so, as it was my fondest desire.

"Perhaps you wonder why his son became so disposed to hate me, Miss Bennet. Can you not guess his reasons?"

Elizabeth kept carefully silent. She felt that at least some of what he was telling her was the truth, but she could not be certain exactly which part—nor could she be sure what he was leaving out. She did, however, understand that giving him any hint that she felt him to be untruthful could lead to his behavior becoming unpredictable. She wished for him to arrive at his point and then leave her alone.

"Why, the reason was pure unadulterated jealousy on his part, Miss Bennet!" exclaimed Mr. Wickham. "Darcy saw how his own father loved me like a son, and he could not abide his father having more than himself in his heart. It was for this reason that he became so vindictive against me.

"In fact, though his father died some years ago, and the family living he had promised me fell vacant, Darcy refused to follow his father's directions and present me with my due, which his father had bequeathed unto me."

Though privately Elizabeth thought that Mr. Darcy, with his adherence to his duty and reverence toward his elders, would be unlikely to go against his father's express wishes regardless of his feelings for Mr. Wickham, she feigned the appropriate level of shock, crying: "I cannot believe it! I have always known Mr. Darcy to be proud and somewhat aloof, but I had not thought him capable of such malicious retribution. Did you have no recourse through the courts?"

The smile on Mr. Wickham's face clearly indicated he was confident that he had succeeded in earning her sympathy. "Alas, no. Old Mr. Darcy's will left the wording of the bequest somewhat vague, no doubt due to his faith that his son would understand what he wanted and act accordingly. There was nothing to be done, as it was not explicitly stated."

"Then how did you come to reside in Meryton?" asked Elizabeth.

"I was left with several thousand pounds, both by my father and by the benevolence of old Mr. Darcy," was Mr. Wickham's reply. "I had managed to invest some of that money, and it allowed me to continue to interact with the society I had been among all my life. It was then that I was fortunate enough to make your acquaintance."

The gleam in his eyes made Elizabeth distinctly uncomfortable, but she bravely held her ground. "Apparently, Mr. Wickham, our meeting was not *too* fortunate. After you were able to use the opportunity to charm me and profess your love, you immediately quit my presence and declared yourself in love with someone else. Do you always profess such feelings to young and impressionable maidens, or was I the only fortunate recipient of your tender declarations?"

"Miss Bennet, you wound me," declared Mr. Wickham, placing a hand over his heart. "You, of all people, should understand that we are all slaves to our emotions. I hold you in the highest of esteem, but from the moment I met her, I knew my wife to be the love of my life. I apologize most abjectly if I have disappointed you, but I assure you that I had no intention of hurting you.

"In fact," continued he, a gentle expression on his face, "I believe I could easily reclaim those feelings if you would give me half a chance. I would very much like to explore the remarkable relationship we had once more."

"I think not, Mr. Wickham," responded Elizabeth with a slight shudder. "Whatever feelings I once had for you have long since dried up."

"That is unfortunate," replied he, still fixing his gaze upon her. He was making her quite uncomfortable with his frank appraisal, and she wished for him to turn his attention to someone else. She would have nothing to do with him.

It was at that moment when the sound of hoofbeats reverberating through the air caught Elizabeth's attention, and she looked up and saw Mr. Darcy approaching them. His face was a mask of displeasure as he regarded her, but when he turned to Mr. Wickham, it became an expression of pure loathing.

He jumped down from his horse and approached the man, his fists clenched with rage. "Wickham! What are you doing here? I told you to stay off my aunt's property. Now, be gone!"

Mr. Wickham's answering smile was all insolence. He bowed to Elizabeth and sneered at Mr. Darcy. "Charming to the last, Darcy. Miss Bennet, I shall take my leave of you."

A moment later, he was gone down a bend in the path, leaving Elizabeth alone with Mr. Darcy.

"Miss Bennet, I really must insist that you do not allow yourself to be alone in Mr. Wickham's company again. You do not know him. You do not know of what he is capable. You must stay away from him and speak to him no more."

"Once again, Mr. Darcy, you are attempting to impose your will upon me," snapped Elizabeth in response, her irritation at Mr. Wickham feeding into that which she felt toward Mr. Darcy. "I am more than capable of handling my own concerns and would ask you to mind your own."

Elizabeth sniffed once in disdain and stalked off in the direction opposite to the one Mr. Wickham had taken. The gall of the man — the sheer effrontery! How dare he speak to her as though she were a wayward child in need of correction! She did not think that she had ever met such a domineering, self-centered man as Mr. Darcy. Even Mr. Wickham did not possess the ability to frustrate her that Mr. Darcy did!

Her time at Rosings was truly beginning to wear on her. From Mr. Darcy's attempts to control her, to Lady Catherine's condescending tones and meddling ways, to Miss de Bourgh's cold antagonism — why, Mr. Darcy and his family would be the death of her! How she wished she could leave and return to Longbourn and the world she knew!

She stayed away from Mr. Darcy for the rest of the day, but complete avoidance was not possible. He cornered her after dinner and attempted to explain himself once more, though she was not at first desirous of hearing what he had to say.

"Miss Bennet," said he, "I should not like you to come to the wrong impression. I have no reservations about your competence or your ability to discern the motivations of others, but I know Mr. Wickham, and he truly is not the type of man with whom you should associate. And you certainly should not be alone with him!"

Elizabeth sighed and rubbed her temples, fearing the onset of a headache. Perhaps she had overreacted, but the man infuriated her so!

"Thank you, Mr. Darcy," replied she after a moment's thought. "I must own that I have some reservations about Mr. Wickham, and the times you have seen me together with him, I have come across him quite by accident. I do endeavor to avoid him, contrary to what you may believe.

"However, my business is my own, and as you just noted, I can determine for myself those with whom I wish to associate. I appreciate your wish to keep me safe, but the manner in which you have castigated me is not appreciated, nor is it welcome."

Mr. Darcy appeared to be truly contrite, and Elizabeth softened slightly toward him.

"I shall attempt to moderate my words of caution then," was his grave reply.

They said nothing further, and a few minutes later, both excused themselves to retire. While Elizabeth felt a little better about his manner, she hoped that he now understood that his interference was not appreciated.

Chapter XXII

Perhaps it was inevitable. After all, Elizabeth appeared to have somehow been targeted by inordinate amounts of hostility (on Anne de Bourgh's part), officiousness (from Lady Catherine), stress (due to her sister Mary's condition), and frustrating meetings (with Mr. Wickham). As these nuisances seemed to be growing worse, Elizabeth's nerves were being stretched to the utmost, and she was becoming less inclined toward putting on a cheery face for the benefit of the world.

What happened next was more a consequence of her foul mood than anything else. She went to the Rosings library to escape Lady Catherine and Miss de Bourgh, and there her thoughts unfortunately moved to darker places. First, she thought of Mr. Wickham. She was incensed at his presence in Kent and felt herself a fool for having ever truly thought he was her suitor. He was the worst sort of scoundrel, and she had been naïve to fall victim to his charms as she had.

From Mr. Wickham, her thoughts turned to Mr. Darcy. Her feelings about him were particularly ambiguous. It was hard to reconcile her anger toward him with the knowledge—though she could barely own it even to herself—that she would be devastated if she never saw him again. But she believed he would never view her in a serious fashion. She was beneath him in consequence, and her dowry was small enough that he had no reason to look her way. She paired with these feelings her resentment toward his previous attempts to control her.

From there, her mind moved to her twin sister, and her thoughts grew utterly black. Mr. Darcy had had no right to separate Jane and Mr. Bingley and nearly ruin Jane's life forever. How could he believe he had the right to interfere in the lives of others in such a fashion? Jane was the sweetest person in the entire world, and he had almost crushed her beneath his boot! It had been a terrible thing to do, and how could she ever forgive him for it?

This was the mood in which Mr. Darcy found Elizabeth. Occasionally, she was glad to see him in the library, but not this time. Today, she responded to his greeting with only a curt "Mr. Darcy" before she turned her eyes back to the shelves without even a how-do-you-do. She picked a book without looking at the title, opened it to a random page, and stared down at it resolutely.

Mr. Darcy evidently did not know to leave well enough alone. "Miss Bennet, is there something wrong?"

"I am very well, Mr. Darcy," gritted Elizabeth, refusing to turn to look at him. Her eyes remained on the book, though she was not reading a single word.

"Miss Bennet, if you are angry with me—"

Elizabeth swiveled to glare at him, bringing the book down to her side. "Of course I am angry with you!" cried she. "You are obsessed with control! Your high-handedness with Mr. Bingley—for I have no doubt that it was you who convinced him to leave Hertfordshire—almost led to the complete ruination of my dear sister Jane's happiness! By telling him to leave, you played with the emotions of both!"

"Miss Bennet," said he stiffly, "I merely counseled my friend to be careful and make certain of his feelings before showing too much preference toward your sister. I did not know her feelings. I believed her indifferent to him and feared her main interest lay in his wealth."

"You believed her an emotionless fortune hunter?" exclaimed Elizabeth, incensed. "How could you say such a thing? Jane is the purest person I have ever known! How anyone who has met her could say such a thing is beyond my capacity to comprehend! Mr. Darcy, you are despicable!"

And then it happened. Elizabeth was shaking the book at him when it somehow flew from her hand and toward Mr. Darcy's head. He managed to duck aside before actually being hit by it, but the fact remained that she had just thrown a book at him.

Her jaw dropped slightly as she stared at where the projectile had landed. Then, flushed, she raised her eyes to Mr. Darcy and waited for him to express his indignation, which would be no less than she deserved.

But that was not *quite* what she received. "Miss Bennet," said he, "it seems you find pleasure not in reading novels but in destroying them. Fortunately, your aim is not nearly as well refined as your propensity for book destruction."

She stared at him for a moment, and he looked back at her. Though his face was serious, there was a sort of encouragement in his eyes. Jesting was not his strong point, yet he was doing his best to alleviate a tense and potentially disastrous situation.

She allowed herself to smile. "I suppose you are right, Mr. Darcy. I indeed feel pity for the state of your aunt's library by the end of my visit." She moved to pick up the book, but Mr. Darcy was there first. He bent over and grasped the volume, which he examined briefly before showing it to her.

"There is no harm done," said he.

"I am glad. I should hate to have to replace another of Lady Catherine's books." She then sighed, turning serious. "Please forgive me, Mr. Darcy. My temper has been somewhat strained lately." She looked down at the book. "And as for my sister, forget I said anything. It has all ended well, and there is no point in arguing about it."

He nodded and said hesitantly: "Miss Bennet, I am afraid I must speak to you about Mr. Wickham." He saw her begin to protest, and he held up a hand. "I am not trying to control you, Miss Bennet. But I have information concerning him which you must know. Please, allow me a moment." When she gave a hesitating nod, he continued:

"Mr. Wickham was the son of the man whom my father entrusted with the management of Pemberley. As a result, my father was very kind to George Wickham, supporting him at school and at Cambridge. My father wished for Mr. Wickham's profession to be that of the church and recommended in his will that I help Mr. Wickham take orders and receive a family living. Miss Bennet, though Mr. Wickham may often seem amiable and all that is good, his character is a dark one indeed. I have often seen him display an utter lack of principles, and I have heard about many of his excesses. He has left behind debts and gambled away disturbing amounts of money, and I fear he has done much else besides.

"When he wrote to me saying he did not wish to be a clergyman, I acceded to his desire for money in place of the opportunity for a church living. He told me that he wished to use it for studying law, and though I did not believe him, I gave him three thousand pounds. After a few years, he applied to me for more money, claiming he had realized he was much better suited to be a clergyman. It was based on this history that I denied his request for assistance.

"Miss Bennet, you must trust me when I say that I have seen ample evidence as to what sort of man Mr. Wickham is. He preys on women with his charms, and he is not to be trusted. In addition, though I hate to speak so without proof, I believe his wife's death was not entirely an accident."

"I see," said Elizabeth softly, feeling foolish. "While I have known for some time that Mr. Wickham is not a good man, I am afraid it was not always so. I might have benefited more from your warnings years ago. Once, I fancied myself in love with him, and I thought he was in love with me. It was not a real love, yet it hurt when he left, and I resolved to avoid dancing as best as I could. It was what I had enjoyed most with him." She gave a half-smile.

Mr. Darcy shifted in place a little, looking uncomfortable and perhaps even agitated. "Miss Bennet—"

"It is quite all right, Mr. Darcy," interrupted she. "I view him with nothing more than distaste now, though I will own that I found him pleasing indeed when I was a young and naïve girl. I know that I should not be seen with him, yet he keeps showing up in unexpected places. It has not been my choice to be in his company; I would be content if he should leave the country and never return. I do not welcome his attentions at all." She tilted her head and looked at Mr. Darcy seriously. "But as we have discussed, I need you to know that you cannot control me. You can give me information, Mr. Darcy, as you just did, but you must not try to direct my actions. I am a bird whose wings must not be clipped, else I should cease also to sing."

Mr. Darcy gazed at her with what seemed to be a warm expression. "I should never wish to clip *your* wings, Miss Bennet. It would be a shame if your song could not echo throughout the world." He clapped a hand lightly on the book that had been thrown at him, which he was still holding. "I shall take what you said to heart, Miss Bennet. I must learn to relinquish some of the control to which I have become accustomed."

"If you can do that, Mr. Darcy, then you shall become an attractive man indeed." Elizabeth flushed—she had not meant to say that—and then she quickly took her leave of him. As she exited the room, she was certain his eyes were on her back.

Her thoughts returned to the book he had been holding. Who would have thought that such a violent move would provoke such an intimate discussion?

As she walked away from the library, she thought about the slight smile tugging at his mouth as he watched her go and the hair across his forehead and the strength in his bearing . . . and how he was quite an attractive man regardless of his occasional infuriating meddling.

She would certainly find it hard to wipe that image from her mind. Yet a part of her did not want to do so. It was far too pleasing.

Chapter XXIII

After her discussion with Mr. Darcy, Elizabeth found living at Rosings was somewhat easier than it had been before. It seemed as though reaching an accord with Mr. Darcy and firmly setting the limits of their relationship had helped to a certain extent. He stopped regarding her with the apprehension which he had sometimes shown over the past few weeks, and he had even made the suggestion of a picnic the day after their tête-à-tête. Though she was surprised by the idea, she agreed to the outing as a distraction.

She *was* slightly concerned when she found out that of the residents of Rosings, she and Mr. Darcy were only ones who were to attend. Mary still did not stir much out of doors, Miss de Bourgh almost never participated in outings which involved Elizabeth, and Lady Catherine felt that picnics were for the lower classes and would not submit to partaking of a meal in such an unclean environment.

Elizabeth had nearly suggested that they cancel the outing, but Mr. Darcy had then informed her he had invited the Bakers to attend. Her concerns as to propriety were thus put to rest, though it left her facing a puzzle that refused to be resolved. Mr. Darcy's relationship with Miss Baker was somewhat of a mystery, and Elizabeth was not sure what to make of it. Why Mr. Darcy would lose interest in such a beautiful woman of good fortune and impeccable connections, Elizabeth did not know, but though he almost appeared to wish to avoid Miss Baker at times, he did on occasion show a great deal of interest in her.

Early the morning of their picnic expedition, Mr. Darcy retired to the late Sir Lewis's study, which he now used to run the estate when he was in residence, stating an intention of completing the estate business for the day before they left the house. Elizabeth, wanting to stay away from the ladies, retired to the library, hoping to lose herself in a book and pass away the time until luncheon.

However, such a respite from her troubles was not to be. She entered into the library and began perusing its shelves, but there was not much to be had — since neither Lady Catherine nor her daughter was a great reader, the library had been largely ignored. With a scarcity of volumes from which to choose, it was inevitable that her eyes would fall upon the unfortunate volume she had damaged.

Immediately, Elizabeth was filled with shame, and she resolutely tore her eyes from the book. She had written to her uncle but had still not received a reply, and she was not certain how long it would take him to procure a replacement.

Shaking her head, Elizabeth tried to clear her thoughts. It would not do to dwell on what had happened. Not seeing anything which piqued her interest, Elizabeth chose a volume at random and sat down in a chair to read. But even that simple pleasure was soon denied to her. After ten minutes in which she stared down at the same page without seeing any of the words, the door opened, and one of the footmen stepped in.

"Miss Bennet," said he, "Mr. Darcy requests your presence in the study."

Elizabeth was tempted to ignore the summons, for Mr. Darcy was a serious menace to her equilibrium as it was. However, knowing that he would undoubtedly come looking for her if she did not respond to his request, she sighed and quit the room after returning the volume back to its place on the shelf.

She knocked softly on the door. On hearing Mr. Darcy's command to enter, she went inside the room, taking in the expensive and ornately carved desk behind which he sat, the bookshelves filled with ledgers and farming treatises, and the bright sunlight streaming in the window on the far side of the room.

As Mr. Darcy glanced up at her, his face broke out in a smile, and he welcomed her to his sanctum. Rising, he opened one of the desk drawers and approached her.

"Miss Bennet, I thank you for attending me. I understand you may think it an impertinence, but I would very much appreciate it if you would accept this book with my compliments."

He extended his hand, and Elizabeth gasped when she saw a copy of Milton's *Paradise Lost* that appeared identical to the one she had damaged. She hesitantly took the book in her hand, peering up at him with no small amount of shock.

Fixing her attention on the volume, she opened the front cover and found a note written on a small piece of paper. It said:

Miss Elizabeth Bennet,

As an apology for startling you, I would like you to have this book which so intrigued you. May you find enjoyment and enlightenment within its pages.

Fitzwilliam Darcy

Elizabeth glanced up at him, noting the soft smile which adorned his features—and the way his gaze was affixed on her. The image was almost breathtaking in its intensity. It was at that moment that Elizabeth wondered what it would be like to be loved by such a man.

Shaking her head, she peered back down at the book, instantly finding the torn page which had been safely ensconced within its confines. But if this was the book she had damaged, then what had she seen in the library only moments ago?

"I sent to London to replace the book," said he, answering her unstated question. "It did not take long for me to receive a reply. I have a good contact in London who is able to obtain a great variety of books in very little time. The replacement copy is already in its place in the library."

His mouth twisted in a mischievous smile. "To be honest, as my aunt and my cousin rarely read, I doubt they would notice if the library suddenly ceased to exist, let alone realize the loss of a single book."

Elizabeth laughed along with him. Then she shook her head, and closing the book, she extended her hand, offering it back to him. "Sir, I cannot allow you—"

"It is already done," interrupted Mr. Darcy gently.

"But my uncle—"

"I have already written to Mr. Gardiner," said Mr. Darcy. "I have explained the circumstances to him and asked him to allow me to act in this matter, and he has agreed."

"But sir, it must have been a very expensive book. I cannot allow you to take responsibility for my mistake."

"Please, Miss Bennet, I wish for you to have it," insisted Mr. Darcy, pushing the hand holding the volume back toward her. "You say you are to blame, yet I was the one who startled you and caused you to jerk the page from its bindings. I wish for you to have it. Indeed, I believe you to be one of the few who can truly appreciate its brilliance."

Elizabeth was unsure how to act. While she desperately wished to avoid accepting *any gift* from him, she could not ignore the conscientious and thoughtful manner in which he had attempted to protect her from her own folly. Who was this man? Was he the controlling and forceful man who watched her, interfering in the company she kept and ruining Jane's happiness, or was he the meticulous landowner and book-savior who stood before her? Had she misjudged him severely, or was he so complex that any attempt to sketch his character was doomed to failure?

Though she desperately wished to refuse him, the intensity with which he regarded her left her breathless, and she found herself accepting his gift and offering thanks to him for his thoughtfulness.

The next few moments were spent in conversation—though she would never be able to say exactly what they discussed—before Elizabeth curtseyed and left him to his business, intending to retreat to her room to sort out her feelings and regain some of her composure.

Several hours later when the time came to depart on their outing, Elizabeth had still not sorted it out in her mind. She *did*, however, feel equal to the company of others and greeted the Bakers, who had arrived by curricle, with every appearance of composure and civility.

Pleasantries were exchanged, and Elizabeth was once again subjected to Mr. Baker's playful conversation. It had become somewhat of a game between them. He paid attention to her with teasing smiles and artful statements, and she responded in kind, aware that he did not feel any significant depth of attachment to her.

Elia Baker's behavior, however, was something which Elizabeth had not yet witnessed in the woman. She spared barely a short greeting for Elizabeth—while directing Mr. Baker's attention to her with little subtlety—and then turned to Mr. Darcy with an enthusiasm Elizabeth had never seen her express before. He greeted her with civility, but her response was so overtly flirtatious and familiar that even the stoic Mr. Darcy was blinking with surprise. By the end of five minutes—when they were preparing to leave—Miss Baker was almost fawning over the clearly uncomfortable man.

Miss Baker's countenance showed her surprise when Mr. Darcy guided Elizabeth to his curricle and settled her in while he himself joined her. Despite her displeasure, Miss Baker nevertheless allowed herself to be helped into her brother's conveyance, much to the obvious amusement of Mr. Baker, and then they set off.

The journey lasted less than twenty minutes, Mr. Darcy expertly guiding his aunt's vehicle to a small glen hidden in the woods of Rosings Park, beside which was a small pond. In short order, the gentlemen had tended to the horses and spread the meal on the large blanket Mr. Darcy had brought. Rather than crafting an elaborate affair with tables and chairs and with a multitude of servants bustling about, Mr. Darcy had decided upon a much more muted picnic, and Elizabeth was glad for the informality.

To Elizabeth's very great surprise, the unpacked wicker basket was revealed to contain her favorite foods. She was even startled to find a generous portion of goat's cheese, a favorite of hers despite its pungent odor and somewhat bitter taste. This surprise was perhaps the greatest of all, as she recalled from a dinner party in London that Mr. Darcy did not find the cheese to his liking.

As they sat down to the feast, Elizabeth noted Miss Baker sitting on the other side of Darcy and regarding the two of them with distaste, though the look was quickly replaced by her normal expression of slightly vague pleasantness.

Mr. Darcy turned to Elizabeth and offered the plate he had prepared to her. Not knowing what else to do, Elizabeth accepted it with a smile. He then proceeded to put food on his own plate, stacking several different items upon it, including two pieces of the pungent goat cheese. Elizabeth leaned toward him, and in a low voice, she said:

"Mr. Darcy, I would certainly never require you to consume anything not to your taste. You need not do it to try to appease me."

"On the contrary, Miss Bennet, I would like to show you that I am serious about not controlling everything in my grasp. If that entails eating foods which are more suited to *your* palate, then I am happy to oblige you."

To punctuate his statement, Mr. Darcy put a bite of the cheese in his mouth. Elizabeth almost laughed at his reaction—which he tried to hide from his expression, though he obviously felt great disgust at the flavor—and she took one of her own pieces and daintily bit off a mouthful.

"Perchance I shall teach you to acquire a taste for some of my favorite foods," said she in a teasing tone.

"Not for goat cheese," muttered he, swallowing his food with some difficulty.

Elizabeth could not help the laugh that escaped her lips, thereby prompting a wide grin from him in return.

"A picnic is such fun!" interrupted the voice of Miss Baker. "I am most obliged that you have included me in your little outing. It *is* truly unfortunate that picnics must be eaten *outside*, however. After all, it is so dirty, and the breeze does play havoc with my hair."

After sharing a glance with Mr. Darcy, Elizabeth turned her attention to Miss Baker, noting the airy expression on her face and the studied nonchalance in which she delivered her inane statement. For the next several moments, Miss Baker kept up a monologue, speaking of everything from picnics, to walking, to the gown she wore at the last ball she attended, allowing for no conversation among the rest of the party. All the while, Mr. Baker smirked at his sister and winked at Elizabeth whenever she turned to look at him. Elizabeth was silent, listening to the woman speak and contemplating her behavior, all the while unable to shake the feeling that there was much more to Elia Baker than first appeared.

The rest of their luncheon was consumed with the unending chatter of Miss Baker for accompaniment, and though neither Elizabeth nor Mr. Darcy were able to say much, Elizabeth laughed every time he ate a bit of the cheese he so detested while he smiled at her and—with the greatest care and diligence—ensured she ate a little of every delicacy he had requested be prepared for her. Elizabeth was grateful for his care and his attention to her tastes, even as she wondered what it meant.

They had just completed their luncheon and had packed the basket with the remaining fare when the sound of horse hooves drumming on the turf intruded on their peaceful scene. The sound grew louder and more pronounced until a single rider broke through the foliage and, spying the company, spurred his mount toward them. His horse was lathered and blowing heavily as he rode up and dismounted, and his livery identified him as a member of the staff at Rosings.

He approached Mr. Darcy and, bowing hurriedly, spoke:

"Mr. Darcy, you must come quickly. It is Miss de Bourgh—there has been an accident."

Chapter XXIV

*D*arcy was waiting.

Normally, he was a patient man, able to keep a cool head in many situations which would have other men flying into a rage or descending into panic. Now, however, he was losing every shred of patience.

All he knew about what had happened to Anne was that she had been in a carriage accident. The messenger had not known any of the details, and Darcy had not been able to see his cousin, though she had been brought home to Rosings.

When the doctor finally exited Anne's room, his face was grim, and Darcy's slim hope was shattered.

"She is suffering from the accident. Her injuries are severe," said the doctor. "They appear to be primarily internal. I fear there is not much I can do for her but attempt to dull the pain, which is considerable."

"Then she—" Darcy hesitated to finish the sentence.

But the doctor knew what he was asking and gave him a knowing look. "Yes, I am afraid so. I believe she will die." He looked Darcy in the eye. "She asked to see you."

Darcy gave a curt nod and then went to Anne's room. Inside, Lady Catherine was standing by her daughter's bedside. She appeared as if all of the wind had been taken from her sails. She was not spouting off advice or commands or even illustrating her supposedly vast knowledge of some insignificant subject. Instead, she was silent, staring hollowly at her only child.

"Anne," said Darcy, hesitating as he stood in the doorway.

"Please come closer, Darcy," said Anne, her voice weak.

Darcy took a few faltering steps forward until he stood at the foot of the bed. But then a slight gesture from Anne had him moving to stand by his aunt's side. A part of him hated to be in here like this—felt as if it were an invasion of the young woman's privacy—but he would not deny his cousin the opportunity to see him while she was on her deathbed.

"Thank you for coming," said Anne. "I have something to tell you."

"Whatever it is, it cannot be that important," said Lady Catherine, arousing herself enough to speak.

"You both need to know," said Anne. "The reason I was in the carriage is . . . I was going to Scotland."

"Scotland?" said Lady Catherine with a frown. "Why ever would you want to go there?"

But Darcy had an idea of what she was trying to tell them, and he said: "You wished to go to Gretna Green?"

"Yes."

"With whom?" asked Darcy.

Anne was quiet for a few moments. Her face was pale, and there was something in her eyes that made it seem as though she had recently acquired a complete knowledge of the world. Finally, however, she told them: "Mr. Wickham."

"Mr. Wickham?" cried Lady Catherine. "Surely you must be jesting!"

"No," said Anne softly. "I have been meeting with him privately for some time, and once the idea of eloping was presented to me, the excitement of it was such a contrast to my normal life that I could not reject it. I felt as if a long overdue adventure had been placed before me. I thought I might finally be able to attain a life of action rather than inaction. Now, however, I realize that he had no real feelings for me. He cared more for my fortune and for the fact that I am heir to Rosings than for me. When the . . . the carriage crashed, he—" Anne closed her eyes, inhaling deeply. "He ran away."

"That blackguard," growled Darcy, infuriated. Lady Catherine, on the other hand, seemed utterly shocked, still trying to take in the fact that her daughter had been interested in such a low-born man.

"My feelings now are nothing like they were. I believe the man wholly despicable, and I must confess, Darcy, that I would not mind if you put him in his place. But he has probably fled far from here. I doubt you will be able to find him."

"Anne, why would you associate so closely with such a man?" asked Lady Catherine, trying to regain some control of her speaking faculties.

"My illness made me feel so helpless, Mother. Did you never think of how terribly restrictive it would feel to be commanded constantly not to venture outside, to be told at every meal which foods were acceptable for consumption and which were not—to be warned even against standing for an extended period of time? Your overbearing nature crippled me far more than the illness that afflicted me with such a weakness of body."

Darcy looked toward Lady Catherine. Her mouth was gaping open, and she appeared to have been struck speechless. Darcy pitied her. It must have been quite a blow for her to hear her dying daughter tell her just how horrible she had made her life.

"Anne," was all Lady Catherine could manage.

But Anne continued without even sparing her mother a glance. "My only hope to escape all this was marriage. But I knew that Darcy would not marry me."

Darcy felt rather than saw Lady Catherine's eyes move to him, but he did not remove his gaze from his cousin's face. Was it true that he had failed her? If he had done his duty, would Anne have lived a longer and happier life? Guilt began to invade his chest, and he clenched his fists together.

Anne continued: "Once, I thought I loved Mr. Wickham. Now, however, I realize that I did not. He was simply my escape. I suppose I was using him just as he was trying to use me." She closed her eyes with a wince, her breathing labored. "Life is full of these ironies, is it not?"

"Rest, Anne," said Lady Catherine in a voice softer than Darcy had ever heard her use.

After saying farewell to Anne, Darcy left the room, his footsteps slow and heavy. His mood was black indeed. His cousin was dying, and that scoundrel Wickham had run away.

Darcy's mood did not improve the next day when the men he had sent to find Wickham failed to recover him. He even searched himself, hoping against hope to find him in some hole. But he had no such news to give Anne, as the man was nowhere to be found, and she finally succumbed to her injuries without knowing anything about the fate of the man who had led to her ruination. It was a Sunday, but the household of Rosings found it difficult indeed to muster any joy in a celebration of the Sabbath.

Chapter XXV

The days following the death of the heir to Rosings were bleak. Though the weather was unstintingly warm and fair, it little affected the residents of the great estate.

Lady Catherine was deeply in mourning and would rarely leave her chambers for many days after Miss de Bourgh's passing. Whereas she had always been a tall and imperious woman, dominating her domain with a single-minded will of iron and molding all to her whims, she now appeared old and tired, a shrunken shell of the woman she once had been.

It was during this time that Elizabeth began to see a different Lady Catherine from the one she had thought she knew. Once, she had believed the lady cared more for appearances than substance. This former belief had been heavily supported by the woman's insistence that her daughter marry Mr. Darcy regardless of the feelings of either party. The lady's reasons were almost completely dynastic and material in nature, her primary motivations being to unite two great estates, make the family more powerful, and keep their current riches within the control of the extended Fitzwilliam clan. She had thus always appeared rather cold to her only child, concerning herself with how to present Miss de Bourgh to her best advantage rather than seeing to the young woman's comfort.

In the days following the funeral, Elizabeth found herself witness to a different person. Perhaps it was because Elizabeth was the only other woman in residence who could attend the lady, as Mary was caught up with her own mourning and the demands of her still difficult situation, but regardless of how it had come about, Elizabeth found herself Lady Catherine's primary source of comfort and support. The situation had even led to a fragile bond of sorts forming between them.

In the course of their discussions, Lady Catherine began to let her heart show. She and Elizabeth spoke of many things, most of which seemed to revolve around Lady Catherine's regrets and her love for her daughter.

Miss de Bourgh, it seemed, had always been a disappointment to Lady Catherine. Her ladyship was a healthy, robust sort of person, and to give birth to a sickly young woman had been almost more than Lady Catherine could bear. As for Lady Catherine's insistence on Darcy marrying Miss de Bourgh, it was a plan that had been borne of desperation. Lady Catherine had been terrified that her daughter would be preyed upon by a fortune hunter after her death and that the estate would be bankrupted as a result. It was difficult for the woman to accept that the very scenario she had feared had been thwarted by nothing more than an ill-repaired carriage wheel.

But though Lady Catherine had schemed and planned throughout the entirety of Miss de Bourgh's life, she loved her daughter wholeheartedly. In fact, the very existence of the lady's desperate plotting was evidence of her great love.

Regardless, once Elizabeth had come to know Lady Catherine through the lady's sometimes rambling words, she began to understand her better, and her opinion of the woman was improved somewhat. Perhaps she would never be one with whom Elizabeth would ever truly be close, but she was not as reprehensible as Elizabeth had originally thought.

For Elizabeth, the desire to depart Rosings forever was stronger than ever before, and she had almost decided to return home on more than one occasion. But the doctor's restriction against Mary traveling had not been lifted, and Elizabeth was still unwilling to leave her sister behind. And now the situation with Lady Catherine had changed, making it impossible for Elizabeth to depart. She was needed by *two* mourning women, and beyond the fact that she was the one on whom they depended, the feeling of being needed was welcome, if sometimes frustrating.

Besides, a niggling little voice in the back of her mind told her, she would miss Mr. Darcy if she left. She felt comfortable in his company and was impressed with the strength of his character and the precision and thought he put into his opinions. The times they had ridden together had been among the most enjoyable outings of her life, and their discussions of common interests had been more satisfying than any Elizabeth had ever known. He was such a complicated man that it was often difficult to understand him, but he had the ability to take her breath away with his thoughtfulness. The picnic in particular had been a completely unexpected but utterly gentlemanly gesture on his part— particularly when he had forced himself to eat her favorite cheese, despite clearly detesting it.

Mr. Darcy was not seen by the denizens of Rosings Park very much in the days following his cousin's death. He seemed gripped by the obsession to find Mr. Wickham and hold him accountable for what he had done. Whenever Elizabeth was in his company, he appeared distracted and exhausted. Unfortunately, his efforts were for naught. Wherever Mr. Wickham had hidden himself was beyond Mr. Darcy's ability to locate.

While his emotional state was uncertain, Mr. Darcy did not appear to be excessively saddened by his cousin's death, exhibiting no more sorrow than that which was due a close relation. He certainly did not suffer as would a young man in love, reinforcing Elizabeth's observation of his utter indifference to Miss de Bourgh as a prospective marriage partner. His manner instead was grim and unhappy, though Elizabeth attributed that to his anger with Wickham and his self-reproach at his inability to predict the man's intentions.

Elizabeth wanted to convince Mr. Darcy that the events which had taken Miss de Bourgh from this world were not his fault, but she knew he took his responsibilities very seriously. He had known of Wickham's character, but he had not suspected him of forming a design on his cousin, and he had thus not forewarned her of Mr. Wickham's character. *That* obviously rankled.

After the fact, Elizabeth was able to put the pieces of Miss de Bourgh's behavior together, and she wished she had been more perceptive before. The looks that Mr. Wickham and Miss de Bourgh had exchanged when the man had first arrived, the way he had often shown up on Miss de Bourgh's heels, the way he had paid attention to Elizabeth in order to distract them from his pursuit of Miss de Bourgh—it all made sense now. But there was little to be gained from castigating herself, Elizabeth decided.

Because Lady Catherine was incapacitated, Mr. Darcy had approached Elizabeth soon after Miss de Bourgh's death and asked her to take on the responsibility of managing the manor house while he continued to handle the estate affairs. At first, Elizabeth was wary of usurping Lady Catherine's position and provoking her ladyship's displeasure, but after attempting to involve her in some of the larger decisions to be made — and seeing that the lady took no interest at all in them — Elizabeth resigned herself to the necessity of the responsibility and shouldered it without complaint.

The management of the manor, she found, was far easier than she had thought it would be. Mrs. Bennet, despite her many limitations, was an excellent mistress and had taught all her daughters how to run a household properly. And though Elizabeth would have thought that managing Rosings would prove to be a much more complex task than managing Longbourn due to its size, in truth it turned out to be much the same. She consulted with Mr. Darcy on matters of import and when she thought it was not her place to make a decision, but he appeared content to simply allow her to do as she liked, as he directed her but little.

Two days after Miss de Bourgh's death, Mr. Darcy made a comment which astonished Elizabeth greatly. They had retired to the drawing room for the evening after dinner, and though they were largely silent, the subject of the elopement and its possible consequences had arisen.

"What will happen to Rosings now, Mr. Darcy? I had understood that Miss de Bourgh was the sole heir of the estate."

Mr. Darcy sighed and slumped down in his chair. "I must own that I do not know. Sir Lewis had no relations for several generations back, and with Anne now gone, there will be some confusion as to who will inherit Rosings. If his will designates an heir after Anne, then that person shall of course inherit. Otherwise, I suppose they will need to investigate further back in the de Bourgh family tree to discover the closest relation. It may become a matter for the courts and may therefore take some time before anything substantive is decided upon."

"I am indeed sorry that I did not see what was happening, Mr. Darcy," said Elizabeth.

"You could not have known, Miss Bennet," replied Mr. Darcy gently. "You were not familiar with my cousin and her habits, and she covered her tracks very well indeed."

A low growl could be heard in the back of his throat. "And Wickham — the man is a blight upon the world. He is a snake who slithers and creeps on his belly until he is ready to strike out at his target. I assure you he is more than capable of performing such a deed without any warning.

"My only consolation is that the carriage he hired to convey them to Gretna was defective and prevented him from realizing his goal. He was likely on his last few farthings and could not afford anything better. For that, I am grateful."

Elizabeth gasped. "Mr. Darcy! Would it not have been better for her to live, even if she were married to him?"

"I assure you it would not," said Mr. Darcy, his voice cold. "Marriage to him would have been a living hell for Anne, and infidelity would have been the least of her worries. I have only suspicions, but I believe that one way or another, she likely would not have been long for the world, even *had* they made it to Gretna."

"Surely you cannot be serious, Mr. Darcy!" exclaimed Elizabeth.

"I assure you, I am," confirmed he. "She is better off dead than married to that rake. I have known Mr. Wickham all my life and am well acquainted with his proclivities. A fragile young lady such as my cousin would not have survived long with him. I mourn her loss, but I have no illusions as to the quality of her life had she actually married him."

Nothing further was said between them that evening, and soon they both retired. Elizabeth could not forget Mr. Darcy's chilly tone or the ominous words which he spoke, and though she wished to refute them, she could not.

Furthermore, it made her aware of her own history with Mr. Wickham . . . and of how she herself had made a fortuitous escape from his clutches.

Chapter XXVI

Anne de Bourgh's funeral fell on the twenty-ninth of April. The day was not dismal, as one always expected the day of a funeral to be, yet neither was it cheery. The sky was clear, but no birds sang. However, the women at Rosings—waiting for the return of Mr. Darcy from the funeral—noticed none of this, cloistered as they were within a sitting-room of the great house.

When Mr. Darcy returned at last, Elizabeth found herself avoiding his gaze. Lady Catherine managed to ask a few questions about the service—the first Elizabeth had truly seen of some return of her ladyship's old self—and Mr. Darcy answered her quietly and with his customary brevity. Elizabeth could not help but wonder if this alternating mood of quiet fury and somberness would shadow his footsteps until at last he came upon Mr. Wickham again.

The sitting-room soon fell quiet, yet it was not long before a visitor was announced.

When Elia Baker entered the room, all eyes slowly went to her. With an air of ceremony about her, Miss Baker moved to Lady Catherine and began offering her condolences. Yet there was a sense of stiffness about Miss Baker, as if she did not truly care about comforting a grieving mother.

At last, however, Miss Baker sat down, and her eyes became affixed on Mr. Darcy, where they remained for most of her visit. The main exception was whenever he spoke a slight word to Elizabeth, for then Miss Baker's eyes would sharply jolt to her and then move back to Mr. Darcy. Her conversation was quite obviously directed at Mr. Darcy, and though Miss Baker and Elizabeth spoke to each other twice during the first several minutes of Miss Baker's visit, there was an undeniable tension between them.

Elizabeth knew exactly what was happening. Miss Baker was using this visit not only as a way to attempt to claim some of Mr. Darcy's attention, but also as a way to watch Mr. Darcy interact with someone she perceived was a rival.

This realization infuriated Elizabeth. Using a time of mourning for such selfish purposes was rather tactless of Miss Baker, and Elizabeth was certain by now that the other woman was more intelligent than she acted.

Elizabeth failed to rein in her anger, and she said stiffly: "Miss Baker, I do not believe this is the proper occasion for a social visit. At a time of grief such as this, I believe it is more appropriate to leave after offering your condolences than it is to linger and force the bereaved to participate in the banalities of unwanted small talk."

Miss Baker blinked at her in confusion and shock, managing only: "Miss B-Bennet?"

Elizabeth—immediately repentant of the rudeness of her words, if not the words themselves—could not help but look at Mr. Darcy to see his reaction. He initially responded with surprise, but his facial expression soon became more pensive.

Elizabeth did not have time to appraise the reasons for his reaction, as she had to handle the aftermath of her words. Lady Catherine appeared not to have heard what Elizabeth said, but Elizabeth's sister had, and Mary rose to begin the process of ushering Miss Baker from the room. Elizabeth assisted, managing somehow to maintain a measure of calmness and civility which conflicted with her inner feelings.

The situation was thus saved from disaster, but Elizabeth knew that the illusion of good will between her and Miss Baker would now be maintained only for the sake of others—not for the sake of relations between the two women.

One development which occurred immediately after Miss de Bourgh's funeral was the dismissal of Mrs. Jenkinson, her companion. Lady Catherine had not been happy with Mrs. Jenkinson, blaming her for her daughter's death and claiming that the woman had not taken enough care in knowing where Miss de Bourgh was and how she was spending her time. Mrs. Jenkinson had shown her gentility by calmly listening to Lady Catherine's diatribe without showing the anger she was sure to have felt. Then, after a brief time defending her actions, she left her ladyship's company and packed her bags, to be gone from the estate at the first opportunity.

It was not until later that Elizabeth discovered that the woman had not been sent away in disgrace, as had seemed to be the case. During a conversation with Mr. Darcy, he let slip—accidentally, Elizabeth thought—that he had provided the lady with a letter of recommendation in Lady Catherine's stead. After much prompting on Elizabeth's part, Mr. Darcy had revealed that he could not blame Mrs. Jenkinson in any manner. Working for Lady Catherine could not have been easy, after all, and Miss de Bourgh's recently found courage and secrecy meant that Mrs. Jenkinson was, in his opinion, being treated unfairly. Once he had made that determination, deciding to right the wrong had been the work of but a moment.

It was another facet to the infuriatingly complex man, and though Elizabeth agreed wholeheartedly with his assessment of Mrs. Jenkinson's merit, his actions served to confuse her even further.

Yet Elizabeth spent little time in Mr. Darcy's company in the days following the funeral, as she was frequently tending to Mary. The time she spent in the company of Lady Catherine, however, was another matter.

Though still resenting the lady somewhat for her behavior, Elizabeth was moved by the elderly lady's suffering. Lady Catherine was now a shadow of her former self. Not only was her countenance overtaken by a most alarming pallor, but her maid revealed to Elizabeth that most of her ladyship's meals were returned to the kitchens largely untouched. A mere look confirmed that Lady Catherine was becoming thinner, almost wasting away before Elizabeth's very eyes. It did not take long for Elizabeth to decide to bring the matter before Mr. Darcy, who had unfortunately been taking little interest in the doings of his aunt.

Before she could, however, the state of the house was changed with the arrival of some new visitors. Mr. Darcy appeared as surprised as was Elizabeth herself—it seemed as if he had had no warning of their imminent arrival. Yet early in the afternoon on the Thursday after the funeral, a carriage arrived, and out stepped three people: Georgiana Darcy, a gentleman who was unknown to Elizabeth, and a lady she had also never before met. Though Elizabeth welcomed them warmly, she could in no way feel sanguine about the addition of Miss Darcy to their party. While the girl was not precisely a bad person, Miss Darcy was undoubtedly spoiled and accustomed to having her own way.

Elizabeth soon discovered that the other two arrivals were Colonel Fitzwilliam, who was a cousin of the Darcys and the son of the Earl of Matlock, and Mrs. Annesley, who was Miss Darcy's companion. Introductions were made and greetings were exchanged, and while Miss Darcy's reaction to her brother was all that it should be—she embraced him in the delighted manner of siblings long separated—she spared only a glance, a barely audible greeting, and a slight curtsey for Elizabeth.

The colonel, however, was a completely different matter. Upon being introduced to the two ladies, he smiled broadly and responded thus:

"I am quite delighted to meet you both! If I had known that my cousin was to meet such agreeable and beautiful ladies in Hertfordshire, I should surely have joined him there."

"Now, Fitzwilliam," began Mr. Darcy with a stern and disapproving expression that belied his fond tone, "I will not have you employing your usual flirtatious manner toward guests in this house. Besides, Miss Bennet is an intelligent and perceptive woman, well able to see through your overly familiar manner."

"Miss Bennet, what have you done to my cousin?" demanded the colonel. "Darcy's manners are rarely ever this open."

"I can assure you that Miss Bennet has done nothing to me," refuted Mr. Darcy. "She has been an acquaintance for several months now, and I consider her a friend."

The colonel had turned an appraising eye on her when Elizabeth, feeling slightly alarmed at this subject, burst into the conversation. "Will you speak of me as if I am not even present?" exclaimed she. "I assure you, Colonel Fitzwilliam, that Mr. Darcy is much as I have known him. But you, sir—you, I can tell, are an incorrigible flirt!"

"See, Cousin?" chortled Mr. Darcy. "She saw through you in a matter of moments!"

The colonel placed a hand over his heart and sighed dramatically. "You wound me, fair maiden! I am devastated that you would think so little of me after only a momentary acquaintance."

The three laughed good-humoredly at his antics, and they soon went inside, along with Miss Darcy and Mrs. Annesley.

They all sat down to tea after a few more words of conversation,

Elizabeth signaling to the staff to provide the refreshment. As she did this, she glanced over and saw a frown on Miss Darcy's face, but since she was immediately engaged again in conversation with the gentlemen, she was given little time to consider the girl's reaction.

"I am surprised to see you here, Cousin," said Mr. Darcy. "I understood that you were with your regiment and would be for some months. Could you not have sent ahead with word of your coming?"

"And miss the chance to surprise and discompose my inscrutable cousin?"

Mr. Darcy waved his hand irritably. "Need you always act with your typical lack of gravity, Fitzwilliam? Must I remind you that our aunt is in mourning?"

The colonel immediately sobered. "No, Darcy, your reminder is not necessary. I had several weeks' leave accumulated, and as my father's health has been so indifferent these past years, I decided I would use my leave and join you here in his stead. I believed my visit might be welcome to Lady Catherine during this trying time."

Darcy nodded. "She will be glad to see you, I am sure. She has been mostly keeping to her room, I am afraid. Anne's death has been very hard for her."

"I suppose it has been," replied Colonel Fitzwilliam. "They were solitary companions for years, after all, and regardless of Lady Catherine's irascibility, Anne *was* her daughter. Once we have finished our tea, we should visit her directly."

Mr. Darcy nodded. "That is for the best. You may still be in for a tongue lashing because you neglected to visit her immediately upon your arrival, though I suspect she has not been apprised of your visit."

"That is indeed the aunt we all know and love."

Mr. Darcy and Colonel Fitzwilliam shared a knowing glance, and Elizabeth could only agree with the sentiment. Lady Catherine could indeed be difficult at times, and Elizabeth suspected that even her familial relations would not be spared her sharp tongue or her meddling any more than would impoverished gentlewomen.

The conversation continued apace for the length of their tea, accompanied by the clanking of cutlery and the tinkling of teacups against saucers. Elizabeth observed Colonel Fitzwilliam and was able to quickly form an opinion of his character. He was a warm and jovial man, quick-witted and friendly, and in his mind and manners, he was very different from Mr. Darcy. He was quite intelligent, and though Elizabeth thought Mr. Darcy to possess the better informed mind,

Colonel Fitzwilliam was by no means deficient. He was also pleasantly handsome, and Elizabeth was certain that had Lydia been there, she would have been fawning over him almost from the first moment he walked through the door.

It was after they had all eaten and drank their fill that Elizabeth addressed the colonel:

"Excuse me, Colonel Fitzwilliam, but are you able to stay in this part of the country for long?"

"Some weeks, I should think," answered the colonel. "As I said, I have several weeks of leave which I intend to use, and I am sure that Darcy could use my assistance here. Especially, perhaps, in the matter of a certain blackguard who has harmed our family one time too many."

He shared a significant glance with Mr. Darcy, leaving Elizabeth in no doubt of his meaning, before continuing:

"And as for Georgiana, I do not doubt that her presence will be a comfort to us both, so I believe she shall stay for some weeks as well." Mr. Darcy confirmed this with a nod. "And you, Miss Bennet? I understand you shall be in residence for some time?"

Though Elizabeth saw Miss Darcy's countenance darken at the colonel's statement, she ignored the girl's reaction. "I believe we shall, but it truly depends on my sister and her health. Lady Catherine has been kind enough to allow us to stay here during the trying months of her confinement."

"Excellent! I shall be very happy to have the opportunity to know you and your sister better."

"The sentiment is returned, I assure you," said Elizabeth. "Now, if you will excuse me, you need to call upon Lady Catherine, while I should see about adding you all to this evening's meal and informing the housekeeper of your presence so your bedchambers may be prepared."

Twin expressions of surprise appeared upon Miss Darcy and the colonel's faces, and Elizabeth immediately realized her mistake. Surely there could have been some other way to inform Mr. Darcy's relations that she was acting as mistress of Rosings in Lady Catherine's stead.

"Miss Bennet is tending to affairs of the house?" said Miss Darcy with a gasp. "What of my aunt?"

It was perhaps an inelegant way of asking the question, but the colonel was clearly curious as well. It was Mr. Darcy who responded.

"Yes, she has been acting as such, for Lady Catherine has been incapacitated due to her grief. Since Mrs. Collins is suffering through difficulties as a result of being with child, Miss Bennet has consented to assist with the running of the house and has been handling the situation masterfully."

Elizabeth was watching Miss Darcy's reaction, and what she saw there was much as she had expected: the girl was clearly unhappy over this new development. Disliking her more than ever, Elizabeth decided that if Miss Darcy caused a scene over the situation, then Elizabeth would cede control of the house back to her without a moment's hesitation. Let her handle it if she was keen to do so! Elizabeth would be quite happy to spend her days walking or sitting with her sister rather than managing a house which was not even her own.

It was not a moment later when Miss Darcy said to her brother:

"I am very certain Miss Bennet has done the best she could under the circumstances, but now that I am here, she shall not have to serve in that capacity any longer. I thank you, Miss Bennet, but I shall be happy to relieve you of that burden."

Elizabeth was about to respond that she was welcome to it when Mr. Darcy spoke, a frown affixed to his face. "Georgiana, I do not believe you will need to step in. Miss Bennet truly has the talent and experience, and you, after all, will still be required to devote time to your studies. Besides that, you have never managed a household before this. I believe Miss Bennet should continue doing so."

Perhaps the only person in the room who was more surprised than Elizabeth that Mr. Darcy would defend her in such a manner was Georgiana Darcy herself. The girl covered her surprise, however, and after glancing at Elizabeth, she turned her attention back to her brother.

"I managed Mr. Bingley's home well enough."

"Georgiana, you were not *mistress* of Netherfield; rather, you acted as Mr. Bingley's *hostess*. Truly, I must insist that you focus on your studies and allow Miss Bennet to continue in the capacity for which she has proven herself more than suited. You will have your opportunity one day, but for now, I believe you had best cede that responsibility to another."

Miss Darcy was clearly unhappy with this development, but she had no choice but to concede, as she obviously disliked contradicting her brother regardless of her own opinion. She did not deign to answer, however, contenting herself with a disdainful sniff. She then rose and walked from the room with her head held high, closely followed by her companion.

Colonel Fitzwilliam stared at the two of them, frowning as if he were puzzling out a mystery. A moment later, he shook his head, and after expressing the pleasure he felt in making Elizabeth's acquaintance, he left the room. Mr. Darcy was about to do the same when Elizabeth stopped him and asked for a moment of his time in the library after he had visited his aunt. Though he appeared curious as to her motive, he acquiesced and then quit the room.

Thirty minutes later, after she directed the staff to prepare the newcomers' rooms and ordered more places for dinner that evening, Elizabeth was joined in the library by Mr. Darcy. She began by expressing her gratitude.

"Mr. Darcy, I must thank you for . . . defending me from your sister." Perhaps she should have put it more delicately, but the words were out now.

"Georgiana?" queried he, a bit of a frown forming upon his face. "I can assure you that my sister was not attacking you. She simply assumed that she should act as mistress since she is a member of the family."

Elizabeth, who fancied she knew his sister quite well indeed, was not as convinced as he was of her benign intentions. Regardless, she was not about to try to point out his sister's faults.

"She has the skills and knowledge to manage a manor house," continued Mr. Darcy, "but at the moment, I think her time is best spent in pursuit of her education. Besides, you have been performing wonderfully, Miss Bennet. I have never seen Rosings run so efficiently as this. I believe you must have a natural talent for it."

Elizabeth colored, embarrassed by his approbation yet thrilled that he thought so highly of her. She told him as much, to which he responded that such praise was well deserved.

"But that is not the reason why I asked you here, Mr. Darcy," continued Elizabeth. "I am most concerned about Lady Catherine's state, and I thought you should be informed."

"Lady Catherine?" asked Mr. Darcy. "She is grieving, I know—"

"She is, Mr. Darcy, but she is very pale, and she hardly eats any of her meals. She has lost a considerable amount of weight, and I fear for her health if she continues in this manner."

The expression Mr. Darcy directed back at her could only be termed one of wonderment. "Miss Bennet, I am astonished. My aunt has not treated you well at all, yet you show such concern for her. I have never before seen such charity in a person."

Once again, Elizabeth felt a blush rising in her cheeks. "I am m-merely concerned, as anyone would be, Mr. Darcy," stammered she.

Perhaps it was a trick of her emotions, which had always been in flux for this man, or perhaps it was merely their proximity—for they were indeed standing very close together!—but as Mr. Darcy gazed into her eyes, Elizabeth focused back on his, and she felt drawn inexorably toward him. In her heart, she felt an indescribable feeling well up within her. Though she had once thought this man to be arrogant and conceited beyond all measure, at that moment she thought there was much to love in the person of Fitzwilliam Darcy, and her eyes fell to his lips.

Unfortunately, whatever was to happen between them was not to be. The door to the library opened with a thump, and Miss Darcy stood looking at them with horror, causing Elizabeth to jump back, an action which Mr. Darcy mimicked, the embarrassment she felt appearing in a like fashion on his face. Elizabeth, unable to help herself, brought a hand up to cover her mouth.

Miss Darcy composed herself immediately, and though she feigned nonchalance, she was obviously suspicious of them, as she attached herself to her brother for the rest of the evening, affixing a most unpleasant glare on Elizabeth whenever she so much as drew near to Mr. Darcy.

It was at dinner that evening when Mr. Darcy informed the company that Mr. Bingley would soon be arriving with Jane and Kitty. Though Elizabeth was first astounded and then excited by the opportunity to see her sisters again, Georgiana Darcy seemed to have other ideas.

"Brother, is it entirely proper to have visitors at this time?" said Miss Darcy, her eyes flicking toward Elizabeth, indicating her opinion over the fact that they already *had* visitors. "We *are* in mourning, after all. Perhaps it is best that *only* Mr. Bingley should come? He is almost family as it is."

Colonel Fitzwilliam peered at his charge, his brow furrowed, as though trying to determine the thrust of her words, but Mr. Darcy only paused for a moment and appeared to be considering the matter. "You are correct, Georgiana, that we are in mourning. However, as the visit was agreed upon previously, I believe that it is well. I spoke with our aunt already, and she decided that she did not care to rescind the invitation based on the circumstances."

What Mr. Darcy did not say was that Lady Catherine was no longer interested in *anything* beyond the confines of her bedchamber.

"Besides," continued Mr. Darcy, "I believe that such pleasant company will help us all to forget our troubles for a while. It shall certainly do us no harm."

"But surely the Bennet sisters need not come," said Miss Darcy, her tone a trifle petulant. "Mr. Bingley is almost family, whereas they are only new . . . acquaintances."

It was all Elizabeth could do not to snap at the girl, but she held her tongue with great difficulty. This was a matter Mr. Darcy needed to handle, after all, and Elizabeth was ultimately nothing more than a visitor.

"Actually, Georgiana," said Mr. Darcy gently, but with an undertone of steel, "I believe that the *Bennet sisters* might actually have more right to visit than Mr. Bingley does. After all, two of their sisters are staying here, and Mrs. Collins will not be able to depart for some time according to the doctor's orders. Mr. Bingley is a longstanding friend, it is true, but he is still only a friend."

It appeared as if Miss Darcy would protest further, but Mr. Darcy said firmly: "I believe that it is time to put this discussion to rest. The decision has been made, and I cannot but feel that we will all benefit from the additional company."

Having been frustrated in her objections, Miss Darcy descended into a brooding petulance which would last for the rest of the day. Elizabeth was well aware that the girl's protests were due to the fact that her chief rival would be in residence, but Elizabeth could not summon much pity for the young woman, believing that what Miss Darcy felt for Mr. Bingley was nothing more than an infatuation. The more important consideration, to Elizabeth's mind, was the fact that the happiness of a most beloved sister was at stake.

Chapter XXVII

olonel Fitzwilliam quickly made himself at home, yet without making a nuisance of himself. Indeed, he was of such an amiable and easy disposition that he could inject levity into any situation without causing offense. Knowing the difference between him and his cousin, Darcy was glad for the opportunity to discuss the present circumstances in Kent with him.

However, despite having other subjects he wished to discuss, Darcy began by inquiring about his uncle.

"My father is much the same as he was when you last visited," said Colonel Fitzwilliam. "Despite his age and poor health, he still manages to order the servants about quite admirably, though he scarcely leaves home except to go to church with my mother. I do not blame him—were I as old as he and as well-placed, I should do whatever I pleased!"

"And your brother?"

"I believe he is still in Ireland tending to a family estate. Personally, I believe it is for the best that he is gone. His mood has been quite ill lately, and if he keeps it up, I dare say I shall have to think of a new nickname for him. 'Billy Boy' simply does not accurately reflect his current temperament."

"I am certain that you shall find a solution to your problem," said Darcy, who was mildly amused despite himself.

"Perhaps," said his cousin with a shrug. His look then became somber. "Tell me, what exactly was this business with Anne?"

Darcy could not help but release a grimace. Thoughts of Wickham's dastardly nature and Anne's untimely death were always enough to bring a foul mood down upon him. Trying to rein in his anger, he explained to his cousin the attempted elopement.

"That unpardonable villain!" said Colonel Fitzwilliam darkly. "I should like to find him and rip his limbs to pieces for what he has done."

"Believe me," said Darcy, his voice low and furious, "I have tried to find him to exact my own retribution on him, but he appears to have all but vanished."

"Well, I shall lend you my assistance. We will teach him what happens to rakes who dare importune our family." Colonel Fitzwilliam had tightened his fists, and he looked down at them and slowly allowed them to relax. As his anger subsided, he looked at Darcy with a curious expression. "Enough of that for the moment. Now, tell me, Darcy . . . what exactly is the situation between you and Miss Bennet? I must own that I am perplexed. You are managing the estate together?"

Darcy turned so that his cousin could not see the slight color on his cheeks. "Our aunt has not been well enough to tend to Rosings, so I have enlisted Miss Bennet's aid."

"And the situation between you?" persisted Colonel Fitzwilliam.

"We are not engaged, if that is what you speak of."

The other man waved a hand. "Yes, yes, but how do you feel about her? Have you turned your attentions away from Miss Baker at last?"

Those certainly were not simple questions for Darcy to answer. He had recently begun to realize that his attraction to Miss Baker was decreasing. He had been interested in her as a pretty little thing whose place in life would match his own well enough that he could justify marriage to her as a fulfillment of his duty to the Darcy name. Now, however, though he still at times found her to be amusing, he was discovering that her moments of obtuseness were beginning to wear on him. Could a life with her ever truly be enjoyable? Even if they married, they could scarcely be true partners, for the inequality of intellect between them was enough to render that impossible.

As he thought about the two women, he reached a startling conclusion. Miss Bennet was far superior to Miss Baker . . . and always would be. There was no contest in his mind. What was more—he had absolutely no desire to marry Miss Baker. His interest in her had vanished like smoke in the wind.

Once, he had believed he could do it. He had believed that she was exactly what he had wanted. Her manner had amused him, and he had thought there was a sufficient personal interest on his part to counteract his dour nature and make the union a viable one. But now that he had known Miss Bennet for so long, he realized he could no longer settle for someone as unstimulating as Miss Baker. The two young women provoked vastly different responses in him, and he doubted he would have realized it had they not been in close proximity to one another. Their being together in the neighborhood allowed him to truly compare them, and it was a sad fact that Miss Baker came up short in every measure in terms of emotional compatibility.

Colonel Fitzwilliam was a good man, yet Darcy wished more particularly to talk to Bingley. His friend would be a great help in assisting him with sorting out his feelings. And so, he said to his cousin carefully:

"I have recently begun to reassess my opinion of Miss Baker. I do not believe I could attain happiness by her side."

"I could have told you that, Darcy," said Colonel Fitzwilliam, giving him a slap on the shoulder. "I have known Miss Baker for quite some time, and I believe she is meant to make some other man happy. Miss Bennet, on the other hand, appears to be a good woman for you. She is just the lively type to put a spring in your step."

Darcy began: "Miss Baker does have her good qualities—"

"Yes," cut in his cousin, "but her qualities are not of the sort which are likely to benefit you. Trust me, Darcy. Miss Bennet is the one whom your eye should watch steadfastly."

The two men continued to speak for a few minutes more before Colonel Fitzwilliam excused himself and left Darcy to his thoughts.

There could be no doubt that the colonel believed Darcy should pursue Miss Bennet. Would Bingley have the same kind of advice? While he suspected that Bingley's thoughts would indeed parallel Colonel Fitzwilliam's, he would not be satisfied until he was certain.

Darcy turned his thoughts to Elia Baker. He had certainly been surprised to hear Miss Bennet's sharp reprimand during Miss Baker's recent visit. Yet though what Miss Bennet had said had been less than polite, Darcy himself had felt the same sentiment, so he could not blame her for it. It was not proper for Miss Baker to linger and make the company of Rosings uncomfortable at such a time, and Miss Baker's presence had not comforted him any more than it had the rest of the party. But she was obviously attempting to bring about a return to the way things had been between them in the past when he had sought to spend time with her and had believed she would make a suitable mistress of Pemberley. Now, he would make a few halfhearted visits to her home, but he was not so certain he wished to be in her company any more, much less marry her.

In fact, he was—ashamed though he was to own it even to himself— trying to use the excuse of mourning as a way to avoid Miss Baker. Yet she still seemed to keep meeting him on seemingly random occasions, particularly when he was outside. He knew she had not been fond of facing the outdoors before, so her motives were not exactly opaque. It was especially irritating when she pushed her brother into conversation with Miss Bennet and then bombarded Darcy with seemingly endless chatter. While James Baker did not appear to be in love by any means, it still irked Darcy to see him speaking with Miss Bennet.

Darcy let out a sigh. He would be glad when he could talk to Bingley. Surely the other man would help Darcy sort through this mess.

Chapter XXVIII

*R*osings, reflected Georgiana Darcy, would have been much more enjoyable without the hordes of Bennet sisters that had invaded it.

Mr. Bingley had just arrived with two more of the Bennet sisters, and though Georgiana did not wish to see the young ladies, she had been ecstatic to see him. Unfortunately, however, though Mr. Bingley had greeted her with civility, she was disappointed in their meeting, for he had immediately turned his attention back to Jane Bennet, as if he had not seen *her* in weeks. To be certain, the lady was beautiful, but she had no accomplishments, was virtually talentless, and appeared to have very few deep emotions. With her perpetually serene countenance, Miss Jane seemed to belong in a painting, not on the arm of someone as filled with life as Mr. Bingley.

Georgiana did not *truly* think ill of the Bennets. They were a pleasant and genteel sort of people, and under other circumstances, Georgiana might have been persuaded to count them among her friends. But with the threat that Miss Jane posed to Georgiana's future happiness with Mr. Bingley, it was impossible for Georgiana to look favorably upon any other members of the young woman's family. And even though Elizabeth Bennet was lively and intelligent, Georgiana could not help but think she was shamelessly attempting to ingratiate herself with Georgiana's brother. It simply would not do. Her brother was the scion of one of the oldest families in the kingdom and could have his pick of almost any woman in England. He was meant for someone better than a fortune hunter from an obscure corner of the kingdom.

When they sat down at dinner that evening, Georgiana was displeased that Miss Jane was seated beside Mr. Bingley at the man's insistence. Furthermore, as they were not standing on formalities, Georgiana found herself seated to the right of Miss Jane, who in turn was seated to Mr. Bingley's right. Thus, Georgiana had no opportunity in such an arrangement to speak to Mr. Bingley.

Fuming, Georgiana ate her dinner largely in silence, listening carefully to every word spoken between the young man and the fortune hunter. And what she heard did not give her much pleasure— they spoke to one another with great animation and laughed with abandon. It was clear that Miss Jane Bennet had not been idle while she had been in Mr. Bingley's company in London.

Finally, however, Georgiana could take it no longer. In a fit of pique, she took the opportunity to reach toward a salt cellar, and in the process, she intentionally brushed her arm against Miss Jane's wine goblet, sending the sparkling liquid cascading out of the capsized glass and directly into the young woman's lap.

Jane jumped up and pressed a cloth against her middle, immediately sopping up the liquid before it could spread and stain her gown any further.

"Oh, I do apologize," said Georgiana, wary of Miss Bennet's eyes upon her and knowing the infernally perceptive woman clearly suspected something more than a mere accident. In an attempt to counteract the woman's suspicions, Georgiana made more of the appropriate platitudes about her mortification over her clumsiness.

Miss Jane, however, merely waved her off. "It is no trouble, Miss Darcy. It could happen to anyone."

Privately, Georgiana felt pleased with herself; after all, the woman would have to leave the table due to the incident. Unfortunately, however, her enjoyment of the occasion was soon dimmed by two events.

The first event involved the object of Georgiana's affections. Mr. Bingley jumped to his feet and fussed over Miss Jane, escorting her from the room to enable her to immediately change and thereby removing himself from Georgiana's company. The second event involved her aunt, who had joined them for dinner that evening.

"Georgiana Darcy!" snapped Lady Catherine. "Watch what you are doing! You are a Darcy with the highest manners and grace, not some inconsequential and clumsy girl. My Anne would never have knocked a wine glass over in such a manner."

Her cheeks flaming, Georgiana mumbled an apology, but she might as well have said nothing, for the reminder of her daughter induced Lady Catherine to silence, and the meal continued in a subdued manner.

A short time later, Mr. Bingley and Miss Jane returned to the table, the latter having changed into a fresh dress. Though she was still angry with the woman, Georgiana asked after her.

Jane Bennet, in that infuriatingly calm tone of hers, responded: "Please, do not worry. I dare say I caught the worst of it in time. I doubt it shall even harm the fabric."

"I am glad to hear it," said Georgiana politely. Inside, she was seething. Would that it had been red wine instead of white!

The rest of the dinner passed uneventfully, and soon afterward, the party was ensconced in the drawing room. Not very many moments had passed when Lady Catherine shook herself from her stupor and addressed Georgiana.

"Georgiana, I must have some music," said she, managing to inject some imperiousness into her tone, though it was nothing compared to her usual manner. "You will play for me now. And none of your somber, ponderous anthems — something cheery, if you please. Perhaps Mozart will do."

This was something in which Georgiana could excel, and furthermore, playing the pianoforte was a talent that Miss Jane did not possess.

"Of course," responded she, dutifully rising and making her way to the pianoforte. Out of the corner of her eye, she watched Mr. Bingley and saw that he was engrossed in his conversation with Jane Bennet, though Georgiana intended to ensure that was not the case for long.

"Miss Elizabeth Bennet," said Lady Catherine. "You should attend my niece and turn the pages for her."

The young woman appeared to be as startled as Georgiana was herself. But Georgiana was aware that arguing would be fruitless, and she sat down at the pianoforte. Miss Bennet apparently came to the same conclusion, for she quickly said something to Georgiana's brother and cousin and then joined her at the pianoforte. Georgiana was by no means agreeable to the idea of sitting so close to the woman, but she was willing to suffer in silence.

Unfortunately, she was not able to begin playing the instrument immediately, as there was no sheet music available. While she had several pieces of music memorized, she preferred to play a variety of different songs. So she stood in frustration, asked her aunt to excuse her while she found the "perfect piece," and then left briefly to hunt down whatever she could. When she at last returned—quite annoyed—she found Miss Bennet was avoiding her gaze. Georgiana inhaled deeply before trying to exhale her frustrations. And then she began to breathe life into the instrument.

This was how she would conduct her campaign, she thought as she played. Miss Jane had so few accomplishments that Mr. Bingley must surely see that he would waste himself upon her if he continued to show her favor.

Georgiana had played through several songs—none of which attracted the attention of her quarry, to her great disgust—when Miss Bennet, in a tone more than usually insolent, spoke to Lady Catherine:

"Lady Catherine, your niece has played through several pieces now. Perhaps she should be given a period to rest. My sister Kitty plays very well indeed and would be pleased to oblige us."

"Oh, yes," interjected Georgiana's brother. "I heard her play when I was in Hertfordshire, and she plays most delightfully. Can we prevail upon you, Miss Kitty?"

Georgiana could not believe her ears. The *blind* girl could play? Smirking, she removed herself from the pianoforte, eager to see the woman make a fool of herself.

But that was not to be. The moment Miss Catherine began to play, Georgiana could tell that she was at least as competent as Georgiana herself. Was there nothing which would show these Bennets to be the pretenders they were?

So the evening continued, and by the end of it, Georgiana found that she had been struck by a most severe headache. She pleaded fatigue and bid the party an early good night. But she vowed in her heart that she would not be defeated.

Chapter XXIX

$\mathcal{C}$olonel Fitzwilliam was generally a merry sort of fellow.
Unless the insult was great or the act heinous — as was the case with Wickham's treatment of Lady Catherine's daughter, which was utterly unforgivable — Colonel Fitzwilliam was one to let bygones be bygones. He disliked dwelling on the past and preferred to remain happily ensconced in the present. However, there was one exception to this, one piece of the past he would never be able to forget. Unfortunately, it was something that continued to cause him pain.

As a boy, Fitzwilliam had stayed at Rosings more often than his older brother — or even Darcy — ever had. Fitzwilliam had enjoyed the opportunity to escape the stern gaze of his father, and he had been close to Sir Lewis, who had viewed him almost as the son he never had. They had been able to speak in a way that Fitzwilliam had never achieved with his father.

As a result of this close connection, there had been some talk of making Fitzwilliam the heir to Rosings. Sir Lewis had seen the ill health of his daughter and believed she would never even make it to fifteen. He certainly would have never believed she could outlive him. Lady Catherine, however, though she had ordered Anne around and seen fastidiously to every aspect of the girl's daily life, refused to believe that her daughter would face an early death, and she had argued against the notion of making Fitzwilliam heir. She had noted that the Fitzwilliams were only Sir Lewis's relations by marriage and were therefore not actually family, and she had proclaimed quite vehemently that Anne would live long and marry Fitzwilliam Darcy, thereby uniting the great estates of Rosings and Pemberley. This was a view she simply would not be divested of, and there had been quite a commotion at Rosings.

Though Lady Catherine won the fight, Sir Lewis was rather angry for a great deal of time afterward, and only he and Lady Catherine knew what words passed between them. With the state of Anne's health, Sir Lewis could not have been blamed for his concern as to who would inherit the estate. Still, there were few who could succeed at winning an argument with Lady Catherine.

At the time, the idea of being heir to an estate (as his older brother was) had held little appeal for Fitzwilliam, though in hindsight he realized it would have been fortunate indeed to be more stationary than the regulars allowed. Yet despite the fact that he would not be inheriting Rosings, there had been something that tied him irrevocably to Kent even after Sir Lewis's death. That something was Elia Baker.

He had first met Miss Baker when they were both quite young. He still remembered fondly the first time they had met. He had been riding his new pony out in the field, and she had been kneeling on the ground and gathering flowers. He had smirked a little at her, thinking the act very befitting of a girl, but she had looked up at him and told him in a matter-of-fact tone: "I am only picking flowers because my mother is forcing me to. I would much rather be doing something else—maybe even riding a horse, which I have not yet done." He had been intrigued, and they had become close friends rather quickly after that. He had even seen to it that she be allowed to ride a horse.

As the years passed, Miss Baker had become less rebellious and every bit the growing woman. Fitzwilliam, who cared for her heart more than for her beauty, developed strong feelings for her, and before leaving to join the military, he had told her: "One day, I will return and marry you." He had meant every word, and he still felt them resonating within his breast.

She had given him a sad smile—had she known even then that it was not to be?—and he had embraced her, throwing all propriety to the wind. As they had said farewell with voices that shook and eyes that were not quite dry, he had found himself wishing very much that he could have been heir to an estate, for then he would not be required to join the military in an attempt to make his way in the world.

A few years had passed before he was able to return to Kent, and when he did, he found with despair that Miss Baker had changed. Gone was the great friend with whom he could have lively and intelligent conversations, and in her place was a woman who appeared to be all beauty and frivolity, with little substance. He did not know for certain, but he suspected her mother had influenced her to value status and wealth over love. And of course, though status was not precisely a problem, Fitzwilliam had no wealth to speak of. Still, he had hoped, and he had resolved to continue as he had planned.

But he had scarcely been able to touch upon the subject of his old promise when Miss Baker told him: "I shall never marry you. Let us talk of it no longer." And then she had begun to talk airily of some inconsequential subject, seemingly unaware of the harshness of the blow she had just given.

To say he had felt crushed would have been to put it lightly. Though he had tried to enjoy his time with the regulars, he had never been able to forget that promise he had made. He had tried to push aside his pain, but it still lingered. Her rejection did nothing to quench the fires of his feelings for her. If anything, he valued her more.

And now, Colonel Fitzwilliam had finally ascertained that Darcy was not truly interested in Miss Baker. And if Darcy was not to marry her, then perhaps there was still a chance that Fitzwilliam could convince her that he was in love with her . . . and that she should marry him.

But Fitzwilliam could not make his move until the break between Darcy and Miss Baker became clear enough to Darcy. Fitzwilliam knew that his cousin held the idea of duty highly, but he hoped Darcy would be able to see that Miss Bennet was much more suited to him.

After all, Miss Baker was *Colonel Fitzwilliam's* true love, not Darcy's. At least, he had been true to her, even if she had not wished to remain true to him.

Chapter XXX

A few days after the arrival of the new additions to the party at Rosings Park, James and Elia Baker stopped in for a morning visit.

James Baker looked upon the prospect of meeting these new arrivals with a certain amount of boredom, and he would likely not have agreed to the excursion at all had he not derived a certain sardonic amusement from his sister's antics.

Simply put, Elia was a huntress, and her prey — to the surprise of no one who saw her in action — was none other than Mr. Darcy. But whereas she attempted to be subtle in her pursuit, to one who knew her as well as Baker, she was as transparent as the glass window in his bedchamber.

She had not always been this way and indeed was very different from her brother, and the reason likely had something to do with their parents. Their mother was the daughter of a duke, and her marriage to Baker's father had been considered somewhat beneath her. However, the old Mr. Baker's estate in Kent was extensive, and he had been active enough politically to have made a name for himself, and that had softened, to a certain extent, the appearance of unsuitability in the match. Still, the connection would not likely have been tolerated if Emma Blascombe had actually been able to attract a suitor who was nearer her own station.

The simple fact of that matter was that the woman had been a shrew, and even her fortune of forty thousand pounds had been insufficient to attract a suitor willing to withstand her character in exchange for her money. At least, not until his father had come along.

David Baker was a good man, and both his children had fond memories of him. Unfortunately, however, he was a second son. Though he eventually inherited Stauneton Hall from his elder brother, he found himself in dire financial straits upon doing so. His brother had virtually bankrupted the estate through his gambling and debaucheries before finally drinking himself to death. Thus, for David Baker, the fact that a woman with the dowry possessed by Miss Blascombe had remained unmarried at the age of three and twenty had been a godsend for his financial needs, if not his emotional ones. They had married after a brief courtship, and then her dowry had been put to good use in restoring the estate to respectable profitability.

Unfortunately, the old Mr. Baker could not boast an equal felicity with the person of his wife as that which he had found with her fortune. Mrs. Baker remained a proud and snobbish woman, and her disposition was simply not compatible with her husband's.

James Baker recalled that his sister had been happy and carefree as a child, unpretentious and kind to all, due in large part to the fact that David Baker had refused to allow Mrs. Baker to teach Elia and James to be overly prideful of their situation.

Unfortunately, that had all changed. As Elia had reached her teenage years, her father's health had taken a turn for the worse, allowing Mrs. Baker to take charge of her daughter's upbringing, without a moderating influence. It was then that this creature who valued money and status had been born, much to James Baker's chagrin. He had truly enjoyed Elia's company as a child, and he was saddened at her change in character.

As for Baker himself, he knew that he possessed a bit of a cavalier attitude. He had had several liaisons with certain lonely widows, though he was always discreet. When he was in town, he had been known to frequent certain . . . less than reputable establishments. And in general, he possessed a playful and pleasing disposition that made him take delight in flirting with any young lady with whom he came in contact.

But he was not a complete libertine. He was well aware of the strictures placed on gently born young women of his circle, and though he might flirt and smile at such young women, he would never stoop to seducing or ruining them.

Such was the case with Elizabeth Bennet. She was an intriguing woman, to be certain, and Baker truly enjoyed their conversations, but she was not much more than that to him. It was not that he did not consider her to be an exceptional woman—certainly not! It was more the fact that he recognized how he himself would not suit her, for she needed someone more serious to balance her tendency toward playfulness. Furthermore, Miss Bennet was a little too headstrong for his tastes, as he wished for a wife who would be somewhat more dependent upon him. All of that was not even taking into account the fact that she was intelligent enough to speak circles around him if she so chose. In fact, she was almost perfect for Darcy, who showed every sign of being completely enamored of her.

Despite this awareness, Baker was more than willing to be influenced by his sister into showing an interest in Miss Bennet. He enjoyed tweaking Darcy's nose (and he had been vastly rewarded with the man's scowls and frowns in this case), and he found that toying with his sister and sabotaging her plans when least expected brought him just as much satisfaction. Perhaps it was cruel and beneath him, but Baker had long ago decided that one must take amusement and pleasure where possible. Besides, any fool could see that Elia and Darcy would not suit each other. Darcy seemed to be coming to that conclusion himself, if his waning attentions were any indication. The sooner Elia realized that, the better off she would be.

Upon entering the sitting room at Rosings, Baker and his sister were introduced to two of Miss Bennet's younger sisters. The elder, Miss Jane, was beautiful and well-mannered, and had that Bingley fellow not been hovering around her, Baker would have thought her the perfect young lady for him to exert his protective instinct upon. The younger sister's response was somewhat playful, indicating a personality similar to Miss Bennet's.

The tea arrived, and the group began making light conversation. It was then that Elia spouted off one of her nonsensical little observances:

"It is truly good to make new acquaintances," said she in her usual flighty manner. "A new acquaintance is so very novel, and I do like having new experiences."

Baker almost snorted at his sister's comment. He knew that she was not as insipid as she often made herself out to be, and he suspected she did it to attract Darcy's attention.

Darcy gazed at her with a pensive air, and the colonel looked on her with some disapproval. But it was the amused smile of the youngest Miss Bennet which caught Baker's eye, and he watched as she responded to his sister.

"A new acquaintance being new," murmured she, smiling slightly behind her teacup. "You truly have a gift with words, Miss Baker. I do not believe I have ever heard anyone refer to the situation in such a manner."

"I thank you, Miss Catherine," simpered Elia. "I do try to infuse my conversation with a little extra interest. After all, the same words spoken over and over again would become very dull."

"And I am sure you succeed, Miss Baker," said Miss Catherine before turning to her sister and beginning to speak with her.

Baker grinned into his hand, trying to cover his amusement with a cough. He was certain Miss Catherine had not been fooled in the slightest by his sister's attempt at subterfuge.

The discourse continued for some time, and though the conversation partners were somewhat fluid, Baker felt himself being quite entertained by the company. Elia attempted to secure Darcy's attention with the use of several pointed hints and comments, but Darcy appeared to be more interested in Miss Bennet's lively conversation. Mrs. Collins was largely silent as was her wont, while Bingley and Miss Jane Bennet hardly had any attention to spare for the other occupants of the room. The colonel was engaged in speaking with all equally, but his eyes often strayed to Elia, and Baker, knowing what had passed between them, pitied him. Finally, Georgiana Darcy spent her time brooding, alternating between scowling at Miss Jane and Bingley and directing sour looks at Miss Bennet due to the attention Darcy was showing her. There was certainly enough happening in the room to satisfy even the most proletarian studier of character.

More and more, though, Baker found his attention caught by the youngest Bennet sister. Baker was somewhat of a vain creature, and he was often wont to laugh at himself because of his vanity. It *was* true, however, that he was a handsome man, and he had used that knowledge many times in the past in his pursuit of the society of interesting and attractive women.

Miss Catherine Bennet, however, was not reacting in the manner in which he had become accustomed. Rather, she seemed to be little affected by his presence. It was intriguing.

As more of his attention was captured by her, he found himself watching her and ruminating over her attractions. She was a pretty girl, though a little more diminutive than he preferred, and she possessed a pleasing and womanly figure. Her face, though perhaps not technically beautiful, was handsome enough to catch the eye, he thought, and her playfulness was pleasing. She was, he decided, much like her sister Elizabeth, though perhaps she was not as overt as Miss Bennet was wont to be in her manners.

A chance remark of Baker's caught her attention, and he saw her face turn in his direction. He was puzzled momentarily, for though he could tell her attention was upon him, her eyes were peering past him.

"Mary, I do believe I would like to converse with Mr. Baker a little. Would you be so kind as to guide me to him?"

Amazed, Baker watched as she stood and, clutching Mrs. Collins's arm, carefully made her way across the room to be seated by his side. It was at this moment that it occurred to him — Miss Catherine was blind!

Immediately, Baker castigated himself as the stupidest creature on the face of the earth. Of course she was blind! She had never looked directly at him, her eyes had shown a tendency to wander, and her hearing was acute enough for her to have heard him speak, though he had not spoken loudly or in her direction.

As she sat, Miss Catherine directed a smile at him. "I must say, Mr. Baker, I am intrigued by your meaning. Did you mean to say that England should not be involved in the war against Napoleon, or were you attempting to make some other point?"

Dumbfounded, Baker had to think back to what he said, feeling immensely stupid that this slip of a girl was able to discomfit him so completely. Taking a deep breath, he concentrated on the conversation and, remembering his words, focused his attention back on his companion.

"No, indeed, Miss Catherine," responded he. "I merely stated that perhaps England is assuming a disproportionate level of responsibility for the prosecution of the war and that other nations had best commit themselves more fully so the tyrant's defeat may be brought about more quickly."

"As an active soldier in His Majesty's army, I cannot disagree," spoke Colonel Fitzwilliam from the side. Baker turned to face him and noticed the sly smile on his face as he regarded Miss Catherine sitting beside Baker. "What say you, Miss Catherine?"

Miss Catherine nodded sagely. "Though I cannot pretend to possess an equal understanding as to the state of our army against the despot, I do believe that Mr. Baker's position is one with which I can only agree."

"I did not know you possessed the soul of a campaigner, Miss Catherine," said Colonel Fitzwilliam with a laugh. "I see I must take care in your presence and not allow my general to meet you. He may not find me indispensable after all!"

Miss Catherine's tinkling laughter enchanted Baker, and he found himself completely captivated by her manner. For several moments, he was unable to say anything; he merely watched her and listened to her conversation as she spoke with the colonel until he was called away by his cousin.

Seeming to sense his state, Miss Catherine leaned closer and spoke in a conspiratorial manner: "Do not worry, Mr. Baker. Your reaction is rather common."

"Reaction?" asked Baker.

"To my blindness. It is quite a common occurrence."

Chagrined, Baker grimaced. "I apologize, Miss Catherine. I did not realize I was being so obvious."

"It matters little. And you were not obvious; I am just accustomed to others' reactions. I am not offended."

"If you do not mind my asking, were you born without the power of sight?"

"Actually, a sickness as a child robbed me of the use of my eyes. I have become accustomed to the loss, though, and am quite content. My sisters often read to me and guide me when I walk, and I still take pleasure in many things."

Her smile turned impish, and Baker found his heart fluttering in response. "I can even dance, Mr. Baker."

"Truly? Is it not very difficult for you?"

"As long as I have a partner who can be trusted to guide me properly, my sisters have taught me so well that I can complete the steps with very little wandering."

Their conversation continued for the rest of the visit, and Baker found himself intrigued by this young woman. It was not long before he could identify the similarities between Miss Catherine and Miss Bennet, but whereas the elder sister could be somewhat intimidating in her intelligence at times, the younger was more apt to make her companion feel comfortable. By the end of their visit, Baker found himself wanting to know her much better indeed.

Chapter XXXI

Though Bingley was, to be sure, reluctant to leave the presence of Jane Bennet for an extended period of time, he was willing—on occasion—to partake in an activity from which she was excluded. One such activity was going on a morning ride with Darcy.

After their first morning ride together in quite a while, the two men retired to the library instead of seeking out other company. The time they had spent together was quiet and serene, filled with dew and mist and the clopping of hooves and not much else. Darcy had been brooding the whole time, and Bingley himself had been considering his friend quite carefully. After seeing Darcy interact with Miss Baker and with Miss Elizabeth Bennet, Bingley thought he knew where the situation *should* stand, yet he needed to learn more. He had to hear Darcy vocalize some of his feelings before he would know how best to be of assistance.

After they were comfortably situated in the library, it felt as if a chasm of silence had opened up between them. Bingley resolved to be the first to bridge it.

"Would you like my advice, Darcy?"

Darcy looked somewhat startled. He had obviously not expected such forthrightness. But Bingley had never been one to unnecessarily delay coming to a point. While he usually tried to avoid being quite so blunt, he had been forced to do an excessive amount of thinking lately, and he had become convinced that matters of the heart were not to be delayed for *too* long. It was not prudent to dive right in, yet neither was it advisable to wait for the seasons to go through their fluctuations several times before making at least a little progress. He had made steps to show Jane Bennet how dear she was to him, and though they were not yet engaged, he felt certain she was beginning to understand the depths of his love for her. And that was what was most important.

Darcy, once he had regained his mental footing, finally replied: "I should indeed like to hear your opinion."

"Just to be clear, we are talking about Miss Baker and Miss Elizabeth Bennet." Though Bingley knew his friend to be astute, he felt that needed to be clarified. Misunderstandings in a conversation such as this could be very detrimental indeed.

"Yes," acknowledged Darcy, looking more uncertain than Bingley had ever seen him. "I know how I wish to handle my situation, yet I do not know if that is best."

"Darcy, I have seen you with both women, and —" Bingley cut himself off, and after a moment's thought, he decided that it was better for Darcy to state *his* impressions of the two young women without prior prompting. Thus, he began again: "Tell me, Darcy — what are your feelings for them?"

Darcy paused for a few seconds, likely to gather his thoughts, and then he responded with careful slowness: "Before meeting Miss Bennet, I was certain that Miss Baker would make an ideal bride. As for my cousin, though I felt in some ways that my duty called for an alliance between us, I did not want to marry her due to our general incompatibility. By marrying someone in Miss Baker's position, however, I believed I could still meet my responsibilities as master of Pemberley."

"You speak of duty, Darcy, but I spoke of feelings."

Darcy gave a slight smile, and Bingley suspected he was marveling over the changes that had been wrought since Bingley had so foolishly abandoned Jane Bennet and departed for London. Certainly, it was strange for Darcy to be seeking Bingley's advice rather than the reverse. But now they were on a more equal footing in their friendship, and Bingley was glad for that. Darcy had been a good friend and advisor over the years, and Bingley was grateful for the chance to return the favor.

"So you did, Bingley. I felt amused by her less than shining intelligence. I believed that amusement would be a good counter to my usual sobriety."

"And Miss Bennet?" prompted Bingley.

"Miss Bennet—" began Darcy, only to pause and sigh. "My feelings for her are much more difficult to describe, for she makes me feel so many things at once. As Miss Baker does, Miss Bennet causes me to feel amusement, yet it is of a lighter variety. With Miss Bennet, I feel frustrated yet intrigued, off-balanced yet awed. The challenge of following her quick wit keeps me from falling too deeply into somberness and taciturnity. With her, I can feel genuinely happy . . . yet I also feel fearful." Darcy colored a little, perhaps out of embarrassment for letting so much of his heart show. "She throws me into a torrent of confusion, Bingley. I am not accustomed to feeling this way."

It was all Bingley could do to keep from bursting out: "You are in love!" Instead, he told his friend: "If you marry Miss Baker, Darcy, then you are a fool. Nothing can replace a loving relationship in a marriage. Money and status cannot act as substitutes. If you cannot respect your wife, you shall never be happy, and finding amusement in Miss Baker's 'less than shining intelligence' does not seem to suggest any measure of respect. Miss Bennet may not have much of a dowry to speak of, yet she *is* the daughter of a gentleman. With that, you can be content."

Darcy gave him half a smile. "And are you content, Bingley?"

"Come now, man!" cried Bingley. "I have my own Bennet daughter, and she has wrapped me around her little finger. She is the loveliest and kindest woman in England. How could I be anything but happy?"

"Mr. Bennet did appear to somehow instill great virtue in his eldest daughters," owned Darcy with a smile. "Bingley, I must congratulate you with regard to your relationship with Miss Jane Bennet. I must say that you have evinced a very un-Bingley-like patience in not asking her to marry you."

Bingley laughed. "It is indeed out of character! But I wish to show her my genuine admiration and solidify the grounds of our relationship. Perhaps you should do a little of that yourself!" He gave Darcy a pat on the shoulder.

A few minutes later, Bingley began to leave the library, hoping that he had succeeded in swaying his friend. When he looked back at Darcy one last time, he noticed that the man appeared thoughtful, and that strengthened his hope. Perhaps they would be brothers after all.

Chapter XXXII

The next several days passed in true pleasure for Elizabeth, for not only had she been joined by her beloved sisters—thereby making the situation at Rosings much more tolerable—but she was also able to see for herself the manner in which Jane's relationship with Mr. Bingley had developed.

It was clear that Jane and Mr. Bingley had eyes only for one another, and Elizabeth was certain that Mr. Bingley would relieve their suspense any day now and propose marriage. Then Jane would have her heart's desire. And deservedly so!

Elizabeth had no qualms whatsoever in doing her own small part in facilitating their relationship. She kept them from being interrupted when they sat next to each other at dinner, speaking together in low voices and ignoring the rest of the group. She encouraged them to walk together, ensured they had ample opportunity to converse when in company by intercepting those who would interrupt them, and supported their gentle affections for each other in whatever ways she could. Not that they truly required her assistance in *that* matter.

Of course, not everyone in the house was as happy as Elizabeth over the developments in her sister's relationship with Mr. Bingley. Miss Darcy's displeasure over the situation was more than apparent to Elizabeth. Thus far, the young lady had done little to show her ill temper other than to glower at Jane and attempt to display herself to greatest advantage to Mr. Bingley. That Mr. Bingley was completely oblivious to her efforts was eminently satisfying to Elizabeth, and at times, she almost found herself laughing at the girl's ineffectual posturing.

What surprised Elizabeth was how Mr. Darcy remained completely ignorant of the girl's feelings and machinations. Though he peered at his sister from time to time, likely wondering about her behavior, he appeared to come to no conclusions as to the true state of matters. Though she suspected Colonel Fitzwilliam had some idea of Miss Darcy's partiality, the young girl tended to keep herself in check whenever he was close by, so it did not appear that he had seen fit to discuss her behavior with her brother.

One evening after dinner, the company gathered together in the sitting room. Mary had been prevailed upon to play for the company, being both well enough and willing, which had not been the case to any great degree of late. Though the worst of Mary's symptoms appeared to have passed, she was still gripped by a crippling melancholy, and Elizabeth did not know how to bring her out of it. Though Mary had held some esteem for Mr. Collins, she had *not* truly loved him — as she had confessed to Elizabeth some weeks previously — but she was now facing the prospect of living her life without a partner, for she felt it unlikely she would ever marry again. Elizabeth did her best to cheer her sister, but privately, she wondered about the futures of *all* her sisters. Jane, at least, appeared to be well on her way toward matrimony with Mr. Bingley, but though the futures of Mrs. Bennet and her daughters were now secure, Elizabeth wondered if she and the rest of her sisters could find partners with nothing more than themselves to garner the interest of a man.

Yet Elizabeth was not made for melancholy, and with a smile, she took her turn at the pianoforte after Mary had finished, playing only a few light and airy pieces before relinquishing the pianoforte to Miss Darcy and taking her seat near Mr. Darcy. The dearth of sheet music had recently been remedied, as Miss Darcy had managed to find several pieces in whatever out-of-the-way location Lady Catherine had stored them. In that, at least, Elizabeth was grateful to Miss Darcy, as it saved her from having to play from memory.

As had now become their wont most evenings in company, Elizabeth and Mr. Darcy quickly fell into conversation, their topics ranging from the state of the household to the territory of literature and current events.

"And how is her ladyship?" asked Darcy after they had dispensed with their pleasantries.

"Much the same, Mr. Darcy," said Elizabeth. "She still takes scant interest in what is happening outside her bedchamber doors. At least I have been successful in inducing her to eat a little more."

"That is something at least. I must own, however, that I wonder how you occupy yourself in her chambers every day. Why, you must spend above an hour daily sitting with her!"

Blushing slightly, Elizabeth responded: "I merely provide a sympathetic ear, Mr. Darcy. We sometimes talk of inconsequential things, and I tell her of the running of the house, but she takes little interest in that subject. For the most part, she wishes to speak about her daughter, and I listen to her stories of Miss de Bourgh's youth, the hopes Lady Catherine had held for the future, and the desolation she feels now that her only child is gone."

"That cannot be pleasant, Miss Bennet," said Mr. Darcy softly. "I commend you for your diligence and forbearance. After all, I am aware of Lady Catherine and Anne's treatment of you, and I am sensible of the fact that you must not enjoy the time you spend with my aunt."

"I am happy to provide assistance. I believe Lady Catherine needs this chance to put her tragedy behind her and heal. She has not been unpleasant to me in the slightest."

"Miss Bennet," said Mr. Darcy, fixing a stern look upon her, "I will not allow you to deflect this praise in any way. I am very sensible of the effect you have had on my poor aunt and can only express my thanks for your assistance. Indeed, we are all very grateful to you, not only for your attention to my aunt, but also for your management of Rosings during this trying time. The housekeeper tells me that she has never seen Rosings house handled so skillfully, even by my aunt, who has controlled it for almost three decades. Please accept my thanks."

Elizabeth was embarrassed — terribly embarrassed — but she was sensible of the compliment this man was paying to her, and she was very conscious of the butterflies fluttering in her midsection at his words and the way he was regarding her with his characteristic intense expression. She found that it was quite beyond her to do anything other than blush and shyly accept his praise, stating that she was quite happy to help.

Not being able to say much more due to her acute embarrassment, Elizabeth soon moved away from Mr. Darcy and ensconced herself next to Jane, who had been left alone for a moment by Mr. Bingley.

Smiling at her sister, Elizabeth sat down beside her.

"Where is your excellent Mr. Bingley, Jane?" asked Elizabeth with a teasing smile, though she could certainly see that the man had moved to converse with Mr. Darcy.

Jane blushed. "He is not *my* Mr. Bingley, Lizzy."

"Oh, I think he is, Jane. And I am very happy for you."

Though Jane still demurred, Elizabeth could tell that her sister was happier than she had ever been. Truly, Elizabeth doubted that it would be long before Mr. Bingley asked Jane to marry him. Indeed, given his obviously besotted state, Elizabeth was surprised that he had not already proposed.

At that moment, Georgiana Darcy, having played several lovely pieces, rose from the pianoforte and, walking past Jane and Elizabeth, directed a barbed statement at the latter:

"Shall you not take your turn, Miss Jane?" She then feigned remembrance and peered at Jane with a condescending air. "Oh, my — I had completely forgotten that playing was an accomplishment which you *do not possess.*"

Though Jane could not have been insensible of the insult, she merely smiled and responded in her calm and placid manner: "Indeed, you are correct, Miss Darcy. Although I love to sing and listen to my sisters play, I have never felt the inclination to learn the instrument myself."

"Jane does not play, but I shall oblige the company," interjected Kitty before moving to the pianoforte with Mary's assistance.

While Miss Darcy did not appear disposed to allow the matter to drop, she bit her lip and turned away.

Elizabeth watched her suspiciously, but Miss Darcy did not press any further. While Elizabeth wished for Mr. Darcy to open his eyes about his sister's infatuation and take the girl in hand, she did not feel it was her responsibility to enlighten him. He would need to open his eyes for himself.

Chapter XXXIII

$\mathscr{E}$ lizabeth smiled as she listened to Kitty play the pianoforte. There was something almost magical about the way her sister touched the keys, bringing forth music that flowed naturally and lacked the artificiality evinced by so many people who concentrated on the mechanics of music rather than its breath. Elizabeth looked over at Jane, who was also smiling as she listened to the tune brought to life by their sister.

The three Bennets were alone in the sitting-room, for Miss Darcy was tending to her studies while Mr. Darcy and Mr. Bingley went out riding with Mr. Baker. As Elizabeth stared at Kitty, she could not help but focus her thoughts on Mr. Baker.

The man seemed as if he were becoming a fixture at Rosings. Something was inducing him to visit more frequently, and Elizabeth, who could never be termed a fool, believed that something was Kitty.

Mr. Baker was undeniably a pleasant man. His conversation was light and amusing, and he was not above laughing at himself. Yet Elizabeth was not certain how she felt about his interest in Kitty. She had the impression that he was *almost* what one might term a rake, but so far, he had always been proper toward Kitty. Still, Elizabeth resolved to watch him. Her sister was wise enough not to do anything foolish, but Elizabeth was uncertain she could make the same statement about Mr. Baker. And *that* was what worried her.

When the gentlemen finally entered the room, Elizabeth and Jane stood and curtseyed, and Elizabeth began to put a hand on Kitty's shoulder to encourage her to stand, but Mr. Baker called out:

"Please, Miss Bennet, let your sister continue playing. There is no need for her to cease."

Elizabeth hid a smile and said: "Certainly, Mr. Baker."

As Jane moved forward to speak with Mr. Bingley, who was moving toward her, Mr. Darcy and Mr. Baker approached Elizabeth and Kitty.

"Good morning, gentlemen," greeted Elizabeth.

"Good morning," said Mr. Baker quickly. "Miss Bennet, might you allow me to sit next to your sister at the pianoforte? I must own that I am entranced by her playing."

With a nod, Elizabeth relinquished her place at Kitty's side to Mr. Baker and stepped a few feet away to stand near Mr. Darcy. But rather than speak to the man, she kept her eyes on Kitty and Mr. Baker.

"Miss Catherine," began Mr. Baker, "I have heard of your skill with the instrument, yet I never believed it could be such as it is. You play magnificently!"

"People often believe blindness to be more of a sorrow than it truly is," said Kitty, her ability to speak and play simultaneously without error evidence of her talent. "Why, I had far rather be blind than deaf! Imagine what it should be like not to be able to hear the chorus of birds outside or the lilt of music inside. These notes could not whisper their secrets to my soul."

"From the way you play, I would say their secrets are magnificent indeed," said Mr. Baker.

"Your sister does play well," murmured Mr. Darcy at Elizabeth's side. "I suspect in part it is because she had such a good teacher."

Elizabeth turned to him slightly and smiled, though she felt taken aback at the intensity of his gaze. "Well, whereas I have put most of my time into books and walks, she has put much of hers into learning more of the pianoforte. Though my sisters and I were not all given such an education as is deemed fit for many young ladies, the avenues of learning were always open to us, and when we wished to learn, we certainly could. We developed our individual skills, and I believe us happier for it."

"Does it make you sorrowful, Miss Catherine?" came Mr. Baker's voice, causing Elizabeth to look at him once more. "Since you cannot see the sheet music, is it not difficult to learn new songs?"

"I have learned to rely on my ears," said Kitty. "Eyes need not be your most important sense. Many people do not realize that. Their minds have been closed to such a possibility; they forget the delight of sounds and smells and even touch."

Elizabeth watched as Mr. Baker gave a small smile. It was a smile that said he was intrigued—a smile that meant he would be watching Kitty further and seeking her out.

Elizabeth moved her eyes to Mr. Bingley, who was speaking to Jane in a low but animated voice, and she reflected back to when Mr. Bingley had first started to pay his attentions to Jane. Elizabeth had known then that he was a good man who could bring Jane much happiness. When it came to Mr. Baker, however, Elizabeth could not help but view his interest with wariness. She *thought* he had a good heart, but Kitty was quite vulnerable, as she could be compromised easily without even realizing the danger looming before her until it was too late. Certainly, Elizabeth could never leave Kitty alone with Mr. Baker. She simply had to ensure that he did not attempt to bring such a situation about.

But as she watched a bright smile spread across Kitty's face, Elizabeth found herself hoping that perhaps Mr. Baker would prove her suspicions wrong. Even if he only became a friend to Kitty, that would be a boon to the dear girl. It was difficult for Elizabeth to reconcile the desire to shelter Kitty with the desire to expand her horizons. Perhaps letting her gain more friends was one way to approach the issue.

Satisfied that the conversation between Mr. Baker and Kitty was going well, Elizabeth turned to Mr. Darcy and began to speak to him, though he was unusually reticent. His eyes kept wandering to the pianoforte where Kitty and Mr. Baker were seated, and soon Elizabeth found that his concerns mirrored her own.

"Miss Bennet," began he, "I must own that there is something which troubles me, though I hope you will forgive me for being perhaps a little meddling."

Elizabeth assured him that she would not take offense and asked him to continue.

"It is concerning your sister, Miss Kitty. It appears as though Mr. Baker is paying an inordinate amount of attention to her of late, and that worries me."

"I assume it is because of Mr. Baker's character?" queried Elizabeth.

"In short . . . yes," confirmed Mr. Darcy. "I have known Baker for some years, and though he is most assuredly not a rake, he is also not the model of propriety. He has been known to be a little frivolous in his attentions to those of the fairer sex. Certainly, he is not as bad as Wickham. I do not believe he would ever take advantage of a gentlewoman, but I do think he should not be trusted with your sister. Unless we curb his attentions, she may be hurt when his eye is inevitably caught by some other pleasing lady."

Elizabeth smiled and reached out to touch his arm in commiseration. "I truly appreciate your concern for my sister and am glad you felt you could speak to me about this subject. She is very precious, and we all take prodigious care of her, as I am certain you have already noticed."

"I could not do anything else. She is a very dear girl, and I would not have her hurt if I can prevent it."

"I thank you, sir," said Elizabeth. "I agree that they must both be observed, but at present, I am not certain there is much to be done. The way he watches her, the way he is solicitous for her comfort—these things hint that his intentions are not simply a passing flirtation.

"Should Mr. Baker ever appear to be treating her frivolously, I certainly think we should intervene. Yet I trust my sister's judgment, Mr. Darcy. Kitty will not do anything which is inappropriate."

"I did not think she would, Miss Bennet," said Mr. Darcy. "I have the highest respect for her morality and honor. I simply wish to ensure that Baker does not hurt her."

"In that case, we must agree to watch them. But I will not interfere unless Mr. Baker behaves inappropriately."

Mr. Darcy bowed in response. "I thank you for listening to me, Miss Bennet. I assure you that whatever I have said here today was merely due to worry. I meant no offense."

"I know, sir, and I thank you for it."

Their conversation turned to other topics soon afterward, and Elizabeth felt they were drawing closer than ever before. Indeed, she sometimes caught him regarding her intently, his eyes smoldering as they watched her, and she wondered what his feelings for her were. Still, she refused to dwell upon such thoughts. The day's events had brought out a lightness of heart which she had not felt for some days. She was determined to enjoy it, for she could not predict how long it would last.

Chapter XXXIV

*J*ane Bennet was a pleasant young woman who had the distinct advantage of being the most beautiful in a family of five daughters. The fact that she was a pleasant young woman with gentle manners and a tendency to see the good in others was further testament to her eligibility as a prospective wife. And though her mother was often almost vulgar in her proclamations of Jane's being "admired wherever she went," the statement itself was certainly not untrue.

Though she had never previously had the experience of being all but courted as her elder sister had, Jane had had her own fair share of admirers since the time she had officially come out. Due to her propensity to think well of others, it would have been easy for her family members to worry that she was a prime target for a rake. However, Jane was in no way mentally deficient. She knew what sort of men to avoid, and she was aware of just what she wanted in life. A healthy income and the trappings of wealth were all fine, but Jane and Elizabeth had spoken of their desires for many years, and neither was willing to settle for anything but the best in a marriage relationship. Jane absolutely refused to resign the last name of "Bennet" until she was certain that she loved her prospective partner and that he returned her feelings.

Mr. Bingley's attentions were clear for all to see. After those desolate weeks when he had left Hertfordshire, Jane had almost given up hope of seeing him again. Since their chance meeting in London, however, he had made his intentions clear, not only by seeking her company, but also by requesting—and being granted—the right to court her. And though Jane had enjoyed this season of courtship, she was impatient for Mr. Bingley to finally declare himself and propose.

On a fine spring morning when the birds were singing tribute to the glorious day, Jane found herself walking through the back gardens of Rosings estate, pleased with her life and the companionship of her admirer. They were both quite happy, their discussion ranging over many subjects, flowing as effortlessly as conversation between two such intimately acquainted souls should.

"Miss Bennet," spoke Mr. Bingley suddenly as they strode through the gardens.

"Yes, Mr. Bingley?" replied Jane.

She stopped to look at him, and a fluttering began in her stomach when she noticed his uncharacteristically serious expression. Mr. Bingley was so affable and good-natured that his acquaintances rarely saw him with anything other than the brightest of smiles upon his face.

"I had wondered . . . That is to say, I wish to know . . ."

He fell silent for a moment, obviously struggling to marshal his thoughts. Jane held her breath, certain he was on the verge of something significant—something she hoped would be a declaration.

At length, Mr. Bingley appeared to gather himself. He inhaled a large breath and then focused his gaze upon Jane, causing her fluttering stomach to overturn itself completely.

"Miss Bennet, I wish to know what you would consider essential in a marriage partner."

"Sir?" queried Jane, nonplussed due to his odd question.

"Please humor me, Miss Bennet."

His smile reassured her and gave her the confidence to answer truthfully. "Mr. Bingley, I am certain I have been very clear over the course of our acquaintance as to what my standards are in a marriage partner, but for the sake of clarity, I shall be specific. I require a relationship where conversation is easy and opinions are respected, a husband who is kind and considerate and who, above all, loves me as much as I love him."

"In that case, my dear Jane," said Mr. Bingley, a soft smile adorning his face, "there is nothing left to discuss."

He reached out and, grasping both of her hands between his own, declared himself thus:

"Dearest Jane, I cannot tell you how grateful I am that I decided to lease Netherfield, as it has led me to you. I have spent these past months since our reunion endeavoring to impress upon you the depth of my regard. Indeed, I love you beyond anything in my life. I never expected to have the good fortune to obtain my heart's desire in such a fashion, and I beg you to grant my fondest wish and accept my hand in marriage."

Tears appeared in the corners of Jane's eyes, and though she wondered if perhaps she was incapable of making a coherent response, she endeavored to tell him that his present assurances were not in any way unequally reciprocated.

"I believe," said she, "that I have made my preference quite clear. I appreciate your care for my feelings, but I have known since our time together in Hertfordshire what my response would be should you offer me your hand. I receive your proposal with pleasure, and I assure you that I would be honored to be your wife."

Mr. Bingley could only respond with laughter, a sentiment in which Jane quickly joined. They continued on their walk, content in their shared love, knowing that they had finally completed their journey toward one another. Now, they could begin the rest of their life together.

At length, their meandering steps led them to Rosings, where they immediately came upon Elizabeth and Mr. Darcy. Their shining countenances must have betrayed their good news, as Elizabeth and Mr. Darcy shared a glance with one another before joining the now declared lovers and waiting for them to speak.

Jane was distracted for a moment, wondering at the two of them. Did Mr. Darcy and Elizabeth share a common feeling of regard for each other? But before she could more fully consider the possibility, Mr. Bingley blurted out their important announcement in his usual ebullient style.

"Darcy! Miss Bennet!" exclaimed he. "I believe I must solicit your congratulations for some very good news!"

"Elizabeth!" continued Jane, engulfing her sister in a close embrace, "I am so happy! Mr. Bingley has made a proposal of marriage, and I have accepted him!"

Her sister returned the sentiment enthusiastically, her gay laughter ringing throughout the room. Her enthusiastic reply, however, was surprisingly equaled by Mr. Darcy's own hearty congratulations to her newly betrothed. It was, in all, a perfect day.

Chapter XXXV

❦

Everyone in Rosings who had not heard of the engagement would of course need to be told, and so it was that Darcy resolved to inform his sister of the development. For the past few days, she had taken to sitting in a small drawing-room where others seldom went, and it was there that he found her.

He stood quietly for a moment, watching her fondly, before she turned. She had begun to paint something which he could not yet make out, and when she saw him, she gave him a slight smile. "Fitzwilliam," said she, by way of greeting.

"Georgiana," responded he warmly. "I wish you would spend more time in company than in this room, but at least you appear to be using your time pleasurably."

She hesitated for a moment before replying. "Solitude can be beneficial at times, though I would not wish to always be thus."

"Yes, it can." He examined her for a moment before speaking again. "I have some news, Georgiana. You must offer your congratulations to Bingley and Miss Jane Bennet, for they are now engaged."

Georgiana shot to her feet, an expression of utter horror on her face. "What?" cried she. "No, William, that cannot be!"

Darcy started to reply but faltered. His sister should have been happy for the pair. Certainly, the engagement had been just on the horizon, so she should not have viewed it as an unexpected event. Why would she react in such a way? It bewildered him.

And then, as he pondered the reason for such a reaction, he suddenly realized just what the cause was . . . and how foolish he had been for not having seen it sooner. The reason his sister had been behaving so strangely was that she had a preference for Bingley herself. Darcy had obviously not been a very diligent brother if he had failed to see her pointed interest in Bingley. He had noticed a certain affability on her part when it came to conversing with Bingley, but he had merely thought it was because Bingley was such a good friend of his. Obviously, he had been mistaken.

"Georgiana," said he, determined to take his sister in hand, as he apparently should have done long before, "I shall not tolerate such behavior. You will not be married for some years yet, and I certainly do not wish to see you acting ill toward such valued acquaintances of mine. I expect you to congratulate Bingley and Miss Jane Bennet, and you shall behave as a proper lady and not as a child."

Now, it was to be said that Darcy was more than a little angry at both himself, for having missed something so significant, and his sister, for having embarrassed him by behaving so poorly. As a result, there was more of angered sternness in his voice than the firm understanding of a loving brother.

Georgiana therefore managed only the first syllable of his name before fleeing the room in tears.

Darcy stared after her for a few seconds before placing a hand over his eyes. He had not expected such a reaction, but perhaps he should have.

Since the deaths of their parents, Darcy had acted as a sort of father figure to Georgiana. He had seen to it that she received a proper education and had all her needs fulfilled. Yet perhaps he had been too much the doting brother. Or perhaps he had simply been blind to the fact that she possessed the burgeoning feelings of a young woman approaching adulthood. She was not a little girl any longer, and he had failed to realize that. He had been too focused on his own problems to give credence to the possibility that his sister might be experiencing difficulties of her own.

She *did* need to be reprimanded. She had to realize that she would not receive what she desired simply by virtue of the fact that she desired it. Yet it was certainly possible that he had been too harsh in his reprimand.

He took a minute to calm himself before he sought her out, knowing it would be better for them both if he was composed when he spoke with her. Once he was in control of himself, he went to her room and knocked on the door. "Georgiana?" called he. After receiving no answer, he called out again.

Finally, the door creaked open, and a whisper of a voice asked: "What is it?"

"I wished to apologize for being so harsh, Georgiana. Please, come out of your room."

After a second of hesitancy, she opened the door further and stepped out. The evidence of her weeping was upon her cheeks, and she truly appeared to be miserable. Darcy's heart went out to her. Her feelings about Mr. Bingley were strong, but Darcy thought they were more in line with an infatuation than any true depth of emotion. That, unfortunately, would not make it any easier for her. Georgiana's contact with men other than her brother tended to be limited to Colonel Fitzwilliam and his father; it was certainly understandable why she would develop a girlish infatuation for Darcy's closest friend, given the sheltered way in which she had been raised. He mentally castigated himself once again.

This time, he spoke with more gentleness. "I had not realized your feelings for my friend until now, and perhaps I made light of them unfairly. I am sorry that your heart was hurt by the news which I bore, but time will heal it, Georgiana. Mr. Bingley and Miss Jane will be quite happy together, and you should be glad for them, though it may mean your own sadness. Loss is part of growing up, I am afraid. But you must simply make amends and move forward."

"Oh, William," said Georgiana before burying her face in his chest. He placed his arms around her comfortingly and gave her a sad smile which she could not see.

When she finally pulled away, he looked at her affectionately. "Georgiana, I am certain in a few years you shall tug on the heartstrings of a man who will bring you more happiness than you can imagine. For now, it is better for you to learn more of the world and be content with your place in it. I am not so eager to give you up to another man, I assure you."

"Thank you," said she quietly. She was no longer crying, but she still appeared to be upset.

"You may take some time to yourself. But please, Georgiana, come and congratulate them. Though it may be painful, you must make a new start."

"Yes, William."

He left her and went to join the happy Rosings party in the largest drawing-room. A little while later, Georgiana entered, and she congratulated the couple as he had requested. She did so without any enthusiasm, but malice was also missing, so he did not reprimand her.

Chapter XXXVI

$\mathcal{W}$ alking through the massive doors which led to the interior of the manor at Rosings Park, Elia Baker gazed about in contentment. *This* was where she belonged, among those who were the cream of society. She *was* the granddaughter of a duke after all.

As the servants stepped forward to guide her and her brother into the house, Elia revised her opinion. It was not Rosings which was the prize. No, *that* honor was reserved for the incomparable Pemberley, the home of the man she meant to marry. She had heard much of the great estate from Colonel Fitzwilliam, and the fact that she had never visited Pemberley *did not* stop her from coveting it. Mr. Darcy *would* marry her. There was no other outcome to be contemplated.

James strode ahead, apparently eager to reach their destination and put himself once more in the company of Catherine Bennet. Elia glared at him in consternation. It was a poor time for James to finally rein in his rakish proclivities and truly pay attention to a young lady. He had recently become a regular visitor to Rosings, while Elia had almost become an interloper. And when he returned home, his conversation was less than scintillating or encouraging, for his focus was not on Elizabeth Bennet, as it should have been, but on her sightless younger sister.

In truth, Elia had nothing against the young woman and did in fact feel a sense of pity for her due to her disability. Catherine Bennet appeared to be a kind and sweet young lady, with many of the characteristics of her eldest sister. The reason Elia was annoyed with the young woman was because the timing of James's sudden infatuation could not have been worse. Now that Elia needed him to distract Elizabeth Bennet so that Mr. Darcy would be left to her, he was busy chasing after the woman's sister. Elia was disgusted with him, but thus far, she had been unable to influence him the way she had in the past.

On their arrival to the sitting room, they were shown in and greeted by the occupants, which included the Bennet sisters, Mr. Darcy, and Colonel Fitzwilliam. Miss Jane and Mr. Bingley were absent, no doubt staring lovingly at one another somewhere on the grounds.

Elia kept her gaze carefully away from the colonel and concentrated on Miss Bennet, who greeted them warmly. Elia assumed her mask and greeted her hostess with her usual vapidity.

"Miss Bennet, how nice to see you."

"Miss Baker," replied the woman. "Welcome to Rosings. I hope you have been well."

"Indeed," said Elia, even as she forced herself to mask the displeasure she felt toward the woman serving as mistress to an estate of which Mr. Darcy was acting as master. "James and I have both been well . . . and who could not be considering the beautiful spring with which we have been graced?"

"I can only agree," was the warm reply. "I can think of nothing better than a walk in the woods of Kent. The area is so beautiful at this time of year."

"A walk *can* be agreeable," said Elia with a sniff. "However, I do wish there were fewer insects, less wind, and less sun. The heat is unbearable, the wind blows my carefully coiffed hair from its restraints, and the insects buzz this way and that without a thought for those they annoy. It is most disconcerting and very thoughtless of them to do so."

As she watched Miss Bennet smile at her, Elia was certain she detected a hint of the other woman suppressing her natural inclination toward amusement at her behavior. Miss Bennet's opinion did not bother Elia in the slightest. If the woman thought her to be daft, then it was all for the better. Perhaps she would discount Elia as an opponent.

"I dare say you are correct," said Miss Bennet. "I try to put such things from my mind and concentrate on the loveliness of nature when

I walk."

"I am certain *you* do," said Elia.

"Please have a seat, Miss Baker," invited Miss Bennet. "I shall order some refreshments directly."

"Thank you, Miss Bennet." Elia turned a sly eye in her brother's direction and continued: "I believe that James wishes to speak to you. I am certain you enjoy his company."

"Indeed, I do," confirmed Miss Bennet. "I will speak with Mr. Baker during the course of the afternoon, I am sure."

With a smile, Miss Bennet excused herself, saying she needed to leave the room momentarily.

Elia watched her go and then began to survey her surroundings. After noting that Mr. Darcy and Colonel Fitzwilliam had left the room during her conversation with Miss Bennet, she chose a seat nearest to the door, where she could snare Mr. Darcy the moment he stepped into the room.

She glanced around and saw that her brother had seated himself beside Miss Catherine, who occupied the piano seat. She suppressed a scowl at the blatant favor shown to the young woman and cursed him once again for his betrayal. As they sat there, Miss Catherine allowed her fingers to move over the keys, playing snippets of various pieces while they conversed. A few of their comments floated to Elia as she sat and listened. Elia did not know what the fuss was. The young woman played well, especially for someone who could not see, but there was nothing else about her which was particularly remarkable. Elia had never learned to play herself, as she had never really possessed the talent, and while she could appreciate a pleasing piece of music, she did not consider it to be especially important in daily life.

"I do not for the most part miss the loss of my sight, Mr. Baker," said Miss Catherine. "It does no good to dwell upon such things, and I would only make myself unhappy if I were to do so."

"I am certain you are correct, Miss Kitty," responded James. "I do not doubt your wisdom in the matter."

Elia started at the more familiar appellation. Had they truly progressed to the point of using such familiarity in the short time since the young woman's arrival?

"But in answer to your question," said Miss Catherine, "I *do* miss colors, but I have compensated for the fact that I cannot *see* them by being able to *feel* them."

Mr. Baker regarded her thoughtfully. "Can you explain?"

"Certainly. Think of the color yellow. It is a warm and vibrant color which puts you in mind of the color of the sun on a beautiful summer day or the pale loveliness of a young woman's summer dress. Blue is much colder, yet still lovely in its way, while red is a bolder, more determined sort of color. Each is different, and if I imagine how the color would feel, then I can still partake in its beauty, though I cannot see it."

Elia had to stifle a snort. It was just like James to be caught up in discussing such frivolous subjects as colors with a blind girl! She turned her thoughts away from the absurdity of her brother and focused on Mr. Darcy while she waited, considering how he had turned out to be such an elusive catch.

Elia had always known that the lure of doing his duty to his family was strong for Mr. Darcy, and she had had to fight to turn his attention toward her and away from the young heiress of Rosings. It had been a hard-fought battle, but she had finally felt that it was one which she was winning, only for him to suddenly disappear for several months. Then Elizabeth Bennet had appeared on the scene, and she had one advantage which Anne de Bourgh had never possessed: Mr. Darcy was truly attracted to her.

Elia was well aware of Mr. Darcy's character. He was a very conscientious man who performed all of his duties to the best of his ability. He was conscious of his image in society and the importance of marrying well and in his own sphere. However, Elia had always suspected that underneath his stern and proper exterior lurked a man who yearned to connect with a young woman on a personal basis. She believed that given half a chance, he would leap at the opportunity to marry a woman for love alone. This part of him was what she had cultivated with him. After all, it was the only way she could induce him to marry her over his cousin.

However, she was also aware of the fact that her relationship with him had always been somewhat false. She knew he felt a measure of attraction for her, but as the front she put up for his benefit was not her real self, she was uncertain as to his true feelings. She had caught his attention by using her wiles, but could she hold his interest, especially with Elizabeth Bennet sniffing about like a bloodhound?

The door opened, and her quarry stepped in, but to Elia's great disappointment, he was accompanied by her rival, and they were laughing together, showing great contentment in one another's company.

Through narrowed eyes, Elia watched Mr. Darcy and Miss Bennet as they continued their conversation. Mr. Darcy was betraying his feelings in everything he did—the way his eyes sparkled as he spoke with Miss Bennet, the times he reached out as though to touch her hand, and the very fact that he was conversing with greater animation than Elia had ever seen him display with *anyone*. All of these things spoke to the depth of his regard. As for Miss Bennet herself, Elia was not able to determine her feelings as clearly, but what was apparent was the fact that she was not unaffected by Mr. Darcy. Elia's observations—especially those she had made at the fateful picnic—were turning out to be accurate. Mr. Darcy—*her Mr. Darcy!*—admired Elizabeth Bennet.

This was not to be borne! She needed to think of some way to turn Mr. Darcy's attention back to her. Somehow, she had to negate Miss Bennet's great advantage of living in the same house as Mr. Darcy. But how?

Then Elia knew just what to do. She would invite Mr. Darcy to Stauneton Hall for dinner! Surely she could show him her superior skills as a hostess, something she was certain Miss Bennet could not boast due to her comparative lack of experience if nothing else. Of course, Elia's beauty and fortune—also virtues that Miss Bennet did not possess—could not help but impress him. Then, she would bring his attention back to its proper place: firmly upon her! He could not help but fall under her spell then!

Chapter XXXVII

$\mathcal{S}$everal months before—nay, several *weeks* before—Baker would likely have been amused. As it was now, however, he was infuriated.

His sister's obsession with obtaining Darcy as her husband was coloring her every action. In extending an invitation for dinner at Stauneton Hall, she had wanted to invite only Darcy, but Baker had insisted it was rude to exclude the others residing at Rosings. And so it was that accompanying Darcy were Colonel Fitzwilliam, Bingley, Miss Darcy, and the four Bennet sisters. Lady Catherine, of course, was still not interested in company, and she had declined the invitation, though in truth, Baker was not even certain that Darcy had extended it to her.

Despite not having intended to invite such a large party, Elia quickly went to work on turning the situation to her advantage, insisting that Miss Bennet sit with Baker in the sitting room before dinner and then proceeding to draw Darcy's full attention to herself. Or at least she attempted to do so—Baker thought, after observing Darcy for a moment, that his attention was at least as much on *Baker's* conversation partner as it was on *his own*, a fact which Elia could hardly miss.

Baker sat with Elizabeth Bennet for a moment in silence before finally releasing a sigh. "I apologize, Miss Bennet," said he in a low voice. "My sister believes that you and I would make a suitable match, though I fear it is for no reason such as our mutual happiness. Rather, she thinks it shall lead to more success in her own pursuits." Here, he turned his gaze pointedly toward Darcy.

Miss Bennet smiled. "It is quite all right, Mr. Baker. I understand that you cannot direct your sister's actions, and I did suspect as much, so what you say to me comes as no surprise."

"She has been rather transparent," said he, shaking his head in exasperation and then glancing at Miss Bennet. "Please forgive me also for transferring my affections so quickly from you to your sister. You must think me fickle. Yet I must own—though it may harm my masculine pride—that you were far too intelligent for me, Miss Bennet. Your mind moves so quickly that I fear I could never have caught it."

Miss Bennet laughed, and he joined her with a laugh of his own.

"Mr. Baker," said she, "your intellect is certainly superior to that of many men whom I have met. I am glad to call you a friend."

"As I am with you."

"Furthermore, I have enjoyed seeing how kind you have been to Kitty. However, I must warn you, Mr. Baker, to be careful with her. I shall not tolerate anyone hurting her." The seriousness in the young woman's voice was unmistakable.

"Do not concern yourself, Miss Bennet," said he, his own tone just as serious. "I shall be careful; I have no intention of harming her."

Miss Bennet smiled at him, and they talked for some minutes.

Alert, as he was, to the machinations of his sister, Baker decided that he was not about to let her have her own way and monopolize Darcy's attention, especially when the man obviously had no inclination for her company. Thus, when they arose for the meal, Baker moved quickly to implement his designs.

"Darcy," said he, "if you will indulge me for a moment?"

The man appeared startled, but he readily assented, approaching Baker after bowing to Elia. Baker was already moving, arranging Elia's dinner companion, lest she spoil his plans.

"Colonel Fitzwilliam, if you would be so good as to escort my sister, I would be much obliged. I am afraid I have some estate questions to ask of Darcy."

It was obvious from the colonel's sly grin that he was not fooled in the slightest, but he nevertheless bowed gallantly to Elia and offered his arm. Elia, left with no other choice, accepted his escort, though she did so with an obvious ill grace.

Not sparing another glance for his sister, Baker turned to Catherine Bennet. "Miss Kitty, if you will come with me?" said he, holding his arm out to the young woman.

Darcy had claimed Miss Bennet's attention in the meantime, and the four of them companionably entered the dining room, where Baker sat Miss Kitty to his right in her place of honor. In the meantime, Darcy and Miss Bennet found their own way to the seats on his left, with Darcy seated in between Baker and Miss Bennet.

Risking a glance at the other end of the table, Baker could not miss Elia's reddening face, but he threw an angry look at her that made her hold her tongue. He would not spare a moment's concern for her plight; Elia had brought it on herself through her behavior and her affected airs. It was time for her to learn that she could not manipulate everyone according to her whims.

The others in the room could not have helped but notice what was happening, but no one said anything, and the changes Baker had insisted upon were made in silence.

Conversation at dinner was somewhat stilted, the diners still feeling the effects of Baker's manipulations, but Baker was able to speak with Miss Kitty, as he had desired. And of course, the fact that Miss Bennet and Darcy were now situated next to him meant that Elia's attempts to keep all of Darcy's attention on herself failed. Darcy was as attentive to Miss Bennet as ever, and Elia was left to stew by herself at the foot of the table, though Colonel Fitzwilliam gamely attempted to draw her focus upon himself. Baker, to be truthful, felt sorry for the colonel. He was a good man who had the misfortune to possess feelings for Baker's superior and shallow sister. If the colonel were to succeed in his efforts to woo Elia, her character would no doubt improve substantially, and Baker could only wish the man well.

After dinner, Baker was careful to keep Miss Kitty with him, and he attempted to keep Miss Bennet and Darcy together as well. Of course, this further angered his sister, but he was certain that everyone else in the room was happier for it.

When at last it was time for the party to leave, Baker told Miss Kitty: "I am sorry that we must part, but I shall look forward to meeting with you again."

"Even I need rest, Mr. Baker, for how else should I endeavor to confound and tease you?"

Baker laughed. "How else indeed!"

A few minutes more, and then the visitors were gone, and Baker was left to face his sister.

"What did you believe you were accomplishing?" came her furious voice from behind him.

He turned toward her. "I know what *you* are trying to accomplish, Elia, and I have only this to say to you. You may do what you wish to ensnare Darcy, and I shall not stand in your way, but you must *cease* trying to bring about some convenient romance between Miss Bennet and me. *That* is something I shall stand for no longer."

"Of course," said his sister with a sneer, "how could I forget your interest in a *blind* girl?"

"Mind your own business!" growled he. "As master of this estate, I hold power over you, Elia, and you would be wise not to forget it."

He stalked away in a fury, enraged at his sister's audacity. She believed too much in her own power, and it led her to do some foolish things. He wanted nothing more than to retire to his chambers and to think of how delightful Miss Kitty was that night during those blessed instances when she had smiled or laughed at him, yet it was difficult to move past his anger at his sister.

Elia would need to tread carefully around him, as he would take no more of her meddling in his life. He had accepted it in the past, but he would do so no longer. Of that, he was determined.

Chapter XXXVIII

*I*t was the twenty-ninth of May when Darcy received a most unexpected visitor.

Mr. Rutledge was the solicitor for the de Bourgh and Fitzwilliam families, and he had been in that position since before Darcy was born. He was a gruff man who frequently eschewed social niceties (such as giving advance notice of his arrival to his clients), but he was well-versed in law and skilled at his occupation, which made it easier to ignore his lapses in proper behavior. Perhaps he was slower in recent years than he had been at the peak of his youth, but there were none who would decry his dedication. If not for the fact that his family had possessed a solicitor of their own for some decades, Darcy might have employed Mr. Rutledge himself.

Yet though Mr. Darcy was surprised at the appearance of the man, he realized he should not have been. With the death of Anne de Bourgh, Sir Lewis's will would need to be examined. Had Darcy been thinking clearly, he would have already attempted to contact Mr. Rutledge. Yet thinking clearly seemed to be the last thing he was capable of doing as of late. His feelings for Elizabeth Bennet had only been growing stronger by the day, and he felt he was close to making a declaration to her.

Darcy pushed these thoughts from his head and closeted himself in the study with Mr. Rutledge. After Darcy saw to the other man's comfort, he began: "I must own that I am surprised to see you, Mr. Rutledge. But after considering the matter, I must conjecture that you are here as a result of my cousin's death."

"Yes," acknowledged Mr. Rutledge with a grunt, making no apology for not having sent a letter to announce his visit. "I am here to discuss Sir Lewis de Bourgh's will."

Darcy gave a slight nod. "I apologize for having been remiss in writing to you for the purpose of discussing that very subject. But we have been facing a number of tribulations here."

Mr. Rutledge offered him a sly smile—something which seemed out of place on what was usually a most serious face. "Yes, well, had you known about the secret provisions of Sir Lewis's will, I suspect you would have been more eager to learn about its full contents."

"I beg your pardon?"

"Sir Lewis was a man with a keen eye, and he was always aware of what possibilities the future might hold," said Mr. Rutledge. "As such, he recognized that his daughter might not ever be able to produce a child due to her ill health. He also believed his wife was too extravagant to properly manage the estate. After considering these matters and discussing the situation with me, he decided to include a clause in his will that if his daughter died before producing an heir, then the property would go immediately to Sir Lewis's only living family. One condition of this was that his wife, for whom he wished to provide, would receive a yearly allotment and be allowed to stay at the estate until her death."

Darcy mulled over Mr. Rutledge's words for a moment. Sir Lewis did indeed appear to have been a far-sighted man. It was wise of him to have made such preparations, even if it had not been done in the usual way.

But then Darcy caught upon a certain phrasing of Mr. Rutledge's, and he said in confusion: "His only living family? Do you mean, perhaps, the Fitzwilliams?"

"I do not. I mean the Bennets of Hertfordshire."

It was all Darcy could do to keep from making a startled exclamation. Instead, he fought his astonishment and said calmly: "I was not aware of any familial connection to the Bennets. What do you know of this connection?"

"You would not have any awareness of it," said Mr. Rutledge with a dry chortle, "for there was some effort to keep it a secret. Mr. Bennet's mother was the sister of Sir Lewis's father. In the de Bourghs' eyes, she did little to recommend herself, however, for she married a lower sort of gentlemen. For a proud family such as Sir Lewis's, this was quite a scandal, and the Bennets were therefore viewed as a disgrace to the family line.

"While this relationship between the Bennets and the de Bourghs is not spoken of and hardly remembered, Sir Lewis and Mr. Bennet were cousins. I believe Sir Lewis found the Bennets to be distasteful, though he did deign to meet with Mr. Bennet once in an endeavor to become familiar with the family which might one day inherit the estate from him. Sir Lewis was a proud man, but he wished for the estate of Rosings to pass on to them rather than into the hands of a fortune-hunter who married his daughter to attain the property. If Miss de Bourgh had produced an heir, then the property would have been in the trust of her husband, should she have preceded him in death, and would have ultimately gone to her child. Yet though it would have been in the trust of her husband, it would have been overseen by the Darcy and Fitzwilliam families to prevent any . . . misuse of the estate funds. Due to Miss de Bourgh's ill health, Sir Lewis believed in taking precautions to keep the estate within the family."

Mr. Darcy paused for but a moment before asking: "What, then, is to be done?"

"I have already spoken with Mr. Bennet regarding Sir Lewis's will, and he has decided the estate shall be managed by his eldest daughter, so you need not worry. In fact, he has entrusted me with a letter to be given to Miss Bennet, whom he informs me is presently a guest at Rosings."

"Yes," murmured Darcy. "Then I suppose I must inform my aunt and Miss Bennet of these developments."

"Indeed," said Mr. Rutledge, reaching into his pocket and pulling out the letter from Mr. Bennet.

After taking the piece of correspondence, Darcy exchanged a few more words with the attorney and then thanked him and saw him out.

He could not help but wonder at the contents of the letter in his possession. But those thoughts were soon superseded by a feeling of dread. If he knew one thing, it was that his aunt would not be happy with the turn of events. Her reaction to such news—particularly at a time when she was still mourning her daughter's death—would not be a good one.

Chapter XXXIX

The day which would change Elizabeth's life forever began much the same as any other day. She left her bedchamber, and after indulging in a breakfast of one of the sticky pastries which she so enjoyed, she adjourned to the small office which had been set aside for her use and inspected the household accounts. Then, after giving the housekeeper her instructions for the day, Elizabeth intended to go out and walk the grounds of Rosings.

A summons from Mr. Darcy to join him in the study did not even come as a surprise, as he often called her in to discuss some facet of the estate or to hear what she had to say of the house. However, on this particular morning, she knew within moments of arriving that some greater issue was weighing on his mind. She was patient, allowing him to make his small talk and come to his point in his own time, sensing that he was trying to order his thoughts.

"Miss Bennet," stated Mr. Darcy at length, "I should be surprised if you failed to apprehend that I have not called you here to exchange pleasantries this morning."

When Elizabeth allowed that she had suspected some more important matter, Mr. Darcy continued:

"Indeed, you are correct. And though I have attempted to determine exactly how to broach this subject, I am as of yet at a loss, so I shall be direct. I pray you will forgive me for blurting this news out, as it were."

Curiosity piqued, Elizabeth sat silently as he reflected once more for a moment and then turned his attention back upon her.

"This morning, Miss Bennet, I was visited by the family attorney, Mr. Rutledge, who had come to me to disclose the disposition of the estate now that my cousin Anne has departed from this world."

"Oh, yes, Mr. Darcy," affirmed Elizabeth. "I know this matter has been of some concern to you. What was his verdict then?"

"It appears, Miss Bennet, that Sir Lewis's heir and the new master of Rosings is none other than your father, Mr. Bennet."

Open-mouthed, Elizabeth gaped at Mr. Darcy. "My father?" demanded she, an incredulous quality inherent in her voice. "Mr. Darcy, is this some kind of jest?"

"I assure you, Miss Bennet, this is indeed no situation for jest," was the man's sober reply.

"But how? The Bennets are certainly not connected with the de Bourghs and therefore cannot be within the line of succession. And did Miss de Bourgh even have a will? And why would she have left Rosings to my father even if she had possessed one? This whole situation reeks of farce and is hardly believable."

"That is because you do not possess all the facts, Miss Bennet. Indeed, until the solicitor's visit, I had no knowledge of these matters, nor was I aware of the provision in Sir Lewis's will which shall cause the estate to devolve to your father. I am as surprised as you."

He proceeded then to impart to her the specifics of his conversation with the attorney, touching on Mr. Bennet's relationship with Sir Lewis and the specifics of the secret provision in Sir Lewis's will, which named her father the heir of Rosings if no other heir were to be produced. By the end of his explanation, Elizabeth was stunned by the enormity of what was happening to her family. Never in her wildest dreams would she have suspected that her father was to inherit such an estate as Rosings!

"Can I get you some wine, Miss Bennet?" asked Mr. Darcy in apparent concern. "This truly must be shock for you. Perhaps a small glass would be advisable to help you regain your composure."

"I am well, Mr. Darcy, I thank you," managed Elizabeth. "I am truly astonished at this turn of events, but I assure you that I am well."

His eyes stayed upon her for several more moments, and he sat in a nearby chair, taking her hand in one of his to comfort her. Grateful for his show of support, Elizabeth calmed herself and forced her eyes to his.

"What does it all mean, Mr. Darcy? Will my father come to live here now? And what of Rosings? Does it have some form of an entailment upon it as well?"

"No, Miss Bennet," said Mr. Darcy. "There is no entailment on Rosings. As I have told you, the estate comes to your father through my uncle's will, and as such, there are no limitations on Rosings other than what your father should determine on his own."

Suddenly, the implications were clear to Elizabeth, and she gasped. "But that would mean that when my father is gone, Rosings will—"

"I believe you are correct, Miss Bennet," confirmed Mr. Darcy. "In fact, if you will permit me," continued he, while rising and walking to his desk, "the attorney has already seen your father and has delivered a letter from him addressed to you."

He placed the missive in Elizabeth's hands, and she looked at it dumbly for several moments before raising her gaze to meet Mr. Darcy's once more.

"I believe, Miss Bennet," said he in a gentle tone of voice, "that it may be best for you to read your letter in privacy. Lady Catherine must be informed of these developments. Shall I leave you and return with my aunt in thirty minutes?"

Elizabeth smiled tremulously. "That would be greatly appreciated, Mr. Darcy."

"Then I shall speak with you again in half an hour," replied Mr. Darcy. Taking her hand, he bestowed a kiss upon it before leaving.

Though she could not help but be curious, Elizabeth stared at the letter for several moments, her mind desperately trying to catch up with the events of the morning. It appeared to be a standard epistle from her father, though it was much thicker than was his wont. And while Elizabeth could not find herself prepared to actually become acquainted with its contents, at length she sighed and, breaking the seal, opened the letter and began to read.

My Dearest Lizzy,

I am certain, my precious daughter, that you are as shocked by these events as I. Please understand that I never thought Sir Lewis would have included such a clause in his will. Certainly, I was never given to expect that such a thing would ever come to pass. Perhaps if I had known of this provision, I might have told your mother some years ago, so as to calm her nerves regarding her future poverty. Or perhaps it is better this way, as doubtless she would have driven me to Bedlam with exclamations concerning the great estate of which she was to one day be mistress, the fine clothes you and your sisters would have, and plots to capture rich husbands. I am certain she would have scarce considered the possibility of Anne de Bourgh producing a child.

But perhaps before I move any deeper into the matter at hand, a small explanation of our relation to the de Bourghs would not be amiss.

I have always known of the connection between our two families. Indeed, my mother told me stories of her childhood at Rosings Park and of her brother, Sir Lewis's father, and in no way did she ever attempt to hide the connection which existed between us.

Unfortunately, the de Bourghs were a different matter. They were a very proud family, both in their heritage and in their fortune and connections. However, they have always been a very small family, as for many years there have been no more than two children in any generation — and in many only one. (I fancy that I am the exception to the rule, as I have fathered you and your four sisters!) Therefore, when my mother married my father, the de Bourghs considered the connection to be beneath them, for though my family has held Longbourn for centuries, we have never been as wealthy or influential. Your great-grandfather de Bourgh held his daughter at arm's length for the rest of his life, a distance which was maintained by his son and subsequently Sir Lewis himself when he became the master of Rosings. I know what the rest of the family thought of my mother, but in the end, she married my father because she loved him. Do not allow any of your other relations to slight your grandmother. She was one of the most exceptional women I have ever had the pleasure to meet, and I am proud that you bear her name, Elizabeth.

I only met Sir Lewis once before his death. I was a young man, newly married and master of my own estate, when I was invited to attend him at Rosings. I arrived and was introduced to his wife Catherine and his four-year-old daughter Anne — who was sickly even then — and spent three days in their company. Sir Lewis died less than a year later when the pox swept through Kent.

I had always wondered at the invitation and the time I spent with my cousin at Rosings. He never gave me any understanding of the reason for the invitation, nor was it ever repeated, though I cannot say whether that would have changed had he lived longer. Now, I can only conjecture that he was testing me, seeing if I could be a worthy successor to the family's legacy. He must have already suspected that he would not father another child and that his daughter might not have been likely to produce a child of her own. He was a proud man, to be certain, but I believe this insight of his shows some greatness of mind.

You might wonder why I never spoke to any of you about this. To be frank, I never felt the need to do so. Since the de Bourghs did not recognize the relationship, you would not be making their acquaintance, and if you did so by some quirk of fate — such as you have — I did not think Lady Catherine would impart the information to you. It seemed pointless to make anything of it. In fact, I believe that the only reason why Lady Catherine allowed you and your sister Mary to stay at Rosings was because you are family. Her pride would likely not have allowed it otherwise.

Now for the particulars of our present situation. I have for some time felt anxiety for the marriage prospects of you and your sisters. Jane's excellent Mr. Bingley notwithstanding, the chances of the rest of you making a good marriage with so little dowry and standing in society have not been not great, as you well know. My health, indifferent as it has always been, has exacerbated this concern. We are no longer, of course, beholden to Mr. Collins, regardless of the sex of Mary's child, and with his having been the last eligible male in the entail, your mother can rest soundly knowing she shall never be thrown out into the countryside to starve. Regardless of this security, however, I would like to do something more to allow you and your sisters some happiness in your lives.

As such, I have instructed your Uncle Phillips to update my will with the following provisions:

First, you have now been designated the heir to all of my holdings. This means that Rosings will be your inheritance, as will Longbourn, unless of course, Mary gives birth to a son — in that case, he shall inherit Longbourn. Perhaps with a great estate as your dowry, you can entice some worthy young man to make you an offer. I have no doubt you will provide for your mother and any unmarried sisters upon my demise.

Second, I have instructed Mr. Phillips and Mr. Rutledge to immediately cede control of Rosings to you, as I believe you will take better care of it than I ever could. You may think I am evading my responsibility in the matter, Lizzy — and I own that you may be correct — but I believe it is for the best. After all, I can hardly take the time to run my own estate, Lizzy, never mind running one more than four times its size! Make certain you have a good steward, allow yourself to get over your disappointment in the matter of that scoundrel Wickham, and find a man with whom to settle down.

There — it is done! At rather little inconvenience to myself, if I may say. I will only add that I wish for you to be happy, Elizabeth. Enjoy your improved status and consequence, and do not allow Lady Catherine to dictate any of your actions. When we meet again, I shall tell you more of my mother.

Please also be advised that I shall not inform your mother of these events for now. It would not do to have her descend upon you and frighten away all the young men who will no doubt be waiting outside your door!

Your loving father, etc.

206 ᔈ *Jann Rowland & Lelia Eye*

Sitting back, Elizabeth released a sigh and considered her changed situation. She was now the proprietor of a great estate! How could this have happened?

She perused the letter again, feeling a faint sense of disappointment in her father. She was certain his health would improve if he could only bestir himself from his bookroom, but in this, he had abrogated his responsibilities yet again. Yet she could not hold it against him. He *was*, in his own way, looking out for her and her sisters, and she knew that he loved them all fiercely.

While she was thus pondering recent events, the door opened, and Mr. Darcy walked in, followed by Lady Catherine, who was complaining at being rousted from her room. Her eyes narrowed as she noticed Elizabeth's presence, and Elizabeth, suspecting this would be a difficult conversation, stood and curtsied to the woman.

"What is this, Darcy?" said Lady Catherine. "I still do not understand why you have asked me to come here. Does Miss Bennet have some question as to the management of the house? I do not understand why you could not come to my quarters to ask me, Miss Bennet." It appeared that being forced to leave her room had roused Lady Catherine from some of her melancholy.

"Miss Bennet has no need of assistance, Lady Catherine. Indeed, she continues to manage this house with an efficiency and flair which is to be commended. However, I do wish to tell you that you shall not be required to manage this house any longer, now or in the future."

The lady's eyes narrowed, and she affixed Mr. Darcy with an imperious glare. "Of what are you speaking, Darcy? I am mistress of this house and will assume my proper role, as I have always intended."

"Lady Catherine," said Mr. Darcy evenly, "the situation has changed. I have just been informed by Mr. Rutledge of the final details of Sir Lewis's will and the implications for the future of the estate."

"My husband's will was executed twenty years ago when he departed this life, Darcy," snapped Lady Catherine. "Do not speak nonsense."

"I am not speaking nonsense, I can assure you. Sir Lewis enclosed a secret provision in his will with instructions as to the disposition of the estate should Anne die before having children. In it, he named Elizabeth Bennet's father as the heir to Rosings. His will has now been executed, and you are standing before the new mistress of Rosings."

Lady Catherine gasped, her face turning white. "That cannot be!"

"I assure you it is, Lady Catherine."

"But . . . No! There must be some mistake. My husband would never have left Rosings to those awful Bennets!"

"I have the documents if you wish to see them."

"I have no wish to see them!" cried Lady Catherine. "You are the one to blame for this, Darcy! If only you had married Anne like you ought, then nothing like this could have occurred."

Elizabeth was not surprised at the lady's reaction to the news, but she was decidedly unhappy at Lady Catherine's words concerning her family, and she resolved to tell her as much:

"*You* may not like my family, Lady Catherine, but I will thank you not to disparage them in my presence!"

"Oh, be silent, child!" barked Lady Catherine. "My father-in-law's sister was a disgrace, marrying such a lowborn thug as your grandfather! You have not the wit to understand how unsuited you are to serve as the mistress of this great estate!"

"Lady Catherine!" said Mr. Darcy. "You are not helping the situation in the slightest. By your words, I can see you knew of the connection. Why did you not welcome the Bennet sisters when they first came here?"

"Because they are not worthy!" cried Lady Catherine. "How could my husband have betrayed me in this manner? What is to become of me? What is to become of Rosings?"

"Miss Bennet will take over management of the estate, Lady Catherine, but you will be given an allowance and will be allowed to stay here until your death."

"Stay here, with Miss Bennet and her . . . *relations* polluting the very stones of this great estate? Never!"

Lady Catherine rose, her countenance flushed and her eyes wildly darting here and there. Her breath was coming in great gasps, and Elizabeth began to be fearful for the lady's health.

"You!" screamed she at Elizabeth. "You must be some kind of witch! You have attempted to bewitch us all, insinuating yourself into the workings of this estate as though you belonged."

Her feverish hands found a vase situated on a shelf, and she seized it, hurling it at Elizabeth, who ducked out of its path.

The lady continued to scream and curse at Elizabeth, even while Mr. Darcy ran to subdue her, calling for the assistance of two nearby servants. The incensed lady was removed from the room to her bedchamber, and Mr. Darcy, fearing for her sanity, called in a doctor to administer laudanum so she could be calmed.

For Elizabeth, the woman's outburst was but another example of her poor manners and breeding. Unwilling to face anyone else that day, Elizabeth retired to her room, and instructed the housekeeper to provide her with a tray at dinner. She spent the time thinking of what had happened, and though she was still shocked, she began making plans as to the disposition of the estate. She hoped Mr. Darcy would not feel compelled to leave Rosings now that it had come into her possession, as she was hoping to have his help in understanding the running of the property. And a small voice inside her whispered that he might find her as eligible as Miss Baker now that she possessed a dowry.

Chapter XL

*E*lizabeth was not certain how precisely to share the revelation of the relationship between the Bennet family and the de Bourgh family and the news of the subsequent fate of Rosings. After seeing Lady Catherine's violent reaction to the unexpected development, Elizabeth knew it could not remain secret for long. Fortunately, however, Mr. Darcy appeared to be aware that the information had to be imparted posthaste, and he calmly made the announcement to those in the Rosings sitting room, including Mr. Baker, who had come for a visit.

Elizabeth's sisters seemed particularly surprised at the turn of events, and there were a few amazed exclamations from Kitty and Mary before Jane ventured: "Lizzy, can it be true?"

Elizabeth smiled. "Yes, it is, dear Jane."

"How delightful!" exclaimed Mr. Bingley. "You must be happy indeed."

Mr. Baker, who was seated near Kitty, offered: "Congratulations, Miss Bennet. I am certain such a grand estate shall do well in your hands." But as soon as he had finished speaking, his gaze returned to Kitty. No change in Elizabeth's fortune would make him alter his preference.

Even Colonel Fitzwilliam offered forth a jubilant congratulation, and once the general commotion caused by the announcement had ceased, Elizabeth went to Jane's side, where the two commenced talking quietly once Mr. Bingley moved away to give them some privacy.

"I am so happy for you, my dear sister," said Jane, her genuine joy filling her voice. "I have been worried about you, particularly since your troubles with Mr. Wickham. And now that you do not need to worry for your future, you shall not find it necessary to marry unless you desire to do so. However, I suspect that such a decision might make a certain attentive young gentleman very disappointed." And just to be sure her meaning was understood, Jane's eyes glided over to rest on Mr. Darcy, who was having his own private conversation with Colonel Fitzwilliam and Mr. Bingley.

Elizabeth blushed but said nothing.

"I suppose Lady Catherine is discontented with this development," said Jane slowly.

"That would be an understatement," said Elizabeth with a laugh. "But I am afraid deciding what to do with the estate was entirely up to her husband. I had no part in it."

"Perhaps she shall soon see that it is a beneficial thing—"

"I doubt that, dear Jane. Her ladyship will never be content with me as mistress of the estate. You cannot make everyone happy."

They talked for a time afterward, but something was weighing on Elizabeth's mind, and she approached Mr. Darcy and asked quietly if he might speak with her in the library. He agreed, and she departed, immersing herself in the many memories created in the room while waiting for him to join her. It was only a few minutes later when he arrived.

She turned upon hearing him enter and put the book in her hand back on the shelf. "Thank you for meeting me, Mr. Darcy."

"It is no trouble at all, Miss Bennet. Might I ask what you wish to speak with me about?"

"Perhaps it is presumptuous of me," said Elizabeth slowly, "but I wished to speak a little of the finances of Rosings."

Mr. Darcy gave a curt and businesslike nod. "I have no numbers to directly give you at present, Miss Bennet, but I can inform you that my aunt's excesses over the years—which I have done my best to prevent—have hurt the estate to a certain extent. However, the estate still remains profitable, and there are no large debts to be paid. Rather, there is always some money available."

Elizabeth nodded, her forehead wrinkled in thought. "I am glad to hear that, Mr. Darcy. You see, I wish to settle some money on all of my sisters for dowries. It need not be much, but I want to help them attract good husbands."

Mr. Darcy looked at her in surprise, but his voice was filled with admiration. "Somehow, I doubt you need worry about that too much, Miss Bennet. Miss Jane is already engaged, and Miss Kitty has a suitor who does not appear to care about her financial situation—"

"This is something I want to do," said Elizabeth firmly. "I wish to aid all of my sisters."

Mr. Darcy's mouth turned upward in a slight smile. "I understand, Miss Bennet. I am certain something can be arranged to your satisfaction." He gave a slight bow and turned to leave.

It was all Elizabeth could do to keep from reaching a hand out to touch him. "Mr. Darcy?" she called as he stood in the doorway.

"Yes, Miss Bennet?"

"Thank you for understanding." She smiled at him, and he stared back at her for a few moments in silence.

"It is my pleasure to do anything to assist you, Miss Bennet." He gave another bow, and then he was gone.

Elizabeth's happiness that day was great indeed. She would be able to help her sisters, and her parents would both have pressure taken off them, though her mother would likely fret until all of the Bennet daughters were married.

Unfortunately, Elizabeth's joy was chipped away in the next few days, as Lady Catherine complained loudly and frequently to all nearby about how the estate of Rosings was going to the Bennets. Her ladyship had calmed somewhat (and was not threatening bodily harm to anyone with words or actions), but she was still quite upset. Her anger only increased when she learned about the dowries Elizabeth was settling on her sisters.

Still, despite the woman's unhappiness, Elizabeth was content with the future. Everything was going well. No matter how many vases were thrown at her, she would not stop believing that.

Chapter XLI

The days after receiving word of the connection between the
Bennets and the de Bourghs were busy as Elizabeth struggled to
come to terms with her new inheritance. While acting as the
house's mistress, Elizabeth had focused on the house, not the wealth
which lay about her. And though her walks through the countryside
had given her an indication of the breadth of the estate's holdings, she
still had no real idea of exactly what she had inherited.

The attorneys were very efficient and quick in their work, and it was
merely a few days after the announcement became known that she was
confirmed in her ownership of the estate. Elizabeth could only take joy
in the fact that the fortunes of her family were assured. Regardless of
Jane's forthcoming marriage to Mr. Bingley, none of the Bennets would
ever have to be dependent upon him; through Elizabeth, and perhaps
Mary's unborn child, the Bennets would always have a means to
support themselves. It was truly an astonishing change from their
situation a few months previous, and Elizabeth could readily imagine
what her mother's reaction would be.

There were, of course, vexations associated with the sudden reversal
in fortunes. For instance, Lady Catherine, unwilling to accept what she
could not change, flatly refused to remove herself from the chambers
belonging to the lady of the house, claiming that they were hers by

right and that she would not stand aside for some upstart. And while Elizabeth was quite content to allow her to triumph in this matter, she was aware that she would eventually need to assert her authority. She had confirmed with the attorneys that the will was specific in that Lady Catherine was to be allowed to reside at the estate, but it did not specify that she must be allowed to stay in the manor house. Thus, upon speaking with Mr. Darcy and Colonel Fitzwilliam about the matter, she decided that the best thing to do would be to move Lady Catherine to the dower house once the woman's temper had cooled. While the house certainly did not possess the grandiosity of Rosings, it was still a large and handsome building, so anyone who lived there would do so in comfort.

Rosings itself was also a large vexation. Indeed, Elizabeth did not know what she would have done had Mr. Darcy not been present to help her through the transition. She had never before understood exactly how gifted Mr. Darcy was in managing the estate. He almost seemed to have some ingrained ability to immediately see through to the heart of a problem, and his advice was invariably sound. Though she was well aware of the fact that he would eventually need to return to Pemberley, she was more than content to continue to allow him to make decisions with respect to the operation of Rosings.

Of course, this threw her already confused feelings into a greater maelstrom of chaos. She was well aware that her unexpected inheritance meant that Mr. Darcy might consider an alliance with her to be far more strategic than he had in the past. There could be no denying the pleasurable nature of their conversations, so could it be possible that he might now consider proposing to her?

Elizabeth was soon given the opportunity to focus on something other than the troubles inherent in her sudden inheritance, for Kitty's birthday was to occur on the Friday following the attorney's visit. Upon giving the occasion some thought, Elizabeth decided to plan a party in her sister's honor.

That day finally dawned with the characteristically warm weather of the beginning of June, and Elizabeth instructed the servants to set up some tables on the front lawn of Rosings. The tables were loaded with sandwiches, Kitty's favorite apple pudding, and other delicacies from Rosings' kitchens. Elizabeth then informed her sister that they would be going for a walk on the grounds and guided her out of the building.

But Kitty was clever, and knowing that her sisters always did something for her on her birthday, she would not be fooled.

"Where shall we walk, Lizzy?" asked she, as innocently as she was able.

"It is not far, Kitty," responded Elizabeth with a smile. "In fact, I believe we have already arrived."

As Elizabeth guided Kitty to sit at the nearest table, her sister asked with a smile of her own: "Have you had some new benches installed in front of Rosings, sister?"

"No, indeed, dear one. In fact, we brought you out here today to celebrate your birthday! It was eighteen years ago to the day that our precious sister was born, and we must celebrate!"

Kitty laughed, and with a bright smile, she embraced her sister. "Thank you, Lizzy!"

The other members of the party—only Elia Baker and Lady Catherine were not in attendance—stated their congratulations, and soon the entire group was seated at the table, speaking with one another and enjoying the repast. Elizabeth, content with the distraction from her problems, watched the rest of the company. Particularly, she enjoyed observing the attentions of one James Baker toward her sister. Indeed, if he could avoid it, he rarely left her side, and he had almost taken up residence at Rosings.

After their meal was finished, they plied Kitty with their presents: some ribbons, a necklace and bracelet set, and some combs for her hair. But Kitty's most treasured gift was received from her admirer, who, seated beside her, pulled an item from his pocket and turned to face her.

"Miss Kitty, though perhaps it is not completely proper at the present time for me to gift you with anything, I also have a present for you. I decided that the occasion warranted my small lapse."

Kitty blushed and, with a slightly unsteady voice, assured him that she was surprised and pleased that he had thought of her.

"It is a wooden carving of a dancing woman," said he, placing it in her hands.

Kitty's fingers ran over the figurine, and she turned to him with a smile. "I thank you, sir. It feels exquisitely done."

"I am glad you feel that way," responded Mr. Baker.

In his smile and in his eyes, Elizabeth saw for the first time the true depth of his regard for her sister. Blinking back tears, she happened to catch the gaze of Mr. Darcy, and in an instant, she knew that he had seen it as well. But while Mr. Darcy seemed slightly relieved at this expression of Mr. Baker's regard, his gaze was intensely upon Elizabeth, and she felt in some measure a sense of his regard for *her*.

Blushing, she turned her attention back to her sister and Mr. Baker, resolving to think upon this evidence of Mr. Darcy's feelings at a later date.

"In fact, Miss Kitty," said Mr. Baker, "I feel I should tell you that this is a unique item, made specifically for you. I carved it myself, thinking of how you will look when I finally have the pleasure of dancing with you."

Kitty gasped and held the carving to her, her hands moving over its surface. "I thank you for this precious and thoughtful gift, sir," said she, her voice almost inaudible. "I shall treasure it forever."

As the servants approached, Elizabeth nodded at one holding a violin, and he began to play a lively tune. Soon, the diners had moved away from the tables and had started to dance on the lawn of Rosings. Elizabeth grinned with delight, certain that Rosings' staid and proper grounds had not been put to such use in many a year, if ever!

It was with great joy that Elizabeth moved through the steps of the dance with Kitty, gaily laughing and enjoying the dance. To her side, Bingley and Jane were moving with abandon, happy in their own situation.

It was not long, however, before Elizabeth saw Mr. Baker approach, and laughing with delight, she yielded her position to him, hopeful for her sister's happy future. She moved to the side of the dancers, noting that Georgiana Darcy—who had become much easier to live with since Jane's engagement—was dancing with Colonel Fitzwilliam.

She was thus engaged in watching the couples when she felt a presence at her side. She turned to see the smiling visage of Mr. Darcy gazing at her tenderly. He spoke not a word—he merely held his hand out to her and led her into the dance.

For the afternoon, Elizabeth was able to forget her troubles, and Rosings and everything else in her life floated away on the music. After what had happened with Mr. Wickham when she was younger, she had thought she would never again be able to give her heart away, and to a certain extent, the supposition was still true. She appeared to have little choice in the matter, as Mr. Darcy appeared to be stealing her heart away without her permission. She could not find it in herself to truly care, though. Losing her heart was proving a most enjoyable experience.

Chapter XLII

A week later, Elizabeth felt her good mood was in danger of turning ill. While inheriting such an estate as Rosings was a blessing to her family, it entailed a lot of responsibility, and it was causing a few adverse reactions in two women of her acquaintance.

Lady Catherine was vociferous in proclaiming her displeasure, and she appeared to have made it her duty to continually pester Elizabeth—and occasionally the other Bennet daughters—about the injustice of Rosings passing to the Bennets rather than to some more illustrious personage found in the family line.

Elia Baker also appeared to have taken up arms against Elizabeth. Her ways were much more subtle, however, and while Miss Baker never directly expressed anger over Elizabeth's inheritance of Rosings, the woman must have been infuriated by it, for the situation raised Elizabeth's appeal as a bride by a substantial margin. Miss Baker seemed to be trying to trump this unexpected "victory" for Elizabeth by showing her face more frequently and denouncing Elizabeth at every opportunity. Though Miss Baker was respectful when Elizabeth was within range of her voice, Elizabeth had at times happened to hear her sharing less than flattering opinions when she had thought Elizabeth could not hear.

Finally, Elizabeth had to face her personal feelings about Mr. Darcy. She had spent an abundance of time in his presence learning more details about the estate, and she was finding it hard to ignore how precious—and almost even torturous—that time with him was to her.

No man had ever been able to make Elizabeth as angry or as happy or as confused as Mr. Darcy could. Even the incompetence of Mr. Collins had not brought her to such extremes as Mr. Darcy was able without even trying. And yet she had no idea how the man felt about her. Sometimes, when she caught him gazing at her intently, she almost dared to hope that she was in his thoughts as frequently as he was in hers. And now that she would bring an estate with her upon marriage, her hopes wished to gain more altitude.

But Mr. Darcy had done nothing definitive to make Elizabeth believe he truly was interested in her. Still, the dance between them at Kitty's party had not been one shared between two people who were friends alone. It had been imbued with a greater significance than that.

This tangle of thoughts and the beauty of the mid-June day brought Elizabeth to the abrupt decision to go riding. She was certain the pleasure she always felt when upon a horse would assist in bringing her calm. While it might not have been advisable for a lady to ride alone, she needed to clear her head, and she had no intention of straying from the estate grounds.

After mounting one of Lady Catherine's ridiculously named horses—"Ringing Bell" this time—Elizabeth guided the silver creature into an open field. But not even nature could distract her for long, and she found herself sinking deep into thought.

Despite her resolution to be careful, the strands of trees around the estate escaped her notice, and without paying attention to her path, Elizabeth unwittingly let her horse guide her into the wooded area. It was only when she heard the sound of hoofbeats that she was jolted back to her surroundings and realized the sort of trouble she was facing.

Swiveling as much as she dared while riding sidesaddle, Elizabeth turned and watched with trepidation as a man with whom she was quite familiar pulled his horse up close beside her.

Her shock was immeasurable. She had thought Mr. Wickham long gone. And to meet him in a wooded region such as this was a terrible misfortune. Her heart seemed to be pounding in her throat as she clenched the reins tighter. She needed to escape his presence.

"Mr. Wickham," managed a shaky voice she was not quite certain was her own. "Why are you here?"

"I have received some interesting news about you, Miss Bennet. While you may be immune to my charms, there is a female servant at Rosings who is not, and she has provided me with some valuable information. It appears, to everyone's surprise, that *you* have become the heir to this estate. You have risen high indeed in the world, have you not?"

Something in his voice made Elizabeth shiver. He must have intended to renew his addresses to her for the purpose of obtaining Rosings, as he had failed to do when pursuing Anne de Bourgh.

"And you have dropped low in the world indeed if you were willing to leave a woman behind to die," returned Elizabeth with a confidence that was at odds with the frantic beating of her heart. "I am now aware of your true character, Mr. Wickham, and you shall not attain Rosings through marriage to *me*. You would do well to leave here now and never return."

He brought his horse up so close to her that it pressed uncomfortably against her legs. In a low voice, he told her with a sneer: "I have no intention of leaving, Miss Bennet. Instead, I intend to claim something that I should have taken some time ago . . . your virtue." He reached out to run his hand down her neck.

Elizabeth shoved him away and drove her horse forward, glad to be freed from the pressure of his horse against her legs.

She tried to increase the speed of her mount. But she was riding sidesaddle and unable to safely spur her horse onward as swiftly as Mr. Wickham could, and he soon caught up to her. The open field was not far away, and it beckoned her. But before she could make one last attempt to surge forward, he leaped from his horse and dragged her to the ground.

His weight pushed against her, and the air rushed out of her chest. She listened desperately to the sound of their horses trotting off.

He pinned her arms to the ground, and he spoke in a low hiss against her ear: "I will compromise you so that you have no choice but to marry me. And getting the wealth that is Rosings shall be much more pleasurable with you than it would have been with frail and pathetic *Anne*. You were always meant to be *mine*, Elizabeth."

She struggled against him, but her maneuverability was limited. Then he released one of her arms so he could pull at her sleeves, and she hit his nose with her palm as hard as she could. That only succeeded in making the lurid look in his eyes grow in intensity.

The swell of absolute fear rose up in her bosom. He would ruin her, and all the gains she had made would be for naught.

Chapter XLIII

*D*arcy was concerned, as Elizabeth Bennet was nowhere to be found.

He had endeavored to help her as much as he was able these past days, knowing what she had endured since learning of her sudden and surprising inheritance. Having been through the same thing himself, Darcy could well empathize, though he knew it was worse for her. *He*, at least, had always known he would inherit an estate.

Recently, watching her had become a torment. Her struggles with her new lot in life were met with the same fiery determination and will to succeed as anything else she did, and he was so far gone in love with her that he doubted he could be *anything* but impressed with her! But he was also aware that the stress of her situation was such that she was reaching a breaking point, so he resolved at last that he would speak with her and do whatever he could to ease her burdens.

He canvassed the servants of the house, trying to determine where she might have hidden herself away. All of her usual haunts—such as the library and the office she had used since she had taken over the mistress's duties—were empty, and he was concerned that she might have left the safety of the house to walk about the estate.

Indeed, he had known she was a great walker since he had met her in Hertfordshire, and he had never been surprised when he found her rambling about the groves of Rosings. However, her situation was different now that she was the proprietress of one of the largest estates in Kent instead of an obscure country gentlewoman. Try as he might, Darcy could not help but feel uneasy at the thought of her on the grounds alone, where someone could come upon her and hurt her without anyone being the wiser.

Determined to find her, Darcy exited the house, intent upon learning whether any of the gardeners or stable hands had seen her departing the immediate grounds. He was in luck, as the first gardener he asked was able to give him the information he desired.

"Yes, sir, I did see Miss Bennet," said the man. "She was riding a horse from the stables. She rounded the side of the house heading west the last I saw her."

"How long ago was this?"

"Oh, about half an hour ago, sir."

Nodding his thanks, Darcy headed toward the stables, to determine whether she had left information concerning her destination. He was about to enter when he heard his name called, and he stopped to see Mary Collins running toward him. He quickly noted her breathless state and obvious distress, and he strode toward her with some concern.

"Mrs. Collins, whatever is the matter?"

"I am very worried," exclaimed Mrs. Collins, pressing a hand to her side.

Darcy led her to a bench and sat her down, allowing her to catch her breath.

"Mrs. Collins, what has distressed you?"

"I was upstairs in my bedchamber, Mr. Darcy," began Mrs. Collins, still somewhat breathlessly, "when I saw my sister Elizabeth riding away from Rosings toward the western groves. In the distance, I saw another rider approaching her, but I do not think she saw him."

"Another rider?" demanded Darcy, his heart filling with dread. "Could you tell who it was?"

"No, sir. I do not know if she is in danger, but I also do not believe the rider was anyone associated with this estate. The rider approached from the north, toward the boundaries. I would not wish her to be caught in the woods without any protection."

Darcy jumped to his feet. "I have not an instant to lose!" cried he. "Thank you, Mrs. Collins, for bringing this to my attention. I shall do my utmost to ensure your sister's safety."

Bowing perfunctorily, he strode away at great speed, heading for the stables. When he arrived, he called out for assistance.

"You there! I need two horses saddled immediately. There is not an instant to lose!"

Then he turned to another stable hand and instructed: "Have my cousin the colonel summoned here at once."

As the two men leaped to do his bidding, Darcy paced back and forth, impatient and fearing the worst. And though it seemed like ages before the animals were saddled and ready, in reality only a few moments had passed.

Colonel Fitzwilliam strode into the stable, and once Darcy had explained to him the situation, both men were on their horses, galloping away from the house.

Darcy mercilessly pushed his horse, soon outstripping the colonel, who had received the inferior mount. Praying that there was nothing amiss, Darcy crossed the ground to the grove in moments, diving into the undergrowth when he reached the border to the woodland.

He had gone only a few yards into the forest when he heard a cry. Urging his horse forward, he was greeted by a sight which at once shocked and enraged him. *His* Elizabeth, while attempting to flee, was knocked to the ground by her pursuer's superior strength and abilities. And then the man—that scoundrel Wickham!—leaped from his horse and assaulted her.

Pushing his horse to cover that last precious distance, Darcy pulled up next to the struggling pair. He threw himself from the saddle, knocking the libertine from away from Elizabeth. Regaining his feet, Darcy strode forward in a fury. When he reached Wickham, he struck him hard in the stomach. Then he grabbed his shoulders and threw him into the dust.

Wickham's breath left his body in a great gasp, and his enraged glare melted into an expression of pain.

Turning, Darcy saw his cousin helping Elizabeth from the ground. Her dress was torn about the arms and the neckline, but she appeared relatively unharmed.

Scowling at the sight, Darcy turned back to Wickham. Seeing the man attempting to stand—no doubt to flee—Darcy grabbed him about the shoulders and hauled him to his feet.

"Wickham!" snarled Darcy. "You treacherous snake! You have imposed yourself on me and my acquaintances for the last time."

Wickham turned white and began pleading for mercy in a most craven and reprehensible manner. Darcy was utterly disgusted with him.

"Since you have pretensions toward being a gentleman," said Darcy, "I challenge you to a duel. Colonel Fitzwilliam is my second. Have your own second meet with him to discuss terms."

"A duel?" said Wickham in response, his countenance fearful. "Surely you cannot be serious!"

"I am, Wickham. Though you are a rabid dog who should be put down, I will not kill you in cold blood. Prepare to meet me on the field."

Desperation apparently brought on Wickham's bravado. "Darcy, truly there is nothing for you to be angry about. I was merely assisting Miss Bennet after she had fallen to the ground."

His eyes shifted back and forth as he spoke, clearly alighting on his horse, which stood grazing some ways off, and calculating whether he could make it to the creature and flee before they could catch him.

The colonel, however, seeing this, smirked in a most unpleasant manner and moved to cut Wickham off from his escape. "I think not, *George*. You will not escape justice this time. I very much look forward to Darcy here giving you your just desserts."

Wickham blanched, but before he could spout some other untruth, Darcy interjected: "Do not insult me, Wickham. You will either meet me in a duel, or my cousin and I shall hunt you and put you down like the wild cur you are!"

Unwilling to speak to the man any longer, Darcy helped Elizabeth upon her horse before mounting his own. Then he moved his horse over to Wickham's, gathering up the brown beast's reins. He began to lead them away from the wood, perversely enjoying the sight of Wickham's distress at seeing his best chance of escape being confiscated.

"Watch him," said Darcy to his cousin as he rode away. "I do not trust the coward not to run."

"He will be there at the appointed time," promised the colonel with a mirthless chuckle before he turned back to Wickham, who was even then trying to hasten away without being seen. "Come, now, George. I have not spoken with you for many months. I believe we have much to discuss."

The ride back to Rosings was accomplished largely in silence. Elizabeth, though she appeared to be calm, was obviously still shocked by her experience, while Darcy was having trouble controlling his temper. How could she put herself in this kind of danger, knowing that

Wickham had been lurking around the estate and had been complicit in Anne's death? What would it take to convince her that she must take greater care?

Their arrival at the house was characterized by the throng of Elizabeth's sisters gathering around to ensure that their beloved eldest sister was well. Darcy was pleased to see Georgiana in the group as well, shyly telling Elizabeth that she was glad she had returned unscathed.

Once the sisters had assured themselves of Elizabeth's safety, the scoldings began, much to Darcy's amusement. Surprisingly, it was sweet and calm Jane Bennet who took the lead in reproaching the young woman.

"Elizabeth! Whatever do you mean riding out into the forest like that without thought of what danger might be lurking inside?"

Elizabeth's response was positively mulish. "How could I have known that Mr. Wickham was nearby? I have walked these grounds extensively since arriving and have never run into any trouble previously."

"With all due respect, Miss Bennet," intervened Darcy. "Then you were simply a young woman of little wealth and consequence in the world, though an extraordinary one to be certain. Now you are the owner of a large estate, and as such, that carries certain responsibilities and risks with which you have never had to contend in the past."

"Mr. Darcy!" exclaimed Elizabeth.

But before she could begin her diatribe, Miss Jane once again stepped in. "Stop it, Lizzy! You know he is right!"

Elizabeth apparently knew when to back down, and the concerned stares of those present were more than enough for her to note that the present company was united against her.

"Miss Bennet," said Darcy in a softer tone of voice. "Please, for the sake of those who love you, do not venture out into the woods without an escort for protection."

Darcy bowed and walked away, but not quickly enough to miss the gasp of surprise from Elizabeth as she understood his implication. By now, he did not care who knew. He was in love with Elizabeth Bennet, and he would allow no one to come between them. Especially the likes of Wickham!

Chapter XLIV

The sixteenth of June was the day of the duel. Though the morning was a pleasant one, it filled Darcy with the firm resolution to burn a lesson forever into Wickham's mind.

Darcy had never been a violent person. Even as a child, he had not been especially keen on playing roughly with other boys. He was physically fit, but as a gentleman, he always held himself with dignity, eschewing the vulgarity of violence. However, upon seeing Wickham assault Elizabeth Bennet, Darcy had wanted nothing more than to pummel Wickham unto death. Even now, the thought that he could end Wickham's life in the duel was proving itself to be a temptation that might very well be difficult to resist. While authorities generally turned a blind eye to duels when no one was killed, they *were* illegal, and if he ended Wickham's life, he could be punished by the courts.

Early, before he went out to face the wretched man, Darcy was met by Elizabeth Bennet. Her eyes were red, and she was obviously distraught, and Darcy felt as if at that instant, he would be unable to deny her anything she asked of him.

"Do you truly mean to carry through with this?" inquired she. Her voice was soft and tremulous, and it had that faint quality of hope that a different answer would be given than was expected.

Unfortunately, he had to disappoint her. "I do."

There was a brief pause before she spoke again. "I beg of you, Mr. Darcy, do not kill Mr. Wickham. No matter what he has done, you must not kill him."

He felt the stubborn and proud part of his heart rear its head. After what Wickham had done, she was worried about him? How could she bear even a shred of pity toward that man?

And then he asked a question that tasted like acid on his tongue. "Do you care for him, Miss Bennet?"

"What?" exclaimed she in surprise. "Of course not, Mr. Darcy. I should be glad if I never rest eyes on him again." She averted her gaze from him. "Rather, I am worried about you, Mr. Darcy."

"About me, Miss Bennet?" questioned Darcy in surprise.

"Yes. Should you kill Mr. Wickham, then there shall be repercussions for you. It shall be seen as murder." There a pleading tone to her voice now. "And should Mr. Wickham prove himself to be a skilled duelist . . ."

Darcy found his heart warmed by her concern. "You must not worry about me, Miss Bennet. Wickham has never been a match for me with either the sword or the pistol. We were boys together, and I am acquainted with the extent of his abilities and his reticence to hone what skills he may have had. I shall return unharmed, and I will speak with you as soon as I do."

She started to extend a hand, as if to touch his arm, but then she pulled it back and gave him a slight smile. "Then I shall await your return."

A short time later, Darcy was riding to the area he and Colonel Fitzwilliam had designated for the duel. It was the same region where Wickham had shown the low depths to which he was willing to sink, and it seemed somehow fitting. Yet despite his eagerness to punish the reprehensible Wickham, Darcy almost felt ashamed to formally oppose one so obviously not a gentleman. Wickham had shown no inclination to send a second to work out the particulars of the duel, so Darcy had told his own second, Colonel Fitzwilliam, to be prepared for any eventuality, including the possibility that the despicable man would try to flee.

When Darcy arrived, Wickham was already present . . . and obviously frightened out of his wits. Yet Wickham was unable to do anything, for Colonel Fitzwilliam, Baker, Bingley, and a couple of trustworthy Rosings footmen were preventing him from escaping.

"You were right, Darcy," said the colonel. "He tried to sneak off like a coward."

"And his second?" queried Darcy heavily. There were no unfamiliar faces nearby.

Baker snorted. "Such a rat as this has no friend to risk his life for him."

Darcy shook his head in disgust. This duel was becoming more ridiculous by the moment. But the grimness on the faces of Baker and Colonel Fitzwilliam told Darcy that they were taking this just as seriously as he was. Wickham deserved to be punished for what he had done, even if he did not deserve the honor of being challenged to a duel by an actual gentleman.

"Shall it be pistols or swords, then?" asked Darcy.

Colonel Fitzwilliam, who was holding Wickham's arm, took his hand from the man and cuffed him roughly on the back of his head to elicit a response. Wickham muttered something Darcy could not hear, and the colonel nodded toward one of the footman. "Swords it shall be."

As the footman moved to first give Darcy his sword, Colonel Fitzwilliam spoke. "Since this beast has no second, I shall decide the particulars of the duel. It shall be fought to first blood. And if you decide, Darcy, that the first blood you draw shall be the result of a sword through Wickham's chest, then so much the better."

Wickham was at last released and given his weapon, and he and Darcy moved into position. But even before Colonel Fitzwilliam had given the signal, Wickham lunged.

Yet Darcy was ready. He neatly sidestepped Wickham's clumsy move, not even bothering to swipe at the easy target before him.

Wickham straightened and held his sword upright. His eyes darted up to meet Darcy's unflinching gaze. Then he stabbed forward once more.

Darcy parried the inept blow. It was all he could do to refrain from making a noise of disgust. Wickham struck again and again, and still his blows were effortlessly blocked.

Darcy had not been exaggerating when he said that Wickham was no match for him. The man had never learned the value of waiting for the right opportunity to strike. Wickham was like a blinded bear, striking out indiscriminately and aimlessly.

It would have been easy for Darcy to plunge his sword into Wickham's heart. Opportunity after opportunity presented itself, but he refrained, letting Wickham tire himself out. With every second that went by, Wickham's desperation and fear grew.

"You have been practicing, Darcy," gritted Wickham as their swords locked.

"And you have not," returned Darcy. "Your days with drinks and dice and loose women have done nothing to help you."

"You are simply jealous of how close I was to taking from Elizabeth Bennet what she has been so desperately longing to give to me."

With a low growl, Darcy struck out, swiping his sword across Wickham's stomach. The blade slashed through Wickham's clothes, drawing a thin line of blood and thereby ending the duel.

Darcy moved up close to Wickham and grabbed the middle of his shirt. In a low voice, he told him: "I shall ensure that you never touch Miss Bennet again."

"And how do you intend to do that?" countered Wickham scornfully, though with a slight tremor to his voice.

Baker and Colonel Fitzwilliam had rushed forward at this point, and they wrenched away the swords and pulled the two men apart.

"You have no friends here," said Darcy in a low voice. "For what you have done, I shall have you shipped off to Australia. I have more connections than you can imagine. And most gentlemen take very seriously the misdeeds of one who feigns to be one of their kind and then shows such reprehensible behavior as you have. You shall never even so much as catch a glimpse of Miss Bennet again."

Letting out an animalistic noise, Wickham struggled to break free of the hold Baker and the colonel had on him. His eyes were flaring with rage and hatred, and Darcy stared back at him. He was serious. He refused to allow Wickham to walk freely in England. He would protect Elizabeth Bennet from this monster.

Chapter XLV

When Mr. Darcy walked into the room, Elizabeth almost fainted with relief. It was a blessing that she was already sitting, for she felt her legs were insufficient to support her. She had insisted that her sisters leave her alone, for she was so distraught she felt unequal to even their company.

The man's reassurances notwithstanding, Elizabeth had known there was no guarantee that Mr. Darcy would emerge from the duel unscathed.

Composing herself, Elizabeth rose to meet the man who had become essential to her life. She greeted him quietly and asked him to be seated.

"Mr. Darcy," began Elizabeth, "I am very grateful that you have returned unharmed."

"Miss Bennet, as I informed you, Wickham has never been my equal, and I was in relatively little danger."

"It was *a duel*, Mr. Darcy!" cried Elizabeth. "You could not have known what was going to happen! What if Mr. Wickham had proven himself more skilled than you had thought? What if you had been injured or even slain during this contest of yours?"

Mr. Darcy was silent, obviously aware that she was upset, if indeed anyone could have missed it. His intense stare soon made her uncomfortable, and she looked down at her hands, trembling slightly.

"I would not have you believe that I am not grateful that you defended my honor, sir," said Elizabeth. "But surely there were other ways to do so rather than putting your life at risk."

"Though it is somewhat of a vanishing custom, it is *still* the province of a gentleman, Miss Bennet."

Elizabeth's displeasure was extreme. "Mr. Wickham is no gentleman, sir."

"He is not," agreed Mr. Darcy. "But his pretensions toward the title, as well as his actions toward you, merited my response.

"Besides, Miss Bennet, Wickham — the cowardly cur he is — would not even have shown up had my cousin not ensured his presence."

Elizabeth felt her annoyance softening. "Please tell me what happened."

Mr. Darcy related the entire morning's events, from Mr. Wickham's reluctant participation, to the fact that he did not even have a second, to the duel's outcome. He told her that he had ensured that Mr. Wickham was handed over to the authorities. Hunsford village contained a single constable and a small gaol, and Mr. Wickham was there awaiting transportation first to London and then to Australia. Elizabeth felt a measure of relief that he would never bother her again.

"I thank you again for your assistance, sir," said Elizabeth once his narration had wound down. "However, I still believe you took an unnecessary risk. If you were intent upon having Mr. Wickham transported, why did you not simply have it done, without having to risk yourself?"

Mr. Darcy considered it for a moment. "I *could have*, Miss Bennet. But I did not believe it enough of a punishment for him. I do not intend to take any unnecessary risks, but I *refuse* to allow *anyone* to offend you!"

Taken aback by his fervent defense of her, Elizabeth gazed at him with no small measure of astonishment. Would that she had had such a defender the first time she had encountered Mr. Wickham! So much of her life might have been different!

"Mr. Darcy, I *am* appreciative of the fact that Mr. Wickham will soon be gone for good. I dare say that he is the last man on the face of the earth that I would ever wish to come across again."

Elizabeth halted speaking and mulled the situation over in her mind. How much could she reveal to Mr. Darcy? Of what should she speak?

And then the answer came to her: everything. This man had

defended her honor, putting his very life at risk in the act. If she could not trust him, then she could trust no one. Still, it was a momentous decision, as even Jane and her father did not know the entirety of what had happened that day.

Squaring her shoulders, Elizabeth turned her gaze upon Mr. Darcy, prepared to tell him what she had not told a single soul. "I believe I never told you of my last encounter with Mr. Wickham when he first came to Meryton."

Mr. Darcy confirmed that she had not, inducing Elizabeth to continue.

"I was fifteen years of age and madly in love with him," said Elizabeth with a wry smile. "In fact, half of the ladies in the village — married or not! — were madly in love with him. You know enough of his ability to charm to doubt it."

When Mr. Darcy allowed it to be so, Elizabeth took up her tale again. "I suppose I must plead the innocence of my extreme youth as the reason that I was fooled by his charming demeanor, but I know in my heart that I was in love with the prospect of being in love. Yet I wish I had known better than to allow my heart to be touched in such a manner by a man of whom I knew nothing. Regardless, I *was* drawn in by him, and it was not until the end of his time in Meryton that I finally became aware of the truth of Mr. Wickham's character."

Taking a deep, fortifying breath, Elizabeth reflected back on the traumatic experience, willing herself to relate it to Mr. Darcy. Perhaps the catharsis of revealing the experience to another would induce her to finally let the past go.

"Mr. Wickham came to Longbourn on that day and asked me to accompany him for a walk. As we had done as much many times previously, I did not think anything of it and gladly accepted his arm. But whereas before we had always walked with Jane as chaperon within sight of the house, my sister had not yet descended from her room on that particular morning.

"I was concerned with his insistence, but as he told me he had a very particular question to ask, I, as a silly young girl, was excited that he should finally propose. So I accepted his assurances, though I never actually strayed as far from the house as he wanted.

"He did manage to get me into a somewhat secluded spot, and after assuring me of his undying love, he attempted to elicit some . . . immediate physical gratification from me in a most shameless and forward manner, telling me that as he was obliged to go away for a time, he wished to have something to remember me by."

Mr. Darcy's face was livid by now, his ire against Wickham undoubtedly raised to new heights. Elizabeth felt certain that he was on the verge of returning to the Hunsford gaol and demanding that Mr. Wickham be hung for his crimes.

Leaning forward, Elizabeth placed the palm of her hand on his cheek, forcing his attention back to her.

"I assure you, Mr. Darcy, I rebuffed his advances and began stalking back toward the house. My thoughts were such a muddle, I was hardly aware of what I was thinking, but I do know that my girlish infatuation was struggling with my anger at his presumption.

"We had a blazing row on the lawn behind the house when he caught up to me. With a sneer, he told me that I was nothing more than a silly girl . . . and that all he had wanted was my virtue, as I was good for nothing else with my nonexistent dowry. He commenced to tell me he had found a *woman* with whom he was in love, and he insinuated that I would never be desirable to any man. He then took his leave."

A smirk formed on Elizabeth's face. "I would imagine he is now repining that decision, considering the events of the past weeks."

Mr. Darcy gave her a half smile, obviously attempting to force down his rage. "I do not doubt it, Miss Bennet. Yet I do know enough of him to be certain that he would never have been that patient, even had he known of it. His wife and her inheritance provided him with a number of years of his dissipated lifestyle, and she died under suspicious circumstances. I would certainly never wish that of you."

Although saddened to hear it, Elizabeth was not surprised, especially when considering the depths to which the man had sunk only the previous day.

"Now you know the entirety of my history with Mr. Wickham, Mr. Darcy. I was a silly girl then, and I hope you do not think ill of me for being so."

Mr. Darcy rose abruptly from his seat and began pacing in agitation. "Miss Bennet, you cannot believe that I feel anything but the utmost regard for you. The mistakes of a fifteen-year-old can be embarrassing, but as a young and sheltered woman, you can hardly be held to the same standard as an adult with years of experience."

"I suppose not, sir," said Elizabeth with a sigh. "It was a traumatic experience for me, and it has taken me all this time to get over it. Even yesterday's events—frightening as they were—are not as scarring as the memory I have shared with you."

Ceasing his pacing suddenly, Mr. Darcy gazed at her, and Elizabeth fancied she could see his heart in his eyes. He approached her, and bending down to one knee beside the settee on which she sat, he gathered her hands in his own.

"May I hope that I have had some small hand in your reclamation, Miss Bennet?"

There was a great tenderness in his face, and her eyes became damp. "You may, sir. In fact, until you appeared in my life, I was quite content to live in a bitterness of spirit, believing that all men were inherently villainous. I am glad to know that those bleak years are over."

"If I have anything to say in the matter, I assure you that they shall never even be remembered," said Mr. Darcy.

He then took a deep breath and stared in her eyes. "I must tell you, Miss Bennet, that I am thankful for Mr. Wickham's lack of foresight. Indeed, you are a woman without a peer, and the fact that he is incapable of seeing past his own interest is nothing more than my gain. I am completely and utterly bewitched by your beauty, your compassion, and your zest for life. There is nothing I would like better than to spend the rest of my life making you happy, and I beg you to accept my hand in marriage, for I love you so very dearly."

By this time, tears were streaming down Elizabeth's face, but she calmed herself enough to assure him—almost coherently—that she welcomed his attentions and wished for nothing more than to be his wife.

An expression of delight spread over his features, but he cast a concerned eye on her. "Miss Bennet, I wish to ensure that you are accepting me for the proper reasons. While I welcome your gratitude, I would not have that as a basis for a marriage. I love you with all my soul, Elizabeth, and I hope that you can feel the same for me in your heart, for nothing else will do."

Smiling through her tears, Elizabeth grasped one of his hands. "And I assure you, sir, that my feelings are a match for yours. I love you with everything I have."

Though perhaps it was not completely proper, Elizabeth allowed herself to be drawn to his breast, and as she rested there, listening to his heartbeat, she reflected that there was a time when she never would have expected such an ending to her history with Mr. Wickham. Here, truly, was the best of men, and she could never think herself as anything but fortunate, knowing that he felt so deeply for her.

"I believe I have loved you for some time, Elizabeth," said he. "But I

234 ~ *Jann Rowland & Lelia Eye*

am most curious as to the genesis of your own feelings. Can you account for it?"

"I hardly know, Mr. Darcy—"

"William," interjected he.

"William," repeated Elizabeth dutifully, a smile jumping to her lips at the intimacy of the name. "As I was saying, we have been so frequently in one another's company that I am unable to name an exact time or place when I fell in love.

"However," continued Elizabeth with some of her old playfulness, "I am almost certain I can claim to have loved you since the incident in the library where you successfully avoided my ill-aimed book."

Mr. Darcy threw back his head and laughed. "A curious way of showing your love, indeed."

"Understandable when you consider my history and my inability to move past the time I spent with Mr. Wickham."

A finger across her mouth silenced her. "Let us leave that man in the past, Elizabeth."

"I agree, Mr. D—" She cut off and flushed before correcting herself softly: "William."

They stayed there for some time, exchanging confidences and increasingly poignant words of love. But at length, they stood to leave the room, for Elizabeth had a number of sisters who were likely waiting to speak with her even now. In spite of all that had happened, Elizabeth was content. She finally felt as though she had returned home.

Chapter XLVI

"What? Engaged? No! That cannot be!" shrieked a voice that Georgiana later decided sounded very much like a goose whose tail feathers had just been plucked. "Miss Bennet, you are a conniver, a bewitching minx, a—a consummate fortune-hunter! You have endeavored not only to place your greedy little hands on Rosings, but also to entrap my nephew!"

Georgiana could not help but wince at her aunt's outburst, and she turned to her brother to see his reaction.

Though he managed to keep calm, he told Lady Catherine in a firm voice: "I should first like to remind you that Miss Bennet is the daughter of a gentleman. Secondly, I would like to note that the clause of Sir Lewis's will was shrouded in secrecy, and Miss Bennet therefore could not have known about the bequeathing of Rosings to her family, nor could she have known that her father would immediately cede it to her. She was not even aware of the familial connection." His expression grew hard. "I shall finally remind you of something else this time and never again. As you are no longer the head of this household, you are not allowed to speak to Miss Bennet in whatever fashion you choose under this roof. And as Miss Bennet is now my fiancée, I expect you to treat her with every courtesy belonging to my future wife, lest you discover that both Miss Bennet and I have the power to make your present life very uncomfortable indeed. Do I make myself clear?"

Georgiana stared at her brother in awe. There had been something very commanding in his tone, and it had been enough to intimidate even the ever-belligerent Lady Catherine.

Her brother repeated his last question once more, and Lady Catherine—who appeared to have deflated—muttered: "Yes." Maintaining some small shred of dignity, she murmured something that might have been well wishes before walking from the room. Yet there was a certain sense of pride missing from her step that almost made Georgiana pity the woman. Lady Catherine had lost her daughter and was now losing her home and matriarchal position. Furthermore, her overbearing nature had won her no friends. Still, Lady Catherine had carved out her lonely place in the world by choice, and whether she softened her stance and allowed others into her life was a matter for her alone to decide.

The other occupants of the room—glad that a possible crisis had been averted—almost all appeared to breathe a sigh of relief, and then the happy congratulations poured in. Georgiana watched as Elizabeth Bennet's sisters went to her and expressed their great joy. They appeared so close and content that Georgiana felt a pang of sadness over the fact that she had not had a sister while growing up.

Turning, she watched as Colonel Fitzwilliam slapped her brother on the shoulder. "Well, Darcy, old boy, I am glad to see you came to your senses. Miss Baker was not the right one for you."

"I would like to second that," said Mr. Bingley jovially. "You shall be very happy indeed with your chosen bride."

"I know," said her brother. "I shall be a very happy man."

As Georgiana stared at him, she realized he was already a very happy man. Something about Elizabeth Bennet had the power to make his face light up in a way that nothing else could. He had frequently been somber and focused on duty since the death of their parents, and Georgiana was happy to see that at last he had done something for himself that would bring him joy. If anyone deserved to be happy, he did.

Her brother noticed her standing a slight ways off, and he excused himself and pulled her to the side. "Georgiana," said he gently, "I would like to speak with you."

She gave a slight nod and waited for him to begin.

"I did consider your feelings before proposing to Miss Bennet. Yet I had to let myself do what I had been fighting against—I had to follow my heart. But I need to know that you shall treat her as she deserves,

Georgiana. She will be family."

By this time, Georgiana's eyes had filled with tears. She lunged forward and put her arms around her brother. "Oh, William, of course I shall treat her properly! I love you dearly, and I *do* wish for you to be happy. I wish I had not caused everyone such trouble!"

Her brother embraced her in return. "I am glad to hear that, Georgiana. I dearly care for you as well."

Steadying herself, Georgiana pulled away and gave her brother a slight smile. Then, though still slightly shaky, she walked over to Miss Bennet, who was laughing with her sisters and paused at the sight of her, as if unsure what to expect.

Georgiana took in a deep breath and then embraced her lightly before pulling away. "I shall be glad to you call you my sister, Miss Bennet. I know you bring my brother great joy."

Miss Bennet—to Georgiana's surprise—smiled back at her and said: "We have plenty of time to begin anew. But please, call me 'Lizzy.' After all, we shall be sisters, remember?"

"All right, Lizzy," said Georgiana shyly. "But you must call me 'Georgiana.'"

"I should be delighted," said Elizabeth with a slight laugh. And then, she and her sisters commenced their excited talking. Yet they were certain to include Georgiana, asking her for her opinion and seeking her advice. And Georgiana's spirits began to lighten, and soon, she began to feel better than she had in quite some time. Though she had never before had a sister, she felt that she would like having Elizabeth for a sister very well indeed.

Chapter XLVII

After she accepted Mr. Darcy's proposal, Elizabeth found that one of the most difficult tasks she faced was the necessity of informing the Bakers—or, more specifically, Elia Baker—of the engagement. Miss Baker's interest in Mr. Darcy had been obvious for some time, and Elizabeth was aware that the woman would not take his rejection well.

When Elizabeth conversed with Mr. Darcy soon after the engagement was announced to discuss what needed to be done, such as obtaining her father's blessing on their union, he told her of his intent to inform Miss Baker in person, citing the previous attentions he had paid to her. There was no gentle or easy way of doing it, and he insisted that he owed at least that much to her.

As it happened, Elizabeth agreed with him, knowing how she would feel if she had been in Miss Baker's situation. And though Elizabeth had never suspected Miss Baker of actually being in love with Mr. Darcy, it would still be difficult for her to hear the news of his pending nuptials.

What Elizabeth disagreed with was Mr. Darcy's determination to inform Elia Baker by himself. That would never do, Elizabeth had declared, and she had instantly resolved on accompanying him on his visit to Stauneton Hall and facing the woman's displeasure by his side.

They were shown into the morning sitting-room of Stauneton Hall, where the two Bakers were awaiting them. While Miss Baker regarded them cautiously, her brother greeted them with a wide smile. Elizabeth instantly recognized that he was aware of what had taken place, and she worried that he would say something to make this endeavor even more difficult than it already was.

As he stood, he greeted them warmly. "Mr. Darcy, Miss Bennet, welcome to Stauneton Hall. And if I may, I would like to take the opportunity to congratulate you. I am very glad you have finally seen what the rest of us have for many weeks!"

Elizabeth colored slightly and thanked him for his well wishes while sneaking a look at his sister. The other woman was nonplussed at his declaration, clearly curious as to what he could be referring.

Apparently aware of Miss Baker's confusion—and the potential for an embarrassing outburst—Mr. Darcy took immediate control of the situation.

"Miss Baker, how do you do?" said he, bowing.

"I am tolerably well, Mr. Darcy," responded Miss Baker. For once, she appeared to forget her affected manners; instead, she merely looked at her two visitors with suspicion.

They sat down, and tea was ordered, but Mr. Darcy did not wait to make his announcement. "Miss Baker, Mr. Baker, I have come here today with Miss Bennet to inform you of a recent development at Rosings Park, though Mr. Baker appears to have anticipated us."

With a sly look at his sister, Mr. Baker allowed that he had. "Even if it had not already been quite obvious, Darcy, I spoke with Colonel Fitzwilliam, and he was positively a font of information."

"My cousin needs to learn to hold his tongue," grumbled Mr. Darcy, though he did not appear especially displeased.

By now, Miss Baker's fidgeting with her handkerchief in her lap was becoming somewhat agitated. She glared briefly at her brother with some displeasure before simpering at Mr. Darcy: "I am all agog, Mr. Darcy. Though my brother neglected to mention this news to me, now you can impart it to me directly. Please do enlighten me."

Though Mr. Darcy appeared as if he would prefer to do anything but that, he smiled tightly and made his announcement:

"Miss Baker, it is my privilege and great joy to inform you that I have requested—and obtained—Miss Elizabeth Bennet's hand in matrimony."

Miss Baker's eyes widened, and her mouth gaped with

astonishment. Her lips quickly tightened into a firm line, however, and Elizabeth watched as the woman clenched her handkerchief and twisted it in her rage.

"Come now, Elia," said Mr. Baker in a jovial tone. "Can you not wish Miss Bennet and Mr. Darcy joy? You must have seen how close they were becoming." He laughed. "I dare say this was the most ill-kept secret in the area!"

Mastering herself, Elia Baker plastered an insincere smile upon her face and peered at Elizabeth. "How . . . fortunate for you, Miss Bennet. You are very much to be envied."

Aware that anything she could say would be considered a provocation at this point, Elizabeth determined to respond simply. "Thank you, Miss Baker. I am very happy."

Elia Baker sniffed. "Oh, yes, I can see that."

Elizabeth certainly did not miss the displeasure which laced the woman's statement, but she was spared from responding when tea was delivered. The four sat conversing for some time, and though Elia Baker had very little to add to the discourse, the loquacity of her brother more than compensated for her lack. Elizabeth did not miss the increased animation of Mr. Baker, though, nor could she fail to notice the sly looks he directed toward his sister. Elizabeth could not in good conscience agree with Mr. Baker's continual baiting of his sister, but she knew on some level that the woman invited it with her behavior.

At length, complaining that the pastries were not up to her standards, Miss Baker left to speak with the housekeeper, returning soon afterward. It was only a few moments later that the housekeeper again entered the room, and after glancing at the mistress in some consternation, she announced to Mr. Baker that his steward wished to speak with him regarding a matter of some importance.

"Is that so?" queried he with a knowing grin. "In that case, I suppose I shall have to take my leave."

He stood and bowed to Elizabeth. "Fear not, Miss Bennet, for I shall return directly."

"Oh, do take Mr. Darcy with you, James," said Miss Baker. "Surely the matter with your steward is much more interesting to a man such as Mr. Darcy than our discussion regarding Miss Bennet's . . . good fortune. And if the talk turns to fashions and lace, I do not doubt the poor man shall be bored to tears!"

The two men regarded her with some skepticism, but she merely gazed back at them with that vacant expression which she seemed to have perfected. Knowing that Miss Baker wished to have her say and feeling it was best to be done with it, Elizabeth smiled at Mr. Darcy, indicating her assent. She almost laughed as he gave her a wry glance, and then he rose and, after bowing to the ladies, followed his friend from the room.

But whatever Elizabeth had been expecting from her companion, complete silence would not have made the list. The woman appeared quite content to sit and sip her tea, completely ignoring her guest. Elizabeth sat quietly with her own tea as well, determined not to surrender to the bitter and ill-mannered woman.

They remained in this attitude for perhaps five minutes before Miss Baker finally unsheathed her claws.

"Well, Miss Bennet, it appears that you have certainly risen in the world. Imagine—a country girl of no consequence rising first to mistress of Rosings and then to fiancée of the inestimable Mr. Darcy, all in the space of less than a month. What an extraordinary conquest for you!"

"I believe you ascribe far too much credit to my ability to control the events surrounding me," replied Elizabeth evenly. "I certainly could not direct the actions of Sir Lewis, nor did I 'conquer' Mr. Darcy as you have insinuated. Ours is a relationship which has developed over many months, and as you are aware, I now have no need to marry for anything but pure inclination, being financially secure."

Elia Baker snorted with derision. "So you think me ignorant of the way you threw yourself at him long before you came into your inheritance?"

"I assure you that I did nothing of the sort."

"And I assure you that I am aware of the type of woman you are! How else could you succeed in stealing away *my Mr. Darcy* from his rightful match?"

"You presume far too much, Miss Baker," responded Elizabeth. The woman was insufferable. It was almost like speaking with another Lady Catherine! "If you had listened to Mr. Darcy's aunt, *Miss Anne de Bourgh* was his only rightful match!"

"You speak as if you think my Fitzwilliam would have ever married such a colorless little mouse!" The sarcasm in Miss Baker's voice had reached new heights, as had the unpleasant nature of her sneer. "I assure you, Miss Bennet, that until you employed your dubious charms and flirtations, Mr. Darcy was on the verge of making an offer to me."

"Mr. Darcy proposed to *me*, Miss Baker. As a woman, I have no say in the matter of who proposes to me, nor did I *steal* him."

Rage flared in Elia Baker's eyes, and she only controlled it with some difficulty. "Miss Bennet, regardless of your recent *elevation*, you are still and will always be an insignificant little country miss, completely unsuited for the rigors of fine society."

"And with this display, I cannot see that *you are!*"

"I am descended from a duke, Miss Bennet!" was the woman's haughty reply.

"And I am descended from the de Bourghs, an old and established line," snapped Elizabeth. "Your descent means nothing when it is not accompanied by a sense of responsibility, respect for your fellow man, and compassion."

"What would *you* know of nobility?" said Miss Baker with a sneer. "I have it on reliable authority that you were brought up in squalor. Regardless of your elevation, you cannot escape your roots."

By this time, Elizabeth had had enough of the other woman's attacks, but she could not quit the room without one final comment. "You know nothing of my upbringing, Miss Baker, so I shall not linger on the subject. However, I shall tell you that Mr. Darcy and I were drawn together by our common interests, our respect for each other, and our assurance that we would be well-matched and happy together. Nothing was done in an underhanded manner, and neither of us entrapped the other into marriage.

"Besides," continued she with a withering glare, "I cannot imagine you would entice Mr. Darcy into matrimony with nothing more than an affectedly empty head and flirtatious manners. If you understood Mr. Darcy at all, you would know that he prizes honesty and integrity above all, something which you have never shown him!"

Elia Baker gasped, and her face became purple in rage. "How dare you!"

"Not nearly as much as you would dare, I should think," was Elizabeth's flippant response.

"Now, Miss Baker," continued Elizabeth before the other woman could formulate a reply, "I must beg leave to return to Rosings with Mr. Darcy. The atmosphere in this room has grown quite oppressive."

"I am *not* finished with you!" snarled Miss Baker while rising to grasp Elizabeth's arm.

"*Yes, you are!*" rang out the voice of Mr. Darcy.

Startled, Elizabeth and Miss Baker both turned toward the voice. Mr. Darcy stood in the door with Mr. Baker, his face, his posture, his very being radiating a fierce displeasure.

"Come, Miss Bennet, we shall leave now. I shall not allow you to be abused in such a manner."

As Elizabeth began to move, she felt rather than saw Elia Baker's rage become an almost physical entity, and as such, she was not surprised to hear the woman's final sally.

"I simply cannot believe you have been taken in by this . . . this . . . impostor, Mr. Darcy! How can you countenance this? It goes against your duty, your honor, and even your character to engage yourself to this Jezebel! I would never have imagined that you could fall so far! Were you not about to make your intentions known to me?"

There was a desperate, pleading quality to her voice which Elizabeth recognized as Miss Baker's last plea to her erstwhile suitor. One glance at Mr. Darcy's face told Elizabeth all she needed to know: he was not amused or moved in the slightest.

"Impostor, Miss Baker? I suppose you would know all about impostors, as you have been one the entire time of our acquaintance. I own I was taken in by your affected silliness, and it amused me for a time, but I am happy to say that I found someone possessed of substance rather than artificiality.

"Miss Baker, I never paid you any improper attentions, nor did I make any promises to you. Your imaginations of our impending engagement are nothing more than your own delusions. I shall marry Miss Bennet, for I love her more than life itself."

The tender expression on his face caused Elizabeth's breath to catch in her throat. She approached him and grasped the hand which was extended to her, blushing when he bent to kiss hers tenderly. He tucked her hand into the space between his arm and his body before turning to Mr. Baker.

"Thank you, Baker, for your hospitality, but I believe the time has come for our departure."

"Indeed, Darcy," said Baker, though his gaze never left his sister. "I apologize for the scene we just witnessed and more especially to you, Miss Bennet, for my sister's words. I believe it is time she and I discussed her behavior."

Elizabeth and Mr. Darcy assured him that they were happy to visit and that he was not to blame, and then they exited. As they did so, they could hear his raised voice berating his sister for her behavior. Elizabeth almost felt sorry for the woman—almost.

Chapter XLVIII

*espite the onslaught of recent events, neither Darcy nor Bingley could forget there was one important duty they had yet to perform. Though each man was loath to part with his newly betrothed, they resolved to journey to Hertfordshire to request Mr. Bennet's blessings for their respective marriages.

As Mr. Bennet was frequently reclusive, neither Darcy nor Bingley was especially comfortable at the thought of approaching him, though it was to be said that Darcy was somewhat better at hiding his nervousness than his friend.

The long trip was made, however, and after many grueling hours of travel, they were at last standing in front of Longbourn.

Bingley threw a look at Darcy. "Are you prepared for this, Darcy?"

Darcy gave his friend a slight smile. "Mr. Bennet has five daughters, Bingley. I am certain he has been expecting a day such as this to come eventually."

"I suppose you are right. Let us go then."

The door was answered, and they were soon shown into Mr. Bennet's study, where Darcy immediately noted the amused smile on the older man's face.

"Mr. Bingley and Mr. Darcy!" exclaimed Mr. Bennet. "I have been expecting to receive a personal visit from you for some time now, Mr.

Bingley. But I am surprised to see you, Mr. Darcy. Have you come to support your friend?"

Darcy sensed a kindred spirit in Mr. Bennet at that moment, and he continued to carry the lighthearted tone held by the father of the love of his life: "In actuality, we are here for the same purpose, Mr. Bennet. Would you like to handle us together or one at a time?"

Mr. Bennet sat blinking in surprise for several moments, likely uncertain as to whether there was an element of seriousness beneath the humor. But Darcy met his gaze, and Mr. Bennet evidently determined at last that he was sincere, as he said: "Well, I have my doubts as to whether I could successfully take on both of you at once, so I shall first handle the man whom I suspect shall be easiest—Mr. Bingley, if you please."

After acknowledging Mr. Bennet's wish, Darcy went out into the hallway. Mr. Bennet was so frequently sequestered from the world that he likely had no knowledge of Darcy's attachment to Elizabeth; certainly, Darcy had fought against his growing feelings for the young woman for some time. Now, he was beginning to have some doubts as to the outcome of the pending conversation. Would Mr. Bennet believe Darcy had coerced Elizabeth into accepting a proposal? Surely he knew his daughter better than that!

Darcy shook his head and smiled at himself. He was merely experiencing the apprehensions of many young men before him. He was a man of high standing in the community; he had no reason to worry.

When Bingley at last exited, he was looking quite cheerful. "He is ready for you, Darcy. Dearest Jane is now mine, and I am certain Miss Bennet shall soon be yours."

After congratulating his friend, Darcy stepped into the study. He was motioned to sit, which he commenced to do, though the action made his anxiety grow.

Mr. Bennet stared hard at him for a minute or two before speaking. "Now, perhaps you will tell me what this business of yours is here. Jane has already been spoken for, and I know you are a man of far too much understanding to be interested in the silly antics of my youngest daughter."

"It is your eldest daughter whom I wish to speak with you about. I have come to ask for her hand in marriage."

Mr. Bennet gazed at him for a few seconds more before exhaling heavily. "A part of me suspected as much, though I am still quite surprised." His countenance took on a slightly dark look as he continued:

"While I do of course care for all of my daughters, I must confess to a particular regard for Elizabeth. Her wit and humor quite often provide a good counterpoint to my own, and her love of reading was inherited from me.

"I do not hold Elizabeth's future lightly, Mr. Darcy. As it was within my power, I have bequeathed Rosings unto her, and I did so with great joy, for she has experienced some sorrows in the past that I feared might have lasting effects on her future."

"If you speak of Mr. Wickham," said Mr. Darcy, startling even himself as he spoke up, "I can assure you that she shall no longer have to see that scoundrel ever again."

"You surprise me once more, Mr. Darcy, but I am certainly pleased to hear that information. Still, I am not quite convinced of your suitability for my favorite daughter. Are you well read? Are you able to challenge her mind?"

"The library at Pemberley is one of which to be proud, and I dare say even you should be impressed. Your daughter and I have had many discussions about literature in the Rosings library, and while she challenges me to look at certain books with a new perspective, I, too, am able to induce her to consider other viewpoints as well. I have fallen deeply and irrevocably in love with your daughter over these past months, and she has helped me to become a better man. Too often did I let myself lapse into brooding in the past . . . but now I have started to experience the same zest for life which so fills your daughter entirely.

"I care deeply for your eldest daughter, Mr. Bennet, and I am certain she cares for me. I can promise you that I shall fight to my dying breath to make her happy."

"And you have spoken with Elizabeth? You are aware that she could not find happiness without a husband whom she can love and respect?"

"I have asked her to marry me, and she has accepted. With the estate you passed to her, any pressure she might have felt to marry and help her situation dissipated. We meet as equals, and we equally cherish and admire each other."

Mr. Bennet smiled. "Very well, Mr. Darcy. I am convinced. You have my consent to marry my daughter . . . though I doubt I should honestly have been able to refuse a man of your stature anything."

Darcy's apprehension took flight like a startled bird, and he felt his heart fill with joy at the thought that every obstacle which had stood between his and Elizabeth's happiness was now gone.

As he joined Bingley, he knew that both he and his friend were facing utter contentment. They had finally secured their futures with the women they loved, and naught but joy stood before them.

Chapter XLIX

Ten years later, Elizabeth Darcy sat in the confines of her private study at Pemberley, attending to her letters and reflecting upon her life.

The years after their wedding had been kind to the Darcys. Their lives together were filled with life and love, and though they disagreed often (after all, two such strong-willed individuals could not help but disagree frequently), their arguments were always short in duration, and their reconciliations all the sweeter.

On that morning, however, Elizabeth's thoughts turned to the preceding years. During that time immediately after her rejection of Mr. Wickham, she had often despaired, thinking herself unmarriageable due to her jaded view of men, and she had been determined to never allow herself to be vulnerable again. But somehow a different man had burrowed his way into her affections and shown her how to live her life without the constant regret of the past.

Sifting through the piles of correspondence, Elizabeth came across a letter she had recently received from her father. Mr. Bennet had continued to be a dilatory correspondent, but with her—his favorite daughter—he was marginally better than he was with most of his acquaintances. His recent letter was much the same as the man had always been, with his love for his family shining through his odd mixture of sardonic wit and quick humor. In particular, he related the recent antics of his eldest grandchild, a precocious child of ten summers who was now heir to Longbourn.

It was a good thing, Elizabeth mused, that Mary had given birth to a boy rather than a girl, and it was even more fortunate that Mary had found true love upon returning to Longbourn after the birth of her child. Mr. Phelps had been one of her Uncle Phillips's clerks, and though the man had not been gently born, his intelligence had been such that he had taken over the management of Longbourn with a certain flair which Mr. Bennet had never possessed. Mr. Phelps positively doted upon his adoptive son, and though he and Mary had not been blessed with children of their own — perhaps a blessing due to Mary's difficulty with her son — he appeared to have no cause to repine.

This of course allowed Mr. Bennet the ability to while away his days in his library or spend them with his grandson, all without the associated guilt of not personally increasing the production of the estate. And though Mr. Bennet always remained in somewhat indifferent health, he had, thus far, defied the doctor's prediction, and he had lived to see several of his grandchildren. His only persistent complaint in life seemed to be that Elizabeth had filled the position of parson at Hunsford with a sensible man named Mr. Johnson. If he could not have a foolishly pompous son-in-law, Mr. Bennet had complained, then the least Elizabeth could have done was to provide him with a similar character in the parsonage under her control, so that Mr. Bennet might study him from afar as he pleased. Elizabeth scarcely responded to these complaints with anything more than an exasperated shake of her head.

Mrs. Bennet was much as she had ever been, remaining silly and flighty, even though her future was now assured with her children married and her grandson as the heir to her home. Both Elizabeth and her husband were relieved that Mrs. Bennet would never have to leave Longbourn — living with her might be far too much for them to take!

Of the other Bennet sisters, Jane had of course married Mr. Bingley about a month before Elizabeth's own nuptials. Bingley, having given up the lease on Netherfield during his time in London, had purchased an estate in a neighboring county to Derbyshire, affording Jane and Elizabeth the opportunity to meet more often than would otherwise have been the case. Jane had already given birth to five children, and a sixth was on the way.

250 °° Jann Rowland & Lelia Eye

Kitty had indeed married Mr. Baker, and they had taken up residence at his estate. Mr. Baker had made a complete change in his character, and he positively doted on his wife and his two children. Kitty, far from being disabled, managed her home with great competence, proving that she was as capable as any other married woman. And though Elizabeth missed her sister due to the distance, she was happy that Kitty had managed to make such a match.

Thoughts of Kitty always brought thoughts of Kitty's sister-in-law, and Elizabeth smirked as she considered the former Elia Baker. The woman had been seriously offended when Elizabeth had married Fitzwilliam Darcy, and her vitriol had been loud and vicious and a serious trial to her brother, who had been in the middle of trying to woo his own Bennet sister.

It was not until after Elizabeth married William that she had discovered Colonel Fitzwilliam's feelings for the woman, a fact which he had confided to his cousin during a night of excessive drinking. After he had sobered up, he had requested—and was granted—permission to stay at Rosings indefinitely in order to further his attempts at wooing Elia Baker. He resigned his commission and took up permanent residence there soon afterward.

However, events did not proceed as he had planned. He was patient, loving, and kind, but Miss Baker by this time had become bitter and resentful of almost everyone around her. The good man put up with her temper for almost six months before he finally decided he had borne enough. On a fine spring day, he had saddled his horse and ridden to Stauneton Hall, where he once again declared his feelings for Miss Baker and urged her to let go of her bitterness.

The woman's response had been acerbic and completely predictable. Apparently, however, the retired colonel had foreseen this, and after her diatribe had lost its momentum, he proceeded to throw her over his horse and ride for Gretna Green. Of that three-day journey, he had never been induced to say much, but he somehow arrived at his destination with a willing—if slightly aggrieved—Elia Baker, and they were married in a most scandalous elopement.

She seemed happy with her situation now, and the Fitzwilliams had added three daughters to their family. And though Elizabeth and Mrs. Fitzwilliam never became close confidants, they were at least able to meet pleasantly in company. In Elizabeth's opinion, it would never go beyond that.

As for the last Bennet daughter, Lydia's story was perhaps the most flamboyant, which was certainly in keeping with the woman herself.

Lydia had spent quite a bit of time with Elizabeth after her wedding in order for Elizabeth to "knock some sense into her," as Mr. Bennet liked to say. And though Elizabeth did her best to educate her sister, in the end, it did little good.

Lydia's time as a Bennet ended rather abruptly when she eloped with an officer in the regulars, marrying at Gretna Green mere weeks after Elia Baker's wedding. They lived primarily in Brighton until Lieutenant Carson's transfer to a regiment stationed in Halifax, Canada. It had come to a complete end after Lieutenant Carson had resigned his commission to try to make his fortune in the new world. The Bennet family had reliable information which suggested that the Carsons had moved down the coast from Halifax to Virginia, but from there, their journey had turned westward, and all contact had been lost.

As for Georgiana Darcy, the disagreements and resentments subsisting between her new sister and herself dissipated with time, and they slowly repaired the rift between them, becoming very close confidants. Georgiana had met the young man who would sweep her off her feet a few years later, and though Darcy was reluctant to let go of his sister, she found her greatest ally in Elizabeth. Georgiana was happily married now and living in Cornwall, the proud mother of two children. And though Elizabeth's husband truly regretted the distance between them—Cornwall was almost as distant as it was possible to live and still be in England!—he was at least comforted by the fact that she was happy.

Perhaps the only downside to having married Fitzwilliam Darcy was that it put her in the company of elite personages quite often, which meant she had come across Lord Trenton more than once. Yet he showed no more inclination to speak to her than she did to him, so perhaps it was not so terrible after all. The man himself was quite the figure of gossip, not only for his conquests, but also due to the fact that he had finally been caught in a compromising position with a young lady of little consequence only two years earlier . . . and had been forced to marry her. Unfortunately, this had not caused him to rein in his lifestyle, but as the woman he married had been thinking of nothing more than costly jewels and fine carriages when she had entrapped him, she, at least, appeared to have no cause to repine.

The door to Elizabeth's study opened, and in walked her husband. Though he was now approaching forty summers, he still retained his devastating good looks and could make Elizabeth's heart race even after all the time they had been married.

"Elizabeth, my love, are you ready to depart?" queried he.

"No, sir," responded Elizabeth, rising to take his hand in her own. "I was just thinking about the twists and turns of our lives. We have truly been remarkably blessed."

"Yes, indeed, my dear," said her husband fondly. "I could not have asked for a better life than the one we lead now.

"Now, come. I wish to make it to our clearing in time for luncheon."

Smiling, Elizabeth allowed her husband to take her hand and pull her from the room. It was a ritual they tried to indulge in as often as they could. It helped keep their marriage exciting and their relationship strong, and Elizabeth suspected they were considered somewhat of an oddity due to how much time they spent alone in one another's company.

As they exited the room and walked the halls of Pemberley, she reflected upon the good fortune that had befallen them. They had four wonderful children, and their two boys were set to inherit two great estates. It was ironic indeed that they had united Rosings and Pemberley in marriage as Lady Catherine had wanted, though certainly not in the manner she had hoped. Yet while Lady Catherine had remained offended for some time, she had finally acknowledged that they made a very well-suited couple. And though she had no grandchildren of her own, she always considered the Darcy children to be such, and her loud pronouncements of how they should commit to their studies or practice the pianoforte filled the halls of Rosings whenever they visited.

Elizabeth had only had the barest chance to obtain the life she now led. The love, the affection, and the companionship she had found were all that she had ever wanted. Through it all, both she and William had managed to find an echo in the heart of the other. And together, they even learned to enjoy dancing.

THE END

About The Authors

Jann Rowland

Jann Rowland was born in Regina, Saskatchewan, Canada. He enjoys reading and sports, and he even dabbles a little in music, taking pleasure in singing and playing the piano.

Though Jann did not start writing until his mid-twenties, writing has grown from a hobby to an all-consuming passion. His interest in Jane Austen stems from his university days when he took a class in which *Pride and Prejudice* was required reading.

He now lives in Calgary, Alberta with his three children and his wife of almost twenty years.

Lelia Eye

Lelia Eye was born in Harrison, Arkansas. She loves reading and misses the days when she was able to be a part of the community theater group in Harrison.

Lelia has enjoyed writing since she won a short story contest in the sixth grade, and she graduated from the University of Central Arkansas with a Master's degree in English. It was while she was obtaining her undergraduate degree at Hendrix College that she took a Jane Austen class which sparked her interest in *Pride and Prejudice*.

She now lives in Conway, Arkansas, with an adorable toddler, her husband, three dogs, and two cats.

Their blog may be found at
rowlandandeye.com

Their Facebook page maybe found at
https://www.facebook.com/OneGoodSonnetPublishing

Made in the USA
Lexington, KY
21 May 2014